D0683550

The QUEEN'S GAMBLE

Books by Barbara Kyle

The Queen's Captive
The King's Daughter
The Queen's Lady

The
QUEEN'S
GAMBLE

BARBARA KYLE

KENSINGTON BOOKS
www.kensingtonbooks.com

KENSINGTON BOOKS are published by

Kensington Publishing Corp.
119 West 40th Street
New York, NY 10018

Copyright © 2011 by Barbara Kyle

All rights reserved. No part of this book may be reproduced in any form or by any means without the prior written consent of the Publisher, excepting brief quotes used in reviews.

All Kensington titles, imprints, and distributed lines are available at special quantity discounts for bulk purchases for sales promotion, premiums, fund-raising, educational, or institutional use.

Special book excerpts or customized printings can also be created to fit specific needs. For details, write or phone the office of the Kensington Special Sales Manager: Kensington Publishing Corp., 119 West 40th Street, New York, NY 10018. Attn. Special Sales Department. Phone: 1-800-221-2647.

Kensington and the K logo Reg. U.S. Pat. & TM Off.

ISBN-13: 978-0-7582-3856-6
ISBN-10: 0-7582-3856-8

First Printing: September 2011
10 9 8 7 6 5 4 3 2 1

Printed in the United States of America

ACKNOWLEDGMENTS

The Queen's Gamble is the fourth in my continuing "Thornleigh" series, and I am grateful to many exceptional people for the success of these books. My thanks go to:

Al Zuckerman, literary agent *extraordinaire*, whose sage advice and guidance I rely on.

Audrey LaFehr, editorial director at Kensington Books, New York, who so ably champions each of my novels. I am fortunate indeed to work with such a gifted and dedicated editor.

Kensington's team of committed professionals, including Production Editor Paula Reedy, for transforming my hard-copy manuscripts into visually beautiful books; Creative Director Kristine Mills-Noble, for the gorgeous cover art; Copy Editor Stacia Seaman, for meticulous fact checking; and Editorial Assistant Martin Biro, for help always cheerfully offered. A special thanks to John Rosenberg, savvy publishing pro, who works such wonders for my books in Canada.

Stephen Best, my husband, an indispensable creative partner in every book I write. There is no better "go-to" guy.

Joy Isley, of Mesa, Arizona, for contributing the winning entry of "Noche" ("night" in Spanish) in the *Name Carlos's Horse* contest that ran on my Web site as I was writing this book. Readers sent in hundreds of excellent names, and I sincerely thank you all.

HISTORICAL PREFACE

When Elizabeth Tudor, at the age of twenty-five, inherited the English throne from her half sister Mary in November of 1558, the country was on the brink of ruin. Mary had bankrupted the treasury by her disastrous war with France, which she had lost, leaving Elizabeth burdened with massive loans taken in Europe's financial capital of Antwerp, and a grossly debased coinage that was strangling English trade.

Danger threatened Elizabeth on every side. Spain, having ruthlessly established dominion over the Netherlands, eyed England as a possible addition to its empire that already spanned half the globe. France, whose queen, Mary Stuart, was Elizabeth's cousin and claimant to Elizabeth's throne, ruled Scotland as a virtual French province, its government run by French overlords, its capital garrisoned with French troops, providing an ideal bridgehead for the French to launch an attack on England. At home, Elizabeth faced seething discontent from a large portion of her people, the Catholics, who loathed her act of Parliament that had made the country officially Protestant. France and Spain sympathized with, and supported, the English Catholics.

If overtly threatened by either of those great powers, England would be vastly outmatched. The English people knew it and were frightened, leading officials in the vulnerable coastal towns of Southampton, Portsmouth, and the Cinque Ports to barrage Elizabeth's council with letters entreating aid in strengthening their fortifications against possible attack. Unlike the European powers, England had never had a standing army. Her monarchs had always relied on a system of feudal levies by which local lords, when required, raised companies of their tenants and retainers to fight for the king, who then augmented the levies with foreign mercenaries. England was backward in armaments, too; while a revolution in warfare was happening in Europe with the development of artillery and small firearms, English soldiers still relied on pikes and bows. Even Elizabeth's navy was weak, consisting of just thirty-four ships, only eleven of them ships of war.

Ten months after Elizabeth's coronation, people throughout Europe were laying bets that her reign would not survive a second year. One crisis could destroy her.

That crisis came in the winter of 1559.

PART ONE

Return from the New World

❧ 1 ❧

Execution Dock

Isabel Valverde was coming home. The brief, terrible letter from her brother had brought her across five thousand miles of ocean, from the New World to the Old, and during the long voyage she thought she had prepared herself for the worst. But now that London lay just beyond the next bend of the River Thames, she dreaded what awaited her. The not knowing—that was the hardest. Would she find her mother still a prisoner awaiting execution? Horrifying though that was, Isabel could at least hope to see her one last time. Or had her mother already been hanged?

The ship was Spanish, the *San Juan Bautista*, the cabin snug and warm, its elegant teak paneling a cocoon that almost muffled the brutal beat of England's winter rain on the deck above. Isabel stood by the berth, buttoning her cloak, steeling herself. The captain had said they were less than an hour from London's customs wharf and she would soon have to prepare to disembark. Everything was packed; three trunks sat waiting by the open door, and behind her she could hear her servant, sixteen-year-old Pedro, closing the lid of the fourth and last one. She listened to the rain's faint drumbeat, knowing that she heard it in a way the Spanish passengers could not—heard it as a call, connecting her to her past, to her family's roots. The Spaniards would not understand. England meant nothing to them other than a market for their goods, and she had to admit it was a backward place compared to the magnificence of their empire. The gold and silver of the New World flowed back to the Old like a river with the treasure fleets that sailed twice a year from Peru and Mexico, making Philip of Spain the richest and most powerful monarch in Europe. Isabel felt the tug of both worlds, for a part of her lived in each, her young self in the Old, her adult self in the New. She had left England at twenty with her Spanish husband and almost nothing else, but he had done well in Peru, and after five years among its wealthy Spaniards, Isabel was one of them. *Money*, she thought. *It's how the world turns.*

Can it turn Mother's fate? She had clung to that hope for the voyage, and now, listening to the English rain, she was seized by a panicky need to have the gold in her hands. She heard her servant clicking a key into the lock of the last trunk. She whirled around.

"Pedro, my gold," she said. She grabbed his arm to stop him turning the key. "Where is it?"

He looked at her, puzzled. "Señora?"

"The gold I set aside. In the blue leather pouch." She snatched the ring of keys from him and unlocked the trunk. She rummaged among her gowns, searching for the pouch. The soft silks and velvets slid through her hands. She dug down into the layers of linen smocks and stockings and nightdresses. No pouch. Abandoning the rucked-up clothes, she unlocked another trunk and pawed through her husband's things, his doublets and breeches and capes and boots. The pouch was not here either. "Open that one," she said, tossing the keys to Pedro. "We have to find it." She went to the brocade satchel that lay at the foot of the berth and flipped its clasps and dug inside.

"Señora, it's not in there. Just papers."

"Look for it!" she ordered.

He flinched at her tone, and she felt like a tyrant. Not for the first time. He was a Peruvian with the small build of his Indian people, which made him look more like a child than a lad of sixteen. He had the placid nature of his people, too, and a deference to authority that had been bred into his ancestors by the rigid Inca culture. When the Spaniards had invaded thirty years ago they had exploited that deference, easily making the Indians their slaves and themselves rich. Isabel hated slavery. Pedro was her servant, but a free person nonetheless. English justice said so. But his docile ways sometimes sparked her impatience, goading her to take the tone of his Spanish overlords, and when she did so she hated herself.

"Take out everything," she told him, less sharply. "Look at the bottom."

"*Sí, señora,*" he said, obeying.

His native tongue was Quechua. Isabel's was English. Neither of them knew the other's language. They spoke in Spanish.

She was rummaging through papers in the satchel, a frustrating search since everything had been repacked when they had left Seville. That had been the destination of their long voyage, since only Spanish and Portuguese ships sailed to and from the New World. Other Europeans were forbidden to trade there by a treaty between those two Iberian countries, sanctioned by the pope. After two days in the port Isabel had booked passage on the first ship for London.

"And hurry," she told Pedro. The captain had made it clear they were nearing the quay. But she would not leave the ship until she found the money. In Seville they had assured her that her Spanish maravedis would be accepted as legal tender in England. Gold was gold, after all. She upended the satchel, dumping out papers and scrolls. No blue pouch. She went back to the third trunk, where Pedro was trying not to disturb its contents as he searched, and she nudged him aside and groped through things helter-skelter. She was on her knees, pulling out her son's toys from the bottom—a wooden caterpillar on wheels, a red rowboat, a yellow tin top for spinning—when the light from the open doorway darkened.

"Isabel?" her husband said. "What are you doing?"

Carlos stood in the doorway, frowning at the open trunks with their spilled-out jumble of gowns, smocks, capes, and boots. Raindrops beaded his close-cropped hair, which stood up like boar bristles, and rain glistened on his black leather doublet. No jewel-studded finery for Carlos, though it was so fashionable with his Spanish peers in Peru. He stuck to the plain clothes of his years as

a soldier on the battlefields of Europe. For a moment Isabel remembered how frightened she had been of him the first time she
had seen him. He had broken a man's neck with his hands.
Twisted his head. She could still hear the *snap*. Carlos had saved
her life.

"Isabel?" he said again.

"I need my gold," she blurted. And then instantly felt how irra-
tional her behavior must look. The pouch held a mere fraction of
Carlos's wealth, and he didn't begrudge her any of it, had always
been content to let her manage their funds, even at the beginning
when they'd had so little. But the money in the pouch would be a
fortune for any jailer. A bribe for her mother's life.

"Now?" Carlos asked. His puzzled look softened to one of sympathy. "All the money is in the ebony chest. Up on deck."

She saw that he pitied her, and it brought reality crashing in.
She sat back on her heels, rocked by the certainty that the hope
she had been clinging to was a fantasy. If her mother was not already dead, she soon would be. Adam's letter had been brief but
clear. Her mother had committed murder. No amount of gold
could alter her sentence.

Carlos said gently, "Come up on deck."

"The rain—"

"It's stopped."

"Really? You're wet."

Again, the look of sympathy. "You need some air."

She needed more than that. She needed the strength to face
whatever they were going to find, and to help her poor father. This
would be killing him. For the hundredth time she asked herself,
how had it happened? How had her parents sunk so low?

She took a steadying breath and got to her feet. "Yes, let's go
up." She turned to Pedro. "Pack the trunks again," she said, and
then added as an apology to him, "Please. There's time."

The pounding rain had stopped, but only as if to catch its
breath, and now came back to pester them as wind-driven drizzle.
When the ship had sailed into the estuary they had finally escaped
the violent Channel winds, but spiteful gusts still followed like a

beaten foe refusing to give up. Isabel winced at the cold drizzle on her face as she and Carlos walked arm in arm past sailors readying the ship to dock. Some coiled the heavy rope hawsers while others climbed the netting of the foremast shrouds to shorten sail. Everything—spars and shrouds and sails—dripped with rain. Seagulls screamed, scavenging in the ship's wake.

A dozen or so passengers huddled in the lee of the sterncastle deck, their faces pale after the rough crossing from Seville. Isabel felt sorry for them but was secretly glad that she never suffered that misery on the water. Since the time she could walk she had often spent days at a stretch on her father's ships. A few of the men, whether hardier or just more curious, stood at the starboard railing to take in the sights as the north riverbank slipped by. Isabel and Carlos joined them, and she gave a nod to an elderly Spanish priest. She had spoken to him briefly when they had boarded in Seville, a neat and quiet man who was bringing a gift of books to his friend Álvarez de Quadra, Bishop of Aquila, the Spanish ambassador in London. Isabel had brought something for the bishop, too. Not books, but news from Peru.

She looked out at the riverbank and felt a tug of emotion. England, once her home, lay close enough almost to touch. Yet she knew the priest and his fellow Spanish gentry must find the sight dreary. Farmhouses squatted in soaked fields. Hammers clanged from rough-hewn boatbuilding sheds. Riverside taverns hulked under the gray rain. Atop one, a weather vane creaked as it veered from east to west, then back again in the erratic gusts. In the chill, Isabel shivered. She looked at Carlos and almost smiled, remembering what he used to say about England. *How can a country be so cold and wet at the same time?* She thought of their home in sunny Trujillo, its earthy heat, its vivid colors, and in the distance its mountain peaks. The two countries could hardly be more different.

"All right?" he asked. He had seen her shiver.

He didn't have to come, she thought. Her family's troubles were her woes, not his, and there was pressing business to keep him home where his silver mine alone took half his waking hours. She wished he hadn't bought that mine. They didn't need the money, and the overseer drove the Indian workers like slaves. But she knew it meant a great deal to Carlos to be accepted as one of the mining fraternity of Lima. It made her grateful that he had insisted on voyaging here with her. Neither of them had wanted to be apart. She tightened her arm, which was hooked around his, and answered, "Better now."

They were passing the grimy little village of Wapping, where the reek of decayed fish rose from the sailors' alehouses and victualing haunts hunkered around the river stairs, when a sound came from some men at the railing, a low grunt. Isabel looked out at the muddy shoreline and saw what was transfixing them. A gibbet stood in the mud, and from it hung a man's corpse. This was Execution Dock.

She felt her every muscle tense. The corpse's skin had turned to the color of the mud. *Will Mother look like that?* She forced herself not to make a sound, but Carlos wrapped his arm around her shoulder with a squeeze, and she knew she had failed to mask her horror. She turned her face into his chest.

"Pirate," he muttered, holding her close.

She looked up at him. How did he know?

"Short rope," he said.

She looked again at the hanged man. English law reserved this special agony for pirates. With a short rope the drop from the scaffold was not enough to break the victim's neck, so he suffered a slow death from strangulation. When his limbs jerked in death throes the people called it the Marshal's Dance, because prisoners were brought here from London's Marshalsea Prison. As a final mark of contempt, the authorities did not cut down a pirate's corpse right away but left him until three successive tides had washed over his head. English law held pirates to be the worst evil in an evil world.

But all Isabel could think of was her mother hanging by her neck from such a gibbet. She felt sick, and looked up at Carlos. "I don't think I can do this."

"Yes, you can. I know you." He added soberly, "Whatever it is, we'll do it together."

She loved him for that.

A flash of red on deck caught her eye. A little boy in a red cap running for his mother. It made Isabel think of her son. She said to Carlos, "Where's Nicolas?"

He shrugged. Then suggested, "With Pedro?"

She jerked out of his embrace. "No. I thought he was with you."

She saw a flicker of concern in his eyes. Their little boy was only four. He said, "Where did you last see him?"

"Climbing a cannon blind by the mizzenmast. The bosun's mate pulled him down and cuffed his ear, which the little scamp deserved. I told him to find you and stay with you while I helped Pedro pack." *Behave yourself, Nico,* she had said. *No more climbing. We're almost there.*

They both scanned the gunwales where six small demi-cannons sat. A merchant ship needed defenses, but the armaments were minimal, and a glance told them that Nicolas wasn't near the cannons. Panic lurched in Isabel. *He climbed up one and fell overboard.*

"We'll find him," Carlos said calmly. "You take the topsides, I'll search the lower decks."

She hurried past sailors and elbowed around passengers, looking in every nook, her eyes flicking along the gunwales, constantly imagining her son's small body tumbling into the frigid gray waves. *My fault. I should have kept him by me.*

He was nowhere on deck. She was sure of it. She hurried down the companionway to the orlop deck, ignoring Carlos's instructions. She was heading toward a victuals storeroom, almost out of breath from her hurry and her fear, when she heard it. A dull *thump, thump, thump.* It came from behind the closed door across from the storeroom. The carpenter's cabin. She threw open the door.

The carpenter, a lanky man, was bent over a table pushing a planing tool that left in its wake a wood shaving curled like a wave. He was saying something about football but he stopped midsentence when he saw Isabel, and the wood wave drifted to the floor. There beside him was Nicolas, bouncing his green rubber ball, *thump, thump, thump.*

Isabel was so relieved she wanted to box her son's ears for the fright he'd caused her. Instead, she swept him into her arms.

"Your boy, ma'am?" the carpenter asked. "He was telling me about rubber trees."

Nicolas wriggled free of Isabel's embrace and dropped to his hands and knees to rescue his ball rolling under the table. "I told him they grow as tall as Lima Cathedral," he said, proud of his knowledge. He popped back up with the ball. "Mama, can you believe it? This gentleman has never *seen* a rubber tree."

"I'd like to, though, lad," the man said. "That's the bounciest ball I ever beheld."

Without a thought, Nicolas offered it up to him with a smile. "Here. I have another."

Isabel saw her son's eyes shine with the gift of giving. Her heart swelled. She was glad she hadn't boxed his ears.

The *San Juan Bautista* approached the customs quay and London loomed. Dozens of oceangoing ships of all nationalities were moored in the Pool, their progress limited by London Bridge. The hundreds of masts bobbed in the choppy water like an undulating forest. The overcast sky had hastened the dusk, and a few torches already flickered at the Southwark end of the bridge, the city's only viaduct and one of its three great landmarks. The first candles glimmered in windows of the merchants' houses and shops that crammed the bridge, some of the buildings rising three and four stories. Beyond the bridge, to the west, was the second great landmark, St. Paul's, thrusting its spire, the tallest in Europe, into the leaden sky. On the north shore, just before the bridge, stood the third landmark, the centuries-old Tower. Once a royal palace, always a fort, and often a prison, it was a forbidding precinct of several stone towers behind stone walls. Church bells clanged from the far northern reaches of the city, and a homey smell of burning charcoal drifted above the reek of fish and dung.

Isabel's heart beat faster as she took it in. The last time she had seen all this, five years ago, the city had been under attack by the small rebel army of Sir Thomas Wyatt, who had reached the walls of London at Ludgate. She had pledged herself to help Wyatt, yet in the end she had helped to close the gate against him. She had done it to save her father's life, but at what cost! Wyatt's men had been cut down. The awful moment haunted her still. Carlos had told her afterward that the rebels' defeat had been inevitable whatever her actions, but Isabel was not convinced. Who could say what might have happened if the gate had been kept open?

She shook off the memory. That day was past, and London lay before her now in all its gritty glory. She felt a flicker of the awe she had felt as a young girl, coming here with her father from their home in Colchester, a day's ride away, and being swept up in the excitement of the brash, brawling capital.

The rain had finally stopped, and in the dusk the customs wharf swarmed with every kind of Londoner out to make a penny or a pound. Lightermen shouted for passengers, offering to ferry them into the city in wherries and tilt boats. Pie sellers hawked mince pies and rabbit pastries. Merchants' agents haggled. Pickpockets silently slipped among the prospects, and whores lounged, their lips rouged, their eyes keen. It startled Isabel to hear English again. Her Spanish was not the best, but speaking it had become second nature, its mellifluous sound a pleasure. These hard Anglo-Saxon voices on the quay jarred her. Not roughly, though. More like being jostled awake. The sound of home.

The customs agents took their time, but finally Isabel and Carlos were free to disembark. They left Pedro on the quay to watch their belongings, and made their way with their son through the crowd toward Thames Street, where, at the corner of Mark Lane, there were stalls with horses for hire. Their destination was Colchester, and Isabel wanted to get there quickly. Sickening though her task was, it would be agony to draw it out. She had to get to Colchester jail.

Carlos swung Nicolas up onto his shoulders, and Nicolas laughed, pointing at a dog that had snatched a pie from a man's hand. It eased Isabel's heart. Her son was seeing everything with a child's happy innocence. And why not? He had never met his grandparents.

Ahead of them the elderly priest from the ship was making his way through the crowd when a well-dressed man who was passing spat at the priest's back. His spittle missed, and the oblivious priest carried on, but Isabel was shocked. At their stopover in Seville she had heard about the changes in England since the death several months ago of the Catholic Queen Mary. Her half sister, Princess Elizabeth, who was Isabel's age, had ascended the throne and immediately declared the realm Protestant. Isabel knew of the country's anti-Catholic bent, but to spit at a harmless priest? After the urbanity of Spanish Peru, she found such behavior revolting.

They reached the horse stalls and Carlos swung Nicolas off his shoulders and began examining the mounts, running his hand over withers, inspecting hooves. As a former captain of cavalry, Carlos knew horses. Nicolas trotted after him as they moved among the animals. "Papa, look at this one. It's got silver dots!"

"A bay silver dapple. An Arab."

"Like in the desert!"

The two of them disappeared among the horses, Nico chattering on.

"Isabel?" a female voice asked.

She turned. A woman finely dressed in green and gold velvet was peering at her as though searching her face for clues. She was heavily pregnant, though not young, her hair touched with gray at the temples under a pearl-studded velvet hat. "Isabel Valverde?" she asked.

"Yes. Yes, I'm Isabel. May I ask—"

"I am Frances. Adam's wife."

Isabel was stunned. Her brother had said nothing in his letter about being married. But then, he had said nothing about *anything* except the dreadful news.

"You didn't know?" Frances said. She seemed very nervous. "I wasn't sure. I mean, I don't know how much Adam told you. About . . . the family."

Isabel's stomach tightened. Her throat seemed to close up. "My mother. Is she . . . ?" She couldn't get the words out. *Alive or dead?* Suddenly, she didn't want to ask. Wanted to keep on hoping. "How did you know?" she said instead. "About our arrival."

"Oh, the ship's boat came ahead with the passenger list. So we heard. We've been keeping a lookout for you for ages."

"Have you?" It made sense. Adam's letter, dated months before she had received it, had been slow on its long journey across the Atlantic to Panama, then on a packhorse train across to the Pacific, then onto another ship down to Lima. She and Carlos had taken passage from Lima as soon as she had read the news, but their journey here had taken months.

"Oh, dear, it's so hard to know where to begin," Frances said, her pale blue eyes blinking, her anxiety plain. "There is so much you don't know."

Isabel was certain now that her mother lay dead in her grave. She felt the strength sucked out of her. She didn't trust her legs to hold her up.

"I'm sorry," Frances said, offering her hand as though she saw how unsteady Isabel was. "This is a sad disappointment for you. You see, your parents . . . your mother. Well, she couldn't be here to meet you."

"She's dead."

"What?"

"They hanged her."

"Hanged? Goodness, no!" she cried in horror. "Is that what you—? Oh dear, no, I assure you she is well. She and your father both hurried here, eager to meet you. We all stood right on this spot and watched your ship come in. But then, just half an hour ago, a message came from Whitehall Palace. They were both called away. Your mother and father are dining at the palace with the Queen."

❧ 2 ❧

The House on Bishopsgate Street

The Thornleighs' great hall rang with excited chatter. Footmen bustled in with the Valverdes' trunks and baggage, calling out to other servants who were rushing in to help. Isabel, almost breathless from asking Frances questions on the way, greeted her old nursemaid, Meg, who burst into tears at seeing her. Carlos switched between Spanish and English as he gave instructions about the trunks to Pedro and to the Thornleighs' chamberlain. Two wolfhounds romped about, barking, and Nicolas chased the dogs, shouting, trying to pet them. Everyone was making noise, human and canine, when Isabel's father came striding in at the far end of the hall, arms outstretched, booming, "Isabel!"

She whirled around. "Father!"

Nicolas gasped. *"El diablo!"* The devil! He pointed at the frightening man and ran to Isabel and clutched her skirt and hid his face in it.

The servants burst into laughter, and Isabel, laughing, too, tugged herself free of her son and hurried to meet her father. When they reached each other a sudden shyness overtook her, for it had been five long years since she had seen him, and she bobbed a curtsy as if she were eight and aware of how to behave in front of her elders.

"What's this nonsense?" he said. "Come here, Bel." He drew her into his arms and hugged her tight, and she had the dizzying sense of feeling eight indeed, when she had been in awe of his apparent omnipotence.

"*El diablo!*" Nicolas crowed again, but this time his face was bright with anticipation, for he had seen how he'd made people laugh and he wanted the same response.

"In English," Carlos told him. "English in England." He made this quiet command to his son as he came forward and offered his hand to his father-in-law, who grasped it and firmly shook it.

Isabel took a long, happy look at her father, thinking that Nico was not far wrong. If the devil had wanted to take a human form, Richard Thornleigh's would be a clever choice. He was imposing, to say the least—tall, robust at sixty-one, with a sea-weathered face and a baritone voice that rang with authority. He wore a maroon leather patch over the eye he had lost before Isabel was born, while the other eye, blue and clear, watched the world with a sharp interest that missed nothing. A self-assured devil, made to beguile converts, she thought. "Papa is right, Nico, use English," she told her son, relishing the moment, "and you must also add your grandpapa's proper title. It is *your lordship*, the devil."

"Ha! Quite right," her father said, amused. "Though I'm not sure what that makes her *ladyship*. By heaven, I can't wait to see her face when she sees you."

"Aye, you're a sight for sore eyes, Mistress Isabel, that's for true," Meg the nurse said, sniffling into her handkerchief. Isabel gave the old woman's shoulder an affectionate squeeze, and her father added with warmth, "Isabel. Carlos. Welcome home."

"And me," Nicolas piped up.

"*This* is for you," her father said, grappling the boy and tickling his ribs. Nico squealed and squirmed, and Isabel looked on, loving it. Two minutes after meeting one another, her father and son were fast friends. *Baron Thornleigh*, she thought, still amazed at how her parents' lives had been transformed. *And Mother, now Lady Thornleigh, at this very moment at Whitehall Palace with the Queen.* Her father had always done well as a wool cloth merchant, but that success was mere chaff compared to the high rank he had been elevated to. Isabel felt almost giddy at what she had learned in the half hour it had taken for Frances to bring them here.

"I hardly know where to begin," Frances had said, looking rather uncomfortable. They were walking up Cornhill Street with Carlos, while Pedro followed with Nicolas and three footmen Frances had brought to carry the luggage. The trunks had been sent ahead in a cart. "You see, the Queen . . . well, Princess Elizabeth back then . . . she befriended your mother and—"

"*Befriended* her?" Isabel said in wonder. "How? When?"

"Well, I suppose it started almost five years ago."

Isabel shared a look with Carlos. *Just when we went to Peru.* "But what sparked this friendship?" she asked.

"The Princess was . . . out of favor, shall we say, with her sister, Queen Mary." Frances paused, looking flustered. "Queen Mary was a misunderstood sovereign. I knew her well, and I will not slander her. Still, it is true that she was harsh with her sister, and that—"

"But what about my mother?" Isabel pressed. She cared nothing about the dead, old Queen Mary.

Carlos said, "Adam wrote that she was in prison in Colchester. Was he mistaken?"

"No."

"And was she really charged with murder?" Isabel asked.

"Yes."

"Who was she accused of killing?"

Frances looked away. "Not merely accused. Convicted."

"But who *was* it?"

Frances continued to avoid her eyes. She said tightly, "I do wish your parents could have met you at the quay. It's they who should tell you all this. I know they wrote to you, but I suppose the letter arrived after you had sailed." She carried on quickly, as though Isabel's question could not be answered, at least not by her. "The nub of the thing is that Queen Mary died, and Princess Elizabeth became queen, and she showed her gratitude for your mother's loyalty by rewarding the whole family. She pardoned your mother of her crime and made your father a baron. And," she added, raising her head with obvious pride in her husband, "she knighted Adam."

Rewards indeed! was Isabel's thought now as she watched Nicolas giggle at her father's tickling. The family's new status was astounding. And the wealth that had come with it! Not least, this huge house on fashionable Bishopsgate Street. From the front door you looked across the busy road at the grand edifice of the Merchant Taylors' Hall. The house was three elegant stories rising above the great hall they stood in, with its long mahogany table and tall stained glass windows and wall tapestries that glowed with silk threads of scarlet and gold and sea green. The grounds contained an orchard and a walled garden with graveled walks and a fountain. And this was just their *town* house; the new Queen had also gifted them with lands and manors in Wiltshire and Kent. She had also appointed Baron Thornleigh to her royal council of advisers, an extraordinary mark of her trust. Isabel found it dizzying.

But so much still eluded her. Had her mother really been guilty of murder? And why had Frances been so reluctant to name the victim? Why did Frances stand quietly now to one side, smiling politely but not joining in the household's high spirits? To be sure, the discomforts of late pregnancy could drain the fun out of any woman. And, of course, she must miss Adam. Frances had briefly explained that he was away on business with the Queen's navy, but Isabel sensed there was more to it. Her father seemed to ignore Frances, seemed almost to snub her, and Isabel wondered why. Yet, as she watched him play with Nicolas, she decided to put aside these mysteries and embrace what was thrillingly clear—that instead of the misery in which she had expected to find her parents, they basked in a friendship with the Queen. They lived in luxury. They were hale. All was right with the world.

"Come, let's sit down to eat," her father said with a clap of his hands. "The moment we knew you were coming your mother ordered a feast." He called to the chamberlain, who was overseeing the servants carrying in the luggage, "James, tell cook we'll sup. And let's have some music."

"Shouldn't we wait for Mother?" Isabel asked.

"She'll be home soon. And she made me promise to see that

you are all fed without fail. I think she believes you haven't eaten in five years."

Everyone laughed, and James headed into the kitchen, calling, "Ho! Victuals!" Isabel was rounding up Nicolas, and Carlos was offering his arm to Frances to escort her to the table, when a man shouted, "Mistress Isabel!"

A wiry fellow loped in from the screened passage. Isabel's hand went to her heart. "Tom! Is it really you?"

He reached her, out of breath, and tugged off his worn wool cap. "Ran all the way from the Spotted Grouse, my lady, soon's I heard you was come."

"Finished your grog first, I warrant," Meg, the old nurse, jibed.

"Nay, that I did not," he insisted to Isabel. "I swear it on my mother's grave."

"A grave she fell into from grog," said Meg with a cackle as she left.

He winked at Isabel. "Can't dispute that, my lady."

She smiled, overjoyed at this familiar face. "Tom, I'm glad to see you." She had grown up with Tom Yates. A clever jack-of-all-trades, he had been part of her father's household for as long as she could remember. He had been a young man when she was a child, and his long, lank hair was now peppered with gray. He wore it swept back and tied in a queue with a grubby bit of leather, just as she had seen him do since she was little. He had always loved colorful clothes, and his jerkin now—what a fanciful affair! It was sheepskin, somewhat mangy, to which he had added an upright collar of red satin and gold tassels on each sleeve cuff that danced with his every move. She was glad that some things never changed.

"Is this your young 'un?" he asked, jerking a thumb at Nicolas.

"It is," she said, bringing her son around, her hands on his shoulders. "This is Nicolas." She saw that Pedro was watching Tom in awe at his forthright manner with her—indeed, the forthrightness of all the servants here. Pedro understood no English, but none was needed to see the absence of servility in the household folk. Isabel felt a twinge of pride at her heritage. English liberty.

Tom reached for Nicolas's head and swiped a hand past his ear. "Is this farthing yours, Master Nicolas?" He held up a shiny coin.

Nicolas's mouth fell open in surprise, his eyes huge.

Tom tossed him the farthing. "It's yours now." Nicolas caught it, and his hand went to his ear as if he hoped to feel another coin sprouting there. A bubble of laughter rose in Isabel. Tom had dazzled her with the same tricks when she was a little girl.

Maidservants were bringing platters of food from the kitchen, and Tom grabbed three empty plates from a passing girl. He tossed a plate in the air, then another, then the third, and juggled them. "Would you pass me another, Master Nicolas?"

Nicolas looked up at Isabel with a question in his eyes, silently asking permission. She nodded. The maid had set the plates on the table and Nicolas grabbed one and then, shy but eager, offered it to Tom. Tom snatched it without disturbing the three plates he was already juggling and tossed the fourth one up, too, adding it to the mix. "And another," he said.

"Hold on, Yates," Isabel's father said. "Last time you tried this the maids were sweeping up broken crockery all day."

"Nay, your lordship, that were but practice. I've mastered 'er now."

Nicolas was watching, enthralled by the flying plates. Isabel saw that Carlos, too, was enjoying the show, intrigued. "Can you do a fifth?" Carlos asked.

"Aye, sir. Try me!"

"Go on, Nico," Carlos said. "Pass him another."

"No, surely it's not possible," Isabel said.

Nicolas looked from her to his father, not sure whom to obey, but clearly wanting to see Tom take the fifth plate.

Isabel laughed. "All right."

Nicolas grabbed a plate from the table. "Now?" he asked Tom.

"Hold your horses," Tom said, his eyes on the four plates he was carefully juggling. Then: "All right. Now!"

Nicolas quickly handed it to him and Tom tossed it up. Servants had gathered to watch in a hush of suspense. James, the chamberlain, crossed his arms over his chest and eyed Tom with the cool interest of a gambler. Even old Meg had padded back in. Pedro seemed positively entranced.

"He can't do it for long," a young maid whispered to another.

"A shilling says I can," Tom said. "To the count of a hundred? Any takers?"

"You're on," said James, which brought an appreciative "Ah" from the others, everyone now eager to see if Tom could accomplish the feat. "Would you count, my lady?" James asked Isabel.

Why not? she thought happily. She started, "One . . . two . . . three," and soon the servants were counting in unison with her, their voices getting louder with expectation as the numbers climbed.

James good-naturedly goaded Tom, "You'll never keep it up, man."

"Said the whore to the bishop," Tom replied.

The others sputtered laughter. Carlos chuckled, and so did Isabel's father, and she shot Carlos a look that said, *For shame, in front of Nico*, but she was laughing inside.

"Thirty-seven," they all chanted with her. "Thirty-eight . . . thirty-nine . . . forty . . ."

Tom's plates flew in smooth loops. The counting accelerated. But beads of sweat glinted on his brow. Isabel thought, *Can* he keep it up?

"Seventy-one . . . seventy-two . . . seventy-three . . ."

A shout came from the kitchen. Everyone tensed. Would Tom drop the plates? A door somewhere slammed. Tom staggered a step. The plates kept flying, but their loops were now wobbly.

"Ninety-eight . . . ninety-nine . . . *one hundred!*" Isabel shouted it as exuberantly as the servants. Tom landed the plates with deft precision, one after another. A cheer went up. Nicolas jumped up and down with glee, crying, "He did it! He did it!" Carlos grinned at Isabel. Her father slapped Tom on the back. "Well done, Yates."

"Thank you, my lord." Tom looked a little wild-eyed after his exertion. He held out a hand, palm up, to James, who dug into his breeches pocket and handed over a shilling, which brought a round of applause.

Isabel's father clapped his hands. "Now, let's eat!"

The family took seats, and Isabel watched Tom guide Pedro into the kitchen, the lad looking as pleased as if he had made friends with a demigod. A manservant poured wine, and maidservants carried in platters of roasted goose, poached turbot, spiced cabbage, and baked apples, the aromas making Isabel's mouth water. Across the table Carlos was helping Frances to a slice of goose, while her father, at the head, bounced Nico on his knee. Musicians had filed into the gallery above the hall and now launched into a gay galliard on their lutes and viols. A robust fire flared in the hearth, making the silk tapestries gleam. Isabel took it all in with a tingling contentment. She looked across at Carlos. He was sitting back, enjoying his wine, and smiling at her with a look that said: I'm happy that *you're* happy. It gave her a little thrill, as if he had slipped his arm around her waist and pulled her close.

Muffled voices sounded in the screened passageway. Some belonged to the servants, but Isabel caught one voice that lifted her heart.

"Where are they? Are they here? Where—" Honor Thornleigh turned the corner to the hall and stopped speaking when she saw them, gazing as though to hold the precious sight forever. "You're here! You're really here!"

Isabel got up and rushed to meet her, and her mother wrapped an arm around her and said, "Oh, my darling girl."

Isabel threw her arms around her neck. "Mother."

The men had got to their feet and Carlos came to Isabel's side, and she turned to include him, feeling too much to speak. He gave her mother a respectful bow of the head, and there was a twinkle in his eye as he addressed her by her new title: "Your Ladyship."

"Carlos," she said, returning the smile. "Dear Carlos."

"It is good to see you," he said.

"And you, sir. Thank you for bringing her safe home."

Isabel wiped away tears of joy, even as she noted that her mother's beauty, at forty-nine, was no longer the blazing light it had once been. It was now a gentle glow.

"Oh!" her mother cried. "This must be Nicolas!"

"Come, Nico, don't be shy," Isabel said, coaxing him forward. Her mother crouched down and gazed at the boy as though he were made of gold, and Isabel felt a flush of pride. Nicolas didn't know what to make of her inspection, but Isabel could see that he immediately trusted this lady who smiled right into his eyes and caressed his cheek. She also noticed, with a pang, why her mother had used only one arm to embrace her. The other, the right one, hung at her side as though useless, as though the sinews at her shoulder had withered. How had that happened? During some violence with the man she had killed? She itched to know, but this was no time to blurt, *Whom did you murder?* The dead arm, though, unnerved her, and when her mother rose again Isabel embraced her with a rush of pity.

Her father called everyone to sit and be merry, and there was a flurry as servants carried in more food and poured more wine, and the dogs barked and trotted about, and the musicians swung into a new tune with gusto. As Isabel took her seat beside her father she saw her mother pause beside him, and she caught them exchange an unguarded look that seemed fraught with unease. If she had not been reaching for a plate for Nico, and her parents had not been surrounded by the swirl of activity that they believed screened them, she might have missed it. Their smiles had vanished, and she heard her father ask in a low voice, "Has she sent him to Scotland?"

"Yes," her mother said darkly.

He looked grim and said, "She has also recalled the Earl of Northumberland."

"Who replaces him?"

A shake of the head from her father, a mute admission that he did not know. The two shared a bleak look. Then her mother carried on to her seat at the other end.

Isabel had no idea what they were talking about, and she would not have minded if it weren't for the tension that had so obviously gripped them. The *she* they had referred to could only mean the Queen. And the troubled looks that had clouded their faces could only mean that all was not well. But the moment had passed, and everyone was now seated, and her father was on his feet, expansive with high spirits again and calling for a toast.

"To Carlos and Isabel—"

"And me!"

"And Nicolas," he added amid the smiles. His tone turned serious. "God be thanked for bringing you all safely to us."

Everyone drank. Isabel felt such a swell of happiness, tears stung her eyes.

Her father banged his goblet on the table and said, "Now, tell us all about the New World."

Isabel was happy to oblige, for she adored their home on the coast in sunny Trujillo. "Well," she began as others started eating, "when we first arrived we were like any dazed immigrants. Utterly confused. Everything looked so strange and different. I didn't know an *encomienda* from an *audiencia*."

"Isabel makes it sound worse than it was," Carlos said with a smile. "We got along fine."

"*You* did, speaking Spanish. It was all foreign to me."

He shook his head and said to her mother, "She made friends with so many people, we dined with a different family every night."

"Ah, but that was because of your success, once you became captain of the viceroy's guard." She was eager to let her parents know this. "The viceroy is Don Andres Hurtado de Mendoza. He is the representative of King Philip and oversees all Peru like a prince. He liked Carlos, and the trust he put in him changed our lives. It happened last year when a group of *encomenderos* rose up in rebellion. Carlos distinguished himself brilliantly in putting them down."

Isabel's mother raised her goblet. "To Carlos. Well done."

He raised his goblet and said with a wry smile, "To the rebels."

They all laughed.

"And because of that," Isabel went on, "the viceroy rewarded him."

"With gold? Land?" her father asked.

She smiled. He always got straight to the point. "With an *encomienda*," she said. "That's what everyone there wants. It's a big grant of land that's worked by the Indians. The whole country runs on the *encomienda* system. But only the King awards the *encomiendas*, through the viceroy, so the competition is fierce."

"These Indians," her mother said. "Are they your slaves?"

"Goodness, no. They've always worked the lands for their own rulers, the Inca leaders. They still live in the same villages they used to. All that's changed is that the rulers are now Spanish."

"Making the Spanish very rich," said her father. He turned to Carlos with a probing look. "It seems that includes you. Am I right?"

Carlos nodded. "The *encomienda* is a good one. Produces more wheat even than the one the viceroy gave himself." *Good* was an understatement, Isabel thought as she shared a look with him. She could almost feel his deep satisfaction. He wasn't arrogant like so many Spaniards, but he was proud of how far he had come. And no one was more proud of him than she was. "And there's our silver mine," Carlos went on. "It's producing well."

"Silver!" Isabel's mother exclaimed, impressed.

"I'll send you a dozen sets of plates and goblets, Lady Thornleigh," he said. "Only the Queen's own will match the quality."

"But what about the climate?" Frances asked. "Do you not die of the heat?"

Isabel was a little startled. It was the first time Frances had joined the conversation since they had arrived home. "No, I love it," she said.

"Ha," her father said. "Just like your mother."

"And the food," Isabel went on. "We pick lemons right off the trees by our veranda. There are bananas, pineapples, coconuts. They have a grain that's like tiny pearls, called *quinoa*. And they prepare whitefish by soaking it in lime juice, no cooking at all, and it's delicious." She knew she was rattling on, but it was such a pleasure to be speaking English again. So easy. So comfortable. "And there's a pear-shaped fruit with black skin rough as a snake, but inside is a luscious, pale green, velvety flesh that's as rich as butter. They call it avocado."

"Sounds wonderful," her mother said. "Oh, for fresh fruit and vegetables." She wrinkled her nose at her spoonful of spiced cabbage to make the point. "I long for spring to sow my garden. Perhaps I should plant some avocado seeds."

"*Seeds?*" Nicolas said with a sputter of a laugh.

"They're very large," Isabel explained. "Big as a baby's fist."

"Goodness me."

Her parents quizzed Nicolas about his favorite things in Peru, and he said making sand castles by the sea, and playing tops with Pedro, and riding Father Bartolomé's one-eared donkey. Isabel listened, tickled by his Spanish accent as he spoke English, and pleased that he was doing so well. She tried to have him keep up his English at home, but having lived all his young life in a Spanish land he was Spanish through and through.

He was yawning.

"Nico," Carlos said, "time for sleep."

"I'll take him upstairs," Isabel said.

"No, stay and talk. Enjoy." Carlos got up, saying to their son, "*Vamos*, Nico."

She kissed Nicolas good night, and he bowed to his grandparents, then to Frances, and then he and Carlos went off, hand in hand.

Isabel looked across the table at her sister-in-law. Frances was idly poking a piece of roast goose with her knife, most of her food untouched. No appetite, apparently. Because of being so heavy with child? It was hard to get used to the fact of Adam being married to this quiet, sad-looking lady who had to be ten years older than he was. Isabel felt sorry for her. "What about you, Frances?" she asked. "We've rattled on about us. I'd like to know about you. Did you grow up in London? Who are your people, your family? And how did you come to wed my wild brother?" She added with a laugh, "I hope you've tamed him."

Frances went still, her face turning pale. Isabel was aware of a heavy silence. Her father set to cutting his meat. Her mother took refuge in a swallow of wine. Isabel couldn't understand their coldness to their daughter-in-law. Frances was clearly upset about something, and their behavior, especially her father's, was downright rude.

"It has been a long day," Frances said. "I shall say good night, too." She got to her feet, making the dogs at the hearth raise their heads.

"Oh, I know what it's like," Isabel said. "I got so tired in the weeks before Nicolas was born. When do you expect to be delivered?"

Tears welled in Frances's eyes. In her effort to subdue them she clasped her hands tightly together above her bulging belly. "A month. God willing."

She's afraid of childbirth, Isabel thought with a rush of sympathy. She stood and reached across the table and took her sister-in-law's hand. It felt chilly and chapped. "You'll do fine," she said, and gave her a squeeze.

Frances offered a hesitant smile. "I hope you'll visit me, Isabel. Later, once you're settled."

"You don't live here?"

"No."

"Their house is on Lombard Street," her mother said. "Frances, thank you for bringing them from the quay. And, of course, you're welcome to stay the night." The words were generous, but the tone was not.

"Yes. Thank you. But I'd rather be home." Then, to Isabel, "Do visit me, won't you?"

"I will."

"I'll call in James to have someone take you," Isabel's father said, not even bothering to look at Frances. He started to get up.

"Don't bother, sir. I'll find him."

Then she was gone. The dogs settled down again at the hearth. Faint sounds of women's chatter came from the kitchen as the maids cleaned the dishes.

In the silence, Isabel's mother said, "Richard, you really must try."

"I do. But, by God, she's the last woman I would have chosen for Adam."

"Well, it's done. Till death do them part. We must accept it."

He seemed about to say something more, but stopped himself and poured another goblet of wine.

Isabel was bursting to ask for details, but feared Frances might still be within hearing. Instead, she allowed herself a verbal poke to her father. "You once said, sir, that Carlos was the last man you would have chosen for me."

They both looked at her, her father with a frown.

Her mother's lips curved in a small smile. "Your father is man enough to admit when he's been wrong. Aren't you, Richard?"

His expression softened. "In your case, Bel, dead wrong." But there was no mirth in him as he added, "In Adam's case, I doubt it."

Isabel was tucking Nicolas in. He had said he couldn't sleep. He missed Pedro, who usually slept with him. In all the excitement, Pedro had been lodged in the servants' quarters. Isabel made a mental note to correct that tomorrow.

"You don't have to check under the bed for ogres. Papa already did," Nicolas told her as she snugged the blanket up to his shoulders. They were speaking in Spanish. He added, as though to break hard news to her gently, "He does it better than you. He checks with his sword."

"There are no ogres in England," she said. A single candle cast its light from the bedside table, making him look small in the big bed, all alone. "They were rounded up and told to leave."

His eyes grew large. "Where did they go?"

"Back to Ogreland. They're having a big feast there now. They're glad to be home, with their brothers and sisters."

"I wish I had a brother. He could play tops with me when Pedro's busy."

"You'll soon have a cousin. Your aunt Frances and uncle Adam are having a baby."

"Tonight?"

"Soon." She kissed his forehead.

"A song, too," he negotiated.

She was singing softly to him, his eyelids growing heavy, when her mother appeared at the doorway. Isabel beckoned her in as she kept singing.

Honor sat down on the opposite edge of the bed, and they both watched Nico's eyelids drift shut as Isabel's song ended. Then she felt her mother's gaze on her. "I've read your letters so many times, Bel, I think I've memorized them."

"I did the same with yours," Isabel said. "But, oh, it was hard to wait the months for the letters to reach us. Especially this last year, hearing nothing after Adam sent the news."

"And so you made that long journey just for me." She shook her head in wonder. "My darling."

"It's worth it, just to see you again." Could she ask now? *Whom did you kill?*

Her mother nodded, smiling. They both looked again at Nico, the living embodiment of their bond of blood. "That was a pretty tune you were singing. I wish I understood Spanish. What was it?"

"Just a ditty the friar sings to the children."

"Father Bartolomé? With the one-eared donkey?"

"The same. He's a good teacher. Nico adores him."

Her mother smoothed a wrinkle in her skirt, as though to avoid comment. Was she disturbed, Isabel wondered, that the priest would be teaching her grandson the Catholic catechism? It tripped her for a moment, realizing that she should have thought of this. She had come home to a country that had turned Protestant. She said quickly, to avoid that topic, "Nico knows his letters so well now. He's quick."

Her mother ran her hand tenderly along Nico's foot, which lay under the cover. "He's a sweet boy." She had to reach across herself with her left hand, Isabel noticed. The right arm hung limp.

"What happened to your arm?"

She didn't answer right away. When she did, the words were terse. "Queen Mary's agents. They got wind of a rebellion plot and detained me. Questioned me. Their techniques are not gentle."

Isabel gasped. "You mean . . . the rack?"

She nodded. Then gave Isabel a searching look. "You're wondering, was I involved in the plot?"

"I'm wondering how you could bear the pain."

She shrugged. "Not much choice."

"Will it heal? In time?"

Her mother shook her head. She seemed to have accepted the affliction.

Isabel had to know. "*Were* you involved?"

"I don't deny that I wanted Queen Mary deposed." Her eyes

locked on Isabel's. "Your sympathies once lay there, too. Wyatt's uprising."

It sounded like an invitation. Or a challenge. "That all seems a long time ago."

"Not so long. Five years."

"Long enough for everything here to have changed. You are fast friends with the *new* Queen."

"I'm proud to say that I am."

"She was grateful to you, Frances says. Was it because of what you suffered for her sake?"

A sharp look from her mother.

It seemed obvious to Isabel. "The goal of any rebellion must have been to put Princess Elizabeth on the throne. Was it for information about her that they tortured you? Frances said—"

"Frances does not always know what she's talking about."

Isabel heard the reprimand. She let the subject drop. Other issues felt more pressing.

"Mother, is there something wrong? Something to do with the Queen? I heard you and Father talking."

"Did you?" was the steady reply. It sounded as though she wanted to say more but was unsure if she should.

"You can tell me. I haven't crossed an ocean to see you just to chat about lemon trees and donkeys."

Her mother's smile was warm. "No. You are made of sterner stuff."

"So tell me. What's amiss?" She sensed a deep anxiety in her mother's eyes that belied her outward calm.

Her mother reached across Nico's sleeping form and took Isabel's hand. It was a gesture of trust, and it moved Isabel. "This must be between us alone, Bel. Matters of state. Promise me that you will keep—"

Nicolas jostled, murmuring incomprehensible words in his sleep. His movement tugged the open collar of his nightshirt away from his throat, revealing the gold crucifix on the chain around his neck. The cross glinted in the candlelight, and Isabel saw her mother's eyes drawn to its glimmer. Something in her face changed, hardened, like a door closing. She withdrew her hand from Isabel's.

"Well," she said, "perhaps we should let the child sleep."

Isabel knew that tone: *I don't wish to discuss this.* It made her feel cold. Why did her mother suddenly not want to confide in her? "He's fine," she said. "He won't wake up until dawn. What were you going to say?"

Her mother looked at her as though gauging how to reply. Her eyes went back to Nicolas's crucifix. "I see you've become Catholic," she said.

"Impossible not to, in Spanish Peru." Isabel had tried to say this lightly, but the heavy significance of her next words was impossible to hide. "Does it matter?"

Her mother was still. Then her face softened. A smile twitched her mouth. "When I was a girl of, oh, seventeen, I think, an academic vicar came to visit my guardian. Sir Thomas was well known for his writings, and often received such guests." Isabel nodded. She knew her mother had been a ward of Sir Thomas More, a scholar and adviser to King Henry VIII. "Sir Thomas had written a book in Latin that was popular, called *Utopia*," her mother went on. "It was about a fictitious island commonwealth in the New World, where the people, though heathen, were morally upright. The vicar had come in all earnestness to ask Sir Thomas for the island's exact location. He intended, he said, to make a missionary expedition to bring to the ignorant Utopians the blessed civilization of the Church." She laughed lightly. "A most delicious fool, for the place is purely imaginary. *Utopia* means 'no place' in Greek."

Isabel smiled. A charming tale. Yet she wondered what the point was.

Her mother's smile faded. "Protestant. Catholic," she said, shaking her head. "I shall never get used to people killing one another over the best way to reach another imaginary destination, called heaven."

Confusion prickled Isabel. The blasphemy was not to her taste, although she admitted she felt the same disdain her mother did for the violence that men committed in the name of God. But what bothered her more was her mother's shift of topic. *Does it matter?* Isabel had asked. She had not received an answer.

Her mother got to her feet. "You haven't said how long you can stay, Bel," she said pleasantly. "I hope we can keep you all here until well after Christmas."

"I hope so, too. Carlos does need to get back eventually, but . . . well, Christmas was always my favorite time."

"Good." Her mother blew her a kiss across Nicolas. "Sweet dreams." She started for the door.

"Mother, why don't you like Frances? You and Father?"

She turned. "I don't *dis*like her. We have accepted her."

"Not the same thing, is it."

"No," she conceded. She looked loath to go on, but then said, "You should know, Bel. Queen Mary's agent, the man who put me on the rack—it was Frances's brother."

Isabel was so shocked, she could not speak. Questions exploded in her mind. Who was this vile man? How could Adam have married a woman whose brother had tortured their mother? But one thing was clear: the reason behind the chilly current that ran between her parents and Frances.

"That's not all. You should know everything. Frances is a Grenville. Her brother was Lord John Grenville."

The name stunned Isabel. And lit fury inside her. The long feud between the house of Grenville and the Thornleighs had brought her family so much misery. "Will those terrible people never leave us in peace?"

"They have now. I killed Lord John."

❧ 3 ❧

Adam's Appeal

Secrets. Evasions. Whisperings. Isabel felt so frustrated she wanted to kick something. Wanted to snatch a snowball from the boys squealing over a pitched battle between the Cheapside shops she was passing and hurl it. But at what? At whom? The boys with their snowballs in the lane were skirmishing with adversaries plainly in front of them, but her adversary was not made of flesh and bone. It was a tension, an atmosphere, a *mood*. Nothing she could stand up to, or even touch. Just whisperings. Evasions. Secrets.

She had been stunned by her mother's calm admission that she had killed Lord John Grenville—though she felt that no man deserved it more for torturing her mother. But when she had asked for an explanation of how it happened she had got an outright refusal. "No, Isabel. It's behind us. I never want to hear that name again." She had asked her father about it the next day, but he was even more terse. "May he rest in the hottest flames of hell. Forget Grenville. And don't trouble your mother about it."

But how could she forget it? She was part of the hostility between the two families, like it or not. She had been there, in her parents' Colchester parlor six years ago when Grenville's father had shot her mother. Isabel had seen her father strike the man down before he could shoot again. Her mother had survived, thank

God, but now here was this thunderbolt—John Grenville had tortured her and then she had killed him. Where would the brutal feud end?

Or had it, with Adam's marriage? Had Frances Grenville been the peacemaker? Frances herself might have shed some light on the matter, but Isabel felt so bewildered by the union of her brother with a daughter of the house of Grenville that she had shirked her promise to visit her sister-in-law.

The mystery was not the worst of it. She might have accepted being shut out of the closet of family skeletons, since it was clear that passions still simmered. Wounds were still raw. Perhaps her parents simply found it too hard to talk about. After all, she had been back amongst them for only three days. In time, her mother might speak her heart. But Isabel knew they were shutting her out of more, and that hurt her deeply. They were involved in some precarious business with the Queen, she could feel it. Though heaven knew she saw little enough of them. They spent all day at Whitehall Palace, and when they came home separately, her mother looking weary, her father looking worried, they immediately put on a front of high spirits for her and Carlos and deflected every question she put to them about the Queen. "Let's have some supper first," her mother would say brightly, and then steer the conversation to inquire what Isabel and the others had done that day. Had Nicolas enjoyed the bear garden? Did Carlos find the Smithfield winter fair amusing? Isabel felt it like an insult. She had crossed an ocean to come to her parents' aid, and they treated her as though she were not even part of the family. Just a visiting guest, someone worth only a false face. Someone to hide secrets from.

Her hurt feelings smoldered—and her curiosity burned. She had visited the servants' quarters in the mews to ask Tom Yates what he knew about it, but was told that Tom had been sent on an errand to her father's country estate. She had then stooped so low as to question a shy young footman, and even Ellen, the businesslike cook. But they had blinked at her in silence, members of the conspiracy. That was when Isabel knew her frustration was making her unreasonable. Conspiracy? How could she think the servants would know about royal doings at the palace? So that morning, after Pedro had taken Nicolas back to the bear garden and Carlos went to see a visiting merchant from Seville, she had gone to the kitchen and apologized to Ellen, bewildering the poor woman even more, then told her she was going out to Cheapside to buy Christmas gifts. She had taken refuge in the brisk walk across the city in the cold air. But then, at Chastelain's shop on Goldsmith's Row, the proprietor's behavior had been the last straw.

"Please send it to my father's house on Bishopsgate," she had told him as he tied a tag to the gold salt cellar she had bought for Frances. She started to tell him the location, but he shook his head.

"No need, my lady, I know your parents' house well. Lady Thornleigh is a valued customer. We missed her during her troubles."

"Troubles?"

He glanced up, and looked as if he had said more than he should. "There now." He quickly tightened the string's knot, evading her eyes. "Will there be anything else?"

Conspiracy was what it *felt* like. Isabel bit back her humiliation and told him that no, that would be all. She asked him, barely civil, if booksellers could still be found at St. Paul's. She slammed the door behind her as she left.

The biting cold air helped. The bustle of shoppers on Cheapside, too, for she was not the only one buying Christmas gifts on Goldsmith's Row. Yesterday, when she had crossed the busy thoroughfare with Nicolas, she had tried to explain that "cheap" had once meant "marketplace," but he'd asked where the pineapples and bananas were, and she realized that Cheapside's array of sumptuous goldsmiths' houses, where the wares gleamed in the windows, did not fit her son's notion of a market.

Pineapples and bananas, she thought. Sunshine and bougainvillea blossoms. The beauty of Peru was so at odds with frigid London, its streets of muddy snow, its pewter-colored sky. A few snowflakes were falling, pristine and pretty as they drifted past rooftops where smoke curled from chimneys, but even the snow became dirty the moment it touched the ground. She had girlhood memories of wonder at London's grand buildings—St. Paul's, Guildhall, the famous livery companies' halls, Westminster Hall—but the city now seemed to her a crowded jumble of smoke-grimed shops, crumbling facades, trash-littered alleys, and smelly ditches. London wore its age like a seedy old man. In Peru, no Spanish building, not even Lima's lovely cathedral, was much older than Isabel herself.

And the London beggars—they seemed to be everywhere. Men, women, children, huddled in rags, scabbed with sores, blank-eyed with hunger. Were they desperate country folk, drawn to the city for sustenance? Had recent harvests been such a disaster? Or was this the legacy of Queen Mary's harsh, mismanaged reign, dying with her a year ago? "Bloody Mary"—that's what she had heard her parents' servants call the late Queen. Whatever the cause, Isabel felt pity for the unfortunate souls in this city of chilly, pinched-faced want. It sent her thoughts back to her sun-kissed house in Trujillo that overlooked the sparkling sea. She and Carlos had dropped everything to come to England, but he could not stay away indefinitely. The viceroy did not permit absentee *encomenderos*. A brief visit to Europe was allowed, but nothing prolonged. The viceroy could retract Carlos's *encomienda* grant and award it to the next deserving man. Very soon, Isabel would have to start planning their return voyage.

What a jumble of emotions she felt. It would be hard to leave her parents after seeing them so briefly. And she longed to know what was troubling them. But if they would not talk to her, what could she do? Their life was here, and she was no longer a part of it. It hurt. And sparked her resentment afresh, a feeling that smoldered as she carried on to find the gift she wanted for her mother, a newly published *Herbal*. Gardening was her mother's passion. She loved getting her hands dirty with daffodil bulbs, rose cuttings, and pear tree grafts. The quest brought Isabel to the end of Paternoster Row, which led into the churchyard of St. Paul's.

The precincts of the massive Norman cathedral were crowded, as usual, and she squeezed past people thronging the ice-slick cobbles. She knew there would be a bazaar atmosphere inside, for Londoners used the cathedral's interior to transact every kind of business. Merchants hailed colleagues to discuss trade news. Gentlemen came to hire servingmen who lounged by the pillars. Ladies strolled arm in arm to gossip. Illiterate folk paid scriveners to write letters to their relations in the countryside. Whores trolled for customers, and pickpockets and confidence men eyed their marks. As a child Isabel had often stood with her father while he and his associates discussed developments in the wool cloth trade, and she had liked watching the lively dramas going on around them. Once, she stood next to a portly gentleman craning his neck to look up at the painted ceiling—clearly not a native of London— and a young man kindly pointed out to him that the place was full of pickpockets so he would do well to remove the impressive gold chain around his neck and conceal it in his sleeve. The visitor did so, with fulsome thanks for such helpful advice. A few minutes later there was a fracas near the doors—some scuffling and raised voices that drew the attention of everyone—and when it died down Isabel saw the look of panic on the visitor's face. The chain had vanished, and so had the friendly young man.

Today she was interested in none of the hubbub inside the cathedral. She made her way to the outdoor booksellers' stalls snugged between the mighty stone buttresses. She navigated between an old woman leading a donkey laden with firewood and a bony dog snuffling at the muddy snow, and she reached the tables where books were laid out under a rough canvas awning that sagged between poles. She stood elbow to elbow with customers who were haggling with the booksellers and let her gaze range over the tomes on mathematics and animal husbandry and astrology. There were beautifully illustrated almanacs, and calendars of celestial events called ephemerides, and manuals for surveyors and carpenters. And there were dozens of pamphlets with sermons. It seemed that Londoners, newly and passionately Protestant thanks to their new Queen, could not get enough of sermons. But amid all these she finally found the *Herbal* she wanted, a freshly printed edition with extensive diagrams, bound in handsome green leather.

Isabel was paying for the book when a shout almost made her fumble her shilling change. It came from around the corner. People from the far end of the bookstalls were scurrying to investigate, disappearing around the cathedral. More shouts, louder, angrier. Isabel felt a prickle of alarm. Best to leave.

She tucked the book into the pocket of her cloak and hurried away from the stalls. Her route led her in the direction of the shouting, but she was careful to skirt the commotion and stay well clear of the crowd. It was growing, though, with people running in from all directions. Like to an execution, she thought uncomfortably. The center of the commotion was Paul's Cross, the raised outdoor pulpit where leading churchmen regularly preached sermons to throngs of Londoners. It held no preacher today, but Isabel saw a wild-eyed man scrambling up its steps, shouting curses. Two men were close on his heels, groping at him to stop him. He was quicker and made it to the top.

"A bastard heretic calls herself our queen!" he cried out to the crowd. There were gasps from the people. "She is a foul sacrilege!" he ranted. "God will smite her! Smite the fornicating heretics who follow her, all of you!"

Isabel was trying to get out of the churchyard, but it was slow going with so many people jammed in, everyone moving closer to the commotion while she was trying to go the other way.

The two men going after the wild-eyed man in the pulpit reached him and one punched him in the face. The other grabbed him by the collar and heaved him down the stairs. He tumbled down and fell in the muck. He struggled to his feet, crying out, "God will smite you all! Every fornicating whoreson dog among you!"

Someone in the crowd yelled back, "Shut your face, you God-rotting papist!" and hurled a rock. It struck the side of the man's head and he lurched, then fell, bleeding. One of the men who had pushed him out of the pulpit came tearing down the steps, his face a livid red. He kicked the fallen "papist" in the belly.

"Hold off!" said a gentleman in a jeweled cap, stepping between them to shield the kicked man. A Catholic sympathizer, apparently. Another "papist."

The red-faced man lifted a dagger and plunged it into the gentleman's shoulder. There were gasps from the crowd, then shouting. The gentleman swayed, clutching his shoulder. Three servants with him reached for him in horror, supporting him, one desperately pressing his bare hand to stanch the blood from his master's wound. The red-faced assailant bolted, running straight into the crowd. People made way for him to escape, calling gleeful encouragement. Then several men among them surged forward and began kicking the fallen, wild-eyed man who had screamed curses from the pulpit. Suddenly, everyone seemed to be running, swarming both him and the gentleman's frightened servants.

Isabel felt the press of bodies pushing her that way, too, and their hot, angry breath as they yelled, "Down with papists!" It was like an ocean tide, impossible to fight. A man's elbow jabbed her ribs. He didn't notice her as he yelled at the mob's victims, but the sharp pain made Isabel stumble. She fought to stay upright, panicked at the thought of being trampled. The panic gave her a jolt of strength and she finally pushed free—at least a little more free, into a pocket of space where the crowd was surging around a lantern post. Her cape had gotten wrenched tight at the throat, and she loosened its strings, catching her breath, glad to be out of the crush of bodies. She was looking for a way out to the street when she saw a black-bearded man pointing an angry finger at her from the edge of the crowd.

"Crucifix!" he shouted.

Her hand went instinctively for the gold cross at her throat.

Several men beside the bearded man turned to look at her in fury. "Papist!" one yelled.

They came at her so fast she froze. Then she twisted around to run. But two more men lunged at her from that direction, including a huge laborer who pushed her shoulders with both hands, the force of it like a board that walloped her backward. She staggered, groping for support from the man behind her. But he stepped aside to let her fall. She hit the ground on her back so hard it knocked the breath from her and pain shuddered up her spine. The faces looking down on her blocked the sky, a blur of hate-filled eyes and shaking fists.

"Filthy papist whore."

She struggled to get up. A boot stomped her chest, pinning her to the ground. Terror flooded her. A primal fear that set her mind screaming for help from Carlos. *"Socorro!"* she cried. Help!

"What's she jabbering?"

"Spanish," the bearded man growled. "A papist trollop, and Spanish to boot."

"If the papists take over we'll *all* be talking Spanish. Or God-cursed French."

"Aye, they'll force it down our throats like the stinking bread they call Christ's body."

The bearded one crouched down and thrust his face next to hers and grabbed the thin chain of her crucifix, his jagged fingernails scraping her skin. "Filth," he growled, and jerked the chain, snapping it off her neck.

Another face loomed close to hers. Broken teeth and red whiskers and a stink of ale. Even in her terror Isabel knew he was not like the others; he was calm. It made him all the more frightening. "Bring her over," he said, jerking his chin toward the church wall. They grabbed her arms and dragged her despite her furious squirming. They took her to an alcove. She felt its darkness. Her fear dug deep. No one could see her here.

They dropped her, but the red-whiskered man instantly grabbed her hand, his eyes on her ruby ring. She wrenched her arm free. "Let me go!" He snatched her hand back and yanked the ring, but could not get it past her knuckle. He whipped out a knife, then looked up at an accomplice. "Keep her still."

Thick legs in boots straddled her. She made a desperate lunge to get up, but the accomplice thudded down on her, sitting on her chest, knees up, his crotch in her face. She could scarcely breathe. This brute clamped a hand around her wrist and forced her hand into the air so that the man with the knife had clear access. Isabel felt sick with terror. He was going to carve off her finger! She kicked wildly and thrashed to get out from under the brute.

"Won't be still, eh?" He bunched his other fist and raised it to punch her face.

Hands from above grappled the brute's shoulders and hauled him off her. Isabel sucked in a breath as his weight lifted. She suddenly saw daylight. Then a face that made her gasp. Adam!

Her brother was fighting the brute. The black-bearded man lunged for Adam, too. Isabel groped for the brute's foot to bring him down, but she could not reach him. Adam took a punch on the chin from one man, a punch in the belly from the other.

Suddenly, two men were at Adam's side, hauling off his attackers. Free now, Adam whirled around to the red-whiskered man with the knife. But the man crouched at Isabel's side and held the knife at her throat. If she moved, the blade would slice her. "Back off!" he told Adam.

Isabel groped for a handful of stony snow and flung it in his eyes. He shuddered, blinking, and Adam kicked the knife from his hand. He sprawled backward. Scrambling to his feet, he took off, plowing into the crowd.

Adam turned to the two men who had come with him. They were finishing with Isabel's tormentors. One of them punched the brute in the face, and the brute staggered back a step, his nose spurting blood, then turned on his heel and slunk away. The other was chasing off the black-bearded man. Adam called to the first man, "Look out, Rogers! Knife!"

His friend whirled around and raised his forearm to deflect the attack of an assailant with a dagger. Then he punched the man in the belly so hard, the fellow crumpled. Bending over, gripping his stomach, he pushed off into the crowd.

Adam was helping Isabel up. She was still catching her breath. Her clothes were askew and her hands were dirty and she could not stop trembling. The moment she was on her feet she threw her arms around her brother's neck. He gave her a quick, tight hug.

"You picked a fine time to go sightseeing."

"Oh, Adam!" She pulled away and saw his wry smile. "But how did you know I—" She saw blood trickling from the corner of his mouth. She pulled her handkerchief from her sleeve to tend his cut, but he took the handkerchief from her and pressed it to her throat, and when he lowered it she saw the smear of her own blood. In her fear, she hadn't felt the man's blade nick her. She felt suddenly shaky, light-headed. She groped Adam's arm for support. She started to ask again, "How—"

Horsemen thundered into the churchyard, a half dozen of the sheriff's men. Adam tugged Isabel out of the way as the horses passed, their hooves throwing up clods of muck. Fistfights had broken out in the furious melee around the pulpit, and amid the blows and shouts the sheriff's men shouldered their mounts into the skirmishing.

Adam said to Isabel, "We need to get you out of here. Can you walk?"

"I think so. Yes."

He turned to the two men with him. One was picking up his cap from the ground while the other scanned the crowd, keeping watch for new assailants. They were dressed in rough homespun clothes, like soldiers or sailors, and were armed with long daggers at their belts. Adam, under his fine blue cloak, wore a sword. None of them had unsheathed their weapons. "Go on ahead," Adam told them. "I'll meet you at the jetty."

"Aye, sir," they said almost in unison, touching their foreheads in a rudimentary salute. They turned to go, and Isabel said to them, "Thank you. Both of you." They glanced back at her, and the one named Rogers gave her a mute nod. They strode away.

Isabel looked at the spot where she had been attacked. "My crucifix," she said. They had torn it from her and left it on the ground. She went back and crouched down to rescue it from the muck. She wiped the cross as clean as she could with her dirty fingers.

"I'd leave it if I were you," Adam warned. His eyes flicked to a man watching them darkly from the edge of the crowd.

She jammed the crucifix into her cloak pocket next to her mother's book, then came back to Adam's side, wanting to get far away from these mad people. He took her elbow, his gaze still on the watching man. "Come."

Once they were out of the churchyard it was a relief to reach Watling Street with its ordinary, calm foot traffic and oxcarts. Isabel still felt shaky, and Adam saw it. Under the sign of the Black Dog he pushed open the door. They went into the alehouse, and Isabel welcomed its fusty warmth. A handful of men who were drinking glanced up with scant interest. Adam spoke to the landlady, and soon Isabel was sitting on a bench by the fire with a cup of warm cider to refresh her and a basin of water to clean her muddy hands.

"That's better," Adam said. "I can't send you home looking like something the cat dragged in."

Home. Carlos. She remembered how she had cried out in Spanish. She shuddered, imagining what might have happened if Adam had not rescued her. Drying her hands with a rough linen towel, she said quietly, "Thank God you were there."

"God may have had little to do with it," he said with a smile. "I came to find you. Father's steward said you'd gone to Chastelain's, and at Chastelain's they said you'd gone to St. Paul's."

She looked at him in wonder. It had been five years. She didn't know where to start. "I hear I must call you *Sir* Adam," she said. "Sounds odd. Like some old man."

"And a little chap now calls *you* 'Mother.' " He shook his head in mock amazement. "I remember you in your cradle with your thumb in your mouth."

She had to laugh. "You'll soon be a father yourself. Hard to imagine. You, a settled homebody."

His smile faded. "Bel, that's why I wanted to see you." He seemed about to say more, but a man who had lumbered over to the bench sat down beside them and settled in to nurse his pot of ale. "I need to talk to you," Adam said to her under his breath. "But not here. Do you feel well enough to walk?"

Her body felt bruised all over, and her spirits were still shaken, but she did long to talk to him. The cider had steadied her a little, and her mind began to hum with questions. "Yes," she said. "I must get home."

"And I have to get to the Old Swan Stairs to meet my men. It's on the way. Shall we?"

They set out along Watling Street to where it curved into Budge Row, making their way toward the river. Isabel was glad of the support of Adam's arm, and as they walked she stole looks at him. He was dark-haired like her, but whereas she had inherited their father's blue eyes, his were as brown as chestnuts, the legacy of their father's first wife. It felt so comforting to have him by her side.

Adam, her stepbrother, nine years older, the hero of her childhood. Adam, who knew everything. How to wade the stream by their Colchester house to show her eggs in the plovers' nests on the island. How to pilfer treacle buns from the cook's pantry when everyone else was abed. How to race around the Colchester church graveyard, jumping to touch the belfry rope on the way. Sometimes he let her be the victor if he hopped up onto the parapet wall and walked it like a tightrope so she could reach the churchyard lichgate first. Now she tried to see in his face any clue of how he had lived in the years since she had last seen him. Almost as tall as their father, he was as sturdy as ever, but the slightest bit thinner, and only a sister would have noticed the new tautness in his face.

"I hear Carlos has become quite the Spanish grandee."

Isabel was surprised by the cool edge in his voice, as though he held some grudge against Carlos. She couldn't imagine why. "Not exactly," she said, then added, glad to show her pride in her husband, "but he has done well."

"Spain," he said darkly. "England's ally, so they claim. We'll see."

She had no wish to talk politics. "Can you come back to the house? Nicolas would be thrilled to meet you. I have spun tales about Uncle Adam ever since he could crawl."

He said he could not, that he had to return to the naval yard at Portsmouth. He was in the capital for just the day, having had a meeting this morning with Sir Benjamin Gonson, treasurer of the Admiralty.

"Hobnobbing with great men. My, Sir Adam, how you've risen in the world." But her teasing was only to mask how pleased she was at his advancement. Adam had worked on their father's ships from the time he was twelve, moving up from deckhand to pilot to captain and master. No one knew the sea better. "Father said you've been at work rebuilding the Queen's navy?"

"Trying to. Took months just evaluating assets and liabilities. An inventory of each ship's tonnage, state of readiness, quality of artillery. Then calculating what it would take, at what cost, to make the fleet into a true fighting force." He shook his head. "Hell of a task. The fleet's just thirty-four vessels, and several of those are mere barks and pinnaces, one brigantine. Of the twenty-one great ships, only eleven are in satisfactory condition, the other twelve so dilapidated they aren't worth repairing. I've assured Her Majesty, though, that she can rely on private vessels as well. If necessary, three dozen merchant ships can be refitted and fashioned for defense."

"Good heavens, you're friends with the Queen, too? Like Mother and Father?"

He shot her a look. "You were away a long time, Bel." He frowned, as though not sure whether to go on. "A lot happened," he said. Then, nothing more.

He's just like them, she thought with a jolt of anger. Why would no one tell her what *did* happen? The rush of emotion made her shaky again, and she stumbled.

"Here," he said, guiding her to a low stone wall that skirted a churchyard. "Sit down."

She did. And took a few deep breaths. The church's tombstones brought back a shiver of her ordeal at St. Paul's. It tumbled together in her mind with her resentment about being shut out of the family's secrets. "I met Frances," she said. It came out like a challenge. She hoped Adam would take it up. Explain.

But he was silent. They were near Thames Street with its smells of fish and seaweedy debris. Shouts of "Oars!" and "Westward, ho!" came from people beckoning wherries. A couple of children ran by chasing a goose. Behind the churchyard wall pigeons fluttered down onto the snow between the tombstones and pecked at the brown grass beneath.

Adam sat down beside her. "I have a favor to ask."

"Of course," she said. "What is it?"

"I have to go away for . . . well, for quite a while. My wife is near her time. She has no mother, no sisters to help. Would you look after her? Stay with her a while to be sure all's well with the babe?"

A while? Isabel thought with a touch of dismay. "How long?"

"A few months. She's not young. It may be a hard birth. Hard for both."

Not young. And not one of us. "Adam," she said, "how did you come to marry a Grenville?"

He looked down the street. "A long story." He stood up.

"But one I want to hear." She stood as well.

He looked at her. "Are you all right now? Can you go on?"

"Adam, I have a right to know. Carlos and I need to start back home soon, but you're asking me to postpone that to stay with Frances. I want to know about her. Did you marry her to end the feud? Or was it *despite* the feud? Do you love her so very much?"

He let out a bitter laugh. "Ask her."

"Stop this. You're as bad as Mother and Father. They go back and forth to the palace in some secret business but never say a word about what it is. They put on happy faces as though they're just going there to play cards, but I know something is seriously amiss."

They stood face-to-face on the busy street. His look darkened. "They're hoping it will all go away. It won't."

"Adam, what is happening? Why won't any of you talk to me?"

"Because what's happening doesn't concern you."

"Not *concern* me? I'm part of this family!"

"Well, you're not part of what's going on in England. Not anymore. You're Spanish."

"I have as much English blood as—"

"That's not what I mean."

"Then what?"

"You're Catholic."

The word fell between them like a tree trunk.

So that's it, she thought with a shiver. Her own family didn't trust her. They thought of her the way those men who had attacked her did, as a "papist." Except her family put on smiling faces. False faces.

She took a deep breath to steady herself, and looked away.

Adam said, an apology in his voice, "Isabel, it's the coming child that matters." She looked back at him and he said, "I care very much about the child."

She saw that he *did* care, deeply, and it touched her. But she had

had enough of being shut out of this family. She put all the steel she could into her voice. "If you want me to do this, if you want me to see to the welfare of your wife and child, then tell me everything. If you won't, I swear I will book passage on the very next ship bound for Spain and then sail home to Peru. Decide, Adam. Now."

❧ 4 ❧

The Borderland Threat

"**Y**ou always were the stubborn one." Adam's frustrated smile told Isabel that he was going to tell her what she wanted to know. They set out walking again, and although she still felt tender and bruised from the rough handling of her attackers, she kept up with her brother's stride, impatient to hear. Turning south on Walbrook, they passed a cluster of livery halls—Chandlers Hall, Cutlers Hall, Skinners Hall—but Adam didn't speak until they turned onto Thames Street. A warren of narrow streets led down to the river a few hundred feet away. He guided her down one.

"First," he said, "Father is advising the Queen's council about buying munitions in the Low Countries. No one knows Antwerp better than he does, and its merchant networks."

Of that much, Isabel was well aware. As a wool cloth merchant with business on both sides of the Narrow Seas, their father had always kept a house in Antwerp. When she was a child the family had lived there for a time. But what was this business about munitions? She put that question aside for the moment and asked, "And Mother?"

"She helped arrange a visit of the Scottish Earl of Arran, all in secret. She kept him in Sir William Cecil's house on Canon Row, and the Queen met him in private." He added with some vigor, "The rumor that the Queen wanted to talk marriage with the Earl is nonsense. It was just a political meeting. She sent him back to Scotland. He can do some good there."

Scotland. She remembered her parents whispering at the supper table about Scotland. "Who is the Earl of Arran?"

He looked at her as if to say, You don't even know *that?*

She tried to keep the angry frustration out of her voice. "As you said, I've been away a long time."

They had reached Adam's destination, the Old Swan Stairs, one of the city's oldest wharfs, and they stopped at the street edge that overlooked the busy jetty. Seagulls shrilled over the fishwives at their stalls and over the housewives and servants shopping for the day's catch. On the water stairs wherrymen beckoned customers into their boats. A young lordling in a crimson cape trimmed with fox fur led a painted lady by the hand into a tilt boat and they disappeared under its canopy.

"You've come home at a crisis, Bel," Adam said. "There's no other way to put it. Look around you. By spring, London could be occupied by French troops."

She gaped at him. The thought was appalling. "How? Why?"

"The Auld Alliance."

"The what?"

"That's what the Scots call it. Goes back over two hundred and fifty years. A pact between France and Scotland, signed by every one of their monarchs for over two centuries, as a hedge against *us.* They've sworn that if either country is attacked by England, the other will invade English territory."

"But I don't understand. England hasn't attacked anyone."

"That's not the point. Over the centuries the alliance has fused the two countries together. Twenty years ago the Scottish King James married a daughter of the mightiest family in France, the house of Guise, the power behind the French throne, and since then Scotland's been a vassal state of France. Even more so since James died with no son, so his baby daughter, Mary Stuart, became Queen of Scots. The French sent her to Paris and married her to their king's son. That son became king a few months ago, so the sixteen-year-old Queen of Scots is now Queen of France, too."

"Then who rules in Scotland?"

"Her mother, Marie de Guise. She governs as the Queen Regent. And back in Paris her Guise brothers, five of them, from dukes to bishops, advise their teenage king. They're the real rulers of France. But here's the thing. Not all Scots have been happy with France running Scotland. Their nobles have been seething for years at how Frenchmen dominate the court in Edinburgh, and the Protestants among them have been seething at Catholic rule. Now they've come together under a leader named John Knox. He's not a lord or even a gentleman, just a common Scot, a Protestant preacher. But he's a fiery one, and clever, and he's organized their forces, and a month ago they rose up against their French overlords. The French responded by sending thousands of soldiers to Scotland. They're about to put down the rebels. That's—"

"Adam, stop. What has all this got to do with England? You said there's a crisis. How?"

"Because of Mary Stuart, Queen of Scots. She has Tudor blood, and since Europe's Catholics consider our queen illegitimate— damn their hides—the Queen of Scots has declared to all the world that *she* is the rightful queen of England. Do you see? The Guise family, running both France and Scotland, are poised to crush the Scottish rebels and then look south to the bigger prize— us. They're using the rebellion emergency as a chance to flood our northern border with troops as a first step to invading England and putting Mary Stuart on the throne."

Invasion. The word held terror for Isabel. Images of blood splashed her mind—slaughtered English defenders, raped Englishwomen, scorched English fields.

"The Scottish lords have asked England for help in their fight," Adam went on. "Our Queen has been reluctant to take sides, but she did meet secretly with the rebel Earl of Arran because he has a claim to the Scottish throne. Her support of him will give the rebels heart."

"Sir Adam," a man called.

They looked down at the jetty where a boat nudged the water stairs. Isabel recognized the man standing in the bow—Adam's friend who'd helped fight off her attackers. The boat was a ship's longboat, and six sailors sat behind him at the oars.

"Rogers," Adam called back, "come up here." As the man jogged up the steps, Adam said to Isabel, "My lieutenant." When Rogers reached them, Adam said, "See this lady home, would you? It's not far, Bishopsgate Street. Meet me back at the ship."

"Aye, sir."

"Give us a moment first." The lieutenant ambled to a diplomatic distance to wait, and Adam said to Isabel, "I must be off."

"But we'll fight them if they dare attack," she said, her mind locked on the French threat. "Queen Elizabeth will surely beat them back."

"How? She has no standing army. She took over a country that her sister left bankrupt. And as I've told you, she inherited a navy that's just a handful of run-down ships."

He made it sound terrible. Isabel had had no idea things were so bad.

"What's worse, she can't be sure of the loyalty of half her subjects." Adam's voice hardened. "The Catholics. Many of them practice their religion in secret, and with growing hostility. Especially in the north—Yorkshire, Northumberland—where the old ways are so rooted. And some of them are very powerful lords. The Queen just dismissed the Earl of Northumberland as Warden of the East and Middle Marches, which is basically the whole Scottish frontier, because he's a known Catholic and she can't trust him if it comes to choosing sides." Isabel bristled at that, but Adam barreled on. "Elizabeth's hold on the throne is so precarious, people are laying bets throughout Europe on whether her reign will see a second year."

His use of the Queen's Christian name sounded shocking. So intimate. "You call her Elizabeth? To her face?"

He scowled. "Isabel, have you heard what I've said? Her throne is threatened from within and without the realm. The French are poised to attack us, and the Catholic holdouts—English traitors—may well join them. She may not survive as Queen."

"I do hear you. But invasion? It seems impossible. The French would not find England easy to subjugate, you know that. *They* must know that. Englishmen will fight fiercely for their liberty.

And as for the Catholics here, respect for the old faith does not make any Englishman a traitor. They too will fight for their Queen."

"Think you so?" He sounded unconvinced, and added with cool sarcasm, "If you're wrong, I won't be able to say 'I told you so' when Father and I are swinging as gallows fruit."

She stared at him, horrified.

"Now you understand," he said in deadly earnest. "If Elizabeth falls, our family falls."

He turned to beckon his lieutenant, but stopped with a look of surprise as footmen set down an open litter beside him and his wife climbed out, the effort a challenge in her very pregnant state.

"Thank heaven I'm not too late," Frances said, looking flushed. "I was afraid I'd missed you."

Adam seemed mystified. "What is it? Is there some problem?"

"No, no. Please, don't worry." Her eyes glowed with affection. "It's just that . . . I got your note."

"It was only to inform you," he said coolly. "There was no need to come."

She tried to hide her hurt. "I wanted to come. You may be gone for . . . so long. I had to say farewell."

He looked out at the waiting boat as if eager to be on it, while Frances clearly ached at the prospect of his going. Isabel did not know the source of their discord—it was hard to understand their marriage—but she felt sorry for Frances. No woman could look more in love. Isabel wanted to pinch Adam. Could he not bring himself to give his wife one kiss of farewell? Or just a tender word? She could not imagine such aloofness if Carlos were about to leave on a campaign. On the contrary, they would make a spectacle of themselves.

Adam gave a formal bow of the head to Frances, scrupulously and coldly polite. "Thank you, madam. Now, get you home and rest yourself. I must go." He called his lieutenant to escort Isabel, made a last rudimentary bow to his wife, and then went smartly down the stairs to the jetty.

Frances gazed after him. Isabel took pity. "I shall visit you, Frances. Soon, I promise."

* * *

"So, I want your opinion on it," Richard Thornleigh summed up, "as a military man."

Carlos looked up from the fire's embers. Thornleigh was waiting for an answer. They were sitting in the parlor, legs stretched out in front of the hearth, while Nicolas played on the floor beside them, lying on his belly to race his wheeled wooden caterpillar back and forth. The thought struck Carlos that anyone would think he and his father-in-law were relaxing over a talk about hunting dogs or horses, not about preparations for war.

Thornleigh added, like an apology, "I know it's a lot to consider."

Too much for Carlos's liking. Not the facts of the situation in Scotland that Thornleigh had just laid out. It was Thornleigh's own deep involvement, both his and his wife's, that bothered Carlos. He had the uncomfortable feeling that his father-in-law wanted an assurance that he, too, would be eager to get involved. For the sake of the family.

"Here, more wine," Thornleigh said, lifting the pitcher from the hearthstone and refilling their cups.

Carlos raised his in thanks and took a mouthful, though he'd already had enough. "It's good," he said, wanting a minute to think. Easy to give an answer right now, but should he?

"Aye, the best burgundy. The French do some things right." He fixed his eye on Carlos. "But can they do *this*, that's what I need to know." *This* meant invade England. "It isn't the first time they've threatened us from Scotland. You know that as well as anyone. You fought there."

Carlos nodded. "For this Queen's brother."

"Unlike her, though, he had a full treasury. In forty-nine he could afford to hire the finest mercenary troops from the Continent."

"Forty-eight," Carlos corrected him mildly. Eleven years ago. The battle of Pinkie Cleugh. Carlos had brought a company of forty light horse over from Germany. They had joined the English army of sixteen thousand as they faced the combined force of twenty-four thousand Scots and French. In all his years of soldiering, at all the godforsaken bivouacs and battlefields he'd seen, whether in Spain, the German lands, the Low Countries, France, or Portugal, he had never been in a place as bone-chillingly miserable as Scotland. Thank God his soldiering years were behind him.

"And despite the odds," Thornleigh said with obvious relish, "you won."

Carlos took another mouthful of wine. Armchair commanders. They saw victory as so simple.

"Oh! Mi oruga!" Nicolas cried.

Carlos glanced at his son. A wheel had fallen off the toy.

"Es quebrada," the boy said in dismay. It's broken.

"English, Nico."

"But, how do you say . . ." He held it up. *"Oruga."*

"Caterpillar."

"Bring it here," Thornleigh said. "I'll fix it."

Nicolas took it to him, carrying the three-wheeled toy as gently as if it were an injured pet. Carlos watched his son and the old man bend their heads together as Thornleigh set the thing on his knee. He straightened the axle pin to fit the wheel back on, Nicolas watching with grave concentration.

Carlos had to smile. It was good for Nicolas to have met his only grandparents. He knew that Isabel was upset about not being a party to their doings, but it seemed to him natural that they had their own life here. Considering what he had expected to find in getting off the ship—her family destitute—the reality was all good, in his view. Her parents were thriving. They were rich. He settled back, stretching his legs out farther to the fire, content to be in this fine room in this fine house, and yet sensing again—an odd feeling that sometimes struck him—that he didn't belong in it. Strange, since he was worth as much as Thornleigh, maybe more. He wondered if he would ever get used to the fact of his own wealth. Him, the bastard son of a camp follower. Never even knew who his father was. And look at me now, he thought, feeling more wonder than pride. In his mind his success was linked with Isabel. He had done it all for her.

He glanced at the window where a light snow was falling. Where was she, anyway? Gone to buy Christmas gifts, the chamberlain had said, but she'd been out for hours. He wished she had taken a manservant with her. This could be a rough city. He had friends in Spain who were shocked at the liberty English women took, going out into the streets with no male kinfolk. But Carlos had seen Isabel manage situations rougher than most people ever had to face.

Still, it was getting late.

And in more ways than one, he thought. Time for them to get home to Trujillo. Past time. He had a lot to see to. The troubles with the Potosí silver mine, for one thing. He had invested a lot in the mine, maybe too much.

"There, good as new." Thornleigh had fixed the wheel. Nico beamed his thanks and took the toy over to Carlos and ran it back and forth along his father's thigh to show him it was working. Carlos absently stroked the boy's hair, still thinking about the mine. He needed information about the problems and was hoping for a letter from Enrique Hernandez, his majordomo. He had told Enrique to send it to the Spanish embassy.

"So," Thornleigh said. "What's your opinion?"

Carlos wanted no part in this developing war, and he hoped Thornleigh wasn't expecting that he did. He could honey the facts, tell the old man what he wanted to hear. Put this English problem behind him and sail back home with Isabel and Nicolas. But he and Thornleigh had been through a lot together. Carlos had no stomach for lying to him.

"The Scottish rebels might hold their own against the French for a while," he said. "The Scots are tough fighters. But they're not soldiers. They never come to the field with more than two weeks' rations. And if it comes down to a battle for Edinburgh, that means the fortress at Leith, which the French hold, and the Scots have none of the big ordnance they'd need against those fortifications. If the French stand on the defensive until the Scots exhaust their provisions, the Scottish fighters will head back to their homes, and their leaders will be forced to yield. Then the French will be in an ideal position to march into England—they'd have a victory under their belts, and massive troop strength, and seasoned commanders. And England?" He shrugged. "No standing army. Few able captains. The Queen could raise a force of experienced foreign troops if she could afford it, but does she have the money?"

"No," Thornleigh conceded bleakly. "She's nearly bankrupt."

"And unless those troops are levied right away, they'll arrive too late." He looked Thornleigh in the eye. "The French have come when your new Queen is weak. England cannot be defended. If the French want to take her, they can."

He watched the full weight of this estimate sink in. Thornleigh rubbed his forehead, thinking. Carlos hoped the old man would not cling to delusions of victory. He had found that people's delusions were often impossible to shake. "What does Adam say?"

"That he has a job to do. Defend England. That's all he sees."

"And you?"

Thornleigh turned to him. He said soberly, "I think you're right."

Carlos was surprised, but relieved. His father-in-law was a realist after all.

"That's why I want to ask a favor of you." Thornleigh lowered his voice, although Nico was oblivious to their talk, busily playing with his toy on the floor. "I'm sailing to Antwerp tomorrow on behalf of the royal council, to purchase munitions. The Queen's border defenses are so meager we need to build them up, and quickly. While I'm away, I want you to promise me something."

"If I can."

"Take Isabel and your son home. I want them out of England, Carlos, before this disaster hits. I want them safe."

❧ 5 ❧

The Ambassador's Agenda

The Spanish embassy in London was lodged in Durham House, a stone mansion that lorded over prime riverbank property on the Thames. It stood between the sprawling precincts of Whitehall Palace to the west and venerable York House to the east, with the busy, cobbled thoroughfare of the Strand at its back. A gatehouse on the Strand led into the embassy's spacious courtyard, but like many of the stately homes of the nobility along this sweep of the Thames, Durham House stood closer to the river than the street, and most visitors used its water gate.

The tilt boat that had brought Carlos and Isabel nudged the water stairs of the landing stage. Other boats bobbed around them, loading and unloading embassy visitors under pillar-fixed torches that flared in the chilly evening gusts. Isabel looked up at the candlelit windows of the private rooms overlooking the river and took a breath to compose herself. The attack on her at St. Paul's had been just a few hours ago, and she still felt tender. As Carlos helped her out of the boat, she winced at the pain in her bruised hip.

"Are you sure you're up to this?" he asked. "If it's too much, I'll take you back. I can see the ambassador anytime."

"No, I'm fine. We've arranged the meeting, and I want to be with you for it."

He growled under his breath, "I wish I'd been there."

She was glad he hadn't been. Almost certainly there would have been bloodshed. When she had arrived home late that afternoon after the attack and her unsettling meeting with Adam, she'd had no chance to speak to her parents about what her brother had told her. Her father had left on his munitions-buying mission for the Queen's council, riding off to Gravesend to sail for Antwerp. Her mother was still at Whitehall Palace. But Carlos had been home, and she had told him about the incident. Just the fact of it, and its flashpoint—her crucifix—not the awful details. That would only have made him more furious at the men who had assaulted her, and what could he do about it? They would never find her assailants. Once she had calmed him down with assurances that she was unhurt, she had explained the far more important situation— the crisis that Adam said threatened Queen Elizabeth. Carlos said that her father had told him the same thing. That hurt Isabel. "Why wouldn't he tell *me?*"

"He's concerned about you."

"Or doesn't trust me."

"What? Why would you think that?"

"He and Mother have always championed the Protestant cause. Anti-Catholic feeling is strong here. The city is seething with it."

"Not your parents, though. No, your father just doesn't want to get you involved, for your own safety."

There had been no time to discuss it, for their appointment with the Spanish ambassador was in two hours, and Isabel barely had time to dress before they had to set out, she whirling her fur-lined cloak around her. Carlos had hailed a tilt boat at the Three Cranes Wharf and they'd climbed in under the canopy and settled on the cushions, a little stiff in their fine attire. Low, humped waves slapped the boat, and the city's torch lights glinted off the choppy water as the two oarsmen toiled upriver against the evening tide.

"Maybe Adam's exaggerating," Isabel said, hoping. "He's so preoccupied with ships and armaments and Mary Stuart's claim to the throne. It's made him see nothing but preparations for war. But that doesn't make an invasion inevitable."

Carlos shook his head. "He's an expert on naval matters. We know that, and so does the admiralty. No, Adam will have got that right. And your father agrees. He thinks this threat is so serious, he wants me to take you home."

"He said that?"

"Made me promise."

"Go home when?"

"Right away."

"And you agreed?"

He nodded. "I think he's right."

She looked out at the watery lights reflected on the river, feeling in turmoil. How could her father want to send her away? How could he think she would not want to help them through whatever was to come? In any case, how *could* she go, after the pledge she had given her brother? "I cannot go so soon," she said. "I promised Adam I'd stay to help with his wife's delivery."

He frowned. "How long?"

"She'll have the baby in a few weeks. I'd have to stay for at least another three or four weeks."

He didn't look happy about it. "Seems we made two promises that conflict."

Isabel could not beat back a nagging sense of dread. "Carlos, it's my parents I'm worried about."

"Why?"

"If France invades England, they'll be in danger. My father would lose everything—his property, his lands. And my mother . . . well, you know about her past."

"That was long ago. Before you were born."

"The church never lifts a heretic's death sentence. Under a French regime—a Catholic regime—she could lose her life."

He was silent for a moment, thinking. Then he said, "An invasion might never happen."

"You mean, you think the Scottish rebels can win? Throw out the French?"

"No, the French will win. But they wouldn't try for England if the Queen had powerful help. Spain is her ally. If King Philip backs her, France won't take on Spain."

Of course—Spain! Isabel happily took heart at this scenario. She didn't know about troop strength and artillery and strategies, as Carlos did. He had seen it all, on battlefields throughout Europe. But everyone knew that King Philip was the mightiest ruler on earth, the lord of Spain and the Netherlands and most of the New World. The treasure fleets from Mexico and Peru paid for his huge armies, which were feared everywhere. And Spain's self-interest was at stake with the tremendously lucrative trade between England and the Spanish-occupied Netherlands. Trade was the very basis of the English-Spanish alliance. King Philip would not let France jeopardize that. If needed, he would come to England's aid. By the time Isabel and Carlos disembarked at the embassy wharf and climbed the broad steps to Durham House, she felt much calmer.

Waiting footmen opened the doors and others took Isabel's cloak, and she and Carlos made their way to the great hall, passing through a sizeable throng of well-heeled English merchants, visiting Spanish grandees with their ladies, and scavenging petitioners and hangers-on. Several of the men cast Isabel approving looks, and Carlos murmured to her, "I told you that gown was the right one."

He had, indeed. The Venetian blue silk gown spangled with embroidered silver stars was her finest, and his favorite. She was pleasantly aware that its success had less to do with its quality than with its curve-hugging fit. Carlos looked quite wonderful himself. At home he was happiest in plain breeches, shirt, and jerkin, but he knew how to dress when it mattered, and his fitted velvet tunic of a green so dark it was almost black looked splendid with its gold-embroidered sleeves and short cape of green satin, while his sword's scabbard was polished to the shimmer of a mirror.

A quick-moving young man with a trim black beard greeted them, introducing himself as Diego Perez, the ambassador's secretary. He spoke with an easy, practiced charm. "Welcome, Señor Valverde, and Señora. His Excellency is looking forward to meeting you. Ah, and before I forget, señor, there is a letter come for you." He sent his clerk to fetch it. "Now, please, do come and meet my lord, the ambassador."

He guided them across the hall to a man who stood near one of the marble pillars, chatting with a plump-faced matron. Perez deftly interrupted them. He presented the Valverdes and introduced to them the ambassador and the lady, a marchioness from Madrid.

The ambassador turned to his new guests with an expectant look. Álvarez de Quadra, Bishop of Aquila, was middle-aged and thin almost to wasting, with an aura of the intellectual aesthete. Isabel had seen the type among the dedicated friars in the missions of Peru. But Quadra had an upright, alert posture that spoke of great energy, and keen gray eyes under the bony socket ridges. As his secretary finished the introductions, Carlos bowed and Isabel made a deep curtsy.

"What a pleasure, Señor Valverde," Quadra said genially. "I was delighted to receive your note." He spoke an elegant Spanish that marked him as Castilian aristocracy.

"The pleasure is mine, my lord," Carlos said.

"And you, dear lady," Quadra said to Isabel. "I have heard of Baron Thornleigh's exemplary judgment on Her Majesty's council, and have heard also of Lady Thornleigh's beauty. I venture to say that their daughter has inherited the best of both parents."

"You are gracious, my lord. If I attain even half of my parents' sterling qualities, I shall count myself blessed."

"I hope to meet your father soon. Sadly, no opportunity has yet arisen."

Isabel understood. It was his job to know everyone of influence at court, but her father's elevation to the minor nobility had been so recent. "He would be honored, sir, by your acquaintance."

Carlos was pulling a letter from the breast of his tunic. "As promised, my lord." He handed it to Quadra. "From Doña Beatriz de Mendoza."

Quadra beamed as he took it. "My dear cousin!"

"And my dear friend," Isabel said with a smile.

"How is she? We get so little timely news from New Spain."

"She is well, my lord," she assured him. "And newly expecting their third child when she gave me that letter for you. Our journey took months, so the babe will soon be on its way."

"I shall read this with the greatest pleasure," he said warmly, tucking the letter into a pocket of his roomy cloak. "Beatriz was my childhood companion. I thank you, dear lady, and you, señor."

Isabel was pleased to have had such an effective calling card. Beatriz was married to a nephew of the viceroy, Don Andres Hurtado de Mendoza, the King's representative. There was no higher society in Peru. Carlos's reputation on its own would have won the ambassador's regard, but her friendship with his cousin bolstered it.

Yet she was sure she saw a shadow of wariness in Quadra's eyes when he looked at her. She had no idea what was behind it.

"I hope you will enjoy your evening here," he said, nodding toward the tables laden with platters of succulent-looking foods and decanters of wine. "I understand, dear lady, that you arrived in London only a few days ago," he said to Isabel with a pleasant smile. "You must find it somewhat bewildering, returning home, do you not? So much is new in England since God took the late Queen Mary to His rest. Such upheavals. Why, look at this place." He waved a bony hand to indicate the residence. "Its walls could speak a testament to the turbulence of the last fifteen years." He asked her and Carlos if they knew the checkered history of the house. Both said they did not, and the plump lady from Madrid declared she was equally ignorant.

Quadra looked happy to inform them. "In 1345," he said with the relish of a scholar, "the Bishop of Durham built the house, and it remained the property of the diocese of Durham, and the London home of its bishops, for the next two centuries, until King Henry VIII decided to add it to his collection of palaces and manors and persuaded the incumbent bishop, Cuthbert Tunstall, to gift it to him." His emphasis on the word *gift* was decidedly sardonic. "When King Henry died and his nine-year-old son Edward became king, he granted Durham House to his half sister, the Lady Elizabeth, for life. Now, thirteen tumultuous years later, she is Queen of England and has housed our embassy here. But pity poor Bishop Tunstall, whose home it was! First, King Henry took the house from him. Then King Edward dissolved the See of Durham, depriving Tunstall of his bishopric, too, and giving the house to the Lady Elizabeth. When the Lady Mary came to the throne she restored Tunstall to his See and gave Durham House back to him. Now he has been deprived of it *again* by the new Queen Elizabeth. The poor man must feel quite giddy with such headlong turnings of the wheel of fortune." He related all this with sociable affability, but Isabel sensed his deep disapproval of the radical wrenching of the realm away from the Catholic Church, both before the reign of Queen Mary and again after it. He was a bishop himself, after all, and there was no mistaking the tinge of disgust when he mentioned the Protestant Queen Elizabeth.

Is that why he offered the little history lesson? she wondered. To see if I share his sentiments? Though she had married a Spaniard, she had been born a Thornleigh. Was Quadra gently probing to see where her loyalty lay?

The lady from Madrid said to her, "You in the Indies are fortunate to live far beyond such disorders." She added with obvious approval, "I understand the heathen Indians have been quick to embrace the one true faith, thanks to the tireless work of our churchmen. Countless souls saved."

"The friars have done wonders, to be sure, my lady," Isabel said diplomatically. She had found that few Spaniards shared her revulsion at the violence done to the Indians in the early days of the conquest—violence sanctioned by the Church. She kept in mind, instead, the many friars she knew personally to be good and sincere men of God.

Perez's clerk arrived with the letter and handed it to the secretary, who handed it to Carlos.

"From Enrique," Carlos said to Isabel. Then, to the ambassador, "My majordomo in Trujillo, my lord."

"Good news, I trust," said Quadra.

"So, your mother is Lady Thornleigh," said the lady from Madrid, eyeing Isabel. "A great friend of the English Queen, I hear. The Duchess of Norfolk mentioned just yesterday that Lady Thornleigh is often in the company of Her Majesty on walks in the palace gardens."

Isabel bristled. Strangers knew more about her mother's closeness to the Queen than she did. She said pleasantly, "My mother delights in all things relating to a garden, my lady."

"And I understand the Queen grows some very exotic plants," Perez offered.

"True," the lady said, failing to hide a smirk. "Heresy flowers in England."

There was a silence at this overt insult to the host country. Quadra's eyes flicked to Isabel.

"And also, I hear, in Scotland," Carlos said.

Isabel stiffened. What was he doing?

He went on steadily, addressing the ambassador, "Will the rebels prevail there, my lord?"

"God forbid it," Quadra snapped.

"The question is," Carlos said, "will His Majesty forbid it?"

Quadra paused for the briefest, tense moment. Then, smiling, he shrugged as though to banish a disagreeable thought. "His Majesty has many other issues to occupy his every waking hour, señor. Particularly the rampaging Turks, who are wreaking havoc against us throughout the Mediterranean. Spain is fortunate in her cordial relations with her dear ally, Queen Elizabeth. And, indeed, with King François as well. We cherish our friends and gird ourselves against our foes, the Turks. In this Scottish situation, His Majesty is completely neutral."

Perez steered the conversation toward Peru, asking Carlos and Isabel about recent fluctuations in the gold market, and for the next twenty minutes the group chatted about a merchant ship that had tragically been lost in the Gulf of Mexico, and about the viceroy's new plan for irrigating Lima's market gardens. The conversation interested Quadra until a clock struck eight, when he excused himself for a meeting with the visiting Count of Feria.

"Neutral," Carlos said darkly to Isabel when they were in a tilt boat on their way back to the heart of London, and her father's house. "Meaning Spain will do nothing to help the Queen."

"I know," she said. She understood why he had pressed his question to the ambassador. And she felt sick about the answer. "England is alone."

* * *

It was late when they arrived. The house was almost dark, the servants abed. The chamberlain was checking through the rooms before retiring, and he told Isabel that her mother had come home an hour ago and gone straight to bed. Isabel looked in on Nicolas, who was sound asleep with his wooden caterpillar snugged up beside his pillow. In the dim light, Pedro stood by the window with his back to her, tossing some rubber balls in the air and catching them. Three balls. Juggling, she realized. Though not very well. He fumbled a ball, and it bounced up to his waist as he fought to control the other two. It bounced again, and on the third bounce Isabel caught it. Pedro twisted around, surprised.

"Pardon, señora," he said, bowing, abandoning the other two balls. "I did not hear you."

"Has Tom Yates been teaching you?"

He nodded, looking nervous. "Is it wrong?"

"Not at all." She smiled, watching the two balls roll away. "Practice makes perfect, I dare say." She tossed him back the ball she had caught. "Is he a good teacher?"

He looked relieved, and his round face softened in a grin. "Tom, he is a master."

She laughed. "That he is. At all manner of foolery. To bed with you now, Pedro." She went to the bedside and bent over Nicolas and kissed his forehead, then left him and her servant to their slumbers.

She passed her mother's bedchamber. The door was closed, the band of space beneath it dark.

When she reached her own room Carlos was sitting in bed, his back against the headboard, reading the letter from Enrique in Peru. He always slept naked, something their Spanish doctor in Trujillo would have called an odd and unhealthy habit, but Isabel liked how the light from the candle beside him burnished his bare chest, the sheet reaching just to his navel. It roused the lovely, familiar flutter low in her belly. And her heart went out to him the way he concentrated on the letter, the words still a challenge. Five years ago, when she had met him, he could barely write his name. He had grown up among soldiers, and in that life literacy was not a skill that mattered, not like prowess on a warhorse or dexterity with a sword. Carlos could have ordered a cavalry charge in five languages, but he could not read or write. Isabel had taught him.

She sat down at her dressing table. "What's the news from Enrique?" she asked as she unfastened her pearl necklace.

"There's a lot." He seemed reluctant to go on, and looked up at her. "Was Nico asleep?"

"Soundly."

"No mention of the horse, then."

"Horse?"

"He was excited about it. Your father, before he left, he told me to pick a mount from his stable, so I took Nico along. I was looking at a bay rouncy, but Nico saw a black jennet stallion and ran to it. Plenty of Barbary and Arab in the animal, so no wonder he liked it."

"He loves *all* black horses," she said, amused, as she rolled down her stocking.

He smiled at his own ignorance. "Ah, I didn't know that. In any case, I told the stable master I'd take the jennet. Nico asked him what its name was, and it was a foolish one, so I told Nico he could give it a new name. He looked at the horse very seriously and said, *Noche.*"

She cocked an eyebrow. "Night?"

Carlos threw up his hands in surrender. "I know, I told him it should be an English name. But he said the rider was a Spaniard—me—and said since I'd always told him a good horseman is one with his mount, the horse should have a Spanish name. He had me there. So, *Noche* it is."

"I like it," she said, getting up barefoot to undress. "Only I hope he didn't talk you into a nag."

"No, it's a fine animal. We used jennets for light cavalry in Andalusia. The boy's got good horse sense."

They shared a smile. Nico, the four-year-old *caballero.*

She unlaced her bodice, her eyes on the lacings though she felt Carlos's gaze on her. But when she looked up at him the letter had reclaimed his attention. She saw the good humor fade from his face.

"What is it?" she asked.

"Bad yield on the silver assay. Bad harvest of wheat, too. It's going to be hard to make the payment on the loan for the mine."

"Can you borrow more?"

He shook his head. "But don't worry. If I get the council seat, it'll pay off everything."

"Yes, of course. Good." He went back to reading, and she unfastened a silver earring, thinking. Months ago he had had his lawyer write to the Council of the Indies in Seville with his application for a seat on the city council of Trujillo. Though he now said *Don't worry,* she knew that *he* was worried. Getting the council seat required the approval of the King, and Carlos was one among scores of petitioners for the lucrative post. An idea came to her as she unfastened the other earring. Ambassador Quadra. He was close to the King. If he gave Carlos his personal recommendation it could tip the balance in Carlos's favor. She would go to Quadra, alone, and ask for this favor.

Only, she would have to be careful. Though Carlos had status as an *encomendero,* the problem was his base birth. Nothing meant more to Spaniards than family pedigree, and the more ancient the lineage, the better. Advancement was usually limited to nobles, or to knights and high-ranking gentlemen who had performed supremely for the King on Continental battlefields or in the service of his government or church. Peru held the single exception—the *conquistadores.* Under Pizarro these men, numbering less than two hundred, had taken the country in their legendary victory over the Inca thirty years ago and carved it up for themselves, becoming immensely rich, and whether they had originally signed on as lowly infantry, blacksmiths, shoemakers, or clerks, they were now so venerated in Peru they enjoyed the reputation almost of deities. Carlos was not a *conquistador,* but his military success in the viceroy's service was marked enough for the Council of the Indies to reward him. But Bishop Quadra? Carlos's mother had been a camp follower in Spain, a whore. He never knew his father. If Quadra learned of this ignominy, he might not lift a finger in Carlos's cause. Yes, she would have to deal carefully with him.

A groan from Carlos.

"What?" she asked. "More bad news?"

"The mine assayer died of a fever. I'll have to hire another. Two days later the strongbox at the mine office was stolen. Two hundred pesos' worth of silver, gone."

She looked at him in concern. "Does Enrique know who took it?"

"The assayer's assistant, he says. The fellow's taken off."

"Has Enrique sent people after him?"

"No point. He comes from the *altiplano*. They'd never find him." He scanned the page. "At the house, the bridge collapsed in the rains. Enrique wants to rebuild farther downstream, but that means moving the road. A big expense, so he won't start until I get back. And the viceroy visited. He's planning a major expedition into that jungle toward Brazil. Wants to talk to me about it."

"Surely not to go along? You're finished with all that."

"No, he just wants my advice. Arming the company, choosing the captains." He looked up at her. "Isabel, we need to go home."

She turned away, taking refuge in the business of laying aside her clothes. She stood in just her chemise. *Go home?* It was hard to sort out her feelings. She shook loose her hair, then came to the side of the bed and sat down. She fiddled with the strings at the neckline of her chemise, thinking. "You know I promised Adam I would stay awhile, for Frances."

He smoothed her hair to one side, exposing the back of her neck. "Three weeks, let's say. She can't expect you to stay longer than that. I'll book our passage."

"What about my parents?"

He brushed a soft kiss on the back of her neck. "We came here to help. But they don't need our help."

"They might if the French cross the border."

"Your father has money and plenty of friends." He slipped the chemise off her shoulder. It sent a sweet shiver through her. He ran his hand up into her hair and kissed her shoulder. Her breath caught in her throat at the feel of his lips, his warm breath, his calloused palm on her neck. She closed her eyes, wanting to keep her mind on the problem. Carlos added, "He has plenty of retainers, too. All the men on his estates. They'd fight for him."

"Farmers with pitchforks against trained French troops?"

"Men defending their homes. A tough enemy." He slid the chemise off her other shoulder. Kissed it. She swallowed at the warmth spreading through her loins. "And don't forget they have the friendship of the Queen," he said. "No matter what happens, she'll see they're protected."

He had bent his leg, and he guided her by her shoulders to lean back against his raised knee. It made her breasts rise and the thin fabric slide down. Her nipples were so hard they caught in the lace trim. She could feel him erect through the sheet at her hip. He gazed at her, his breathing rough.

"The Queen . . ." She forced her mind to stay focused, though her body ached with desire. "She couldn't protect them if the French learned my mother is a convicted heretic."

"They've survived worse."

"Years ago."

"Your mother is clever. And your father always lands on his feet."

"They're not young anymore."

"*Mi amor* . . ." He pulled the chemise skirt up over her knee. She gasped softly as his hand smoothed up the inside of her thigh. He kissed her mouth, a kiss rough with want. Her thighs seemed to melt. He pulled her leg to one side to get his hand higher. She could hardly breathe as his fingers slid along her hot, wet cleft.

She gripped his wrist to stop him. "Carlos . . . please." She straightened, pushing away his hand, catching her breath. She tugged up the chemise to cover her breasts.

He let out a quick, sharp breath, accepting. "All right, let's talk about your parents. What do you want to do?" He added with gentle mockery, an attempt to make her smile, "Fight the French yourself?"

"No, I . . . I don't know."

"Me, then? I would fight a wild mob for you, Isabel, but I can't take on the whole French army." He was half smiling as he said it, but she heard the exasperation in his voice.

"I just wish . . ." She shook her head and said again, helplessly,

"I don't know." She turned to look at him. "I just wish I could get them away from here."

He shrugged. "Then let's do it."

"What?"

"Take them to Trujillo. They can live with us."

She stared at him. The idea was like a bright light beaming on her, making everything suddenly clear, blazing her worries away. "Of course! They'll be safe with us. We can take care of them. It's perfect." Wonderful images swirled in her mind. Her father bouncing Nicolas on his knee. Her mother training bougainvillea vines up the porch pillars to blossom in a canopy of blooms. Spirited conversations at the dinner table. Quiet talks with her mother. She threw her arms around Carlos's neck. "Oh, my love, you are so . . . so . . ." She showed him with a kiss. A happy, grateful, heartfelt kiss. He returned the kiss with passion.

She pulled free and jumped up from the bedside. "I'll tell her right now."

"Who?"

"My mother. I can't wait. It solves everything."

He grinned and caught her wrist. "Let her sleep." He pulled her back down with pretend violence, landing her on her back with a thud that made her laugh. He kissed her hard, and when his hand reached her breast, she gasped in pleasure. "That can wait until morning," he said. "I can't."

➷ 6 ➷

The Visitor

Morning came with sunshine so bright it blazed through the staircase windows of the Thornleighs' London house, warming Isabel as she hurried down the steps still tying the lacing at the back of her bodice. She felt full of hope. Ice dripped from the eaves, melted by the strong sun. Birds chittered in the garden hedges. It felt like spring. *She* felt like spring, felt as eager as an April robin. She was bursting to tell her mother what she and Carlos had decided.

She found her at the east end of the great hall, where the bay of the oriel windows was festooned with a small jungle: flowering plants, vines, cuttings, seedlings, and sprouts. Her back was turned as she lifted a watering can to sprinkle a hanging vine.

"It looks like the rain forest of Peru," Isabel said.

Her mother turned with a start. "Oh, you frightened me, my darling. I didn't think you were up yet."

She said this lightly, but Isabel saw the tiny lines of worry that radiated from the corners of her eyes. They hadn't been there five years ago. And the way her right arm hung lifeless at her side, was it still painful? It had to be horribly cumbersome, at the very least. For all her mother's verve and intellectual curiosity, there was a new weariness that she could not hide. Isabel felt a pang of pity. "You look like you didn't get much sleep," she said.

"I never sleep well when Richard's away."

"I'm the same when Carlos is gone. The moment he leaves, the murderers and ogres circle the house, waiting to get at me and Nicolas. The moment Carlos comes home, they slink away."

Her mother nodded, amused. "Amazing, isn't it?"

They shared a smile.

A ginger kitten lay on its back, batting a dead leaf between its paws like a practice mouse. There was an earthy smell from all the potting soil. Isabel realized she had always associated the smell of spring earth with her mother. As a child, looking for her, she had often found her in the garden.

"Shall we breakfast together? Is Carlos up, too?" Her mother pinched a sprig of sage from a tier of herbs and handed it to her. "Ellen has made barley bread, and there's fresh churned butter."

"No, no breakfast just yet." Isabel twirled the sage between her fingers to release its fragrance. "I want to talk to you."

"Oh?" Her mother set down the watering can and picked up a pair of scissors. She inspected a tendril of English ivy and snipped off a brown leaf.

"You told me Father was going to Antwerp to see an old friend. But I know the truth. He's gone to buy munitions for the Queen. And you've been helping her, too."

Her mother turned, the leaf stilled between her fingers. Her face betrayed no hint of emotion. "Who told you that?"

"Father did, told Carlos. But I heard it from Adam, too." She gave a quick account of the mob at St. Paul's, and Adam coming to her rescue.

"Good heavens! Did they hurt you?"

"No, I'm fine. That's not what I want to talk about. Adam told me about the crisis in Scotland. The huge buildup of French troops. The fear that they might invade England. How weak Queen Elizabeth's position is. Mother, there's no need to pretend anymore. I know the peril you face."

There was the merest flicker of unease. "My. He told you a great deal."

Isabel could not forget Adam's other words: *You're Spanish now.*

You're Catholic. Was her mother thinking the same thing? She hated this barrier between them. "Mother, you can *trust* me."

"Certainly, my darling. I just didn't want you to worry. None of this is your problem."

"Of course it is. Your problems are my problems. Adam said that if England falls, our family falls. Under a French regime they could burn you at the stake."

The horror of it hung in the air. Her mother said quietly, "All the more reason to hope that England does not fall."

"But there's no need for you to take that risk. Carlos and I want to help you."

"Help?" Her mother fixed her eyes on her, and Isabel saw something new there, a flash of keen interest. "How?"

Nicolas dashed into the hall. *"Mami, mi conejo tiene hambre!"*

Isabel sighed. "In *English*, Nico."

"My bunny. He wants to eat."

"Say good morning to your lady grandmother."

He bowed. "Good morning, Grandmama."

"Here," her mother said, snipping off a bunch of leaves. "Take him this for his breakfast."

"Gracias!" he said, grabbing it, and ran out.

"Radish seedlings," she explained to Isabel with a smile, sounding relieved that Nicolas had changed the course of their conversation. "I hope to plant them outside soon."

Isabel could not return the smile. Why would her mother not acknowledge the danger she was in? Voices sounded faintly outside. They both looked out the window at the garden. Beyond the far brick wall, tendrils of smoke from the city's chimneys rose in the still air. The gardener and his apprentice, digging in the winter-barren flower beds, were greeting Nicolas as he dashed to them. A wooden cage sat nearby under the hawthorn hedge. Nicolas, on his hands and knees, opened the cage and pulled out the rabbit and hugged it so tightly it made his handful of radish leaves spill to the ground. The rabbit squirmed to get to the greens but Nicolas clung tight.

"He'll smother that creature with love," Isabel's mother said.

THE QUEEN'S GAMBLE 73

There was unmistakable fondness in her eyes as she watched her grandson.

It touched Isabel. Good for Nico, she thought. It reminded her of what was important. "Mother, wouldn't you like to live where you could garden in the out-of-doors every day?"

"Mmm, that would be lovely." She turned to a hanging plant and poked through its foliage.

"You can. In Trujillo."

"Where?" she asked absently, barely listening.

"Peru. My home." She took hold of her mother's shoulders and turned her so they were face-to-face. She was so glad to be able to say this—like giving a gift. "Come and live with us. You and Father. Leave this unstable country. Leave all this frightening uncertainty behind. With me and Carlos you'll never have to worry again."

Her mother stared at her for a long moment, the words sinking in. Then she gave a light laugh, as if the idea was preposterous.

Isabel bristled. "I do not jest, Mother."

"No, of course not, and it is very thoughtful of you, my darling. Very generous." She patted Isabel's arm. "I do thank you most sincerely. But no, the New World is not for your father and me."

"You're not well, Mother. Your arm. And the constant strain you seem to be under. You cannot bear the shocks you bore when you were—" She didn't finish.

"Young?" her mother challenged, almost smiling.

"If you won't think of yourself, think of Father. He's not as strong as he was. How can you answer for him?"

"Your father and I have sparred about all manner of things over the years, but on this topic I promise you we are in complete agreement. We'll stay where we are."

So that was the end of it? She had made this enormous offer and this was her thanks? Summary refusal? "But you haven't even considered—"

"I don't have to. I shall never leave England again."

"That's just foolish. In Peru you'd be safe."

"In that ferociously Catholic land?"

"But not a soul there *knows* you! There's no one to betray you."

"Enough, Isabel. No."

"How can you be so stubborn!"

"Stubborn?" Anger flashed in her eyes. "You have no idea—" She stopped. Took a breath. When she spoke again it was with a wry smile. "Elizabeth, now *she* was stubborn."

Elizabeth. She used the Queen's Christian name just as Adam had—so startlingly personal. "Is she the reason you won't leave? The Queen?"

Her mother seemed annoyed by the question. "Of course. What else?"

"What is she to you? What is this *hold* she has on you?"

Her mother's face softened. She came closer and caressed Isabel's cheek with the back of her finger. "Bel, there were times in these last years when I missed you so much. Wished that I could just talk to you, be assured you were all right. Elizabeth is exactly your age, you know. She often reminded me of you. Strong-willed. Clever. But sometimes too impetuous." A noise outside made her turn again to the window. "Ah, I see Carlos is up after all."

"Up before me, actually." She watched Carlos stride along the gravel path toward Nicolas. She was still struggling with how to convince her mother. "He went to the stables. He likes to see to the horses first thing. Old habit."

"I'm so glad you have him, Bel. And he you. So glad to see you happy."

"Mother, come back with us, please. You can have a happy life, too."

"Sometimes, my darling, we need to think beyond our own happiness."

"Even if it means courting death?" She could not believe this was happening. "Why won't you let me help you?"

Her mother turned to a tier of seedlings. She lifted a small clay pot where a green shoot, just three fragile leaves, trembled in the slight current of air. "I have seen four reigns here," she said, touching the tiny plant with a kind of caress. "Four Tudor monarchs. I knew King Henry. He cared only for his own magnificence. At his worst, he was a tyrant. King Edward was a mere boy, bullied by powerful dukes, sickly to the day he died. Queen Mary was a pitiful woman, vicious in her weak-minded obsession with her religion. None of them thought of what was best for England." She looked up at Isabel. "None, until Elizabeth. She has a heart that beats in sympathy with the English people. She senses their latent vitality. This poor realm is a seedling, Bel, struggling in the cold, harsh wind of an early spring. In Elizabeth's hands it can flower, fresh and vigorous. Without her, tyranny can so easily trample it again."

Isabel saw the passion in her eyes, and it gave her a shiver. She felt as though her mother was slipping away from her. "This is no answer."

"It is *my* answer."

"But—"

Voices sounded in the screened passage. Timothy, the young footman, appeared, followed by a man who strode in with a brisk air of business.

"Sir William!" her mother said in surprise. She sounded pleased at the interruption. Isabel was not. She tried not to glare at the man for intruding on them. He appeared younger than her mother by perhaps five years. His clothing was costly but somber.

"Honor, forgive the early hour," he said as he reached them. He looked at Isabel and added affably, "The business of state keeps no hourglass."

"Well, I trust the business will allow you to join us first for breakfast? Isabel, this is Sir William Cecil."

Isabel was taken aback. What exalted circles her mother moved in! She knew Cecil to be the Queen's first minister and closest adviser. "Sir," she said with polite deference as she curtsied.

"Sir William," her mother said, "allow me to introduce—"

"Your daughter. I know. And no, no breakfast." His brusqueness might have seemed rude in someone else, but Isabel sensed a familiarity between him and her mother that spoke of a comfortable friendship. He gave Isabel a courtly bow of the head. "You, Señora Valverde, are the reason I am keeping you and your good mother from breaking your fast. I trust your evening at the Spanish embassy was pleasant?"

Isabel was astonished. How quickly gossip spread. "Very pleasant, sir. Bishop Quadra was most gracious."

Her mother said wryly, "Really, my friend, do you have a spy in every closet?"

"No need for spies, Honor, not with a steadfast ally like Spain. Friends simply pass along to me what's newsworthy." He was tugging off his leather riding gloves, but his eyes were still on Isabel. "For example, I am told that you and Ambassador Quadra have a mutual friend in Peru."

"We do, sir. His cousin. He was pleased to receive our news about her."

He said with a warmth that surprised her, "Yes, family is everything. For us all. Your mother has told me how delighted she is to have you here. Your parents are such dear friends of mine, I feel I know you already. And although you are a married lady, I can think of you only as a Thornleigh. Do you mind?"

"I consider it a compliment."

He smiled. "Just as it was intended. Which is why I have come to see you. Tell me, did the ambassador make any mention of the situation we face with the French in Scotland?"

His directness took her aback. He had indeed come on the business of state.

"I presume you do *know* about the buildup of French troops on our border?"

"I do."

"Well, it has become dire. We now have reports that the Marquis d'Elbeuf has sailed from Dieppe in command of a fleet bringing seven thousand more French troops."

"Sir William, is this necessary?" her mother said. The rebuke was mild but held an unmistakable tension.

"It's fine, Mother. Sir, I hesitate only because I fear you will not find this news agreeable. My husband, in fact, asked Ambassador Quadra outright how Spain stood with respect to the French posting thousands of soldiers so near England. I expected no declaration of Spanish policy, of course, but I did hope to hear him confirm that England could rely on her alliance with King Philip if needed. Instead, he replied, diplomatically but quite clearly, that Spain intends to remain neutral."

Cecil nodded, considering her words. "Thank you. Very helpful to know." He seemed unperturbed by her report. Isabel had the feeling that it was actually not news to him at all. If so, why had he come to ask her? She looked out the window at Carlos playing with Nicolas on the gravel path. Carlos held the boy high in the air, then swung him down and tucked him under his arm the way he would a saddle. Nicolas laughed in delight, squirming to get free.

"Sir, may I ask a question?" she said to Cecil. "I understand everyone's fear that if the French defeat the rebels they will be poised to invade England. But *would* they?" Could everyone be wrong? She was fervently hoping so. "After all, what possible pretext could they use?"

"Oh, they have made no secret of their designs. The Queen of France is Mary Stuart, queen also of the Scots since she was a child. She has Tudor blood—she is our Queen's cousin—and she is publicly trumpeting her native right to sit on the throne of England. She and her young husband, King François, have brazenly quartered the arms of England on their own coat of arms. And they have declared to all the world that they would save England from heresy. They are urging the pope to declare Her Majesty Queen Elizabeth illegitimate, the bastard daughter of the heretic, Anne Boleyn. *Their* words, trust me, never mine. Her Majesty has quite rightly recalled our ambassador from Paris. This is where we stand."

Isabel shook her head in mild disgust. "Battles of religion, always." She gave her mother a pointed glance. "A lethal battlefield."

"Which is why we are building a new country," her mother said. "One where people will not be persecuted for how they worship God."

"Is Queen Elizabeth's new church really so different?" Isabel asked. "Everyone still has to conform. It's illegal not to."

"But not a capital offense," Cecil pointed out. "Our late Queen Mary sent hundreds of poor wretches to the stake to perish in the flames. Her Majesty Queen Elizabeth merely imposes a fine. For repeat offenses, imprisonment. She does not kill."

"A new tolerance?" Isabel asked skeptically. The men who had attacked her at St. Paul's had shown little sign of it.

"Politics," Cecil replied smoothly. "When Her Majesty came to the throne she needed the support of both camps, so she forged a compromise, a nationwide religious settlement. Former Catholics still grumble that it went too far, and radical Protestants grumble that it did not go far enough, but no blood has been shed. For this rational arrangement your mother can take much credit. When we were drafting the legislation, she advised Her Majesty."

Isabel looked at her mother in wonder. "Really?"

"I made a suggestion or two."

"Ha. She is too modest. Five years ago I asked her to take the young Lady Elizabeth under her wing. She did better than that. She took an unruly princess and turned her into a queen."

Extraordinary, Isabel thought. Her mother's letters had sometimes mentioned Princess Elizabeth, but always as though she were a personage whose doings she followed at a distance, with no hint of this close relationship. The five years Isabel had been separated from her mother felt like twenty.

"Ah, Bel," her mother said, "the new England will be about far more than religion." She sounded eager to explain. "It will be about learning, about opening minds at our universities. About voyaging for exploration, daring to imagine an English presence in the New World."

"What? Those lands belong to Spain and Portugal."

"The lands claimed so far, yes. But English trade with the Indies could open up more. Ask Hawkins of Plymouth, who is building three ships for that purpose with the Queen's blessing. Ask Adam, who has dreamed of it for years and backs Hawkins's enterprise. And there are mathematicians, astronomers, musicians, poets, so many inventive souls ready to build a new society."

Isabel did not doubt her mother's passion. If only passion could change the world. "I hope it may be so," she murmured.

"Honor," Cecil said, "I believe I will accept your invitation for a bite to eat after all. I must ride to Walthamstow today. Left the

house with Mildred still abed. Will that be an inconvenience for
your cook?"

"Not at all, sir. I'll tell Ellen you are staying. Isabel, will Carlos
join us, too? Ask him, would you?" She crossed the hall to the
kitchens.

Left alone with Cecil, Isabel felt rather ill at ease. He had a way
of looking at her as if inspecting her. She looked out the window at
Carlos and Nicolas, who were now sparring in a swordfight, using
twigs as their blades. Nicolas thrust his small arm high to stab his
father's ribs. Carlos dropped to his knees, clutching his side. He
toppled in a great show of being mortally wounded and lay on his
back, spread-eagled. Nicolas scrambled on top of him, crowing in
victory. Carlos rolled him over onto his back and set to tickling him
mercilessly. Nico was laughing so hard it seemed he could not
catch his breath. His breeches will be all dirt, Isabel thought, not
caring, loving Carlos for how he loved their boy. She wanted more
children. So did he. A miscarriage in her fifth month almost a year
ago had shaken them both. Now she was eager to start another life
growing inside her.

"I hope your mother and I do not weary you with our talk,"
Cecil said. "These mazes of religion can become a fixation."

"In truth, sir, I do not give a great deal of thought to such things.
I have much to do just to see to my family's welfare."

"The issues may be one and the same."

She looked at him. How much did he know? "May I ask, sir,
have you known my mother long?"

"Long enough to know that she would be in danger if the
French ever did take England. The Guise family runs France,
telling their nephew, the boy king, what to do, and the Dukes of
Guise are fanatic enforcers of the Catholic faith. They have
burned Calvinist and Huguenot dissenters in the hundreds."

The message was clear. He knew about her mother's past, her
conviction for heresy. It was why the family had fled to Antwerp
when Isabel was a baby, returning only years later. Oddly, it gave
her a sense of relief that Cecil knew. And she felt grateful that he
so obviously cared.

"Their regime is ruthless," he went on. "They cut out the victims' tongues first so the poor wretches cannot pray or sing hymns at the stake. The only mercy shown is that those who recant are strangled before they burn. What's worse, the regime has passed a new law that anyone who fails to denounce to the authorities a person whom he suspects of being a heretic is guilty of heresy himself, and is to be burned."

Isabel shivered. If he meant to horrify her, he had succeeded. "She talks about mathematics and poetry," she said, "but poetry will not save her from the fire."

"Your mother dreams large. She imagines the future. I deal with the present."

"So do I. I have asked her—begged her—to come and live with me. She and my father. But she refused. She insists on staying."

He nodded. "She will never leave England again."

The very words her mother had used.

"Oh, sir. I wish I could do something to help her."

"Do you really?"

She had made the statement with a sense of powerlessness; he had pounced on it with authority.

"There *is* a way that you can help." He said this with such a mix of urgency and conviction, Isabel was certain it was the real reason he had come. "In fact, you—with one foot in our world and one in Spain's—may be the only person who can."

❧ 7 ❧

The Test

Isabel found the great hall of Durham House almost vacant. Gone were the crowds of merchants, petitioners, grandees, and gossipers who had been milling under last night's candelabra and wall torches. Perhaps it was the hour—at midday most people were at dinner. Or perhaps it was the weather, a cold misty rain that shrouded London. Whatever the reason, her heart beat a little faster as she crossed the hall in the stark light of day, passing a scatter of lounging servingmen and hangers-on, their eyes on her. She felt exposed, almost like an actor in a play. So be it. She knew her role.

"Good day, Señor Ramos," she said as she reached Secretary Perez's young clerk. He stood at his desk handing a letter to a porter.

"Señora Valverde." He bowed, looking mildly surprised at seeing her again so soon, and sent the porter on his way.

Isabel threw back the damp hood of her cloak. "Is Señor Perez available? I come bearing gifts." She held up a pear-sized muslin bag of candied apricots tied with a gold velvet ribbon. She had told Carlos she was coming to visit Maria Perez, the secretary's wife. Women's talk, she had said, so no need for him to accompany her. "A delicacy from my mother's kitchen," she said now to the clerk. "Her ladyship's cook is known for these confections."

"Charming," he said. "Unfortunately, Secretary Perez was called away on business. Perhaps I can help you?"

She knew Perez was out. She had timed her visit for it. Perez was an experienced social administrator. This junior clerk would be less so. "No matter," she said. "Would you see that this is delivered to his wife, with my compliments?"

"With pleasure, señora." He took the little bag. "Will that be all?"

"No, I am here to see the ambassador."

"Oh? He did not mention—"

"I have a message from Sir William Cecil."

His eyes widened a little. Cecil was a name that opened doors.

"Of course, if you feel that my visit would inconvenience him—"

"Not at all, señora. This way, please."

She followed him out of the hall and down a corridor where a row of portraits of former Bishops of Durham gazed down with such stern looks she almost felt they knew her mission. Rain spattered the narrow windows that overlooked the courtyard. A couple of workmen blacked with coal grime sat in their coal wagon under a makeshift canvas awning, their shovels stilled as they looked out at the rain. Otherwise the courtyard was deserted, all the household chores paused for either dinner or the rain. As Ramos padded ahead of her, Isabel heard her own footfalls echo on the stone floor as though she were alone.

At the end of this chilly corridor he opened a door, asking Isabel to kindly wait a moment. As he went in she saw that the room was a private refuge, warmed by a fire in the grate, plush with tapestries, and bright with the colored leather bindings of two half walls of books. Ambassador Quadra's library, apparently. Quadra and another gentleman, a florid, paunchy man, looked up from their chess game in front of the fire. The clerk bent and murmured in the ambassador's ear. If Quadra was surprised, he made no show of it. He said something to his guest, and both men rose as the clerk ushered Isabel in. Speaking in Spanish, she apologized for disturbing their game.

"Not at all, señora," the guest replied, stretching as though to ease a kink in his back. "I would have had my lord bishop in checkmate within three moves in any case."

Quadra chuckled. "Sometimes, sir, capitulation is our best tactic. I humbly concede."

"Very wise," the guest said genially. "I'll move on to the chapel, if your fellow here will show me the way?"

When they were alone Quadra invited Isabel to take the chair opposite him. "Baron von Breuner is expert at many things. Chess is not one of them."

"Then you are a diplomat indeed, sir," she said as they both sat.

He gave her a sage smile. "Ah, he needs all the entertainment he can get, poor man. He came here in the summer as the envoy of the German emperor to offer the emperor's son's hand in marriage to Queen Elizabeth. Her Majesty is still pondering it, so poor von Breuner has been cooling his heels all these months."

He offered Isabel wine. She declined. She noticed at his feet a wicker basket in which a honey-colored spaniel lay contentedly looking up at him. Quadra settled back, crossing one narrow leg over the other. "Now, Señora Valverde, to what do I owe this pleasure? Ramos mentioned Sir William Cecil. I presume you left that gentleman in good health this morning at your father's house?"

She could not hide her surprise. Did he have the house under watch? Or was it Cecil's movements he watched?

He smiled thinly. "Sir William follows my schedule with equal interest, I am sure. He and I get along very well."

"Sir William is a friend of my parents, my lord. Today was the first time I met him. I bring no message from him. Forgive me, but I used his name only so that you would see me."

She could not tell if the sharp look he gave her spoke of irritation or interest. "And now that you have my exclusive attention?"

"It is about my husband. I would ask a favor, my lord."

"Ah." He was clearly used to hearing this kind of thing. She sensed an amiable cynicism in him, having no doubt heard the grandiose ideas people had of their own worth or that of their relatives. He reached down to the basket and picked up the spaniel and set the dog in his lap. "How can I be of assistance?"

"He has served his excellency the viceroy with great distinction, as you know."

"I do, indeed," he said, idly stroking the dog. "My cousin Beatriz writes of the high regard in which Don Andres de Mendoza holds Señor Valverde. A bold captain of cavalry. I am aware that without your husband's daring success in the last rebellion, His Majesty's authority in Peru might have been destroyed."

"Thank you, sir. Since then, my husband has sent the Council of the Indies in Seville his application for a seat on the city council of Trujillo. As you know, this requires the assent of His Majesty the King. My lord, would you graciously give him your recommendation?"

He regarded her thoughtfully. "It is good that Mendoza rewarded your husband so generously. A rich *encomienda* with hundreds of vassal Indians, I understand?"

"Yes, sir. We deeply appreciate his excellency's trust." This was the real basis of Carlos's reputation. Military prowess was admired, but only landed wealth marked true success.

Quadra stroked the dog's ear. "I do not have the pleasure of acquaintance with your husband's family. In what region of Spain do they live?"

Here was the challenge—Carlos's base birth. His mother had been a camp follower, a whore, and he never knew his father. If Quadra learned this he would almost certainly decline to help Carlos's cause. But Isabel had come prepared to work that to her advantage.

"My husband is a fine man, my lord, but his family is not one he can be proud of." She lowered her head, pretending shame, letting him believe that this evasion of his question was her acknowledgment that she was on shaky ground. Then she looked up, cleareyed. "I know how the world goes, sir. I have asked a favor of you. Please, allow me to reciprocate."

A shadow of distaste flickered in his eyes as though she had offered him a bribe. He held up a hand to refuse.

"Information, my lord. I believe it may be of some use to you, and to Spain."

He lowered his hand. "Information?"

"Eight days ago Her Majesty Queen Elizabeth had a meeting with the Scottish Earl of Arran. He came to discuss marriage. He came in secret, and was hidden in Sir William Cecil's house on Canon Row."

Now Quadra was interested. Isabel rejoiced that he had taken the bait. The rebel lords in Scotland backed the Earl of Arran's claim to the Scottish throne. Adam had told her that, and Cecil had confirmed it—and told her much more.

"The rebels are eager for this alliance with the Queen," she went on. "Marriage with her would greatly enhance their cause— would make it legitimate in the eyes of many. In the meantime, they have asked for her outright support. Money, men, and munitions."

A keen new energy was apparent in Quadra. She could see that he had known nothing about the Queen's secret meeting, and was intensely interested.

She pressed on. "I am pleased to tell you that the Queen refused both. No marriage—she sent the earl home to Scotland with that answer. And no help for the rebels." The first was true. The second was not yet decided. Isabel had come for this very reason. It was the Queen, through Cecil, who needed information. "Her Majesty wants to send the rebels aid," Cecil had told her. "She needs them to defeat the French. But it would be a dangerous move, with the eyes of all Europe on her, and before she will commit herself she needs to know Spain's position."

"But we *do* know it," Isabel had said. "As I told you, the ambassador told Carlos that King Philip will remain neutral."

"A public statement only, the official position," Cecil had said. "I must know what the King actually intends."

Quadra set the spaniel back down in its basket. "May I ask, señora, how you know all this?"

"My mother told me," Isabel said without hesitation. "As I'm sure you're aware, she enjoys the friendship of the Queen. She arranged the details of Her Majesty's private meeting with the earl."

"And yet, Lady Thornleigh is not one to babble secrets."

"She did not, my lord. I overheard a little of it as she spoke with

Sir William Cecil. Later, in private, I asked her to explain, and she did. Perhaps because she felt I might ask elsewhere and she wanted to prevent that. In any case, she knows that she can trust me."

"Can she?" He made no pretence of subtlety.

Isabel matched his bluntness. "Just as I trust you to do what is best for us all. For Spain."

His gaze seemed to bore into her. Isabel felt her confidence desert her. He doubted her, she read it in his look. Doubted that *he* could trust her, because of her parents. He did not see her as a loyal subject of Spain. He saw her as a Thornleigh.

He stood. "Señora, forgive me, but I must cut short our conference. Baron von Breuner is waiting in the chapel. We are holding a mass in honor of his wife's safe delivery of a son, so I must bid you farewell. Unless, of course, you would like to join us at mass in commemorating the eternal sacrifice of Our Lord?"

A mass? Caution prickled her scalp. To hold or attend a mass, the supreme Catholic rite, was an illegal act in this new England. "But, sir, how can—"

"The Queen, wisely, grants this crucial right to me and my Spanish staff."

But not to English people. She saw that he was setting a test: Would a Thornleigh refuse?

"Do join us," he said again, and she knew that she was looking into the steely eyes of a bishop. He added, barely concealing his interest in ferreting out her true allegiance, "Unless you have not the time today?"

The chapel was a sanctuary for the senses. Every object soothed the eyes, transporting the worshipper to a place both peaceful and mysterious. Stained glass windows depicting the ecstasies of saints bathed the space with liquid beauty. The Virgin Mary, a sculpture gorgeously painted in azure and gold, welcomed all to her forgiving embrace. Silken banners and tapestries glimmered. A rood screen of delicately carved wood segregated the people from the priest in his lavishly embroidered vestments, and through the screen they watched him at the marble altar, preparing to transform bread into the body of Christ, and wine into His blood. Candle-light glinted off the golden chalice and paten on the altar beside child-high candlesticks of pure silver, and the rood screen was crowned with a shining cross of gold. The only sounds were the shuffling of worshippers' feet, the priest's soft Latin prayers, and the gentle tinkle of the sacring bell. The chapel's aura was the soothing, enveloping security of the womb.

Isabel, though, found it impossible to relax. Yet she needed to, to convince Quadra. He sat beside her, the two of them alone on the cushioned front bench, Isabel on the aisle. His eyes were on the chaplain who was officiating at the altar, the service about to begin, but she felt that his whole concentration was on her, waiting to gauge her response to the rituals of the mass. Four or five other men—Baron von Breuner and some embassy clerks—sat behind them in silent, prayerful contemplation. A stooped old man stood to one side, perhaps still uncomfortable with the benches, an innovation unknown in the days of his youth when the whole congregation stood.

Isabel kept her own eyes fixed on the exquisite reredos behind the altar, two paintings, one of St. John and the other of the Virgin, and focused on their beauty to compose herself. She had been in one of the new Protestant churches, the one in her parents' parish, and found it bleak. She had heard that at the death of Queen Mary last year the London radicals had attacked the churches and stripped them of all Catholic trappings. They had shattered the stained glass windows, smashed the statues, burned the paintings, shredded the priests' vestments, hacked the wooden saints with axes and gouged their faces with knives. She shuddered, imagining the mob, the same kind of furious men who had attacked her in St. Paul's churchyard. Now, by law, all churches throughout England were barren of the trappings of "idolatry"—no carvings, no statues, no paintings. No mass was held, only a communion. The altar was a plain wooden table. The priests wore simple black.

What foolishness to banish beauty, she thought. Although she had seen this happen before. In Antwerp, where she had lived as a child, the Protestants had been ascendant, and strict. When she had married Carlos and moved to Peru, she had accepted Catholicism. The change did not trouble her. The day-to-day demands and pleasures of real life were enough to engross her. The mysteries she left to God.

A sound made her look ahead to a narrow door beside the rood screen that partitioned the chancel from the nave. The door opened and several more people entered the chapel. Perhaps nine or ten of them, men and women, they slipped in through the door with a furtive shuffle. As they filed past Isabel, heading for the benches behind her, she heard a man whisper to a woman, "Don't fret, Dorothy, you'll be back before they know you're gone." English voices. The man's cowhide jerkin gave off an odor like that of a butcher's shop, and the woman wore a plain linen dress and a cap like a maid. Another man wore the satin finery of a gentleman, and a few others were equally well dressed, but there was a young man in an apprentice's blue smock, and another whose clothes were dusted with flour, a miller or baker. These newcomers seemed to come from all ranks. The humbler folk looked awed but determined. Being English, they were risking fines, perhaps forfeiture of their property, even imprisonment, just by being here. Their bravery moved Isabel.

She glanced at Quadra on her other side. He was watching the newcomers file in, his benign smile welcoming them. He obviously prided himself on being the shepherd of this little flock of English Catholics in need of a secret shelter to practice their faith.

Then Isabel spotted a face among them that made her stifle a gasp. It was Frances. Several bodies were between them, almost blocking Isabel's view of her, but there was no doubt that it was her sister-in-law. And, from the way she set her eyes on a rear bench as though it were *her* spot, it seemed she had been here before. Shocked though Isabel was, she realized that she should have suspected it. Unlike the Thornleighs, the Grenvilles had always been a staunchly Catholic family. Did Adam know that his wife frequented the embassy chapel for mass? Impossible—he would never allow it. She finally caught a clear view of Frances, who had not yet seen her. She looked exhausted, so heavy with child, and rather frightened as she clutched her rosary, her pale lips moving in a silent, fervent prayer. Isabel's heart went out to her, for she looked so alone. She thought of her promise to Adam. Frances's fear, she was sure, was not just about the risk she was taking by being here. It was about her impending labor.

She felt Quadra's eyes on her. Checking for any sign in her of disgust at these English lawbreakers? It kindled an idea. Frances had reached the rear bench and was about to sit. Isabel got up and went straight to her. Frances froze at the sight of her. Her eyes went wide as though in fear.

"It's all right," Isabel whispered. She slipped in beside her, standing with her at the bench, and wrapped an arm around her shoulders to reassure her. She could feel Frances's rigid muscles. "It's all right," she said again.

Frances blinked at her. "Please . . . Adam—"

"Shhh, it is our secret," Isabel whispered. "Here, you need to sit." She gently lowered Frances onto the bench. Frances looked up at her in wonder. Isabel sat beside her and patted her knee. "There. All right now?" she murmured.

Frances's eyes filled with relief. She nodded.

Isabel looked ahead, up the nave. Ambassador Quadra was watching her.

Mass was over. The English worshippers had left as furtively as they had come. Isabel had rejoined Quadra, and as she walked with him out of the chapel and down the stone corridor he was like a different man, chatting easily without a hint of lingering mistrust. She had not only partaken of mass with reverence, her show of solidarity with Frances had clearly pleased him. He asked her the identity of the lady she had comforted, for although he knew who most of the well-to-do worshippers were, this visit had apparently been Frances's first. When Isabel told him the lady was her brother's wife, he looked very satisfied to know that more of her family were secret Catholics. Isabel felt quite victorious. She had passed the ambassador's test.

He returned to the topic of Carlos's application for a seat on the Trujillo city council, told her that it was always a pleasure to do what he could to advance men of promise, and that he would send a letter recommending her husband to His Highness with the next post bound to the court at Valladolid.

Isabel could not have asked for more. She thanked him most sincerely. Now it was time to find out what she had come for. The information that Cecil needed for the Queen.

"My lord, might I ask your advice on another matter?" She slowed to a stroll so that the two clerks walking behind them, deep in a private conversation, could pass them.

Quadra assured her that it would be his honor to advise her in any way he could.

They were now walking alone. "My husband and I plan to stay in London until Easter," she said, "but this situation in Scotland has me wondering if that is quite sensible. We have our little boy with us, and I'm rather alarmed at all the whispered talk I hear of an invasion by the French. A friend even suggested that we should get out as soon as possible, to be safe. What do you think? Is this just alarmist talk, or should I plan our return sooner?"

"It might be wise, indeed, to advance your departure."

"Really? But if the French do dare to threaten England, His Majesty the King will surely come to the aid of his ally, Queen Elizabeth, will he not?"

"Not if these heretic rebels gain strength." He inclined his head closer to her so that he could keep his voice low as they strolled on. "You, as a loyal daughter of the one true Church, can appreciate Spain's sacred position as defender of the faith." Isabel knew that he was speaking now not just as ambassador but as Bishop of Aquila. "His Majesty is the most pious prince in Christendom. I assure you that he will *never* allow a heretic Scotland allied with the heretic Queen of England. He will back France."

❧ 8 ❧

A Promise Fulfilled

"For the baby," Isabel said, offering the gift. It was the size of a small book, and wrapped in silver satin.

"How thoughtful." Frances, moving with a ponderous gait, so great with child, had come to greet her as the footman led Isabel in from the front door. If she felt surprise at Isabel's visit at nine o'clock in the evening, she did not show it. "Thank you."

The calmness was a mask, Isabel thought—Frances was itching to speak of their meeting that morning in the Spanish embassy chapel. So was Isabel. It was partly why she had come. But it was not a safe topic with servants near—the footman lingering for further instruction, and a maid passing by with a coal scuttle. Servants talked.

It was the first time she had been at her brother's house. Despite its fashionable address, it was old and felt dim and cramped— not at all what she would have expected Adam to choose. But then, perhaps he hadn't. He was so often away on navy business, her mother had said. Because he preferred to be away from his wife? Isabel wondered. She nodded at the gift in Frances's hands. "Open it."

Frances unwrapped the satin and lifted out a pink coral for teething. It was plum-sized, its original spines smoothed to gentle bumps, and was mounted on a handle of silver shaped like a tad-pole. She smiled. "How sweet."

She invited Isabel upstairs to the birthing chamber to show her the other gifts. An old woman sat in a rocking chair by the fire, knitting. Her face was lined with deep ridges like the bark of a walnut tree, and she was wrapped in a brown shawl that had seen such long service the wool was fuzzy as a caterpillar. Frances intro-duced her: Mistress Dauncy, the midwife. Apparently, she had been brought in preemptively and was staying—more proof of Frances's anxious state about the coming ordeal. Her first child, at the age of forty-two. The room smelled musty, Isabel thought. Every window was shut tight, the heavy brocade curtains drawn against the darkness. Candles flickered on the sideboard.

Frances told the midwife she could retire for the night.

"I'll rest me bones by the kitchen hearth for a spell if you don't mind, my lady," the old woman said, struggling out of her rocking chair. "There's grumbling wee devils in me joints, bad with this wet cold." It took her some time to gather up her basket of yarns and needles. Waiting, Isabel dutifully praised the baby gifts laid out neatly on a table: tiny lace caps with white silk strings, little shirts of the finest Dutch linen, embroidered bibs, a silver rattle.

"Your mother sent the swaddling clothes," Frances said, finger-ing the coral as she watched the midwife. "And Lady Gonson sent the christening gown. Is it not fine?" It was exquisite. Ivory taffeta shot with silver threads, with a soft little ruff of lace.

The old woman waddled to the door, her movements so slow that Isabel wondered about her competence. But Frances appar-ently felt lucky to have found her. "A goodwife of the good old ways," she whispered pointedly. Isabel understood. In every parish, only midwives approved by the church were allowed to practice their art, because if the baby seemed likely to die before a parson could arrive, the midwife had to baptize the child. It had al-ways been this way, but now the official orthodoxy was Queen Elizabeth's reformed church, and Isabel doubted that Frances would put her baby's soul in the hands of a Protestant. This woman must be an adherent of the old church, practicing unlaw-fully.

The moment they were alone Frances grabbed Isabel's hand and said with quiet fervor, "It gladdened me so to see you at mass. What a joy to know that you are one of us!"

Isabel stiffened. Us? Meaning the Grenvilles? No, Frances would not make such a blunder. Catholic, she meant. "I was the ambassador's guest," she replied, realizing it sounded like an excuse.

Frances did not seem to hear that note. "A good and pious man," she said. "I do not know him personally, but I thank God for him. His chapel is our refuge." She asked, looking very anxious, "You will not tell Adam you saw me there, will you? He wouldn't . . . understand."

No, he would not. "Of course I won't. And Frances, please, you must tell no one about *my* being there. If my parents heard . . . well, you know."

"My dear, I shall not breathe a word." She squeezed Isabel's hand and lowered her voice to a conspiratorial murmur. "It goes hard for us, Isabel, we of the true faith. But we can rejoice in the fellowship of our own kind."

Isabel could not share the zeal. She slid her hand free. "Our secret, then. Good."

Frances smiled. "And thank you for this, truly," she said, indicating the teething coral. She set it down alongside the other baby gifts and stroked the neatly folded swaddling clothes. Her smile faded. "The midwife says my time draws near." Isabel saw the slight tremor of her fingers as she touched the baby things. "Is there much blood?" she whispered. "I know there is pain, but it's . . . it's the blood that I—"

"You'll be fine, Frances. You are hale, in good health." She laid her hand gently on her sister-in-law's arm. "And I have come to stay with you, to help in any way I can."

Frances looked at her in wonder. "Stay?"

Isabel had not been looking forward to this chore, but she had made a promise to her brother and meant to keep it. Besides, Frances looked so frightened and lonely with no kinswomen to lighten the time. Her mother was dead and she had no sisters, while her sister-in-law, the widow of Lord John Grenville, had al-

most certainly shunned her since Frances had married a Thornleigh. Isabel was still uneasy about Adam marrying into the family
that had brought her own family so much pain, but none of that
misery was Frances's fault. "That is, if you want me to."

"Oh, yes. Yes!" She almost beamed.

"Good. Adam wanted to be sure that you are well taken care
of." She hoped it might cheer Frances to know that.

"Did he?" She seemed desperate to know. "Did he really?"

"Yes, indeed. He said so, just before you came to bid him good-
bye." Isabel left it at that. *It's the child that matters,* he had said, and
she could not forget the stiff formality of his farewell to Frances at
the Old Swan Stairs, and the yearning in Frances's eyes. She found
it rather pitiful, especially since Frances seemed well aware of
where she stood in her husband's affections. What wife isn't? she
thought. "Now, let me begin by doing the office of your maid and
seeing you into your bed." She guessed that between her discomfort and anxiety, Frances was not getting much sleep. She looked
quite haggard.

They reached the bedchamber, a cheerless room with old-
fashioned dark paneling. The air held a strong smell of vinegar. Isabel sent a maid downstairs for some spiced wine, then helped her
sister-in-law undress. She eased Frances's cumbersome body onto
the mattress and under the covers, then plumped the pillows as
Frances fussed with her prayer book. Crossing herself, she tucked
the book under her pillow, then sank back with a sigh and gave Isabel a wan smile. "You are very good to stay with me, Isabel. I am
most grateful."

"Nonsense, I'm glad to help."

The chamber was chilly. A bird had made a nest high in the
chimney, Frances explained, so the fireplace could not be used
until the sweep arrived to clean it. Isabel asked if she wanted to
order a brazier of hot coals for warmth, but Frances shook her head
as though she had no energy to even consider such things. Isabel
was glad when the wine arrived.

"Here," she said, handing her a goblet of the warm, spiced
claret, "this will help you sleep."

But later Isabel, too, found sleep difficult. Her small chamber down the corridor from Frances had no fireplace at all and was stone cold. She lay under the covers, curled up for warmth, and stared through the window at the sliver of moon, sharp as a blade, hanging high in the black sky, and thought back to her meeting with Sir William Cecil. After leaving the Spanish embassy, she had gone to his house on Canon Row to report what Ambassador Quadra had told her.

"God help us," Cecil had muttered. She had sensed that he was not panicked, only digesting the information, but his words had chilled her nonetheless. He saw dire trouble ahead for England, and the reason was Spain. "Just as I feared," he said. "King Philip will not sit quietly by if Scotland looks ready to fall to Protestants."

"What will he do?"

"Who can say? Perhaps send his own troops to crush the Scots rebels. And bestir the pope to send his. The French are already urging the pope to declare that any of the faithful who can depose our queen will win his endorsement." He shook his head in dismay. "The worst scenario? An open Catholic League—the forces of Spain, France, and the pope—rampant on our very border, and casting ravenous eyes southward on us. If they cross that border, it's catastrophe for England."

Invasion—Isabel saw it looming. Saw that Queen Elizabeth would stand little chance of beating back such a fearsome alliance of foes. And then, she thought, what will happen to the people of England? To my parents, so closely tied to the Queen? To Adam, a captain in the Queen's navy? Standing there in Cecil's study, she had hated the sense of helplessness. Was there not something more she could do? she had asked him. "I might be able to learn more from Ambassador Quadra. If information from that quarter would be of use, sir, I will gladly try."

"Not yet. I shall impart to the Queen what you have told me." He had looked at her for a long moment, as though weighing risk and gain. "Be prepared. Her Majesty may want to speak to you."

She was astonished. "Me? Why?"

He frowned. "Do you want to help or not?"

Did she? If it meant enmeshing herself in the crisis? The answer came in a heartbeat. "Yes."

But the secrecy that Cecil asked for did not sit well with her. He had asked her not to tell her mother about her visit to Quadra, which Isabel did not mind, since she did not want her mother to know of her attendance at the mass, but he had also insisted that she not tell Carlos, and that felt difficult. She had never kept secrets from him before. Yet she sensed it was necessary. Carlos, for all his generosity in offering shelter to her parents in Peru, did not feel the same concern that she did about what happened to England. She was surprised herself to find how very deeply she cared. It felt oddly stirring, as though she had been given a second chance. A chance to atone for her actions five years ago at the Battle of Ludgate.

The memories of Sir Thomas Wyatt's rebellion crowded back now as she looked up at the stark slice of moon. She had been nineteen, and so naïve. Wyatt was planning an uprising against Queen Mary, and Isabel had eagerly pledged to help him, for she had thought herself in love with one of his captains, a young man as naïve as herself. Wyatt and his two thousand men had marched north from Kent toward London. The Queen's forces brutally cut them down, but a few hundred straggled all the way to Ludgate in London Wall. By then, Isabel's father had joined them. When she learned that an assassin hired to kill her father lurked inside the wall, she had to choose between her father and her pledge to Wyatt. She chose—and helped Londoners close Ludgate on Wyatt and his men. The Queen's forces set on them, killing most, capturing the rest. In the mass executions that followed, Wyatt was hanged. Queen Mary had triumphed, and England had suffered for it—in the few years of her reign she burned hundreds of men and women at the stake for their beliefs—and Isabel felt in some small way responsible. Carlos had assured her that Wyatt's forces had never stood a chance from the very beginning, but a nagging question lingered that she could never quiet: *If I had helped keep Ludgate open, might Wyatt have rallied to claim the day?* Now England stood to suffer again if the French invaded, and their occupation would be harsher than Queen Mary's rule. Cecil was asking Isabel to help prevent that, and she welcomed the chance. It felt like a chance to redeem herself.

Carlos would not understand that.

I'm not so unlike Frances, she thought with a shiver as she lay in her cold bed. We both love our husbands, but we're keeping secrets from them.

She had not been asleep for more than an hour when a scream jolted her awake. It came from down the corridor. Isabel jumped out of bed, the floor icy on her bare feet. She whirled a robe around her shoulders and snatched a guttering candle and hurried to Frances's chamber. The way was dark, the air frigid. She found her sister-in-law quaking in her bed, her eyes wide with terror. She kneaded the sheet in fists on either side of her distended belly.

"It's all right, Frances. I'm here." Coming to the bedside, Isabel saw that the mattress was soaked.

"Is it blood?" Frances gaped at her in fear.

"No, no," Isabel quickly assured her, "not blood." The poor woman was too terrified even to look at the sheets. "Your water has burst, that's all. It's—"

"Will I die?"

"Of course not," she soothed. "It's perfectly normal. It just means the baby is on its way. You're going to be fine." She took Frances's hand and stroked it to calm her. "Now, how far apart are the pains?"

"Terrible . . . terrible!"

"All right, let's get you to the birthing chamber."

"No!"

"But it's so cold here, and everything is ready there for—"

"*No!*"

Isabel was shocked at the panic in Frances's eyes. Nothing was going to induce her to move. "All right, all right," she said calmly. "Don't worry. I'll fetch the midwife here. Try to breathe slowly, deeply." Frances gulped frantic breaths, and Isabel didn't have the heart to correct her. It was more important to soothe her with support. "That's right. Even more slowly. Good, keep doing that."

She hurried down the corridor. Behind her she could hear Frances moaning. On the stairs she stopped a sleepy young maid who was padding up with an armful of kindling, and asked where the midwife was. The girl blinked and scratched her neck. "I know not, mistress. She were in the kitchen after supper, asking cook for a lemon."

"What's your name?"

"Nan, mistress."

"Go to Lady Frances's bedchamber, Nan, and stay with her. Her time has come. She must not be alone."

A sharp cry came from Frances. The girl looked startled, but Isabel nudged her and the girl went on up the stairs. Isabel carried on down. The house was dark, most of the servants asleep. As she hurried through the great hall she sent two dogs scrabbling to their feet from their slumber, one barking. She found the kitchen, a cavernous space of brick and stone, and dark but for the red glow of embers in the hearth that sent shadows flitting over the crockery piled on the table. But it was warm. Two children, scullery boys, lay asleep on straw mats under the table. The midwife was sprawled in a chair at the hearthside, fast asleep.

Isabel shook her shoulder. "Mistress Dauncy. You are needed."

The woman jerked awake with a snort. Spittle seeped from a corner of her mouth. "Wha—?"

"Lady Frances is in labor."

"Ah." She rubbed her eyes with gnarled fists. "All right, my lady, lead the way."

Isabel first woke up the scullery boys and told them to rouse the other kitchen servants and have them build up the fire to start boiling water for the midwife. The old woman took her time struggling up the stairs to the birthing chamber. Isabel, impatient, went on ahead and found Nan standing outside the doorway, hugging herself, frowning in alarm.

"What is it, Nan? Is she all right?"

"Don't know, mistress."

"Why have you left her? Go in, girl."

Nan shook her head, nervous but adamant. "I be a spinster, mistress. It ain't right."

Isabel gritted her teeth. Tradition again. Only married women were allowed into the room at a childbirth. And, of course, no men. Nan took a step to slink away, but Isabel took her by the arm. "Go and fetch clean linen cloths. And find someone to bring a brazier of hot coals to warm the room. Go!"

Frances was moaning, staring in stark-eyed fear. Isabel's heart went out to her, sure that such searing fear made the pain worse. She was glad to see the midwife set about her business, asking a servant who had arrived, disheveled from sleep, to bring in her satchel from the birthing chamber. Meanwhile, Isabel did her best to calm Frances, sitting on the edge of the bed and offering comforting words as she smoothed her hair back from her damp forehead. Frances groped for her hand and almost crushed Isabel's fingers in her grip.

The midwife clucked in disapproval. "Leave her be, my lady. She must do this labor on her own." She shooed Isabel away from the bed. Frances groped the air, frantic for a human touch. But the midwife insisted, so Isabel reluctantly moved away and sat down on the window seat. A maid came with the brazier of coals and set it in its wall fitting, glancing in dismay at Frances's suffering. She finished her task and fled. The coals barely warmed the frigid air. Isabel's teeth almost chattered as she watched the midwife unpack her wares and set them on the bedside table in full view of Frances. A long, coiled, black tube. Pincers the size of a man's hands, rusted at the ends. A knife. A burlap bag of dried herbs that gave off a rank smell. A long grubby cloth with a fringe of knots. The black tube gave Isabel a shiver. To administer an enema? It seemed revolting, a further assault on poor Frances in her agony of fear. She thought how different her own labor had been, thanks to Pedro's mother and her gentle Indian ways.

Frances moaned, looking almost delirious. Her lips were parched and looked pale blue in the chill air. She writhed in the grip of a wave of pain, and cried out. The old woman paid her no mind, but settled herself down on a stool at the foot of the bed and went about untying the knots on the grubby cloth, one by one like some ritual, and muttering a mournful incantation. Isabel could not understand how she could ignore Frances's fearful state. She noticed the leftover cup of claret on the sideboard and jumped up and brought it to the bed. Holding it to Frances's dry lips, she encouraged her to sip some.

"Nay!" the midwife said. "To a laboring woman, drink is poison!"

Frances heard. In terror, she knocked the cup away. Wine spewed over the sheets, staining them red.

Isabel felt a jolt of fury at the old woman, who shooed her away again. Isabel paced, watching Frances labor on in lonely agony as the old woman untied the knots, crooning her dirge. Time crawled by, an hour at least. The whole household was up now. Young servant girls scurried outside the chamber, leaving water and cloths, but never coming in. The male servants stayed downstairs. Frances groaned as she labored. She writhed, and sweated, and screamed.

"All of her's shut up too tight," the midwife muttered. She hobbled around the room, opening drawers and cupboards. Isabel watched in dismay. She had heard of this senseless superstition, actions to coax the womb to open. What folly! It was sheer terror that was paralyzing Frances.

Another hour. Frances writhed. Sweated. Moaned. "Adam!" she screamed, a sound of such raw pain that tears of pity stung Isabel's eyes. She had never witnessed a labor so hard.

After another agonizing hour Frances lay back shuddering, racked with exhaustion. Her face was white and damp, like raw pastry, and her nightdress clung to her with sticky sweat. The midwife beckoned Isabel, who rushed to the bedside. "Prepare the lady for death," the old woman told her. "Fetch a priest, if you can find one."

Isabel was horrified, for Frances had heard. She snatched Isabel's arm, her fingers like claws. "Priest! Can't die . . . without . . . rites. *Please!*"

"Shhh, Frances, you're going to be fine," Isabel assured her as calmly as her fury at the old woman would allow. "There's no need for any priest. The baby's almost here, and we're going to help you bring it."

She turned on the hag, gripped her elbow and hustled her away from the bed, then lowered her voice, putting steel into it. "Get out."

"What? I was called by her—"

"Leave at once, or I shall report you to the parish vicar."

"Report what?"

"Fetch a priest, you said. That's enough to land you in the stocks. Now go! And take these wretched things with you." She scooped up the black coil and other paraphernalia, threw them into the satchel, and thrust it at her.

The woman hobbled out with her wares, grumbling. Isabel turned to the three servants who were watching, wide-eyed. One was a stout middle-aged woman with a sensible look about her. "What's your name?"

"Margery, my lady."

"Is there a washtub, Margery? A big one?"

"Aye," she said, bewildered. "In the kitchen."

"Go and tell the kitchen folk to build up the fires and boil water, buckets of water. I want the washtub filled. Go!" Margery hurried out and Isabel turned to the others. "Is there a strong man about?"

They blinked at her. "Bartholomew, the porter," one said. "He's a wrestler."

"Fetch him here. And you," she said to the third one, "help me get your mistress into a fresh nightdress."

Frances was so rigid with fear, it was hard to calm her enough to change her shift, but they managed it. The porter arrived, but would not step into the room. Isabel went to the doorway and told him to carry Frances down to the kitchen. He balked, said birthing was women's work. "Bartholomew," she said quietly, "we may lose your mistress and the babe unless we can make her relax. Now carry her downstairs, or be prepared to answer to Sir Adam Thornleigh for the death of his wife and heir." That got him moving.

The kitchen looked like a smithy's workshop, a dozen servants at work around the roaring fires in the two huge hearths as Isabel ushered Bartholomew in carrying Frances. Footmen slogged in from the scullery pump house with pails of water to fill the kettles at the hearth, and women poured steaming water from the kettles into the wooden washtub. Isabel tested the water in the tub. Too hot. "Warm, like blood," Pedro's mother had said. Isabel ordered some cold water poured in, then tested it again. It was fine.

"Lower her into the tub," she told Bartholomew.

He stared at her, shocked. The kitchen quieted, all eyes on Isabel. Frances blinked at Isabel, bewildered and still stiff with fear. "Frances, the water will ease your pain. It will be good for you, and good for the baby."

"No! I'll drown!"

"You shall not, believe me." She gently took Frances's face between her hands. "Do you trust me?"

Frances stared at her in an agony of doubt. Then managed, in a small voice, "Yes."

"Good. Let this man lower you into the water. Do it now, Bartholomew."

He didn't move.

"*Now.*"

He shook his head as if to say that he would not be responsible for drowning the mistress, then set her down in the tub, immersing her bulky body up to her waist, her shift billowing under the water. "Dear God!" she cried, her face screwed up in fear. She threw her arms over the sides and gripped the tub edge as if for dear life.

There was a hush, everyone waiting for catastrophe.

Then Frances's face unclenched. A sigh rushed out of her mouth. She half sat, half floated in the tub. Isabel relaxed, too. She remembered the feeling well, the water buoying up her heavy body, taking the awful strain off her back. The warmth of the water easing her taut muscles. All of it easing her mind. "This is how my son was born," she said. She ordered that a curtain be hung to give Frances privacy, and sent a young maid for cider to give Frances strength, and sent Margery for twine. Once the curtain was up, she ordered all the servants to stay behind it. She could not risk their reaction to what she was going to do.

Alone with Frances, she stood behind her and laid her hands on her shoulders and gently kneaded. The muscles felt like wire. Another wave of labor pains made Frances tighten again with a gasp, but Isabel kept massaging her shoulders and back, slowly and gently, and murmuring encouragement, just as Pedro's mother had done for her, and gradually Frances's stiff body loosened. The labor pains came in waves that got closer together, but now

Frances was able to ride with them until they ebbed. Though exhausted, she was much calmer.

After another hour, the pains crested. The baby was coming. Isabel perched on the side of the tub. "Push, Frances. Push, just as your body wants you to."

"But . . . no, I must come out . . . the child—"

"Your baby will be born into the water."

Frances gaped at her in horror. "He'll drown! No! Let me out!"

Isabel held her back, gently but firmly. "He will not drown. A watery bed has been his home all these months. He will not need to breathe until his face touches the air. Frances, look at me. I swear to you, Nicolas was born this very way." Doubt swam in Frances's eyes. Isabel willed her to trust, and to believe.

A wave of pain overtook Frances.

"Now, push!" Isabel said.

Frances took a deep breath. She lifted herself so that she was half floating, and she pushed.

"It's coming . . . your child is coming," Isabel crooned. "Push!"

The baby floated out into the water, as unperturbed as though it were still dreaming in the womb. Frances gasped. Isabel cried out, "You have a daughter!" On her knees, she reached into the water and scooped up the warm little being. "Margery, the twine!" Margery threw open the curtain and rushed in with the twine.

Slowly, Isabel brought the baby girl to the water's surface. The child went rigid. Then gasped in a breath. And let out a lusty yell. Isabel laughed with joy.

With the slippery, squirming child in her arms, she instructed Margery, who kneeled, and with trembling fingers wrapped the twine around the umbilical cord and tugged, pinching the cord tight, severing it. Isabel gently laid the warm little body on Frances's heaving breast. Frances blinked, still catching her breath, sweat gleaming on her face. A shadow of a smile struggled over her pale lips. A smile of awe at her baby. And a tired but glowing look at Isabel.

A boy darted across the street in front of the horses, making Ambassador Quadra's gelding shy, hooves up. He rocked back in his saddle. Carlos reached across from his mount and hooked his finger in the gelding's bridle and steadied the horse. The ambassador settled, looking relieved. "Thank you, Valverde."

"Your servant, my lord." They were riding west on busy Newgate Street, going at a walk, on their way to a dinner the French ambassador was hosting at his Charterhouse lodgings outside London Wall. It was the first time Carlos had taken out this horse he'd chosen from Thornleigh's stable, and he was pleased with its quick reflexes. A strong, steady animal. Handsome, too, black as a raven. *Noche*, his son had named it. A good name. *Night*.

"There'll be good food and wine, I can promise you that," Quadra said, adding with a dry smile, "The French do *some* things right."

Carlos smiled back to be polite. Food was food and wine was wine—he had never understood the skirmishing that Frenchmen and Spaniards wasted their time on over who cooked a better sauce. He wasn't sure why Quadra wanted him along at this dinner, either, but he was glad to keep abreast of the man's network of contacts.

He noticed a girl shaking a sheet from a second-story window, and his thoughts went to Isabel, shut up with her sister-in-law. Had the baby come yet? he wondered. As soon as she was done there they could leave for Spain and then, finally, sail back home. He was itching to go. So much to see to, what with the troubles at the Potosí mine. He was sorry her parents had refused to go back with them—sorry for her sake, because he knew she was worried about them. But her mother had made the decision, and now he was keen to go, and he hoped that being shut up with Adam's wife had made Isabel keen, too. Staying indoors for days on end was not her favorite thing. He smiled to himself, remembering her happy look when he had taken her to see the house at Trujillo for the first time. She loved that house, its sunny courtyard, its open verandas, its view of the mountains. It had made him glad to be able to give her that. He hoped he could hang on to the house. But if his debts at the silver mine piled up much higher, he'd have to consider selling the place. He would hate to do that to Isabel.

"Have you met Ambassador de Noailles?" Quadra asked.

"No."

"Well, get to know him tonight. He's something of an alarmist—the French so often are—but in this case, in Scotland, he may have cause. France has enjoyed such a long alliance with that country, until the recent dilemma." Quadra gave Carlos an appraising look. "Are you familiar with the latest developments?"

"Only that the rebels hold Edinburgh." Though he had fought in Scotland years ago, he had never seen their major city. "But I understand the French have landed over seven thousand troops, and they will have strengthened the nearby fortress."

"At Leith, yes, on the coast. But the rebel dogs have camped their tents right out into the fields past Edinburgh, forcing the Queen Regent to take refuge with the Leith garrison. Rebels—bah! Too meager a word. An unholy band of heretics. When they rampaged down from Perth, they ransacked all the churches in their path. They sicken His Majesty. They sicken all of Spain. They are an affront to God Himself." He gave Carlos a pointed look. "I trust you understand my meaning?"

He did—that it was not in Spain's interest to allow the rebels to win. "You want a French victory."

Quadra did not say so, but his nod made it clear. Carlos wasn't surprised.

They were approaching the arch of Newgate in London Wall, where Newgate Prison rose three stories above them, and white-faced prisoners stared out from barred windows. Carlos and Quadra passed under the arch, the clang of their horses' hooves echoing off the frosty stone walls.

"The hair in the ointment is the English Queen," Quadra went on doggedly. "She is anxious about so many Frenchmen on her border. His Majesty wants no quarrel with Queen Elizabeth, for she is his ally, and he has proclaimed his neutral position. However, neither can he allow the attacks of these Scottish curs against the one true Church, and in this goal he is united with the King of France. They are kinsmen, after all, since His Majesty last summer wed the French King's sister. These two great kingdoms are now handfast friends. More important, they are united in their dedication to doing God's holy work."

So much for neutrality, Carlos thought.

"Señor Valverde, it pleases me greatly that you have proved yourself such a loyal servant of the King. In her letter my cousin Beatriz wrote a glowing tale of your exploits in putting down the traitor Mendez's rebellion. Others who know Peru have told me the same, and it seems no exaggeration to say that you saved his excellency the viceroy from a defeat that would have gravely undermined the King's authority in that land."

Carlos nodded. He was glad of the rewards the Peruvian campaign had brought him, but had little interest in going over old ground. He looked to the road ahead, where a dozen or so cattle plodded toward him and Quadra. A farmer trudged at the rear of the cattle. Here, outside the city walls, there was a stink from the tanneries to the south, where livestock entrails were slopped into the Fleet Ditch. To the north lay Smithfield fairground, not busy today with no horse market. Past it, frozen fields.

"Tell me," Quadra said, "as a military man, how do you rate the chances of our French friends?"

Isabel's father had asked him the same question. Carlos hadn't changed his mind since then. "Is Leith the only fortress the French hold?"

"No, there are more. Principally, Dunbar and the island of Inchkeith."

"What about the stronghold of Edinburgh Castle? Have the rebels taken it?"

"No, Lord Erskine commands it, ostensibly for the Queen Regent, though he has proved unwilling to turn his guns on the rebels."

"But he hasn't gone over to them?"

"No."

"Who commands the French troops?"

"Monsieur D'Oysel. He has advised the Queen Regent for many years, and she trusts him completely."

But can he fight? Carlos let that question go. "How many troops have the French landed?"

"Seven thousand at the Leith garrison, and we know that the

Marquis d'Elbeuf is readying at Dieppe to sail in forty ships with six thousand more, and cannons."

Battle-hardened troops against a ragtag army of clansmen who had no artillery and would turn and walk home to their hovels when their few weeks of rations ran out. There was no real match here. "The French will succeed," he said.

"Indeed, we must hope so. But hope is no substitute for action, I'm sure you'd agree. Although in this case our actions must be circumspect. Which is why I hope that you will accept a mission in His Majesty's name."

Carlos looked at him, taken aback. "Mission?"

"To Leith. As our military liaison to the French commander. We need someone of your caliber close to the decision making, to safeguard Spain's interests."

Carlos kept his eyes ahead on the approaching cattle, hiding his alarm. A posting to Scotland was the last thing on earth he wanted. He had put soldiering behind him. He was a gentleman now. *I earned it, damn it.* But he couldn't say any of that. He answered carefully, "I am always at His Majesty's service, my lord."

Quadra gave a courtly nod. "As are we all."

"However, his excellency the viceroy has requested my return, and I am his to command. I am sorry to disappoint you, my lord, but I expect to sail to Peru almost immediately."

"Not until Easter, your wife said."

Carlos looked at him, surprised. "My wife?"

"She came to tell me about your application to His Majesty's Council of the Indies. For a seat on the Trujillo city council? She asked me to add my recommendation."

Did she? "Of course," he said, not wanting to seem unaware of his wife's doings. He was pleased, actually. It was a good idea. Clever Isabel. He wanted that Trujillo seat badly. It would be expensive, what with the fee to the Council of the Indies, but well worth the cost. The position was permanent, and carried the authority to sell scores of minor offices and pocket the cash. It would bring in so much, he could keep the house and give Isabel everything she would ever need or want, and let him build a fine patrimony for Nicolas.

"I would like to assist your application," Quadra said. "Naturally, only those who have proved their loyalty to His Majesty can be considered for such an honor. As you have so capably done, Señor Valverde, and will, I am sure, continue to do. May I rest easy that I can entrust this Scottish mission to you?"

So that was it. Carlos felt the heavy weight of the ultimatum. To win the seat that would discharge his debts, keep the house that Isabel loved, and build the legacy he wanted for his son, he would have to endure a God-cursed billet in stinking Scotland. "My lord, please consider my position," he said, making one last stand. "The viceroy does not allow absentee *encomenderos*. By staying away from Peru I could forfeit my *encomienda*."

"Oh, your land holdings will in no way be jeopardized. I will personally assure the viceroy of the necessity of your mission, and your indispensability to His Majesty."

Carlos gritted his teeth. No way out. He answered as calmly as he could, "In that case, my lord, I am His Majesty's servant to command."

Quadra smiled. "Excellent. Don't worry, Valverde. If you're right about the superior French capability, and I pray to God that you are, this whole thing could be over in weeks."

9

Departures

Isabel was delighted with Frances's quick recovery. The change was remarkable. Within a day the bloom had crept back into her cheeks, and she was sitting up in bed contentedly reading a friend's note of congratulation. Isabel had immediately sent a message to the Admiralty to be forwarded to Adam, telling him about his baby daughter, who was quite perfect, she added, and assuring him of Frances's good health. It tickled her to imagine her devil-may-care brother as a father, but she knew the role would please him tremendously. Frances had named the child Katherine.

Isabel had encouraged her to dismiss the hired wet nurse and suckle the baby herself, and by the following day little Katherine was nursing well. Frances had regained a hearty appetite, too, and ordered her kitchen to prepare roast capon and baked cinnamon apples for herself and Isabel, arranging the details with brisk efficiency. Isabel sensed that she was seeing the real Frances emerge. Cowed before by her fear of childbirth, she had confronted that demon and conquered it, and now, eager to get on with life, the able manager in her came striding forth. Isabel loved sitting with the baby in her arms when Frances napped. She would watch the tiny fingers curl around her own finger, and dream of having another babe of her own. Carlos wanted more children, she knew. It made her long to get back to her parents' house. Could she leave yet? Frances was certainly well enough. She decided she would stay one more night, make sure that Frances was comfortably settled in the morning, and then go. Tomorrow night she would be lying in Carlos's arms. A daughter next time, wouldn't that be wonderful?

That evening, as she was about to undress for bed, Frances surprised her by coming into her room. "Is everything all right?" Isabel asked.

"Yes. Katherine is sleeping."

"As should you."

"I will. I just wanted to say . . . Isabel, I don't know how I can ever thank you enough. I believe you saved my life. And my child's."

"Nonsense. You did all the work. I only fussed."

"No. I owe you everything, and I shall never forget it."

Isabel couldn't resist. "No odd effects from the water? A mad desire to swim? Fishy scales on the babe?"

Frances laughed. "I'll tell her when she's older how her aunt made me face down my fears in a washtub."

They embraced, Isabel feeling happy that she had so faithfully discharged her promise to her brother, and even happier that she would soon be going home.

Frances pulled away. "I am leaving tomorrow. I just received a note from Adam."

"Ah! You are going to join him?"

"No." Frances looked down, her sadness all too plain. "He is not coming home. His duties keep him away." Isabel felt sorry for her, all alone in this house with only servants. She had invited her to come to the house on Bishopsgate Street, but was not surprised when Frances declined. Isabel knew there was little love between her sister-in-law and her parents.

Frances looked up, and a brisk new energy straightened her back. "I will not pine," she said. "I am going to visit my brother Christopher at his house in Northumberland. It will cheer me. And the wholesome country air will be good for Katherine."

Isabel felt a prickle of alarm. Another Grenville, this Christopher. She had never met him, and hoped she never would. But that was not the only cause of her concern. "Are you sure you can manage such a journey?" she asked. It would take three weeks at least, over ice-hard roads. And Frances was still recovering.

"I will go in a litter. I *must* go, Isabel. Must get away from London. Katherine has to be baptized, and I will not have it done in one of their filthy churches."

"Things are no different in Northumberland."

"Ah, but they are." She lowered her voice. "If one knows where to go."

The cryptic comment sounded conspiratorial, as though they shared a secret. It opened a dangerous door, Isabel thought. To partake of a mass held by the Spanish ambassador was one thing; he was an eminent dignitary privileged by his position. To join country people in outlaw worship was something else altogether. Isabel was about to urge her to reconsider, when a maid came to the doorway.

"A letter for Mistress Valverde," she said as she curtsied.

Isabel opened it. It was from Sir William Cecil, a brief note, but one that sent a shiver through her. The Queen, he said, required her presence at Whitehall Palace.

"Not bad news, I hope," said Frances.

Isabel forced a smile. "Not at all. Mother wants help with the Christmas preparations." She folded the letter and tucked it away. "Frances, since you're leaving tomorrow—"

"Yes, of course, do return to your parents' house. I am sorry to have taken you from them." The formality of her words sounded as though she was trying to hide how much she would miss Isabel.

"Mistress Valverde. Wake up."

Isabel surfaced from a dream of swimming in a sunlit sea with a naked newborn in her arms. "What is it?" She blinked in the glare of the candle flame held near her face.

Frances's servant girl, Nan, stood near the bed. "Your husband. He's asking to see you."

Isabel sat bolt upright. "He's here?"

"I told him you were sleeping, but he—"

"I'm coming." She got up and whirled a robe around her shoulders, kicked her feet into slippers, and hurried down the stairs. At the bottom, the murky light of dawn from the stairwell windows made Carlos a shadowy form standing at the front door. He turned when he heard her coming, making his spurs clink and his sword glint in its scabbard.

"What's happened?" she asked as she reached him. "Is it Nico?"

"No."

"Mother?"

"No. She's fine."

He looked so serious, she knew something was wrong. Why was he booted and spurred? "What, then?"

"Is your sister-in-law up?"

"At this hour? No. Did you get my message? About the baby?"

He nodded. "Isabel, I came to say good-bye. I'm on my way north."

She blinked at him. "Good heavens . . . where? What for?"

"To Edinburgh."

"Edinburgh! Why?"

"Quadra." He explained: The ambassador was sending him to the French garrison at Leith. He was to be Spain's military attaché to the French commander. He added bitterly, "Why? Because I happen to be in this cursed country."

She stared at him in shock. He was going to help the *French?* A voice in her screamed *No!* And it was no peacetime posting . . . *He'll be in the fighting!* Her stomach twisted at the horror of it. She fought to speak rationally. "But . . . how can he ask this of you? You're not involved in that anymore. Soldiering. You have property in Peru that—"

"It's about the seat on the city council. I won't get it unless I do this. He made that clear."

Her hand flew to her mouth to bottle up a gasp. "Oh, no. I asked him to endorse you. This is *my* fault."

"No, he told me you asked him, and I'm glad you did. His word carries weight. I'll get the seat faster."

"The seat doesn't matter. It's *you* I care about."

"It does matter. I need the money. *We* need it. It'll cover our debts."

"The money's not worth it if you get hurt or—" *Killed* was the appalling, unspoken word. "Carlos, you can still refuse. Tell Quadra about your commitments to the viceroy. He has said he needs you back to—"

"No, Quadra's settling all that. The King's service comes first." When she opened her mouth to say more, he held up his hand to stop her. "Enough. Isabel, I've agreed. I'm going. Listen, what I came to tell you was . . ." He stopped, as though he found the next words difficult.

"What?"

There was a scuffling sound at the top of the stairs. He looked in that direction. It was Nan, yawning as she came down. It made Carlos even more reluctant to go on with what he had started to say. Instead, he told Isabel, "Have my things sent, would you? Clothes. I'll travel faster without baggage. Send it after me. Quadra's secretary will tell you where."

She could scarcely believe this was happening. The crisis had sucked them both in . . . and was pulling them apart. *We're on opposite sides.* It so stunned her, dizziness shot to her head. She swayed.

Carlos grabbed her arm to steady her. "You've worn yourself out caring for Adam's wife. Do you need to sit down?"

"No. No," she insisted, struggling to come to terms with the devastation of her world. She fought to respond as he would expect, and heard words come out of her mouth: "How long will you be gone?"

He shrugged, grim-faced. "Until someone wins."

Should she tell him everything? Tell him she had offered to help Cecil, to help the Queen? No, she had promised Cecil her silence. She cursed that promise now, hating to lie to Carlos, lie to him by her very silence. The longing to explain made her say, "About Ambassador Quadra . . . I've had a message from . . . the palace. The Queen has asked to see me."

He looked astonished. "Why?"

"I don't know." It was only half a lie. Cecil had sent the summons but no explanation of what it was about. "Maybe because we're friendly with Quadra . . . so maybe she thinks I've heard some useful information." It was half the truth.

He frowned, puzzled. "About Scotland?"

She shrugged, mute with misery. She had already said too much.

He shook his head with a look of impatience, as though he thought it a waste of time to discuss something neither of them knew the facts of.

Muffled clangs sounded from the kitchen, servants starting their morning chores. And preparations for Christmas, Isabel thought bleakly. It was just a week away. She looked at Carlos. "Nicolas will hate Christmas without you."

It seemed to prod him with a new urgency. "Isabel, I came to tell you something. If French troops surge into England, things could get bad here." He took her by the shoulders, gently but firmly. "I want you to go home."

"I am. Today," she said, not caring. "Frances is fine now."

"I mean *our* home. Trujillo. I want you to get Nicolas and take the next ship to Spain, and then sail home. I've left all our money for you, all but enough to get me by. Take it, and take Nico, and go home."

She stared at him, unable to speak. Leave without him? Everything in her said *no*.

"And talk to your mother," he said. "Convince her that she and your father should go with you."

"They won't. I've tried."

"Try again. But no matter what, you and Nico get home. You hear me?"

No, she could not agree to this. If it became necessary she could send Nicolas to Spain to stay with Beatriz's family in Seville. He would be well taken care of there. But she would not go home without Carlos. Nor even leave England herself, not yet. She had promised. She said, "Nico and I can go to Seville and wait for you." When he looked about to argue the point, she added flatly, "Carlos, you must trust me. I'll do what has to be done."

He frowned as though not quite satisfied, but then nodded. "All right. Seville." He heaved a tight sigh. "Now, I must go."

They stood looking at each other, both unwilling to say the awful word *good-bye*. Her devastation that they were on opposite sides was swallowed up in sheer anguish that he was going at all, putting himself in harm's way—that this was the last she would see of him for . . . how long, God only knew. "I'll come out with you," she managed.

The air was frigid as they stepped outside, and Isabel snugged her robe tightly around her. Fog shrouded the street. She could hear a wagon rumble over the cobbles but it was invisible in the misty gloom. A horse whinnied nearby, and Isabel could make out the shape of two waiting horses, one with a rider. It was Pedro. He would have left Nicolas asleep in bed. It gave her a shred of comfort to know that Carlos would have someone with him who was a part of their life. They walked hand in hand to the horse that Pedro was holding for him, and she greeted the lad.

"Señora," he replied with a nod.

Carlos turned to her, ready to go. "We'll get through this," he said. "Come summer, we'll both be home." He added, trying to sound lighthearted, "You'll be on the veranda telling me to take my boots off before I come in the house." But the tightness in his voice betrayed his emotion. He took her face between his hands and kissed her. She could barely respond, for her heart was breaking.

A burst of laughter came from the street—two apprentices hustling to work. They were laughing at some jest as they went on their way, unaware of Carlos and Isabel, but it was enough to pull him away from her. He mounted his horse. Isabel gripped the bridle, madly wishing there were some way she could stop him from riding off. She laid her hand on his knee and said, "Be careful." Paltry words! She hated them. Hated Quadra. Hated that she had no power to stop this.

"And you," he said with feeling. He covered her hand with his and squeezed. He looked as though he wanted to say more. But there was nothing more to say.

Isabel said to Pedro, *"Tome cuidado."* Take care.

"Gracias, señora."

Carlos turned his horse's head, easing it into a walk. Pedro followed him. Isabel watched them go—past the neighbor's house, past the baker's shop, then on into the gloom beyond, the horses'

hooves clacking on the cobbles. She closed her eyes, finding it un-
bearable to watch Carlos disappear, on his way to help the enemy.

At the sound of galloping hooves her eyes sprang open. He was
cantering back to her. He swung down from his horse and pulled
her into his arms and kissed her with all the passion he had intended before the apprentices had interrupted them. She held
him tight and gave herself to the kiss with all the longing she knew
would haunt her cold nights to come.

"Vaya con Dios," he whispered. He kissed her forehead tenderly,
then swung back up into the saddle. Just before he turned his
horse, he looked down at her and said, "Isabel, be careful with the
Queen. You and I are subjects of Spain. Make sure she honors
that."

She shivered, watching him ride off until the fog swallowed
him up.

‟ 10 ‟

In the Presence
of the Queen

Whitehall Palace teemed with the activity of a town. Built three centuries before by the Archbishop of York as his London house, it eventually became the home of Henry VIII's chancellor, Cardinal Wolsey, who had enlarged it and made it magnificent. So grand was the place that when King Henry abandoned Wolsey to ruin and death, he took Whitehall for himself and made it his principal London residence—it was convenient for hunting in his nearby forested deer park, St. James's. The palace kept growing, with additions and constant rebuilding, and by the time Queen Elizabeth took the throne it contained well over a thousand rooms. Every day it housed scores of courtiers—lords and gentlemen and their ladies—with their retinues of serving men and women, as well as a resident army of clerks and servants, all of whom jostled in its corridors and courtyards alongside visiting foreign dignitaries, merchants, and place seekers, each with an entourage. The site included houses, shops, barracks, stables, gardens, brewery, an outdoor banqueting pavilion, bowling alley, tennis courts, a pit for cockfights, and a tiltyard for jousting. These sprawling precincts, like a burgeoning village, straddled the public road that ran right through the palace and on to Westminster.

Isabel barely took it in, so anxious was she about meeting the

Queen. She walked beside her mother, who was leading her and Nicolas through the labyrinth of busy streets, alleys, and courtyards. They passed a group of splendidly dressed lords chatting under a scaffold where workmen were hammering at an eaves trough. Isabel tightly held her son's hand to keep him from dashing into the path of a farmer's cart clattering by to deliver sides of mutton and baskets of cabbages.

"Look!" Nicolas pointed to a company of mounted horsemen of the Palace Guard trotting in under a stone arch. He strained at Isabel's hand to pull away. "It's Papa!"

"No, it's not," she said, tugging him back. "Hush!"

Her mother shot her a look of concern. She had been highly displeased when Isabel had told her that Carlos had gone to Scotland to see to the interests of Spain. Isabel herself still felt stricken. His mission had cracked her world apart. Then, last night her mother had come home from the palace in an angry state, saying that in her presence Sir William Cecil had told the Queen how he had sent Isabel to Ambassador de Quadra. "How dare he?" she had fumed to Isabel. "He had no right to press this problem on you."

"He pressed nothing, Mother," Isabel had insisted, relieved, at least, to be lightened of the burden of the secret. "The country could face an invasion, and that endangers you and Father. And since you won't come to Peru, I did what little I could to help."

Her mother had looked at her in surprise, but with a touch of admiration. "You did it . . . for me?"

"Of course. For you—for England. And I managed to get some useful information."

"Yes, Sir William explained. Spain's true position." She shook her head in sad acceptance of the fact. "Elizabeth needed this news, however unwelcome." Impulsively, she embraced Isabel. "I hate to see you involved, Bel, but I do thank you. You did well."

Now, as they entered the palace's main block, Isabel felt horribly on edge about this audience with Queen Elizabeth. *What will she ask of me? And how much do I dare do for England, with Carlos pledged to Spain?* Adding to her unease, the royal summons had included her mother and Nicolas. Isabel did not appreciate the

Queen's insistence on making this a family visit. It would only ag-
itate her mother more. She would far rather have come alone.

They went up a broad staircase crowded with courtiers and their
servants. Two angry gentlemen were shouting at each other, apparently over a gambling debt. Isabel had heard that gambling was
a passion here at court, among men and women alike. People laid
bets on everything from cockfights, dice games, and tennis
matches to a courtier's chances of landing an earl's daughter as
wife, and since all gentlemen went armed with sword or dagger,
their disputes, when tempers flared, could get bloody. As Isabel's
little party reached the door of the Queen's private apartments,
she heard scuffling and shouting and the clanging of swords, and
she glanced back toward the staircase to see officers of the Queen's
chamberlain pulling the brawlers apart.

Guards stationed at the Queen's door ushered her and her
mother and Nicolas into the antechamber. A few courtiers were
lounging, looking over maps on a table. One of the royal gentle-
women approached, her arms outstretched. "Lady Thornleigh,
what a pleasure. I have been at home in Devon so long, I missed
you."

They clasped hands. "I trust your family is well, Kat?"

"All hale, I thank you. Is this lady your daughter?"

Introductions were made. The gentlewoman was Mistress
Katherine Ashley, the Queen's former governess and her longtime
friend. Isabel nudged Nicolas to bow to her, which he did, and
Mistress Ashley looked charmed but faintly distracted. She led
them through to the Queen's private chamber. Isabel's stomach
tightened. In a moment she would be face-to-face with Queen
Elizabeth.

As they entered the room, though, she saw only young ladies-in-
waiting amusing themselves. Three stood chatting at a sideboard,
inspecting bolts of silk in gorgeous colors of peacock blue and
cherry red and spring green. Two more sat in a wide window seat,
tossing a yellow ball back and forth. Between them was a basket
where a plump calico cat lay suckling a litter of kittens. Servants
bustled, laying covered silver dishes of food on a small table by the

fire, presumably for the Queen's dinner, since it was almost noon. Isabel smelled onions and a fresh scent of thyme. Mistress Ashley introduced her to the young ladies, and they welcomed her and made a spirited fuss over Nicolas, laughing as he caught the yellow ball. One of them tousled his hair. Isabel knew they were daughters of noble families who would have lobbied hard to win them these choice positions. She guessed that all of them were under the age of twenty. At twenty-six, she felt quite the matron.

"An anxious morning for Her Majesty," Mistress Ashley explained. "She has been shut up since eight with her councilors." She lowered her voice and added, "Scotland."

Isabel and her mother shared a glance. Scotland had them all on tenterhooks.

"Some wine, ladies, while you wait?" Mistress Ashley asked, beckoning a maid.

"Thank you, Kat."

They sat on cushioned stools to wait, sipping claret, as the young ladies at the window seat enlisted Nicolas in their game, tossing the ball back and forth to him. Isabel almost relaxed as she saw him join their fun, for there was nothing he liked better than playing with a ball. He soon became a kind of live net between the two young ladies, his face aglow at the challenge of jumping higher each time to try to catch the ball.

Mistress Ashley expressed an interest in Isabel's life in the New World, and Isabel answered her questions politely but briefly, her thoughts everywhere but there. She had learned that people were usually interested in only three things: the heathen Indians, the treasure hoards of silver and gold, and how do you bear the dreadful heat? Once she had satisfied the lady's curiosity about these topics, Mistress Ashley turned to chat with her mother about the latest suitors who were vying for the Queen's hand in marriage. Archduke Charles of Austria. The Duke of Saxony. King Eric of Sweden. Isabel barely listened. Scotland was all she could think of. What had happened to make Queen Elizabeth and her council deliberate all morning? Since Carlos had left, Isabel's thinking on the Scottish crisis had crystallized. Before, she had only an inchoate hope that the rebel Scots would win their fight against their French overlords, because that would stop the French in their tracks before they could invade England. Now she wanted a Scottish victory more than anything, and fervently wanted it to be a swift one, because that would bring Carlos home.

Nicolas darted past her, running for the ball as it sailed high, right across the room. One of the ladies, laughing, cried out, "Catch it!" and Nicolas jumped, but missed. He landed unsteadily, his arms windmilling to stay on his feet, when the door opened and the ball hit the floor and bounced up into the face of a young woman. She lurched back in alarm, and Nicolas skidded head first into her skirts.

There were gasps from the young ladies. The ones who were seated shot to their feet. The servants bowed low. The young ladies bobbed curtsies. Isabel's mother and Mistress Ashley rose from their stools. Isabel rose with them, appalled at her son's blunder. This was Queen Elizabeth!

Nicolas thumped down on his backside at the Queen's feet. The ball had rolled between her embroidered shoes, and he scrambled onto his hands and knees and thrust his hand between her feet and grabbed the ball. He jumped up, grinning, and turned to his playmates with the trophy held high. "I got it!"

The Queen snatched the ball from him. "No, young sir, I have it."

He gaped at her, stilled by her imperious tone. The room was utterly silent.

"Nicolas, come here!" Isabel ordered in a whisper.

He looked around at all the grave faces, bewildered by what was happening.

"Nicolas," Isabel said tightly.

"Do not move, sir," the Queen ordered him. "I know this yellow ball. It is Mistress Arnold's. Are you a thief?"

He stared at her.

"Speak up. Is it the stocks for you, Master Thief?"

"No, madam. She . . . we were just playing."

"Playing catch?"

"Yes."

"Well then, let's see how high you can catch." She tossed the ball high in the air. Nicolas leapt and caught it, a perfect reflex despite his baffled state. Landing on his feet, he hesitated, his eyes flicking between the Queen and young Mistress Arnold as though uncertain which one had the better claim to the ball. After a moment he boldly held it up as an offering to the Queen.

"Ha!" she laughed. "A little courtier!"

The young ladies giggled. The older ladies laughed. Isabel had to smile, too.

A clerk hustled into the room behind the Queen with an armload of papers. He stopped and took in the scene with the look of a man who knows he has just missed something. "What's happened?" he asked.

"Avoid a career in the theater, man," the Queen said wryly. "You lack a sense of timing."

More laughter from the ladies. Nicolas sensed the light new mood and came to Isabel and pressed against her leg with a contrite look up at her. She kissed the top of his head to show him he was forgiven. He glanced with curiosity back at the Queen, and Isabel, too, felt intensely curious. She knew that the Queen was exactly her own age, but was surprised at how young she looked. Perhaps it was her slender body, or the quickness of her movements, or the straightforward interest that shone in her dark eyes. Just as surprising was the way she was dressed, not in the opulent raiment Isabel had heard she wore for her public appearances, but in a simple dress of black velvet with white satin sleeves embroidered with tiny flowers. Isabel had the feeling that the unfussy black-and-white effect was deliberate, because it beautifully set off the Queen's red hair, coiled at the nape of her neck. A monarch, she thought, but still a woman.

Isabel was startled to see Sir William Cecil in the room. He had entered so quietly behind the clerk. He stood by the table where the clerk had put down the papers. He kept his gaze on the floor, and his rigid stillness and the hard line of his mouth told her he was seething with anger. From the council meeting? The Queen ignored him—quite pointedly, it seemed to Isabel. Why? She knew from her mother something of the close relationship between Cecil and the Queen. He had been her adviser since she was a princess in her teens and he had held the honorary post of steward of her lands, and during the perilous years of her sister Mary's reign, when many feared that Queen Mary would execute her, Cecil had stood by the Princess. For half her life she had relied on his counsel. What had happened to come between them now? Isabel longed to know.

"Lady Thornleigh," the Queen said, "is this lady your daughter?"

"She is, Your Majesty."

Isabel sank into a deep curtsy. Etiquette forbade her speaking until the Queen addressed her directly.

"Señora Valverde, is it not?" she asked Isabel.

"Yes, Your Majesty," Isabel answered, catching the emphasis on her Spanish name.

"You may rise. And this is your son?"

"Yes, Your Majesty. His name is Nicolas."

The Queen kept her eyes on the boy even as she continued to question Isabel. "I hear that your brother is newly a father. It is a girl, I understand. His wife, is she well?"

"Very well, Your Majesty. Mother and child are thriving."

There was a trace of sadness in her eyes. "What joy for your brother." Isabel was sure she heard regret beneath the words. She remembered the warmth in Adam's voice when he had spoken of the Queen. What secret current flowed between these two? she thought in wonder.

The Queen lifted her head with a snap of pride, as though to banish unwelcome thoughts. "You are most welcome here with us," she said with fresh energy, "for your mother is my well-beloved friend. Indeed, your whole family has done me stout service." She cast her eyes over the three of them—Isabel, her mother, and Nicolas. "So, three generations, eh? Yes, I heartily welcome all branches of the Thornleigh tree, thorny or smooth."

Isabel felt a little overwhelmed at this effusive greeting. Had she been wrong in thinking she had been brought here to speak to the Queen about Quadra? Was this audience to be merely a casual family visit instead? She glanced at her mother, who was smiling fondly at the young Queen. It gave Isabel the tiniest prick of jealousy to see the bond between them, almost like a mother and daughter, a bond forged in the five years that she had been away.

"Leave us," the Queen told her ladies. "All but Lady Thornleigh and her daughter. And the lad."

There was a flurry of skirts and perfume as the young ladies swept out of the room. Mistress Ashley followed, and then the servants.

Cecil, however, did not move. "Your Majesty," he said, "I would speak with you."

"But I, sir, would speak with my guests," she snapped.

"I beg your leave to wait."

She glared at him. "Suit yourself."

He cast his eyes down again in angry silence. The tension between them was almost palpable. The Queen pulled out the gilded chair meant for her at the table and sat down with obvious relief after her strenuous morning of business. She ignored the covered platters, reached for a silver dish of sugar-dusted almond macaroons the size of coins, and popped one into her mouth. Munching, she sat back and stretched her legs straight out. "Master Nicolas, watch those kittens in the basket, if you will. They like a tickle. But be gentle, or their mother will scratch you."

"I like kittens," he said, dropping to his knees beside them.

"Good lad. So do I."

She turned to Isabel, and a new graveness settled over her features. "Now, Señora Valverde, I have been told of your visit to Bishop de Quadra. I cannot say that I like the information you got from him, but I thank you for bringing it to us."

Isabel was taken aback. Business, after all. It was hard to know where she stood with this queen. "I only hope it may serve useful, Your Majesty."

"It already has. It has set our new policy."

A grunt escaped Cecil—a clear and caustic disapproval. The Queen glowered at him, an equally clear and caustic rebuke. Is-

abel did not know what to make of their discord, but she took the
Queen's introduction of the subject as an invitation to speak. She
was eager to do anything she could to help end the crisis in Scotland, for the sooner it was over, the sooner Carlos could come
home. "Your Majesty," she said, "if I may be of further use, I am
your servant. I will visit the ambassador again, if you wish."

The Queen looked barely interested, the matter closed. "Do,
yes," she murmured. "That will be helpful." She picked up another macaroon, but only toyed with it, as though her worries had
stifled her appetite. She looked at Nicolas and said, "Master
Kitten-Tamer, do you like sweetmeats?"

He shot a puzzled look at Isabel. He didn't understand the
word.

"Dulces," she translated. Sweets.

His eyes went wide. *"Sí!* I mean, yes!"

"Good lad," the Queen said, "so do I. Here, catch." She tossed
the macaroon at him, high in the air. He leapt up and caught it. She
chuckled.

Isabel wasn't sure she liked her son being treated like a per-
forming dog. And was there to be no more discussion about
Quadra? About Scotland?

"Madam, enough!" Cecil said. Everyone looked at him,
shocked at his outburst. "Forgive me, but I can no longer abide
this charade. The crisis is too dire, much as you try to avoid it.
Please, let me say—"

"I shall not!" the Queen said with a blast of fury. "We have been
through this, ad infinitum. I know your mind, sir. I wish you would
take more heed of *mine!"*

He bowed to her. He looked overwrought, pale, almost as
though he were ill. "Indeed, madam, it is my duty and pleasure always to do your will. I assure you that I will never pursue a policy
of which you do not approve. And since I am certain that you are
mistaken about the peril in Scotland, I cannot carry out your
wishes effectively. Therefore, I humbly request that you transfer
me to other duties. My only wish is to faithfully serve you. Allow
me to do so, please, in matters on which we are in harmony."

She gaped at him, stunned. Isabel looked from one to the other

in astonishment. Cecil was refusing to carry out the Queen's policy—or was as near to refusing as any minister of a monarch
anointed by God dared go. Isabel's mother, too, was staring at him
in amazement. And something more. Anger. "Sir," she said tersely,
"if you think you can coerce Her Majesty into—"

"Coerce?" he shot back, insulted. "My life is Her Majesty's to
command. I will serve in any capacity that furthers her welfare and
good government for the people of England. But this policy," he
said, turning to the Queen, "does everyone ill. I cannot, in conscience, promote what I abhor. Transfer me elsewhere, madam, I
beg you."

It was the Queen's turn to look pale. Her mask of power
dropped. "Sir William," she said, looking very vulnerable, "how
can you?" Isabel suddenly saw her as the green ruler she was, inexperienced and untested. "How shall I do without you?"

"Do *with* me, madam!" he implored. "Heed my counsel. Help
our Scottish friends. I know your heart is with their cause."

She raised her head as though to master herself, and said simply,
"*Their* cause, sir? Nay, my heart is with the cause of England." The
sincerity of it struck Isabel.

"Their cause is our cause," he said, "and if—"

"Sir William," Isabel's mother interrupted, "we *all* support their
cause. But not to the point of committing suicide. We cannot prevail against the combined might of France and Spain."

"You leap to outcomes, Lady Thornleigh," he said. "We need
only devise a way to aid the Scots in their fight without France or
Spain getting wind."

"Which cannot be done," was her stern reply. "Please, sir, you
know their network of spies. Nothing goes unnoticed."

"We will not know that unless we try."

Watching them spar, Isabel felt hungry to understand. Her
mother was arguing the Queen's position of noninvolvement.
Cecil was urging engagement. Who was right?

"And if King Philip finds out?" her mother challenged. "He already considers Her Majesty a heretic. If he sees her aiding a
Protestant rebellion he will intervene, to our utter ruin."

"He will not have time if we act first," Cecil insisted. "The Scots can win this, if we help them. They are ill funded and ill equipped, unable to pay their men and starved for adequate munitions. If we can provide the money to build their strength, they can win this fight."

"Spain has far more strength," her mother countered, "and the King will consider it a holy crusade to use it. He has said so, through his ambassador, to my daughter. He will never abide a Protestant Scotland allied with a Protestant England. And if Spain lands troops to crush heresy in Scotland, he will come to yoke England next and call it the crown of his crusade."

"Which is precisely why we must help Knox's rebel force *now*, immediately, before Spain can act."

A log in the fire lost its footing and tumbled, flinging sparks. It seemed to cut through everyone's thoughts. A spark was exactly what Isabel felt. *Mother is wrong. Cecil is right.*

But that seemed far from clear to the Queen. She looked into the fire with a look of dread, as if searching for an answer to her problems. Isabel felt she was seeing the core of the woman laid bare—young and inexperienced, but driven by a fierce love of her country. "It is too late, sir. I have written to the Scottish Queen Regent assuring her I will do no meddling in Scottish affairs."

"Irrelevant," he said, and his keen eyes glittered at her note of wavering resolve, as though he felt he might now sway her. "Since then she has asked France for aid, and her Guise brothers have shipped thousands of soldiers to her, with thousands more on the way. *They* have altered the situation. You, as a sovereign queen, must adapt."

She looked at him gravely. "No. Lady Thornleigh is right. The risk of antagonizing Spain is too great."

"The risk of doing nothing is greater," he shot back. "If we allow the French to subjugate Scotland, they will not stop there. They will come for England. And to try to stop them then will take more money and men and arms than we can ever muster. Your Majesty, I implore you. Help the Scots fight now, or risk a bigger fight that we can only lose."

The Queen looked anguished. "A gamble. That is what you are asking me to take. A gamble that we can help the Scots without enraging Spain."

"A necessary gamble," he said steadily. "If we wager nothing, we could lose all."

Listen to him, Isabel thought, bursting to speak. The longer this war festered, growing ever more malignant, the longer she and Carlos would be on opposite sides. *Strike now, help the rebels win, and end this.*

"But help them *how?*" the Queen demanded. "Quadra has his hired eyes and ears posted in every second doorway. So have the French. Anyone we send north with gold would not get past those spies without being spotted, perhaps captured."

Isabel said, "Any *man*, perhaps."

They all looked at her, startled.

"That's right," she said, "send me."

Her words held them all silent, as if locked in a fairy's spell. Isabel herself hardly knew where her voice had come from, so strong and clear. But she knew she could say the words again, and just as steadily.

Cecil was the first to speak, and he did so with fresh energy. "This is a fine idea. A messenger no one would suspect."

"No, it is too risky," her mother said. Isabel sensed her inner battle, as though she was proud of her daughter for offering—but dead set against the idea. "You've done enough."

"If I can do more, I will, and gladly," she said. "Your Majesty, please let me go. I can do this."

The Queen, however, looked darkly skeptical. Her eyes seemed to bore into Isabel's. When she spoke, a new coldness hardened her voice. "You could," she said. "If I could trust you."

Isabel was so shocked, she wondered if she had misheard. "Pardon, Your Majesty?"

"That statement you got from Quadra, was it before or after you kneeled beside him at mass?" She added with icy precision, "You see, señora, I too have extra eyes and ears."

Fury leapt in Isabel. How many times must she hear this attack on her allegiance? First her mother, then Adam, now the Queen. *You're Catholic*—that was all they could see. *I am one of you!* she wanted to shout.

Her mother surprised her by coming to her defense. "Elizabeth," she said sternly, "Isabel has always been loyal to your cause. Five years ago she helped Sir Thomas Wyatt in his attempt to curb the tyranny of Queen Mary, an attempt undertaken in your name."

Isabel felt a rush of gratitude. Turmoil, though, clouded her mother's face, for she seemed to realize that she had endorsed Isabel's offer.

The Queen rose from her chair. "Did she, indeed?" she said, still skeptical. Her eyes had not left Isabel, and she came forward, stopping within a few feet of her. They were the same height, the Queen perhaps an inch taller, and now they stood face-to-face. "But that was before she married a Spaniard. One who has now gone to Edinburgh to help his king against us."

Isabel fought to stay calm. Where did this woman *not* have spies? "It is not so, Your Majesty," she managed to reply. "He has gone merely as an observer."

"Is he not a loyal subject of King Philip?"

Here was the trap. "He is. And, as such, he is eager to preserve Spain's long alliance with England."

"And you? Of which crown are you a loyal subject?"

"I am English, Your Majesty. Nothing can change my blood."

The Queen seemed struck by that. "Blood ties. Ah, they are strong indeed."

"And think, Your Majesty, no one would be watching me, for I am not one of your court. My sister-in-law is about to travel north to visit her brother. What if I traveled with her? Who would suspect two ordinary ladies plodding north to visit family? Her brother's home is in Northumberland, almost on the border with Scotland. I can slip across to Edinburgh, deliver your gold, and return to London, all while the Spanish ambassador's spies are busy looking elsewhere."

The Queen considered this in silence, studying Isabel for a long moment, the slight frown of skepticism still lurking. She said to

Cecil, "If I agree to this, no gold must go to that toad, John Knox."
It was an order, delivered in an irritated tone. "I will give no succor
to the author of that monstrous book."

Isabel did not follow. What book? But a cautious excitement
flooded her, for there was no mistaking the Queen's meaning. She
had agreed. They had convinced her. She would send money to
the Scottish rebels, and Isabel would deliver it.

"No need for that, Your Majesty," Cecil said, magnanimous in
his victory. "Mistress Valverde can deliver your gold to the duke.
Hamilton is our steadfast friend. Or to the Earl of Arran, if you
wish. We shall keep Knox at arm's length."

"I would keep him in a dungeon," she growled.

"Unfortunately, he is essential to their cause. The fighting Scots
follow Knox."

Isabel felt a shiver. What had she got herself into? She knew
none of these people—a duke, an earl, this man Knox whom the
Queen clearly hated. And what a dark new world she glimpsed,
with spies, dangerous borders, fighters, and the punishment of a
dungeon at the Queen's command.

The Queen said to her, with a wary look still in her eyes, "Well,
mistress, it seems you have won the mission. Is that what you
wanted?"

There was no going back. "I will serve you to the very best of
my ability, Your Majesty."

"Will you, indeed?" It sounded not like a question, but a challenge. Without waiting for a reply, she went to the table and
reached for the dish of macaroons. She turned to Nicolas. "Come
here, young sir." She held the dish up to lure him.

What is she doing? Isabel thought with a prickle of alarm.

Nicolas came to her slowly, hesitant. Isabel knew he wanted the
sweets but was nervous about the Queen's domineering tone. The
Queen held the dish high. "Closer," she said.

He crept to within a long stride of her. She reached for his hand
and yanked him to her side. He tried to resist, struggling against
her grip, whimpering, "No, I don't want to . . ." but she held him
firmly by her. He cried, "Mama!"

Isabel could not move, torn between the fear in her son's eyes and her duty to respect the Queen's authority. *What is she doing?*

"Godspeed to you, Mistress Valverde," she said. "Account yourself well in Scotland, for as you can see, much depends on it." She held Nicolas's hand tightly in hers. "While you are away, Master Nicolas shall remain here. He will be my guest."

The meaning stunned Isabel. *A hostage.*

"Mama, no! I don't want to stay!"

She did not think. She lunged for her son. She grabbed him and wrenched him free and pulled him to her.

"Isabel!" her mother cried.

"Madam!" Cecil said, equally shocked.

Her mother gripped her by the shoulders, holding her back, and whispered tightly, "Bel, we must obey. It is done." Cecil guided Nicolas back to the Queen's side.

"Mama?" Nicolas looked stricken with fear, his tears brimming. "I don't like this place. I want to go home!" He reached out for her.

It was all she could do to hold back. His tearful face wrenched her heart, but she would only increase his terror if he saw hers. "It's all right, Nico. Just a little visit." She forced a smile. "You can play ball with the nice young ladies." Her eyes locked in hatred on the Queen.

The Queen's voice rang with the steel of a monarch in command. "As you love your son," she said, "so I love England. Understand this. The welfare of the two is now entwined."

Christmas Day. A sunny morning, bright and crisp. Isabel, feeling none of the day's joy, rode in the midst of Frances's domestic entourage of servants and baggage train as they plodded over the snow-packed ruts of Bishopsgate Street, their slow pace dictated by Frances's horse-drawn litter, for she was still recovering. The Queen's gold was packed in leather satchels disguised as part of Isabel's wardrobe strapped to a packhorse. Frances had been delighted when Isabel had told her she would travel with her as far as her brother Christopher's house in Northumberland, then continue on to Edinburgh to see Carlos. The lie was convincing, since visits by wives to their military husbands were not uncommon. In Peru, Isabel had visited Carlos at various outposts where he had been stationed with the viceroy's troops. Frances had no knowledge of the royal cargo her train was carrying as they reached the city walls and passed through Bishopsgate, leaving London behind.

Two maids riding mules laughed at something Tom Yates said. Isabel heard his voice spinning a lively yarn from his mount between them. He had returned yesterday from his errand to her father's country estate, and her mother had insisted that he accompany Isabel north. As Frances's party had assembled, Tom had entertained the other servants with magic tricks involving the miraculous appearance and disappearance of an angel coin. The household folk were missing their Christmas and needed cheering. Tom was doing a good job of it.

Nothing, though, could cheer Isabel. Though well screened in their midst, she felt exposed. The sun shone down on her so brightly from the vast blue sky, she felt that all the spies of France and Spain must have their eyes on her, whether in the faces looking out of cottage windows they passed, or masquerading as the farmers and laborers who trudged the road. She felt that they could hear her every thought carried on the cold, still air. Her horse shivered as though it, too, knew the dangerous path she was on. If anyone hostile to England discovered her mission, she could be captured. Imprisoned.

But what shook her far more deeply was how her family had been pulled apart. Carlos, drawn into the camp of the French. Nicolas, a royal hostage at Whitehall Palace. The Queen had made that chillingly clear. It had almost broken Isabel's heart as she had said good-bye to her son, putting on a cheerful face for him as though the charade of the Queen's hospitality were real. She had never hated anyone as she hated Queen Elizabeth. Yet she was pledged to do her all for the woman. Her only hope of getting Nicolas released was to succeed in her mission.

And if she failed? She glanced back at London as it disappeared in the wake of the baggage train. Was Nicolas at that moment sitting with the young ladies-in-waiting, trying not to cry, terrified by the disappearance of his mother? She looked ahead, up the Great North Road toward the imagined snows of Scotland. Was Carlos at that moment inspecting the French garrison's artillery, offering advice on how to defeat France's enemies?

I have to succeed, she thought, or I may never see either of them again.

PART TWO

Through the
Enemy's Gates

❧ 11 ❧

The First Encounter

Gale winds in the North Sea lashed at Adam Thornleigh, blurring his vision with frigid sea spray. Yet he could see well enough the fleet of French ships scudding north-northwest toward him off his starboard bow. At least twenty, he reckoned. *God help us.*

He was captain of *Elizabeth* alongside seven other ships of Her Majesty's navy under Admiral William Winter, and they had barely made it alive this far. They had left Gillingham after Christmas as a fleet of fourteen, but a witch's brew of storms had ripped into them off the Yorkshire coast, damaging six ships so badly they'd had to limp back in the hope of reaching port. Just eight had carried on toward Scotland, beating their way to the North Sea in the teeth of the gales, riding under bare poles but for storm tops'ls. Only yesterday, finally, had the winds abated enough to let them carry more sail.

Adam wiped the icy sea spray off his face and looked up at his sails, their edges tattered from the furious winds. Three months ago, in warm autumn sunshine, he had overseen the refurbishing of *Elizabeth* from stem to stern. He had been so proud to see her freshly painted and tarred, her hull caulked, her guns oiled, her gun deck loaded with grapeshot and round shot, her masts stepped at a perfect angle to make her fly. But for three days now she hadn't been flying anywhere, just prowling the approach to the French coastal fortress of Leith off Edinburgh, lying in wait for the enemy ships coming from France. He and his men had been battered by the roaring seas as the decks pitched under ice-crusted rigging, leaving Adam and the crew so cold some had lost feeling in fingers and toes. But though his body ached and he was chilled to the bone, fresh energy surged through him when he saw Admiral Winter's flagship swing onto a downwind course to face the French galleons. *This is what we came for.*

"Master Curry!" Adam called to his first mate, shouting above the howl of the wind. "All hands lay to!"

"Aye, sir!" Curry turned and yelled to the crew in the waist of the ship, "All hands lay to!"

Seamen jogged to their posts. Adam called orders to his helmsman, and as *Elizabeth* swung onto the downwind course, gusts billowed her sails, and the shrouds let out cracks like pistol shots. They were charging toward the French fleet.

The two dozen soldiers aboard weren't used to the lurching deck, and they gripped handholds at the gunwales. The French were close enough for Adam to see that the gales had hit them hard, too, their fleur-de-lis flags half shredded. But, God in heaven, they looked strong. At least twenty ships, maybe more. Reports he had heard before leaving Gillingham said this French fleet was coming from Dieppe with five thousand soldiers to reinforce the garrison at Leith. Among them were ten huge warship galleons. Against eight of ours, Adam thought, and only three of them galleons, the rest much smaller. *Elizabeth,* at just two hundred tons, could perch on one of the French quarterdecks. His heart thumped. He knew he must not show fear to his men.

"Prime all cannons," he ordered. "Load grape. Action stations!"

Curry shouted the orders, and Adam glanced over his shoulder at *Pelican* under the command of Matthew Lockhart, carving the waves as she turned to face the French. Off his port bow was *Golden Lion,* one of the three English galleons, froth flying at her bow and in her wake. Beyond her, *Tiger* and *Swallow* and *Minion* alongside *Mary Willoughby,* all joining the charge.

Their orders were to harry the French to prevent them landing the troops, but not to fire unless fired on first. Also, if any English were captured, they were to say they were acting on their own initiative, with no connection to the Queen. Desperate demands, Adam thought. Elizabeth had no standing army, and only this meager navy, since her sister's reign had left the treasury bankrupt, and for months she had been unable to do anything but watch as the French had built their strength in Scotland, knowing that if the French beat the Scots they could then pour south to conquer England. But now the danger was so clear, she had roused herself to dispatch Winter on this covert mission. About time, Adam thought. He had once urged Elizabeth to use ships as "walls" to protect her realm, and she was finally doing it. But his mission wouldn't end here on the sea. His father, working with the Queen's agents in Antwerp, had been quietly buying armaments and ammunition and shipping them home, and Adam had loaded *Elizabeth*'s hold with two demi-cannons, crates of arms, powder, and shot that he was going to deliver to the rebel force under John Knox.

If I survive today, he thought as they closed on the French. He had never been in a naval battle—or any battle. His mouth was dry with fear. He knew his ship was up to the challenge—he had built her himself—but was *he?* He had lived most of his life on the sea, but always in peaceful trade. He'd seen hard service with the Merchant Adventurers' tragic expedition to Russia, losing friends in those unforgiving seas, but this was something else. Enemy cannonballs that could blow your head off. Musket shots that could shatter a leg, shred an arm. Down the companionway he glimpsed his men on the gun deck loading the brass culverins, small cannons called "bastards," five on each side set behind gun ports. And up here on the main deck they were loading the twenty-pounders at bow and stern. But these guns were nothing to match the French galleons' mighty cannons. *Any one of them could blow my ship to hell.* And if the enemy boarded, that would be a different kind of hell, close combat. He looked across the tumbling waves at the hundreds of troops crammed on the decks of each of the French ships. If cannon fire crippled *Elizabeth* and the enemy closed to board her, those soldiers would swarm aboard with pistols, pikes, swords, and axes, while their archers let loose a storm of arrows. He imagined an axe caving in his skull.

He shook his head hard to shake off such thoughts. And reminded himself of the letter in the pocket of his sea-sodden jerkin. A daughter, Isabel had written, born a week before Christmas. Frances had had a rough time. Katherine, she had named the baby. Adam felt a fierce desire to see his child. *That's why I have to survive*, he told himself. *For Katherine.* He would get through this. He would make it into Edinburgh to deliver the arms to John Knox's rebels. And he would do anything else in his power to help Elizabeth. But all other thoughts of her he would put out of his mind, all remembrance of their brief, bright time together—his lips on hers, her body under his, her glory in his arms. He had been hoarding that treasure trove of memory for too long. It was time to let it go. Elizabeth had never truly been his, and never could be. He looked out across the deck at his seamen and soldiers all staring grimly at the ever-closing French, and saw a gunner make the sign of the cross on his chest. Saw a soldier unsheathe his sword and kiss the hilt. Adam looked up at the angry clouds roiling in God's heaven, and he made a silent vow. *If I survive this, I will commit myself to my family.* Treat Frances more kindly. Build a world for Katherine. And hope for a son next time.

He plowed toward the French.

It began as a chase, Winter strictly obeying the Queen's orders. The French fleet bore off southward, and the English ships followed, nipping at their heels. But then the French turned. A cannon shot from them, perhaps meant as a warning aimed to cross *Mary Willoughby*'s bow, instead tore away her bowsprit. The fight was on.

The swirl of battle swallowed the *Elizabeth*. A furious confusion of scudding ships, booming guns, men's cries above the shriek of the wind, the smell of gunpowder in the sodden air. On Adam's decks men scrambled for balance at their posts, lurching each time he maneuvered the ship through fast tacks, hardening her into the wind to chase an escaping French frigate, then bearing off to narrowly miss crashing into a monster galleon. He heard his fellow captains bellowing orders, heard French yells. Heard his own voice hoarse from shouting commands. Beyond *Mary Willoughby* wallowing in the confused seas, he glimpsed *Swallow,* half her mainmast blown away, the men aloft trapped in the wind-whipped mess of sails and rigging.

"Captain!" Jack Curry yelled. "The *Pelican!*"

Adam turned. Beyond his stern a savage broadside had blasted *Pelican,* blowing away much of her forecastle deck. She did not look mortally hit, but men were running and shouting, and in the commotion the helmsman lost control when a monster gust heeled the ship onto her side. *Too far,* Adam thought in dismay. A man aloft at the topsail fell, screaming. He pitched down past the anti-boarding netting and plunged into the sea. The ship kept plowing ahead on her side, like a limping wrestler refusing to give in to an injury, but she was heeled at such a severe angle she could not right herself. Water would be roaring in through her gun ports, Adam thought. Within minutes she was sinking. Men leapt overboard from the listing main deck, screaming.

"Lower the longboat!" Adam ordered.

"Aye, sir!" Curry confirmed.

Elizabeth's boat splashed into the water and six crew clambered into it and rowed furiously between the lumbering ships, heading for *Pelican*'s survivors, who thrashed in the frigid, heaving waves.

"Fire!" The shout came from Adam's main deck. He twisted around. The gaff-rigged sail on his mizzenmast was aflame. Tongues of fire licked out at the mainmast. If it spread to the mainsails, the fire would engulf the ship as fast as *Pelican* had gone down.

"Cut down the mizzen, Master Curry!" Adam ordered.

"Aye, sir." Curry yelled to the crew, "Axes! Buckets!"

Men hacked at the base of the mizzenmast while others scurried for water buckets, just as Adam saw the bow of *Minion* bearing down on them. Her captain, Doan, a friend of his, was pulling the helmsman off the binnacle where he was slumped, blood pouring from a head wound. Adam ordered his own helmsman to tack immediately, and they swept past *Minion,* her bowsprit swinging across *Elizabeth*'s stern, not three feet between the hulls. Adam could hear her timbers creaking.

He looked up at the fire eating his mizzen. The swift helm maneuver had saved them from a collision but had put them on a course that made the wind whip the mizzen's flames closer to the mainsails.

"Cut her down, men," Adam shouted. "Be quick!"

They chopped furiously. Jack Curry jogged forward to organize the line of water buckets just as the mizzenmast toppled. Curry didn't see it coming at his back. The massive oak timber felled him as it crashed on the deck, flames leaping, sparks flying.

"Jack!" Adam grabbed a water bucket and bolted toward him.

Men with buckets swarmed the mess of wind-whipped sails aflame on the deck, dashing water on the fire, and Adam jumped over the blazing rigging to reach his first mate. Curry lay moaning facedown beneath a mast spar that pinned his legs to the deck. His breeches were on fire. Adam heaved the water from his bucket onto Curry, dousing the flames, then tossed the bucket and yanked off his own leather jerkin, shouting for a crewman to give him his as well. Wrapping the leather garments around his hands, he shoved his hands under the glowing red spar and pried it up off Curry.

"Haul him out!" he told his men.

They pulled Curry by his feet and dragged him to safety. The others had doused most of the fire, and some had pulled off their jerkins to beat the last of the flames, coughing in the smoke.

Adam batted sparks from his shirt sleeves. The leather had protected his hands, but the spar had burned his forearms, branding a red welt across each. No time to think of the pain. The wind had veered, and a French galleon loomed to starboard. He had to think fast whether to beat north to windward to escape the cannon broadside that was sure to come blasting from the galleon. The only other choice was to go south and run before the wind, but that course would take him right into the middle of the French fleet.

He heard his third in command, young Hendricks, order the helmsman into the wind to flee from the galleon that now towered above them. They were hardening up to tack.

Adam leapt over the mast debris and dashed back to the wheel. "Belay that order!" he said. That course would doom them to the huge galleon's cannons. The only way out was to go through. On his command they swung southward, heading straight into the maw of the enemy fleet. His men watched in horror, as if their captain had lost his mind.

South they went, racing before the wind through the massed galleons. Adam looked up to see the menacing three-deck cannonades rush past them. The big guns were silent, as he'd gambled. The tall galleons on either side of him could not risk firing at this lone, low ship, for their broadsides would have ripped into each other. He scudded through the center of the enemy fleet. *Elizabeth* was through. His men cheered.

They had escaped, but Adam saw that his ship was too wounded to fight on. They would have to head for shore, seek a sheltered Scottish bay to hide in and repair what they could. Adam set the new course, and watched as the smoke and booming of guns diminished in his wake. The French might rip apart the last of the admiral's ships and slaughter Adam's friends, and there was nothing he could do about it. He felt cheated, angry.

That's when he saw the French ships ahead. Two of them, hugging the coast. Not big galleons, not warships at all. These were galleys, likely supply ships. Supplying the French troops at Leith? Adam felt a blast of vindication. He would take those galleys, or die trying.

❧ 12 ❧

The Road to Edinburgh

Tom Yates pointed at a cloud. "That one's a mermaid, my lady.
Do you mark her fishy tail?"

Isabel studied the cloud in question sailing high above the
snowy East Lothian moors. The game had helped to pass the long,
cold hours on horseback. That morning she and Tom had crossed
the border into Scotland, alone but for her packhorse laden with
the satchels of the Queen's gold. Isabel had wanted no armed escort to draw the interest of French spies, so she was travelling in
the plain homespun garb of a farmer's wife. "I see a haunch of
roast venison," she said, "and if you see a mermaid, Tom, you're
daft."

"You're just hungry, my lady, that's what's making you cross-
eyed. She's a mermaid, I warrant. See her seaweedy hair, all wavy
like? And those two fair, round paps? They'd lure any seaman to
his doom, and right willing to go."

She almost laughed. Who but Tom would see a woman's breasts
in a cloud? "You're right about one thing. I'm so hungry I'd pay a
prince's ransom for a hot meal at the next inn. I don't mind if it's
oat gruel, I'll gobble it down."

"Lucky thing, since oaten gruel is all these Scots heathen eat, so
I hear." He cocked his head with a mock, mad glint in his eyes.
"When they're not devouring their babes, that is."

She smiled at his foolery. His cheeky jests had lightened her spirits a little as their horses trudged this lonely landscape. She had needed it, for every mile northward they went, the wider the chasm she felt between herself and Nicolas. And the more she hated Queen Elizabeth. She did not doubt that her son was being well treated, perhaps even cosseted by the Queen's young ladies, but she could not forget the fear on his face, nor his confusion and dismay at her acceptance of the Queen's edict. How his tearful look had pained her heart! And now, was he utterly dejected, wondering where his parents had gone? Was he frightened at night with no father to sweep his sword under the bed to clear away ogres and no mother to sing him a lullaby? Had the wretched Queen shunted him away into some corner of the palace to be minded by a stern official of the chamberlain's staff? It was horrible to think of him bravely trying to obey a taskmaster's regime all day and crying into his pillow at night. Before she had left that awful royal interview, her mother, trying to hide her own dismay, had asked the Queen to allow him to stay at her house, but she had snapped a refusal. Nicolas was the Queen's hostage, a surety against Isabel's betrayal, and the palace was his prison. Pampered he might be, but a prisoner nonetheless. Isabel would never forgive Elizabeth.

But helping her was the only way she could free her son, so she had pushed herself and Tom at a hard pace along the Great North Road. At Alnwick they had parted company with Frances, who had gone on to her brother's, Isabel maintaining the lie that she was going to Edinburgh to see Carlos. The sooner she could deliver the gold to Knox's rebels, the sooner she could return to London and reclaim Nicolas. Over the long, cold miles it had become a silent chant inside her head: *Give them the gold, go back for Nico....* *Give them the gold, go back for Nico.* She could only hope the money would let the rebels buy enough arms and pay enough soldiers to bring them a speedy victory, for only when this war ended could Carlos, too, come home. Her silent chant for her son alternated with one for Carlos. *Let them win, send Carlos home.... Let them win, send Carlos home.*

Tom was whistling a ditty. Isabel took a deep breath of the

frosty air to clear her head of her worries. Her toes felt nearly frozen, and she had balled her fingers into fists inside her gloves for the tinge more warmth that offered, and she took comfort in knowing they were just a day from their destination. Strangely, the wide-open landscape helped soothe her. They had crossed the border in moor country, barren and windswept, but unexpectedly beautiful. She had not seen a winter in five years. Peru's sunshine and greenery and flowers had so completely satisfied her senses, she had never thought to miss the cold, dead season of this island. But here, in the wild country between the Scottish Lammermuir Hills and the North Sea, she was reacquainted with the bold beauty of winter as though with a childhood friend. Not the grimy winter of London, where rooftops and chimneys cut off the light, and mud and dung befouled the streets' snow. Here, the sky was a vastness of clean blue, and sunshine sparkled on the snow-smoothed hills that rolled westward like ocean swells held in a northern fairy's spell.

It was not, however, a countryside kindly to people. The popu-lation was sparse and hungry looking, for they struggled with flinty soil and a cruelly short growing season. The dwellings Isabel had seen were little more than sheds, flimsy huts of piled rocks, mud and thatch that could be thrown together or taken down in a few hours. "Dog kennels," Tom had called them. "Woof, woof." Even the cattle were small, stunted. The largest town they had passed, Haddington, was just one main street with cramped alleys leading off it. Pigs ran freely. Any Englishman would call it a village. Spaniards would call it a pigsty.

"There, my lady," Tom said now, "see that stub of a chimney?"

"Tom, that cloud is no more like a chimney than I am like a pea sprout."

"No, I mean the smoke, yonder."

She looked ahead. Wispy brown smoke curled up from behind the next hill. "An inn?" she asked hopefully. "Or perhaps just a cottage."

"Even a cottage would have vittles." He lowered his voice. "If its folk are alive."

His tone gave her a chill. "Why wouldn't they be?"

"Mayhap raiders have burned the place."

She had heard gruesome tales about these lawless borderlands. The murders, the maimings, the burning of houses and crops, the stealing of cattle. It sprang from the deadly feuds between clans, so fierce they sounded more like savage tribes. Their life was thieving and reiving and raiding, and they often swept down into England, where the long frontier was poorly controlled by the Queen's deputies in the garrison towns of Berwick, Alnwick, and Carlisle, fortifications on a line that swept like a sickle around the dangerous border areas. That morning Isabel and Tom had stopped in a churchyard to eat cold bread and sausage from their saddlebags, and in the church porch she had seen a red-smeared glove—the "red hand"—stuck on a spear point, some clan's silent challenge to an enemy clan.

"Just how hungry are you, my lady?" Tom asked with a wry look.

Isabel gauged the sun low in the western sky. The winter days here were short. Nights came on fast. Ahead, an icy stream gurgled over its stony path, and a heron rose up from the water. She watched the bird wing its way across the barren wastes. She longed to press on, too, and get to Edinburgh, but a peddler they had passed around noon had told them they would not make it there before darkness.

"Very hungry," she said, "and soon in need of a bed. Let's go see."

Fear is at its worst as an expectation. That was Isabel's thought two hours later as she and Tom sat down at the inn's rough supper table among people who were blatantly not murderous raiders— the landlord's impoverished family and two other road-weary travelers slurping their supper pottage. The landlord was pale and quiet and thin as a sapling, and his careworn young wife was burdened with two babies, one balanced on her hip, the other asleep in an empty crate doing service as a cradle. The only color in the whole drab place was on Tom's fanciful jerkin, the mangy sheepskin that he had tricked out with a red satin collar and gold tassels on each cuff. "Inn" was too grand a name for such a humble place—a low-ceilinged common room dominated by the hearth with its smoky peat fire, a kitchen behind it, and four cramped rooms above. But Isabel was grateful as she dug her spoon into her wooden bowl brimming with cabbage and morsels of rye bread in barley broth. It was surprisingly tasty, and blessedly hot.

Tom, as usual, had attracted the children around him, the landlord's brood, two boys and a girl, all under ten, who had served the travelers their supper and small beer. The children wore shabby clothes and no shoes, but had bright faces as they stood entranced by Tom's magic tricks. He had pivoted on the bench to face them, and now drew a penny from behind the ear of the little girl. Her breath caught in wonder at the magic. Her brothers, too, were wide-eyed.

"By gum," one of the travelers said in amazement around his mouthful of pottage. "How'd he do that?"

"He's a master, sir," Isabel said proudly. Tom had dazzled her with the same marvels when she was little.

After supper Tom entertained everyone with a guessing game that involved three walnut shells under which he had hidden a pea. Then the other traveler, a coal merchant's agent, pulled a tin pipe from his pocket and tweedled a jig. Tom got up and danced a parody of a sailor's hornpipe, and that got everyone laughing, even the work-wearied hosts. Isabel pressed three shillings into the hand of the oldest boy and whispered to him to give it to his father. The lad walked away, eyeing the windfall in amazement. Isabel hoped it might buy this family some shoes, at least. Would the war brewing in Edinburgh touch their lives? she wondered. Scratching out a living from season to season was their whole world, and she doubted that it mattered a whit to them whether the far-off lords were Scottish, English, French, or even Spanish. War was a thing for great nobles and armies, not for quiet folk such as this.

"You overpaid the lad, my lady," Tom told her later as they sat alone by the fire. He was whittling a stick with his knife, the two satchels of the Queen's gold lying at his feet. He would spend the night sleeping beside them. Isabel was keeping him company before going up to bed, for she did not want to leave the gold until she was sure the others had retired. The children already lay asleep on straw pallets in the corners.

"You're not one to talk," she said. "That little girl is a penny richer, and you're a penny poorer."

"Is she now?" he said with a sly look. "Were you, at her age?"

Isabel dug into her memory. Good heavens, she thought. "Tom Yates, did you tell the child to give it back so you could show her a more wonderful trick?"

"Which she did, like you did, my lady. Then got lost in the walnut shells, like you did."

Isabel laughed. "And forgot all about the penny."

He smiled as he skinned the stick. "Folks are the same, young and old. Easily led onto a new path, so long as they think it's got roses."

She gazed into the glowing peat fire, remembering how, as a child, she had loved to help her mother tend the roses in her garden at their home near Colchester. Damask roses, red and white. "How are they, Tom, all the folk at Speedwell House?"

He gave her a puzzled look. "My lady?"

"It's been five years, so I've lost touch." She knew he had recently returned from there, and she was interested in news of the place where she had spent her girlhood. "Does Fat Mary still rule the roost in the kitchen? And old Peter Brewer, is he still making the best ale in the county at our brewhouse?" Tom was looking at her so oddly, she wondered if she had misunderstood. "You were just there, were you not?" she asked.

"No, my lady, not there. At your father's new manor in Kent." His brow furrowed in concern. "You don't know about Speedwell House?"

The news, she sensed, could not be good. Had one of the longtime servants died? "Know what?"

"It's gone, my lady."

"Gone?" Had her father sold the place?

"Burned to the ground. Last year."

Her hand flew to her mouth in dismay. "I had no idea." Why had her mother not told her? The thought was awful—her old home, vanished. "How did it happen? A kitchen fire? A lightning strike?"

He let out a grunt that sounded like he was in pain. "If only it had been. Leastways that would have meant God's hand was in it. No, my lady, this was the work of the devil. And the devil's name is Grenville."

A shiver touched her scalp. "Lord John Grenville . . . burned our house?"

"Attacked us, he did. Thundered in with a band of brutes. I was there. Midsummer Day, it was. All calm and quiet, and sweet with the blooms of summer on the air, and all of us house folk lazy from our dinner in the noonday sun. I were jesting with Fat Mary about her sweetheart, a swaggering captain that made her smile, and she and me was chuckling over the pudding, when out of the clear blue rides Baron Grenville, crashing through the gates with his mounted brutes alongside him and murder in his eyes." Tom shook his head in sorrow. "And murder he did that day, the devil. Someone sounded our alarm, and Peter Brewer—you say aright, my lady, he brewed the finest grog—he dashed into the courtyard, and that band of murderers cut him down. He lay bleeding on the cobbles, and nothing anyone could do, for we were all in a uproar, men searching for weapons, women crying out, and your father and uncle running to meet the marauders with sword and bow. They felled your uncle, an arrow to his heart."

Isabel gasped. "Uncle Geoffrey!"

"And Grenville himself," Tom went on, "he struck down your father so he lay senseless. They killed more of our menfolk. Fired the house. Slaughtered the livestock. And carried your father away."

She asked, still shocked, "Carried him . . . where?"

"To Grenville Hall." He lowered his voice, as though what he had to say was too vile for anyone to overhear. "And kept him chained to the wall in his lockup, not able to lie or sit. Kept him suffering like that for three long days."

"So, my mother . . ." She could not find the words.

"Aye. She rode to Grenville Hall alone. And there, in front of all the baron's folk, to save your father, she stabbed that devil over and over and over. Killed him dead."

Isabel listened, stunned. *Murder . . . in cold blood.*

Could I do what she did? Isabel asked herself later as she lay sleepless on her straw mattress in the dark. She felt ashamed that when she had first arrived home she had been so irritated with her mother, angry at her for keeping secrets. Now she understood why her mother had not wanted to speak about this. And also why her father acted so coldly to Frances. It left her more mystified than ever about Adam's marriage. How had he come to wed Grenville's sister? Isabel liked Frances, and felt sorry for her in her loveless marriage, but she was glad she had not accepted the invitation to break her journey with a visit to Frances's other brother, Christopher. She had never met this new head of the house of Grenville, but she doubted she could be civil to a man whose family had brought her own family so much grief.

Round and round these thoughts went in her head, and always she came back to the desperate action her mother had taken, and the question: *Could I do murder, knowing I would hang?* Only the new Queen's pardon had saved her mother. Isabel hated Elizabeth for keeping Nicolas a hostage, but she had to admit the immense debt her family owed her.

The next morning Isabel finished her breakfast of porridge while Tom saddled their horses in the cow byre. The other two travelers had already left, riding north together. Isabel was paying the landlord, ready to go, too, when the door burst open and the two travelers rushed back in. They were out of breath and looked shaken.

"Raiders," one said. "They're swarming the road ahead."

"Must be twenty or thirty of 'em," the other said, taking a chair to steady himself. "They were hooting and hollering at us like banshees. We turned and raced back."

"Jesu," the landlord said, crossing himself, "that'll be the Douglas clan. Word was they were riding hell-bent for a skirmish with the Murrays in the vale yonder."

Isabel saw the men's fear and felt it creep into her too. "What will they do?" she asked the landlord.

"Mayhem, that's for sure. The Douglases will go for the cattle, but the Murrays will be awaiting them. It'll be a battle."

"Are we in danger?"

"Not if we stay put. It's each other they're out to maim. But there'll be no traveling north now. No one's getting through that lot."

Isabel was dismayed. She was so near her journey's end, she hated to delay. Clearly, though, it would be foolhardy to try to pass these murderous raiders. "I'll tell my man," she said, angry but resigned as she started for the door. "We'll have to stay another night."

"Mistress, those brutes will be swarming for *days*, what with their kin riding in to join them, and all of them fixing to do battle. You hunker down with us and wait it out, that's all there is for it."

"Days?" she cried.

"Once, they were bashing each other for nigh on two weeks."

"No, that's not possible. I must get to Edinburgh."

"You won't be getting anywhere with your throat slit."

It was terrifying—and infuriating. But what choice did she have? She went out and told Tom. "Buggers," he growled, but he agreed that the only thing to do was wait. All day they sat, she and Tom, the other two travelers, and the landlord's family, everyone silent with fear as they listened to the faint whoops of the raiders in the distance. The common room was barely warmed by the low peat fire where the landlord's wife had gathered her children around her at the hearth. Late in the afternoon the weather turned foul, with rising winds and an onslaught of snow.

"Maybe this bad weather will send them away, send them home," Isabel said, standing at the window to look out at the driving snow.

"Those devils care nothing for snow," said the landlord's wife as she suckled her baby. "They were whelped in snow and ice. They'll stay."

Night fell. The wind howled around the inn. Isabel sat on the edge of her narrow bed, thinking. She could not spare two weeks, nor even two or three days. She had to deliver this gold, and then get back for Nicolas. She got up and went downstairs for Tom. He sat by the hearth whittling a stick. The others had gone to bed, exhausted from fear. She told him what she had decided.

"What? Out in that storm?" he said in dismay.

"Yes. Tonight. Now."

"We wouldn't be able to see beyond our noses!"

"And those raiders won't see *us*."

He looked far from convinced.

"Tom, I cannot stay. Those men might come here—to steal the horses, or for food. If they do, they'll find the gold. And if they don't kill us in taking it, once it's gone I might as well be dead."

He heaved a hard sigh. Then looked out the window, steeling himself. "Bundle up, my lady."

They left without a word to anyone. As they made for the byre, the wind whipped Isabel's cloak and tugged at her tightly drawn hood and scarf. When she was mounted, Tom tied a rope between her horse and the packhorse so it would blindly follow her, and another rope between her horse and his. He took the lead of this blind train and they set out northward, and blind they were indeed in the darkness and the wind-driven snow. It blasted Isabel, scouring her face whenever her scarf wrapping slipped. She could barely see Tom ahead—he was a mere ghostly shadow—and she knew he could see no better, letting his horse pick its way by instinct along the road, the animal veering back whenever it felt the spongy ground off the road. The animals plodded with heads lowered against the wind. Isabel had never been so cold. And never so frightened. The creeping pace was excruciating when she knew that all around her men were camped with daggers, axes, and claymores.

She did not know how long they had been plodding on when the first feeble hint of dawn crept over the distant hills. Her fingers were sticks of ice. Her cheeks were frozen slabs. A headache pounded from the battering of the wind and the stress of her fear. Her toes were numb. Her *mind* felt numb, for she realized that the wind had dropped—realized that she *could* see the hills ahead. Never had she been so glad to see a sunrise. She looked all around for signs of encamped raiders. There was no one, only snow-swept barren fields. They had made it.

Tom turned in his saddle to look back at her. He had tied a scarf around his head, and it was a clump of icy snow. "Had enough exercise, my lady?"

She smiled, though it hurt her cheeks. "Quite enough."

"Then let's get us to that cottage ahead and beg for some grog to thaw us out."

Low, barren hills overlooked Edinburgh under a gunmetal sky. Refreshed from a hot meal at the cottage, and dry clothes, Isabel waited on horseback on the most southerly mound, her horse dancing nervously on the spot as it sensed her tension. She had felt it too risky to ride into the city with her packhorse laden with a small fortune in gold, so she had sent Tom down into the narrow streets to quietly seek out the rebel leaders—John Knox, or James Hamilton, the Earl of Arran—and tell them she was here. But he had been gone for hours. Where in God's name was he?

This southerly rise gave her a full view of the capital and the fields beyond. Edinburgh Castle sat atop its high crag at the city's western end, while at the other end lay the royal residence of Holyroodhouse. In the middle rose the crown-shaped spire of St. Giles Church. She knew that Knox's rebel force was in command of the capital, and she could see indisputable evidence. Their encampment stretched beyond the city walls, out toward the coastal village of Leith that lay two miles distant on the Firth of Forth, an estuary of the North Sea. The open fields between the city and the coast were thick with tents, and dotted with men moving at ease among tethered horses and carts. She could make out the threads of smoke from their cooking fires curling lazily upward in the faint breeze. The sense of such a huge host of Scottish rebels gave Isabel a rush of hope. Not only were they in possession of the capital, they had pushed the French troops into their garrison at Leith—she knew that from Cecil, who had also told her that the Queen Regent had fled Holyroodhouse and sought protection with her garrison. Of course, that was before the French had

landed seven thousand more troops to swell their strongholds of
Leith and Inchkeith.

Isabel gazed across at Leith, straining to make it out at this distance. Leith, she knew, was no mere village. Over a decade ago, in
their war here against England, the French had enclosed it within
strong walls. She could make out the encircling earthen ramparts,
and three high stone bastions. It gave her a thump of dread. Carlos
was inside that fortress, living among the French officers. It looked
like a formidable stronghold, standing guard against the dark water,
its gates closed. Behind its high ramparts, the enemy seemed not to
stir. It put Isabel in mind of a giant, asleep. Or waiting.

But a brazen Scottish leader, a commoner, had cornered the
giant behind those gates. "A firebrand named John Knox," she remembered Cecil saying as he had briefed her. "He leads the
Congregation. That's what his Protestant army of followers call
themselves, and the nobles who've joined them call themselves
the Lords of the Congregation. And none of them call themselves
rebels, but reformers. They swear it is not royal authority they
mean to destroy but papist idolatry and wickedness. Interesting,
for Knox himself was once a Catholic priest. But there is nothing
more bloody-minded than a convert, and now he's the most mili-
tant of Protestants. A hardened soldier, too, captured thirteen years
ago by the French. They made him a galley slave for two years,
then traded him and others in a prisoner exchange with our King
Edward. He's also a scathing author. And a blistering preacher. His
Scottish soldiers love him. Her Majesty cannot abide him."

"Why?"

"For a book he wrote condemning women rulers. *Blast of the
Trumpet*, he titled it, and in it he blasts indeed at female rulers,
calling them unnatural and monstrous."

But the Queen needed this cantankerous Scot, Isabel realized,
and she wondered now: Is Knox the fearsome warrior who will slay
the French? She prayed that he would. Only then could Carlos
leave here and come home.

A noise made her tear her eyes from Leith and look down to the
base of the hill. Three horsemen were cantering up the slope to-

ward her, their spurs and swords and harnesses a-jangle. She tugged the reins to keep her horse still, but could do nothing to calm her quickened heartbeat. The men's boots and capes were dirty from service in the field, their faces lean, their chins dark with beard. She spotted a fourth man at the rear and saw that it was Tom. Thank God. These Scottish strangers must be Knox's men.

Then a sudden fear gripped her. What if they were not Scots at all? Had three French outriders captured Tom and forced him to lead them to her?

❧ 13 ❧

The Rebel Camp

Tom did not look like a cowed prisoner, and when the three strangers got closer Isabel saw that the blanket one man had slung over his shoulder like a cape was a Scottish plaid. *Friends,* she told herself with a rush of relief. *Calm down.*

They reached her in a thunder of hooves and jangling harness and surrounded her, hauling back on the reins as their horses capered to a halt.

"Isabel Valverde?" one of the men gruffly asked. He appeared to be the oldest of the three, perhaps forty, with a barrel chest and stout legs, and the lower half of his face bulked by a thick black beard. He was glaring at her in suspicion. Isabel guessed why. Her Spanish surname. She saw the eyes of all three men flick to the nearby farmer's shed as though wary of an ambush. All had laid their fighting hands on the hilts of their swords.

"I am, sir," she replied. Her own need to establish identities was as strong as his. She had taken the precaution of keeping the Queen's gold out of sight, tethering her packhorse behind the farmer's shed. "And you are . . . ?"

"Excuse my manners," he said, still wary. "Alexander Cunningham of Glencairn." The Earl of Glencairn, she realized. She had been briefed by Cecil. Glencairn introduced the other two.

Archibald Campbell, the Earl of Argyll, a wiry young man. And Patrick, Lord Ruthven, keen-eyed and fair-haired. Both looked not yet thirty. Glencairn said cautiously, "Your man said you bear a message from the English Queen."

Isabel looked to Tom. He caught the question in her eyes and gave her an easy nod. That satisfied her. Besides, she had heard the Scots burr in Glencairn's English. "A bright message, my lord," she replied. "One that will cheer you." He still looked skeptical, as though unable to get past her foreign name. To clear away his misgivings, she said, "My father is Baron Richard Thornleigh, Her Majesty Queen Elizabeth's loyal servant."

His stern look vanished. He asked with a sudden, piercing curiosity, "Are you kin to Sir Adam Thornleigh?"

She was astonished. "He is my brother. Are you acquainted?"

The three men exchanged a look and a happy laugh. "I'll drink his health when I *do* meet him," said Glencairn.

"Have you not heard the news, madam?" Ruthven asked. "About Admiral Winter?"

"I have heard nothing, sir. My man and I have been on the road from London for three weeks."

"Ah, then you have some rejoicing in store. The Lord knows we have done our share. The French fleet was on its way here with thousands more troops, but Winter's ships intercepted them and scattered them, sending the poxy French back out into the gales. Only a few of their ships reached Leith, and they landed less than nine hundred soldiers. Sir Adam Thornleigh captured the two French supply ships that lay off Leith with their stores of ammunition and provisions. Your brother was the hero of the day."

Joyful news, indeed! "Have he and the other captains returned home?"

"I know not, madam. But I can tell you they have the thanks of all the Lords of the Congregation. Their brave action has gladdened the hearts of our fighting men."

Argyll said soberly, "It was the blessed hand of God, for He is watching over us."

"Aye, with a little help from the English Queen, I warrant," said Glencairn. He added to Isabel, as though to probe her, "Though we heard of no such naval order from Her Majesty. Have you, madam?"

"I, sir? How would I?" But she thought it would be like the anxious Queen to send her navy on a covert mission. Fearful of Spain, Elizabeth clearly intended to keep secret *all* her intervention here in Scotland. Isabel only hoped that Adam had sailed home, safe.

"Now, my lords, to our business," she said, tugging her reins to turn her horse. "Please follow me, and I will deliver my message."

Glencairn asked, puzzled, "You did not bring it with you?"

She smiled. "It is somewhat heavy."

He took it the wrong way. "Bad news?"

"Far from it!"

They followed her, and when they reached her packhorse at the shed she dismounted with Tom's help. She lifted the flap on one of the packhorse's satchels to reveal the gold to them. "Three thousand pounds," she said.

The faces of all three Scots lit up. "Thanks be to God," Glencairn said with feeling. He added quickly, "And, madam, to your noble Queen."

He moved his horse closer and reached for the packhorse's bridle, but Isabel tugged it, turning the horse's head beyond his reach. "Pardon, my lord, but I have a commission to deliver this gift only to the Earl of Arran or to his father, the duke." Again, Cecil had briefed her. James Hamilton, the Earl of Arran, was the nobleman who had recently come to London in secret to negotiate for marriage with Queen Elizabeth, for he claimed the right to the Scottish throne after his father and Mary Stuart, Queen of Scots. The elder Hamilton had been governor of Scotland and regent to the infant Queen of Scots, who was now the wife of the French king, and to keep him on their side the French had made him the Duke of Châtelherault, with rich estates in the heart of France. But then John Knox had come along, inflaming the Scottish people against their French overlords in a grassroots revolt that had swept the country, at which the Hamiltons, father and son, had turned Protestant. The Duke of Châtelherault was now the rebel movement's leading noble, and his son, the Earl of Arran, a leading fighter. "Is the earl in the city?" she asked.

"No. At his father's house at Kirk o' Field, a few miles hence. Allow me to escort you."

"No, I wish no more delay." She wanted only to hand over the gold as the Queen had instructed and then return to London. The sooner she left, the sooner she would see Nicolas. "Is the duke also at Kirk o' Field?"

"No, here, in the city."

"Then please take me to him directly."

Glencairn's scowl returned. "Madam, our camp is no place for a lady. My friends will escort you into town, where you will be shown to a comfortable lodging. I will see that this gift from your queen is safely delivered."

"Pardon me, sir, but that will not do. I will stay with the Queen's gold until I give it into the hands of his grace the duke."

The ancient church of St. Giles, Edinburgh's patron saint, lay in the heart of the city. Isabel and Tom followed Glencairn through its crowded nave, and she marveled at the host of men camped throughout the church.

There were hundreds. They lolled on blankets, strolled the aisles, lounged on the floor playing at dice and cards. The arched stone ceiling reverberated with their voices—bored chatter, bursts of laughter, occasional shouts of complaint over a dice game. They were soldiers, but were dressed in such an array of dirty, unkempt clothing they looked like no cohort Isabel had ever seen. There were women among them, too. A skinny young woman in a ragged dress crouched beside a cooking fire, turning a spit where a haunch of pork sizzled. Isabel could smell the sweet fat. She saw a man sharpening his dagger on a whetstone wheel. Saw dogs foraging in the litter of bones and scraps that were crammed into corners. Saw a goat tied to one of the central stone pillars.

The military encampment did not unnerve her, but the desecration of the church did. It was all around. Every article of Catholic ritual had been ruined or removed. She had heard about the sacrilegious spree of these rebels. They had sacked churches in Perth and St. Andrews and all through Fife on their march to

Edinburgh, and had driven the monks out of their monasteries. Still, the extent of the defilement here shocked her. The church must have had many altars at the various chapels and family monuments, but every one of them had been smashed and the marble still lay in dusty chunks, littering the stone floor. The walls, which would have been resplendent with paintings, were bare, and some of the canvases still lay in shreds. The niches that would have held statues of saints had been stripped, and on the few statues too high to reach, the saints' noses had been chipped off by pistol shots. Beside a cooking fire Isabel saw a jagged panel of gorgeously wrought woodwork, a former rood screen. They had smashed this work of art for firewood. She could not express her alarm to Glencairn, but she glanced behind her at Tom, and even he, a dutiful Protestant, shook his head in dismay.

They passed a chapel nook where a half dozen people sat in a tight circle—three rough-looking soldiers, a prim-looking young woman, a man in the homespun garb of a servant, and another older man in much finer clothes including a russet satin cape, clearly some lord. They all held books on their laps—Bibles, Isabel saw—and were listening to one of the soldiers speak. It was startling to see people of such differing classes sitting and chatting together like equals.

"This way," Glencairn told her.

They followed him to an open door off the chancel. A soldier leaned against the doorjamb, picking his teeth with a wood splinter. Glencairn told Tom to wait here with the soldier, then ushered Isabel inside. It was a snug, paneled room, formerly the priest's office, she guessed. Five men were playing a game of darts. Gentlemen, judging by the better quality of their clothes, though their jerkins and breeches and boots were almost as dirty as those of the common soldiers. It was their superior weapons that spoke of their status—costly swords and engraved steel cuirasses that lay around the room. Isabel was taken aback to see that the target they were using for their darts was a painting of Saint Cecilia. The bull's-eye was her mouth.

Glencairn told them to leave, and the officers gathered their things and filed out with curious glances at Isabel. "Make yourself comfortable, madam," Glencairn said. "I will tell his grace you're here."

Left alone, she looked around the room. On a table there were other games—a backgammon board, Primero cards, a red ball made of rubber. She picked up the ball and bounced it on the floor, thinking of Nicolas, of how he loved to play with a ball. It stung her with a longing to see him. As she caught the ball she noticed a silver goblet half full of wine. Not just any goblet, but a chalice formerly used in mass. A priest had once blessed the wine it held, transforming it into Christ's blood, but now it was just a cup to satisfy an officer's thirst. Isabel surprised herself by how quickly she was becoming inured to this sacrilege. Of course, these people didn't see it as sacrilege. They felt they were ridding the country of "idolatry."

She thought of that ill-assorted group out in the chapel reading the Bible together. Cecil had told her that these rebels were unique. For centuries, he'd said, the uprisings that had sporadically occurred throughout Europe had been nothing more than mobs of peasants. None had attracted nobles to their cause, because no noblemen—even enemies of the monarch—would tolerate a peasants' attack on authority. They always joined ranks with the crown and put down the rabble uprisings. But here in Scotland the Protestant rebels under John Knox had won over aristocrats who supported them not only in word but in deed. There were earls—Arran, Glencairn, Argyll. There was Hamilton, the Duke of Châtelherault. There was even a nobleman with royal blood, Lord James Stuart, the illegitimate son of the late King James. These Lords of the Congregation, as they called themselves, rode with the common men. It was extraordinary.

She heard a soft sound behind her. She turned and was startled to see a man just inside the door. He had come in so quietly.

"Is there anything you need?" he asked.

It was the servant who'd been sitting in the circle in the chapel. "No, I'm fine," she said.

"Are you sure? A cup of water, perhaps?"

He was looking at her with an intensity that irritated her. Perhaps curious at seeing a lady in this soldiers' camp, she thought, though she was dressed as a common farm wife. The way he stared was almost insolent. She realized that she still held the rubber ball, and she set it back on the table, saying, "I told you, I need nothing."

He made no move to go. "Your journey must have been tiring."

His Scottish burr sounded harsh to her ears. "I am waiting for his grace the duke. His presence is all I require to restore me."

He smiled. "That's what Jeremy Calder was just saying about Our Lord."

She didn't follow. "Lord who?"

"Our Lord Jesus Christ."

She felt a pinch of annoyance. These lowly Protestant Scots were so forward, it was hard to get used to. Yet she felt she should make an attempt. "This Jeremy Calder, was he one of your group? I saw you in the chapel."

"Aye, Bible study. Every day at three. Join us tomorrow, if you're still here. You'd be welcome."

This was more than she could allow. "That will be all, thank you. I will wait alone for the duke."

"Why do you want to see him?"

She was so taken aback, it was her turn to stare. "Goodness, man, that is none of your—"

"Forgive me for keeping you waiting, madam," a man said, striding in. Glencairn was behind him, and two soldiers. "James Hamilton, at your service." The duke, she realized. He was tall and lean, with an air of easy arrogance born of his noble rank, yet Isabel was astonished to realize that he was the lord she had seen sitting in the Bible study group. These people were so bewildering! She dropped into a deep curtsy, for a duke was almost a prince. "Your Grace."

"I see that you have met Master Knox. Good."

She almost stumbled as she rose. The servant . . . was Knox? Nothing in his manner had changed. No bow to the duke. No lowering of his eyes from hers as she stared at him. She had barely noted his appearance, but now she took it in all at once. He was short, but broad-shouldered. Had coarse black hair, but limpid blue eyes. A swarthy complexion, but cheeks that were as round and ruddy as a baby's. A narrow forehead, but bold bushy eyebrows. A man of contrasts who seemed to fit no type at all.

"Three thousand pounds," said the duke, rubbing his hands. "Madam, you have brought salvation to men thirsting in the wilderness." He turned to Glencairn. "Muster the men, Alex. Tell them they're getting paid." Glencairn left, and the duke went on to Isabel, "I cannot express thanks enough for this generous gift from your queen."

She pulled herself together. "My lord, I will convey to Her Majesty your thanks."

"Do. The thanks of all of Scotland." He lowered his voice. "Now, where is the gold?"

The glint in his eyes put her in mind of a pirate. There was something of the cutthroat in this nobleman. "I will have my man bring it to you, my lord."

"No, no. Not to me." He gave a short bark of a laugh. "For my sins, madam, for my sins. No, have him hand it over to Master Knox."

She was almost too astonished to speak. "But, my lord, Her Majesty requested—"

"Ah, but you are in Scotland now, not England, and there's a world of difference. We've had to rely on a patchwork of funds to keep body and soul together in the hard days of our march here. Contributions that dribble in from supporters. Rents confiscated from greedy priests. On the way, well, some irregularities occurred. A shivering man may pull on a patchwork that's not his, you understand, to get warm. So we decided there was only one man we all trust to hold the funds. That man is Master John Knox."

"I see." Clearly, there was nothing to be gained by arguing. "In that case . . ." She turned to speak to Knox. He was gone.

Knox took delivery of the gold in the churchyard. His sergeant and another man shouldered the satchels that Tom relinquished. Isabel requested a signed receipt from Knox. He replied that it would be sent to her lodging. The business was concluded.

Despite the rough-and-ready circumstances, Isabel was happily relieved to have it done. She felt cheerful as she walked back into the church to meet Glencairn, who was going to escort her to her lodging. After the weeks of worry about Nicolas, she could now return for him. Already, she could see his bright, smiling face as he ran into her arms. Her hopes for the rebel army ran just as high. Having seen for herself how strong their force was, she sensed that victory was within their grasp. This crisis that held her whole family in its thrall might soon be over.

She was passing soldiers in the church nave, looking for Glencairn, when Knox caught up with her. "I need to talk to you," he said. With a glance at the throng of men, he added under his breath, "Not here."

He took her up to the church belfry. Dusk was closing in, and Isabel shivered as they looked out over Edinburgh, where the first torches flared in the dim streets. Campfires dotted the fields that stretched beyond the city, looking like fireflies in the gloom. Again, she was heartened by the sight of so many Scottish soldiers. "It is wonderful," she said, "how your army has taken the capital."

He shook his head. "But not the castle." He jerked his chin toward the end of the street, where mighty Edinburgh Castle was perched on its stone crag above the city. "Lord Erskine commands it. He will not allow us to enter. He has trained his cannons on the street."

"Is he allied with the Queen Regent and her French troops?"

"No, he backs neither them nor us. He declares he will relinquish the castle only to Parliament. But Parliament broke apart in turmoil months ago. In the meantime, Erskine has said he will turn his guns on whichever side attempts to enter his stronghold."

"Well, sir, your rebel army is so formidable, the French may quietly take to their boats and slip home."

She had hoped to raise at least a smile from him. Instead, his gaze on her unnerved her. "We are not rebels," he said. "We are reformers. We dispute not the Queen Regent's authority, only her decrees to impose wicked idolatry."

"Reform. Is that what you call the desecration of churches and the despoiling of monasteries?"

He surprised her with a smile, though a rueful one. "Looters.

Early in our march I stopped them, but it went hard with the men. They felt a right to a small pinch of the riches the priests have reveled in for so long, with their concubines and palaces and barns packed with grain bought with rents of these very men whose children go hungry. So I turned a blind eye." He was unapologetic, and Isabel got the impression of a skillful politician, a man as attuned to the popular will as Cecil was. She knew the two men corresponded.

"Why do you care about such things?" he asked with that disconcerting directness. "You come to us from Queen Elizabeth, yet your name is Spanish."

The same suspicion again, she thought, annoyed. "My husband is Spanish."

"You live in Spain?"

She was unwilling to tell this man that Carlos at that very moment was across the fields with the French in Leith. She answered simply, "No, in Peru."

"Ah," he said with a knowing disdain, "then you have Indian slaves. A lady of leisure."

She did not care for his tone. However, nothing could dampen her high spirits that evening, for she was done here. "A lady, sir, who will set out for London tomorrow morning. If there is a message you wish me to convey to Sir William Cecil, I will be pleased to do so."

"Aye, to Cecil and to Queen Elizabeth. It's why I came back for you."

"I will gladly inform them of the readiness of your army."

"Ready they are, aye. And stout of heart, God knows. And yet . . ." He rubbed the back of his neck, and frowned as though he needed a moment to order his thoughts. He looked out over the flickering campfires of his men, and beyond to the French fortress of Leith. "I was once a prisoner of the French, you know. For two years I rowed in the bowels of a galley ship with my fellow captive Scots. Down the Seine, round the coast of Brittany to Nantes. Whenever the wind dropped, we rowed. Twenty-five oars, each forty feet long, six men to an oar. We were chained to our benches day and night, had no shoes, lived on biscuit and water, with soup three times a week. And we lived in fear of the whip." He looked at Isabel. "They unchained us to go to mass, but we Scots refused to attend—refused, to a man. I told the captain's mate that I would go to mass on condition that I could stab the priest, not otherwise." Again, that rueful smile. "Slackness at the oars he punished mercilessly with the lash, but piety concerned him less. And there were many of us. We prevailed."

She heard the steel in his voice. There was no doubt in her mind that he had organized the religious revolt of the galley prisoners. He did not look like a storybook leader, but she had a glimpse of why men followed him.

"Stout hearts can do much," he went on, "but they cannot stop cannonballs. Nor can green farmers match trained and battle-hard veterans of Continental wars. We have pitchforks and knives where they have cannons and cavalry. Unless we get more aid—money, trained men, munitions—we are doomed."

She could not have been more astonished. "But you have thousands of men. Surely you will prevail."

He did not answer. His icy blue eyes seemed to bore into her. "You will not start for London tomorrow. I need you to stay. Before you return to Queen Elizabeth, you must understand the reality."

❧ 14 ❧

The Garrison at Leith

Carlos was finishing his report to Ambassador Quadra, but it was hard to concentrate, what with the din of Frenchmen eating and drinking and playing cards, even though he sat at the end of a table as far away from them as he could. He dipped his quill into the silver inkpot he'd borrowed from D'Oysel, the French commander, and scratched the final words. Usually the mess hall noise didn't bother him. He had lived among soldiers all his life and could tune them out at will. It was the writing. Remembering how to form the letters always took his full attention. It had been only a few years since Isabel had taught him. When they'd begun he had cursed his slowness. He could clean, load, and prime an arquebus pistol faster than write a five-word sentence.

And today he wanted to be fast, to send Pedro off to London with the report. He didn't much care about the report, or Quadra—what he wanted was for Pedro to bring back news of Isabel. Had she left for home with Nicolas as he'd told her? Had she convinced her parents to go with her? If she'd been quick she might be sailing right now out of Seville toward the warm waters of New Spain. It felt strange, this hoping she was gone. He hated them being separated. Besides, an ocean voyage always held the chance of peril. But if she had gone, he could at least rest easy that she and

Nicolas wouldn't be ground under by a French invasion of England.

Although he was beginning to wonder if he had misjudged the situation here in Scotland. The French weren't looking as strong as he had believed before he arrived. A virulent sickness had put hundreds of men out of commission. Worse, the French fleet bringing thousands more troops had been intercepted by the English and scattered into the winter gales. He had told Quadra about it in his report. The locals said the English ships were renegades, pirates, but that was nonsense. One of the two French vessels that had made it into Leith reported seeing the flagship of Admiral Winter, although not flying its colors. Obviously, Queen Elizabeth had sent her seadogs on a covert mission. It had shaken Carlos when he'd heard that one of the English captains was Adam Thornleigh. He was said to have captured two French supply ships, a spectacular action. Carlos had not put that detail in his letter to Quadra. He didn't need the ambassador fuming to him about his Thornleigh relations.

Damn Quadra, he thought, for sending me on this God-cursed mission. Damn the English admiral, too. This setback would only prolong the French standoff with the rebels, keeping him here longer. Damn them all, Scots and French and English and their God-cursed war. He wanted no part of it. Wanted only to get back to his *real* life, with his family, back to Peru.

"All alone?"

He looked up. The blond. D'Oysel's woman.

"Letter to your sweetheart?" she asked with a smile.

He couldn't remember her name. She was one of the locals, as poor as the other women who hung around the garrison. When he'd first arrived she had seemed glad to find that he could speak English. "The frogs' jabbering hurts me head," she had told him with a wink. Since then, she had come by to talk to him a few times.

He folded the letter, glad to be finished with it. "Just business," he said.

"Ah, I warrant you're keeping the juicy bits until you see her. Lucky lass."

She was a good-looking woman, and he noticed several men watching her. He got up. "Must send this." He scanned the crowd of Frenchmen.

"Looking for your heathen lad?" she asked.

He nodded. "Pedro."

"He's in the slop kitchen, chumming with Lieutenant Goncourt's groom. Teaching him to juggle, it looked like."

He looked at her, impressed. "You keep a watch on everyone around here?"

She smiled right at him. "Only on who I want to."

Any man breathing could read the invitation in her eyes. Fenella, that was her name.

He heard a shrill whistle. They both turned. Across the hall, Jorge Rodriguez was beckoning him. Carlos gave Fenella a mock salute with the letter. "Thanks," he said, then set out across the crowded room to see what the Portuguese artilleryman wanted. Infantrymen lounged at the long communal tables over their food and card games. Melted snow was puddled on the stone floor under their boots. He reached Rodriguez, who got up, leaving his fellow card players, though he kept hold of his tankard of ale. He took Carlos aside.

"*Mãe do Deus*, didn't you see me waving you off her?"

Carlos didn't follow. "I heard your banshee whistle. Half the garrison did."

"Banshee?"

Carlos wasn't sure where he'd heard that word. Gaelic. From Fenella? "A fairy," he said, his mind elsewhere. "Screams a warning about death." He was looking toward the kitchens, wanting to find Pedro and get the letter sent.

"It'll be *your* death they scream about, Valverde, if the commander sees you with her."

Carlos looked at him. The only good thing about godforsaken Scotland had been coming across his old comrade-in-arms. They'd fought together in several campaigns. Eight years ago, for a German captain on a wooded battlefield near Augsburg, where Rodriguez had saved Carlos's life by pointing out a sniper. Later, for a Polish prince-bishop on a boggy riverbank south of Prague, where Carlos had saved Rodriguez by yanking him out of the path of a cannonball. "You mean D'Oysel's woman?" he asked.

"He is *louco* about her. *Insano.*"

Carlos chuckled. "Did you try to bed her, Jorge?"

"No laughing matter. Listen, I've been here five months, I know. A jackass arquebusier from Nantes spent a night with her, and what did D'Oysel do? Cut off the jackass's ear. He posts his lieutenants to tell him who's sniffing around her. Stay away from her, *meu amigo.* She's bad for your health."

This didn't match Carlos's own judgment of the French commander. "Doesn't sound like D'Oysel. He's a rational officer. Calm, unemotional."

"Not about her." Rodriguez knocked back a gulp of his ale and wiped his mouth with his sleeve. "And not about the Scottish prisoners, either. He likes to carve a finger off them before he hangs them. Behind his back the men call him Monsieur Doigt Rouge." Mister Redfinger.

A man hustled past them spattered with mud and sounding out of breath. He knocked Rodriguez's arm, making him spill his ale. Rodriguez growled, clutching his crotch, "Eat this!" The man hurried on, taking no notice. Rodriguez gave Carlos a look that said, Who the hell was that?

Carlos recognized him. One of D'Oysel's spies, a turncoat Scot. The fellow was heading for the staircase that led to the commander's rooms. Carlos watched him rush up two stairs at a time. Urgent news? If so, he should check. There might be more for his report to Quadra. He tucked the letter in his jerkin, about to follow the Scot. "Check Picard's sleeve," he told Rodriguez with a nod at one of the card players. "He's got a king."

The Portuguese looked at the Frenchman, outraged. "Poxy frogs!"

As Carlos climbed the stairs he heard Rodriguez bark a barrage of threats at Picard, and had to smile at the inventive obscenities.

He reached the upper corridor where officers and their body servants passed him, going about their business. From a window he could hear voices of the troops at ease down in the courtyard.

The door of D'Oysel's room was open and he could see the Scottish spy bowing to the Queen Regent. Commander D'Oysel stood at her side, a short man but one with a reputation as a tough fighter. Carlos thought of him cutting off prisoners' fingers, and his estimate of the man dropped a notch. He'd seen enough torture to know it was never about getting information. It was about taking pleasure in power. Something to keep in mind about D'Oysel. He knocked on the open door.

"What is it?" D'Oysel asked irritably in French. Then, seeing it was Carlos, he beckoned him in, saying more genially, "Yes, yes, come in, Valverde."

Carlos made a bow to the Queen Regent, a courtly gesture, not servile like the spy. She had been kind to him in the few meetings he'd had with her. Marie de Guise was in her early forties, he guessed, and she was the face of French power here. When he had first presented his credentials with Ambassador Quadra's reference, she had told him she was grateful that King Philip cared enough about her in her hour of need to send a military attaché, for she was beset with enemies, she said, and welcomed every friend. She had told him all this in French, of course, but Carlos had no trouble following it. No man could spend almost twenty years as a mercenary in Europe without knowing French.

Now, though, she barely acknowledged him, just gave him a wan, distracted look. Something's happened, he thought. The politics here were always shifting, but he knew the basic situation. Sister of the powerful Duc de Guise in France, she had married King James of Scotland twenty years ago. He'd died, leaving their infant daughter as queen—the people called her Mary, Queen of Scots. At age six she had been sent to the French court in preparation for marrying the French king's young son. That king had died last summer, so the young couple, still in their teens, became the King and Queen of France. Here in Scotland, Marie de Guise was acting in her daughter's place as Queen Regent, and Carlos had heard that she was fanatical about protecting her daughter's Scottish throne. When the rebels took Edinburgh she had been forced to take refuge here with her troops, and he thought the strain was taking a toll on her. She looked tired, almost sickly.

"Well, what news?" D'Oysel asked his spy.

The Scot, still catching his breath, answered in English, "My lord, I was watching the Earl of Glencairn, like you asked. This afternoon he rode out with the Earl of Argyll and Lord Ruthven. Up Grouse Hill they went, south of the city. There they met a woman. They brought her into town, to St. Giles."

D'Oysel frowned his annoyance at the man's thick Scots accent. He and the Queen Regent spoke only serviceable English. He turned to Carlos and repeated in French what the spy had said and asked if he had understood correctly. Carlos confirmed that he'd got it right. This back-and-forth translating was going to take time, Carlos thought, so to speed things along he asked the spy the obvious next question. "Who was the woman?"

"I canno' tell ye that, sir, for I know it not. A lady, though, the way they acted with her, though she were dressed poor. And by her saddle I'd say English. And she brought a heavy-laden packhorse."

When Carlos translated this, the Queen Regent cried in horror, "An English emissary!" then vented her fury in a stream of French. "No doubt sent by that Jezebel, Elizabeth. She has sent succor to these rebel vermin, I am sure of it. And after she assured me in that fawning letter of hers, queen to queen, that she would *never* acquiesce to their pleas for aid. The Jezebel!"

"We do not know that, madam," D'Oysel said to calm her, though Carlos could tell that he believed it was true. It had been a huge blow to the commander to lose those thousands of troops sent from France, chased by the English into the North Sea gales. He had told Carlos over wine last night that he was certain, as Carlos was, that Queen Elizabeth had sent them. Now he bottled up his anger at this further interference from England, and told Carlos in French the instruction he wanted given to the spy.

Carlos gave the man the order. "Find out the identity of the woman."

The spy made his servile bows again, and when he had gone

D'Oysel and the Queen Regent fell into a discussion. Mostly, it was her asking anxious questions. Should they request more troops from France? Could such troop ships make it here through the foul weather? Were the English so-called pirates still maintaining a blockade? Was there any chance the rebels could take Edinburgh Castle?

Carlos moved away to let them talk. He wanted no part in their deliberations, but that didn't mean he had no opinion, and it was changing in light of the spy's report. He stopped at a window and looked out at the water. The fortress commanded the estuary, the Firth of Forth, a long, narrow arm of the North Sea. Leith was a port, and a few local fishing boats bobbed in the choppy waves, looking like cockleshells beneath the fortress guns trained on the sea lane approaches. *This news could change everything,* he thought. The rebels were notoriously in need of funds, and if Queen Elizabeth had sent money, they could buy artillery, soldiers, powder and shot. That might put them in a strong enough position to attack. Over Marie de Guise's dead body, he thought.

"Señor Valverde," she said, startling him. He turned from the window to find her moving toward him. "I am going to attend mass," she said. "Please send my respects to Ambassador Quadra."

"I will, madam."

"Tell him how much we value our Spanish friends. God has given me the task of preserving this kingdom for His anointed, my daughter. Your king knows it is her right, and knows, too, that a heretic horde usurping her would be an abomination, damning our subjects' souls to hell."

He nodded, uneasy at the desperation in her eyes.

When she had gone, D'Oysel beckoned him to a chair and poured them both a goblet of wine. They sat facing each other beside the commander's desk, littered with maps and scrolls, the wine decanter, and a half-eaten bowl of cold mutton stew. D'Oysel stretched out his legs, relaxing now that he was in male company. Yet not really relaxed, Carlos could see.

"Roque did an inventory of our stores," D'Oysel said. "We're seriously depleted."

"In victuals or ammunition?"

"Both. That captain who captured our supply ships—God help me, if I had him here I'd slice off his balls and make him eat them."

Carlos studied his wine. That captain was Adam Thornleigh. "There's food enough to be had from the country people," he said. He looked up at the commander. "If this action doesn't last too long."

D'Oysel grunted. If he knew his king's intentions, he was keeping them to himself. "It gets worse. Three of those English sea hornets have not sailed for home. The *Minion, Elizabeth,* and *Tiger.* They sting us still."

Carlos was surprised. "Here in the estuary?" *Elizabeth* was Adam Thornleigh's ship. Adam was daring, but not insane. The fortress guns would sink him like a sieve.

"They got by us via the north shore at night. Now they're sniping and raiding all along the banks of the Forth, in Fife and West Lothian."

This was bad. "Must be supplying the enemy. Or they wouldn't venture so far west."

D'Oysel nodded with a grim look. "I agree. As for our lost fleet, I've had reports of ships being dashed all along the North Sea coast, bodies washed up all the way to Denmark. The Marquis d'Elbeuf was commanding, and I hear he struggled back to Dieppe, so I'm confident he'll soon send me more troops, and stores, too." D'Oysel reached for the decanter and topped up Carlos's goblet. "Nevertheless, my options for now have dwindled. Like my stock of powder has. So I'm inclined to keep it dry until the marquis resupplies me. On the other hand, I must consider the enemy attempting an attack." He poured wine to refill his own goblet. "What do you think, Valverde?"

That I'd rather be in sunny Peru, but Carlos bit those words back. The thought that plagued him was, *Who do I want to win?* If France was victorious and then conquered England, it would be bad for Isabel's parents, if they'd stayed. Under an occupying French army, they would suffer. But if the rebels mounted a successful attack and captured the garrison, Carlos could be taken prisoner. He could expect Quadra to negotiate his release as a noncombatant, but that could take months, assuming the rebels even acknowledged such rules of war. If not, he might *never* get home. Besides, he had another reason for backing France, one more deeply ingrained. All his life as a fighter he'd been loyal to whatever commander paid him, because without such a reputation you didn't get hired for future campaigns. He wasn't hired now, of course, but in every real sense his paymaster was Philip of Spain. Everything he had earned in Peru—the *encomienda*, the grand house, the silver mine, the gentleman's life—all of it came from the King. And, because of Carlos's base birth, he held on to it only at the pleasure of the King. And what the King wanted in Scotland was a French win, to rout the heretic rebels.

He made his decision. And hoped that Isabel had convinced her stubborn parents to leave England with her.

"I think you shouldn't wait," he told D'Oysel. "If the English Queen has sent them money, they'll soon buy men and artillery. Don't give them that chance."

"You mean, attack?"

Carlos nodded. "Cut them down. Now."

The bugler sounded the Stand to Horse, a blast through the cold air.

Carlos gulped down the last of his breakfast beer, shoved a crust of barley bread in his mouth, and left the officers' mess. D'Oysel doesn't waste time, he thought. Last night the commander had explained today's plan, but this was early, the sun barely up. A few candles still guttered from supper. Well, the French hadn't risen to power on Europe's battlefields by being sluggish. He was still fastening his leather jerkin as he strode into the thin morning light of the courtyard. He wanted to check that Pedro had left before dawn, as he'd ordered. Best to have him on his way with the report to Quadra before this action began. *Wish I could be gone too,* he thought.

Throughout the garrison men were falling out of barracks, forming into companies in the forecourt amid a roar of voices and boots and horses' hooves. Good discipline, though, Carlos noted. He imagined the sleepy Scots waking up in their tents, totally unprepared. Poor bastards. D'Oysel was an experienced commander, his troops highly trained and battle hard, and he was about to launch them in a full assault.

Decent cavalry, too, Carlos thought as he passed a lieutenant barking orders at his horsemen. Grooms scurried with harnesses and saddles. Officers' body servants buckled on their masters' cuirass breastplates and swords. Horses snorted steam in the cold air and danced with pent-up excitement, harnesses jangling. In the gallery above the mustering men, a dozen or so women, officers' bedmates, lined the railing, still in nightdress. Some were shivering, some leaning on the railing, but all were chattering as they watched the companies form up. A scarlet shawl caught Carlos's eye. Fenella. She was watching him.

He climbed the stairs at the side of the stables, knowing Pedro slept there in the loft with the grooms. He found the loft empty, nothing but messy heaps of straw that were the grooms' beds, and a few scattered pieces of their clothing. Good, he thought, Pedro must have left. He went to the edge of the loft and looked down at the grooms leading out the last of the horses. It felt strange to just watch, not be saddling up himself. Strange, but just fine. His soldiering years were behind him, and all the misery of that life, too. The old pain in his right knee from a German lance gave a twinge as though in reflex at this battle preparation.

"You might want to see this." A woman's voice.

He turned. Fenella stood in the loft doorway. She jerked her head to indicate the courtyard behind her. "Your lad."

He followed her out, and she pointed down to the courtyard. Pedro stood with a French captain who seemed to be yelling at him. Carlos felt a stab of disappointment that Pedro hadn't gone. God only knew when he could get away now. He seemed to be almost cringing, as though the Frenchman was haranguing him. What the hell was going on?

"Thanks," he said to Fenella as he hurried down the staircase.

He was crossing the courtyard, pushing past horses' rumps and passing men buckling on swords, when he saw the captain slap Pedro so brutally it drew blood.

He reached the Frenchman and grabbed him by two fistfuls of his collar. "Leave the boy alone."

"Who the hell are you?"

"Nobody. Hit the boy again, and you can tell the commander that nobody broke your jaw."

Pedro wiped blood from his mouth, apologizing to Carlos, *"Lo siento, señor. Él me paró."* Sorry, sir. He stopped me.

Carlos tightened his grip on the captain's collar. "You stopped my servant? Why?"

"He was taking a horse, for God's sake."

"It's *my* horse, you fool." He let the man go with a shove.

Maybe he shoved too hard. The captain staggered backward, stumbled on a cuirass breastplate on the ground, and sprawled on the cobbles. Carlos saw the humiliation and anger in the man's eyes, and regretted the push. He knew how seriously these Frenchmen took their precious honor.

He turned to Pedro, who was still shaken from the slap. "Come with me," he said, and led him away, squeezing the back of the boy's neck to calm him down. "Let's get you some breakfast."

The kick from behind surprised Carlos. A sharp boot at the back of his knee that made him lurch and almost lose his balance. He whirled around to see the French captain's fist coming at him. He jerked aside enough to miss it smashing his nose, but the blow glanced off his cheekbone. Christ, the idiot wanted to *fight?* Carlos shoved him again, a flat-handed thump on the man's chest, and this time with no regrets. "Save it for the Scots," he said.

"They needn't tremble," a woman shouted from the gallery in a taunt. "Renault's all push, no poke."

That brought laughs from dozens of men. The laughter inflamed the fury of the captain, apparently named Renault. Carlos groaned as the Frenchman pulled his rapier. He lunged at Carlos. Carlos chopped Renault's forearm sideways to knock the blade from his hand, but it didn't break the Frenchman's grip. Renault slashed with the rapier, and Carlos jumped back, the blade an inch away from slicing his throat. He took advantage of Renault's follow-though and kicked his rapier hand so hard, Renault finally dropped the weapon. It clattered on the cobbles. Men and officers stepped back, sensing the danger of the captain's fury. Renault went to snatch up his weapon. Carlos grabbed him and spun him around, took his wrist, and bent his arm up behind his back. It immobilized Renault.

If Renault had accepted defeat, it would have been over. Carlos wanted it over. Instead, Renault gave a roar of rage and tried to turn on him. Carlos heard Renault's arm bone crack. The man cried out at the pain. Carlos let go. Renault staggered in agony, looking about to collapse.

Soldiers moved in, shouting in alarm. Two grabbed Renault to prop him up. D'Oysel pushed through the crowd, the sun glinting off his steel helmet. "By God, I'll whip the hide off any man brawling—" He stopped in surprise when he saw it was Carlos. He looked at Renault, who was moaning, his face gone white. D'Oysel said, "Christ, Valverde, what have you done?"

"Captain Renault's arm is broke, sir," one of the men said.

D'Oysel looked dismayed, but held his anger in check. He gave brisk orders for a sergeant to take Renault to the surgeon, and for the others to resume forming up. He called over a cavalryman, a ramrod rider who was clearly alarmed that his captain had been sidelined. D'Oysel told him he was promoting the next man in line under Renault. "Fetch him. It's Lalonde, right?"

"Yes, sir," the man said nervously. "But the Scottish ague hit Lieutenant Lalonde this morning. Didn't you get word, sir? He's puking his guts out. Can't stand, sir, let alone ride."

D'Oysel shot Carlos a hot look of disdain that said: *You're responsible for this.* "Renault is the nephew of a duke, Valverde. There's going to be hell to pay."

Carlos felt a surge of fury. How could he be blamed for an idiot like Renault? But his fury was partly shame because he knew he *was* responsible. The idiot's arm didn't break by itself. Worse, he'd just jeopardized his own reputation. If word got back to Quadra that he'd been brawling and had injured a duke's nephew, he could kiss good-bye his hopes for a seat on the Trujillo city council, or for any advancement at all. He'd be lucky to hold on to his *encomienda*.

D'Oysel scratched his chin, looking worried, and grumbled, "After Lalonde it's Roux, the brainless bastard of a bishop who dumped him here. Doesn't know a hackbut from a halibut. We'll suffer, that's the truth of it." He made a snap decision. He ordered a stand down, then sent word for all officers to attend him in his quarters. After a last glare at Carlos, he headed back inside.

Carlos followed the officers, and D'Oysel ignored him as he came in to sit in on their meeting. D'Oysel asked for his officers' opinions. Should they postpone the action until Lalonde recovered? The feeling was that Lalonde would be ill for days. Could Roux, then, handle the commission? The response was clear—no one had confidence in Roux. Carlos listened with mounting concern. He imagined the cavalry unit on the field straggling out of formation, leaderless. Imagined them getting swarmed by the Scots, by their sheer brute numbers, and taken down. The Scots had far more men, so this attack would work only if it was total—a disciplined, lightning assault. Otherwise, D'Oysel might have to call a retreat, and then the war would drag on and on, and Carlos would be stuck here. When D'Oysel was about to speak again, Carlos gritted his teeth and spoke up. "Could I have a word alone?"

D'Oysel took him aside as the men went on talking. "I could lead the company," Carlos offered.

D'Oysel looked startled, but almost instantly there was a keen interest in his eyes. "You would do that?"

"For a favor."

"Which is?"

"No mention about Renault to my king's ambassador." He thought grimly, *If I make it back.*

D'Oysel called the men's attention, told them Carlos would lead the company, and explained that he had served with distinction as a captain of cavalry in many Continental wars, had even fought the Scots years ago, fighting then for England. The announcement brought enthusiastic looks of relief. Carlos knew some of these officers from card games, and they trusted him. He cursed himself one last time for getting himself into this mess, then told D'Oysel, "Give me an hour to talk to the company."

An hour later the gates of the fortress flew open, and two thousand French troops surged out with Gallic war cries. Mounted in half armor in a borrowed cuirass, on a warhorse he hadn't trained, with a sword he hadn't had time to hone, leading men he barely knew, Carlos rode at the head of the company. He cursed all Frenchmen as he raised his sword and galloped forward to rout the Scots.

❧ 15 ❧

The Bridge

Isabel was getting dressed after the first deep sleep she'd had in her weeks of rough travel. She was pulling on her stockings when she heard shouts from the street. Another prisoner being locked up? Glencairn had lodged her on the High Street in the house of a shipwright's widow, and the tiny attic room she had been given was across from Edinburgh's tollhouse, which held the jail. Nine or ten of Knox's men were billeted in the widow's lower floors, and last night, as Isabel was getting ready for bed, she had heard them spill out into the street to jeer a prisoner being admitted to the lockup. They hated turncoats more than anything. Looking out the attic window, she had caught the fearful look on the prisoner's face. He had seemed eager to get inside the jail where Knox's men could not slit his throat.

Now the sun was up as she went to the window to investigate the shouting. Horsemen cantered past, over a dozen, heading for the city gates. Among them she glimpsed Glencairn and the two other rebel earls who had met her yesterday on the hill—Argyll and Ruthven. A bell was clanging from a church tower, and people were scurrying out of houses and shops and side streets. What was happening? She craned to look down the street and saw men trooping this way, at least a hundred. They didn't look like a military company in their mismatched clothes, but they marched like one. People fell in beside them—shopkeepers, laborers, house-wives, children—watching with expectant looks as if a traveling troupe of actors had just come to town.

Isabel whirled on her cloak and ran down the stairs. The house seemed empty, the billeted soldiers gone. She had slept so soundly she hadn't heard them leave.

"Tom!" she called down the cellar stairs. "Tom—" She stopped, seeing him already hurrying up the stairs, still tucking in his shirt.

"What's the commotion?" he asked.

"The soldiers are marching out."

"Are we under attack?"

"It can't be. People are flocking to see."

They both hurried out the front door as the rebel company marched past, people following in their wake. Isabel stopped an elderly man who was limping, trying to keep up. She asked him where the soldiers were going, and his eyes glittered with nervous glee.

"Master Knox and the earls are hurling their army at the Frenchies!"

"At Leith?"

"Aye, mistress. Now we'll see some frog blood flow!"

Tom said, "Does it run green?"

The old man wheezed a laugh. Isabel knew Tom's jest was to mask his concern, but she could not share it. She felt as excited as the old man. Within hours, perhaps, the rebels could be victorious! She thought of Carlos and thanked God that he would be out of the fray. He had no part in these hostilities, and wanted none. He was a civilian, and there were laws of war. She knew such niceties could get trampled in combat, and that gave her a moment of alarm. But Carlos was so experienced, and clever, too. He would know how to take care of himself.

Oh, let this be a day of victory for Knox and his men! He had alarmed her last night with his dour words and his insistence that she stay to see for herself how weak his force was, but she had already seen enough, and could not believe his grim assessment. He was exaggerating so that she would carry his plea to Elizabeth for more money, that was all. These scores of soldiers in the street were marching to join the full rebel host encamped in the fields between the city and Leith, and they were several thousand strong, while the French had fewer troops and were likely unprepared, too. She felt a rush of pity, for men would surely die, on both sides. But after this one battle it could all be over, and that would *save* lives. *Please, let this rebel army send the French packing!*

The soldiers were out of sight now, gone out through the gates, their footfalls becoming faint. The people following had disappeared after them, but many were left—the old, the young mothers, the fearful. The women snatched their children, and soon they all stole back into their houses and shops, and closed their doors. The street became oddly quiet.

Isabel could not bear to shut herself in, ignorant of what was happening beyond the city walls. "Tom," she said, "get the horses ready. I want to go and see."

He looked dismayed. "Pardon, my lady, but that's daft. Blood will flow out there, be it green or red."

"That'll be miles away. Come, I must have a look."

In the stable they could not find her horse. She questioned the barefoot child who mucked out the stalls. He shrugged. "Gone, mistress. Soldiers."

"What?" she said, appalled. "They took my horse?"

"For the glorious cause," Tom said with a growl. "Now, my lady, let's you and me go back inside and sit us down and wait, like the sensible folk of this town. We'll know the upshot soon enough."

"No. Your horse is sound enough for two, and we'll not go far. Come, saddle up."

They rode out through the city gates at a trot, Isabel riding astride behind Tom and holding onto his sheepskin jerkin. They weren't alone. Men and a few women straggled along on foot, curious, all eyes on the distant horizon. The few tents in the nearby fields were abandoned, the soldiers gone ahead, leaving a muck of trampled snow and mud. Their exodus had been abrupt. Isabel saw cauldrons that steamed above still-smoking cooking fires. A few women crouched blank-eyed by the fires. One was slinging satchels onto a mule, preparing to flee. Isabel and Tom rode on up the road. The farther they went, the fewer people they passed.

"All right, my lady, seen enough?"

"I haven't seen anything. Go on, Tom."

He grunted his displeasure but kicked the horse's flanks to carry on. They were approaching a narrow wooden bridge over a stream when Isabel saw smoke on the horizon, a mere thread. Birds flapped by above her head, fleeing. She felt a shiver go up her spine. Where was the smoke coming from? There were no crops to burn in the dead of winter, and neither army would bother razing the farmers' miserable huts. "Is it the fortress, do you think?" Her throat had gone dry. Carlos was inside there.

"Or maybe the thick of the camp tents up yonder," Tom said. "Canvas burns quick."

She heard it before she saw anything. Faint clangs and shouts. The sounds of battle. But so far away, it was impossible to know what was happening. Then came a low rumble that she felt steal up from the earth into her bones. She didn't need to see. "Cavalry," she said. And at that moment she knew the rebels' camp was burning. Only the French had cavalry.

Tom had halted the horse on the bridge, as though he sensed, as Isabel did, the threshold they had reached. Before their eyes the horizon now came to life. It happened so slowly it was mesmerizing. Small, indistinct figures spread across a wide swath, growing larger. The rumble of hooves became louder. Crows shrieked in the sky. A company of riders was racing this way.

Isabel stiffened in dread. *I was mad to come here.*

"Back we go," said Tom, jerking the reins.

"No. We need to hide."

"There's nowhere—"

"Go down," she told him. "Under the bridge."

He instantly understood. "Right."

They jostled down the bank. Halfway down the slope the horse found the footing slippery in the snowy tangle of weeds, and balked. Isabel kicked its flanks and the horse then bolted down to the stream. They splashed through the water, icy droplets stinging Isabel's face. The bridge was low. Bushes reached almost to the underside. Too low for her and Tom to stay mounted. He jumped off the horse and helped her down. The water was ankle-deep and frigid. They dashed through it, Tom leading the horse, and they reached the bridge. They stood crouched, crammed together beside the horse, catching their breath, eyes cast upward to the mossy boards just inches above their heads.

The riders thundered overhead, a hollow roar of hooves on wood.

It was over quickly. A smaller group than Isabel had thought. Much smaller, just eight or nine. When they had passed, she ventured a few steps from the bridge and watched them gallop away. The sight froze her. Their colors. Not a band of French cavalry. Rebel officers in retreat.

The horse whinnied. Tom gave a strangled sound. Isabel twisted around to see a filthy, bearded man grappling Tom backward against his chest, his arm around Tom's neck.

"Go quiet, and I'll nae cut your woman's throat."

Isabel saw in horror that he wore the colors of Glencairn's company. A deserter. He had wrapped the horse's reins around a bush before grappling Tom. He meant to take the horse.

She forced out her voice. "Let him go," she demanded.

"Aye, soon's he's quiet."

Tom's hands were free and she saw him slowly pull his dagger. "Tom, don't!" she cried. The deserter looked desperate, vicious. "Let him have the horse."

Tom obeyed, and stilled his hand. But the blade was already out.

"Good lackey," the deserter said. He punched Tom in the ribs, a blow so hard it made Tom gasp and drop his dagger and sink to his knees.

Isabel ran to help him. The deserter gripped her by the throat. She staggered on the spot, choking.

"Fine lady, eh? Must have some lady's gold." He groped inside her cloak for her purse. She tried to stop him, but his other hand was a muscled claw squeezing her windpipe and she had to fight just to breathe.

She saw Tom, a blur behind the man, struggle to his feet. He lunged for the man's back and grabbed him and yanked him away from Isabel. She staggered free.

The deserter whirled around on Tom. He pulled a long knife. Tom stood helpless, his own weapon on the ground near Isabel.

She snatched it up, about to throw it to Tom to defend himself. But before she could, his legs buckled and he sank to his knees. She saw in horror that blood covered his side. The deserter's earlier punch to Tom's ribs had been more than a punch—he had stabbed him with this knife. Tom stood on his knees, blank-eyed from the pain. The deserter stood before him and lifted his blade, poised to slash Tom's throat.

Isabel's body worked before her brain did. She raised Tom's dagger high in both hands and plunged it down into the man's back. He jerked with a grunt of surprise, then clawed at the knife in his back like a man scratching. He twisted around and gaped at Isabel. He dropped to his knees. She stood panting, dry-mouthed, both men kneeling before her in shock.

The thief gave a roar, and his hand shot out and snatched her ankle. In panic, she kicked, breaking his grip. He toppled sideways toward the stream and landed sprawled in the shallows. His eyes went glassy. Water gurgled around him, turning pink with his blood.

She backed away from him in horror. "Tom . . . Tom, come!"

He managed to get to his feet, clutching his side where blood seeped between his fingers, but he could barely walk. She threw her arm around him and dragged him to the horse. He was too weak to mount. Nothing she tried helped. Sweating from the effort, she stood still, trembling, trying to think what to do. She looked up at the bridge.

"Tom, can you make it to the bridge?"

He nodded, so dazed with shock he seemed to smile. She half led, half dragged him up the bank and midway across the bridge, then guided him to the edge. She scrambled back down and loosed the horse from the bush and struggled up into the saddle. She nudged the horse forward, her hands shaking as she held the reins, until she was directly beneath Tom. He looked down at her from the edge of the bridge and seemed to understand. He managed a crooked smile. "I'm no fairground acrobat," he said.

"Yes, you can do it." It was a short jump, but he looked so

ashen. "We can't stay here, Tom. They're coming. You've got to hop on."

He looked uncertain, but nodded again, and shuffled forward so his toes were over the edge. Then he let himself drop. His body fell against her back like a sack of grain. The horse staggered. Isabel said, "Hold tight!" and Tom held on to her shoulder and she got control of the horse. She kicked it gently to get it moving. They stumbled up the bank, awkward and barely balanced, and finally made it onto the road.

Isabel headed back to Edinburgh. She heard the battle clamor behind her, far away at first, then getting louder. Two horsemen galloped past her. She barely glanced at them. Her concentration was on getting to the city to find a surgeon to see to Tom's wound. She longed to gallop, but Tom was too weak to hold on. Every jounce made him groan. She had to keep the pace slow or risk him falling off.

More riders cantered past her in twos and threes. Then men on foot, running. And men driving carts, with soldiers lying in the carts, bloodied and moaning. Isabel didn't need to look behind her to know this was a terrible retreat. But she could not think of that. Tom's grip on her shoulder was slipping. He was slumped against her back. She felt the wetness of his blood, soaked right through her cloak. And he was so quiet. She reached back to grip his arm. She felt him slip off. Heard him thud on the road.

"Tom!"

She lurched to a halt and slid off the saddle and ran back to him. Men and horses surged past her. She dropped to her knees beside Tom and bent over him and took his hand. "Tom, look at me!"

His eyes were open but glazed. Blood soaked the side of his sheepskin jerkin. His face was white as chalk. Isabel sank back on her heels and cradled his head in her lap. Tears burned her eyes and her throat. Men and horses and carts eddied past. She looked up and cried out to a man driving a cart, "Help me! Please, stop!"

The man drove on.

Then, a voice behind her. "Mistress Valverde!"

She turned, and through her tears saw a horseman lurch to a stop. Glencairn.

"Help me, my lord! My servant is wounded!"

He looked appalled to see her. "What are you—"

"I beg you, sir, help me get him to a doctor."

"Good God, woman, there are hundreds wounded. And dead."

She shook her head. "A doctor . . . that's all he needs. I just—"

Glencairn swung off his horse and grabbed her arm. "Get up, madam. You cannot stay here."

"No. Tom needs—"

"That man is dead. Come away."

Edinburgh's High Street looked alien through her fog of misery. The rebels limped through town, bleeding, moaning. Townspeople slammed their doors. Housewives hurled apples at them. Prisoners in the tollhouse shouted curses. A bakehouse in the Cannongate was in flames. Isabel let her horse follow Glencairn on his, both of them surrounded by the straggling soldiers of Knox's army. They were falling back westward, to Stirling, she heard someone say. She followed . . . nowhere else to go . . . fighting to not think of Tom's body left behind on the road.

❧ 16 ❧

Stirling

The town of Stirling, thirty miles west of Edinburgh, had held strategic value dating back to the time of the Romans. Its importance lay in its position. It controlled Stirling Bridge, the farthest inland crossing on the River Forth; the land to the west was bog and marshland, making it impossible for armies to cross.

Built on a crag high above the river was Stirling Castle, easily defended because of the cliffs beneath it on three sides. Since the twelfth century it had been one of the principal strongholds of Scottish kings. In 1500 James IV had added a monumental great hall, the largest banqueting hall in medieval Scotland, with two high, elegant oriel windows that bathed the royal dais in sunlight, and five huge fireplaces to heat the space. Forty years later his son, James V, added an entire new palace to celebrate his marriage to Marie de Guise, designed to be as splendid as anything his bride would have known in her much richer home in France. Fifteen years after James V died, leaving his widow as Queen Regent, John Knox was raising the Reformation storm throughout Scotland, and in the summer of 1559 the townspeople of Stirling had welcomed Knox and his army. The Lords of the Congregation had taken control of the town and the castle, forcing Marie de Guise to flee to Edinburgh. When Knox had marched to Edinburgh, she had then taken refuge with her French garrison at Leith.

Now, in the dark January of 1560, the French attack on Knox's men at Leith had turned the tide of the rebels' success. The rebel army, reeling from the French assault, had beat a retreat to Stirling. Edinburgh was now in the hands of the French.

For hours, rebel soldiers had been straggling across Stirling Bridge and in through the castle gates, many of them stumbling from their wounds. Bleeding, numb from the cold, dazed by the disaster, they barely looked up at the towers that flanked the gate, their conical turrets shining with gilded stone lions and unicorns. Plodding in through the castle's central door, they took no comfort in the emblazoned royal coat of arms, the Lion Rampant, displayed above it. They crammed the banqueting hall and collapsed on the stone floor in exhaustion after their long and miserable march. The floor was iced with muck tramped in from the snow-packed courtyard. Torches on wall brackets flared in the cold drafts. Moonlight from the high oriel windows blanketed the men with a thin sheen that gave no warmth.

"Can you lift your head?" Isabel was on her knees, offering a tin cup of water to a man whose left arm had been hacked off to the elbow. He lay on the floor surrounded by other wounded. She slipped her hand under the back of his neck to lift his head, and he gulped the water, parched from his ordeal. Too eager, he gagged on it. His head lolled in a delirium of pain. Isabel gently lowered his head, but she could not hold back a shudder. The filthy bandage wound around the stump of his arm was soaked with blood. Her hands and skirt were already stained with other men's blood. *Some of it is Tom's.* Every thought of him brought a stab of grief.

She sank back on her heels, and with the back of her hand wiped sticky strands of hair off her damp forehead. The misery all around her was overwhelming. Women and children were doing their best to tend to the injured, but the suffering was awful. Men lay moaning, weeping, dying. It wasn't just their injuries that had felled them. It was the devastating sense of defeat. No one was more devastated than Isabel. She knew now what the French were capable of. These simple country Scots had no chance against such a war machine. Knox had been right.

"Yes, get some rest," she murmured to her patient. Futile encouragement, for she doubted the poor man would survive the night. He did not hear her, in any case. He had sunk into unconsciousness. *Futile*, she thought, *like this whole desperate enterprise.* The rebels' cause was hopeless.

She heaved herself to her feet. Bone-weary, she longed to lie down on the floor, too, though it was fetid with bloodied rags of bandages. A man grabbed her ankle, and she turned. His lips were moving but no sound came. He was so weak his grip on her slackened and his eyes closed. She wished she could help him, but his gashed chest had been bandaged and there was nothing more she *could* do but pray. She stared at his bloodied shirt, and her thoughts shot back to Tom, dear jesting Tom, left dead on the road. Her last sight of him had been of retreating rebels tramping past his body, blood still oozing from his side. *He'll be lying there still. Alone. Abandoned. No burial.* She thought of him sprawled under the moonlight. Had his body been rifled by corpse robbers? Mutilated by carrion? The thought made her sick. She balled her fists, digging her nails into her palms to dam the sickness and force back the tears. *Knox was right. If I had believed him, I would not have ridden out beyond the walls. Tom would still be alive.*

A murmur came from many throats. Isabel turned to see the three earls—Glencairn, Argyle, and Ruthven—moving through the crowd of maimed men. Prostrate soldiers were feebly calling out to them. The commanders moved slowly, offering a word of encouragement here, a nod of pity there. Glencairn made his way to Isabel. "Come with us," he told her. "Master Knox wants words with you."

Why? she wondered. To give her the receipt she needed for the Queen's gold and then send her on her way? Or—a terrible thought—were the French coming? Was Knox planning a further retreat? Or even surrender? Whatever it was, she would be leaving Scotland, and that gave her a twist in her stomach. She had done what the Queen had asked, and had every reason to flee this place of death and defeat. Yet something in her balked at flight, a voice inside her murmuring that what she had come to do was not yet finished. She followed Glencairn and the other lords out into the frigid night, and went with them across the street and into the church.

It was packed with men, the able-bodied of their army, all in dirty, sweat-stained clothes, their tired faces streaked with grime. Had they been mustered here or had they come to the church on their own? There were so many they stood elbow to elbow, and Isabel read expectation in their faces. They're waiting for something, she thought. She stood at the rear, flanked by Glencairn and Argyle.

"Has the whole army been called here?" she asked Glencairn.

"What's left of it."

She understood his grim tone. Their ranks were so depleted. "So many casualties," she said in pity.

He grunted. "And worse. Deserters."

A coldness slid down her spine as she remembered the bearded deserter under the bridge jamming his knife into Tom's ribs. Remembered the frantic moment when she had plunged Tom's dagger into the man's back. The dull crunch of metal on bone . . . his gaping, uncomprehending look at her. She had committed murder. But it had not saved Tom. That guilt tore at her. It felt like *she* had murdered Tom.

Knox was climbing the steps to the pulpit. He looked out at his soldiers with sunken eyes red-rimmed from fatigue. The men watched him and their voices hushed. The church fell silent.

Knox cast his eyes toward heaven. "O shepherd of Israel!" he called out, his voice quivering with emotion. "Thou that leadest Joseph like a flock, stir up thy strength and come and save us. Turn us again, O God, and cause thy face to shine, and we shall be saved!"

"Eightieth psalm," Argyle murmured, watching Knox, as rapt as the lowly soldiers.

"O Lord God of hosts," Knox cried, "how long wilt thou be angry against the prayer of thy people? Thou feedest them with the bread of tears, and givest them tears to drink in great measure."

"Aye, tears!" a man called out in a raw voice. Men around Isabel nodded, and groans of agreement rumbled from all parts of the church. They knew their desperate situation.

Knox stretched his arms heavenward. "O Lord God of hosts, look down from heaven and behold the branch that thou made strong for thyself. It is burned, it is cut down. They perish at the rebuke of thy countenance."

"Aye, we perish!" someone groaned.

Knox's tone suddenly changed from a lament to an urgent plea, vibrant with fresh energy. "Let thy hand be upon the man of thy right hand. Quicken us, and we will call upon thy name." The men quieted. Their hard faces softened with hope. "Turn us again, O Lord God of hosts," Knox beseeched, "and cause thy face to shine, and *we shall be saved!*"

Isabel heard breaths slowly sucked in around her, as though these men were filling themselves with Knox's vigor.

"We began alone!" he thundered, looking down at his soldiers, his eyes ablaze. "We have suffered. We have lost brave men. God has tested us, and has not found us wanting! We began alone— many thought so. But we *never* were alone. God was with us. He is with us still. And He will deliver us to victory!"

Every face was upturned to him, thirsty for his words. He launched into a fiery sermon, his voice ringing loud and confident as he called the enemy weak with sin, called the loyal men of Scotland strong with righteousness. He switched between biblical quotations and his own muscular exhortations, never pausing, his energy infectious. Many men were smiling now. One man wept, smiling.

"God is with us!" Knox thundered in conclusion. "And He will deliver us to victory!"

The men cheered.

Isabel watched them and marveled. Knox had turned these weary soldiers around. He had transformed their despair into euphoric determination. "They will follow him anywhere," she said in awe as he came down from the pulpit to be mobbed by his men. "Follow, and fight."

"As will I," said the Earl of Argyll, his eyes shining with joyful tears. "Fight on, even if only twenty horsemen ride with me!"

"We must," Glencairn muttered, no euphoria in him, just grim resolve. "Or else each take our turn with the hangman."

Another cheer from the men around Knox. He was grinning, slapping backs, grabbing hands as he moved among them. They pressed in tightly, eager to be close to him.

Isabel marveled at how he had kindled fire in them. For months they had slogged and gone hungry and slept on snow. Today under the French onslaught they had fallen and bled and seen kinsmen die. Yet they were not giving up. Knox's words had drilled into each man, down to a core of fortitude. To endure what they had endured and still be so keen to fight on—it amazed her. Why did they do it? For God? No, men did not feel God in their blood. They called on Him for the strength to fight, but He was not what they fought *for*. Did they do it to put a Scot on Scotland's throne? No, most would return to hack out a living from their stony fields no matter who won this lethal contest. Did they fight for their kin? That was it, she realized. They were risking their lives for brothers and fathers and cousins and sons who had fallen or who still stood beside them. For wives and mothers and daughters who kept the hearths warm for their return, and would perish if they did *not* return. The bond of blood. *Nothing is stronger.* It humbled her.

Knox had kindled a spark in her, too. Was it possible that if they fought on they could actually *win?*

The meeting took place in Knox's lodging, the high-ceilinged second floor of a coal merchant's house that overlooked the River Forth. Eleven men, summoned to strategize. And Isabel, summoned for she knew not what. The room was gloomy, lit only by a candelabra whose candles guttered in the draft. No one had come to dine or relax by a fire. Some of the men stood, some sat on chairs turned away from the barren dinner table. Hamilton, the Duke of Châtelherault, was the ranking nobleman, and all the others present were lords, but plain master Knox was clearly the leader. Isabel sat on a stool near the cold hearth, listening in silence to their talk.

"This dishonor will not stand," said the duke's son, James Hamilton, the hotheaded Earl of Arran. He was pacing before the cold grate, his narrow face pinched with anger. Isabel had heard that the rank-and-file men thought him arrogant, for he never mixed with them. She remembered that Queen Elizabeth had secretly met with this young nobleman to discuss marriage. Isabel's mother had arranged the tryst. But nothing had come of it, for the Queen was not impressed. Nevertheless, Arran had a reputation as a capable fighter in the months of skirmishing that Knox's men had been engaged in with the French. He often rode out with Lord James, the illegitimate son of the late king, another daring fighter, although to Isabel the two seemed very different. The dark-haired Arran was intense and quixotic; fair-haired Lord James, leaning back in his chair across from her, was all quiet coolness. "No, by God," Arran said, thumping his fist on the hearth mantel, "we will not let it stand!"

Knox ignored the young man's outburst. "News first," he said to the others. "The French have recalled their ambassador to London. Monsieur de Noailles has been replaced by Michel de Seurre."

Glencairn groaned through his thick black beard. "That's a weathercock."

"Aye," Lord James grimly agreed, "it shows who's in control at the French court. The party of the Constable Montmorency is out, and the party of the Duc de Guise is in."

"A weathercock that blows us more ill," said the duke, rubbing his red nose on a dirty handkerchief. "Their boy-king's a spindly puppet and his Guise uncle is the devil that jerks him."

"And every day he and his brother the bishop burn scores more of our brethren in Christ," said Lord Ruthven, one of the youngest there, his beard mere downy fuzz.

"What's most significant about it," Knox said sternly to pull them back from these side paths, "is that the Constable's party always insisted on steady relations with England, but not so the Duc de Guise. He is bent on having his niece make good her claim to the English throne. This may stiffen the will of Elizabeth of England to lend us more aid."

They all looked at Isabel. It gave her a shiver of suspense. Was this why Knox had called her in? She understood the politics. The

Duc de Guise's niece Mary, the sixteen-year-old Queen of France, was also Queen of the Scots and stood next in line to inherit the English throne, too, because of her Tudor blood. Pressed by her powerful uncle, she was publicly claiming her right to take that throne immediately, since Catholics everywhere considered Henry VIII's divorce from his first wife invalid, his marriage to Anne Boleyn illegal, and therefore his daughter Elizabeth a bastard. It was a threat that Elizabeth could not ignore. And Knox is using that, Isabel thought with a touch of awe at his shrewdness. He was hot passion and cold calculation in one focused force. No wonder men followed him.

He'll send me back to entreat the Queen for more aid, she thought. She could do it, easily. Then take her son home and be finished with this dangerous business. But was it enough? That unnerving voice inside her still murmured that what she had come to do was not yet done. She could not stop thinking of Tom.

"Forget their far-off dukes and ambassadors," Glencairn said. He got up, bandy-legged but strong looking with his barrel chest. "It's the Queen Regent's men thirty miles away who can cut our throats. *That's* the news we need—news of what's afoot at Leith. We must know, is King François sending another fleet with more soldiers?"

"Of course he is," said Sir William Maitland, as lean as a scarecrow. He was the scholar and wit among them, but he had seen battle, and his cheek and neck bore livid red welts. "D'Elbeuf will have already sailed from Dieppe with thousands more."

"Not if the reports about the Huguenot uprisings are true," said Ruthven with hope in his voice. "The King and the Duc de Guise need all their troops to keep our Protestant brethren from overwhelming their throne."

"Wishful thinking," scoffed Maitland. "The duc will send his sister reinforcements, count on it. Marie de Guise will be expecting them. It's just a matter of when."

"Aye," Glencairn agreed. "Our plans must be under way before those troops arrive."

"Attack first!" said the hothead Arran. "That's our only course."

"No," Knox said firmly, ending the discussion. "Our course is the one we've already agreed on. We concentrate on holding Fife and the southwest."

Isabel listened as they discussed some successes they'd had in the skirmishing with the French throughout Fife. A couple of Admiral Winter's ships had supplied them with arms. "Thanks to Sir Adam Thornleigh," Glencairn said with a respectful nod at Isabel, and again they all looked at her. She felt a rush of pride for her brother. He was so bold. Too bold? she suddenly wondered. He was alone with just his crew in a hostile territory. She remembered Knox's chilling talk of being captured by the French, and the years he had spent in forced service on their galley ships. Chained to the oar bench. No shoes. Bread and water.

"Friday we march out. We will divide our force," Knox said. "Two days here to see to our wounded and bury our dead. Then we march south." He detailed how the duke and Glencairn would go to Glasgow with their men, while Arran and Lord James and their men, and Knox himself, would go to St. Andrews. The other lords were given their orders, too. A discussion about tactics, monies, levies of men, and friends to contact went on for another half hour. Then Knox dismissed them. He asked Isabel to stay.

When they were alone he called for a servant to build a fire. Then called for some food. "Are you hungry?" he asked her.

"Very." She was famished. The last she had eaten was a hunk of stale oatmeal bread from the saddlebag of a kind sergeant hours ago and a cup of icy water on a riverside rest during the long ride to Stirling.

"And weary, I can see," he said, pulling up two chairs to the fire. He beckoned her to sit.

Weary, indeed. She sank into the cushioned seat. An old woman brought the food, two wooden bowls of rabbit stew that smelled deliciously of onions, which she set down on the dining table, then left.

"No, no, do nor bestir yourself," Knox told Isabel, and he brought the bowls over to their fireside chairs. Isabel gratefully took the bowl, warm in her hands from the brown, steaming stew. Knox dug a spoon into his. But the moment Isabel saw the sheen of fat on the surface her stomach recoiled. She feared she might be sick, and set the bowl down on the floor. It was her grief for Tom, she thought. It made her feel almost faint.

"Not to your taste?" Knox asked, spooning stew into his mouth. He called back the woman, and she soon returned with wedges of wheat bread fresh baked with currants, and a small winter apple. This plain fare suited Isabel well. She was relieved to munch on both.

She glanced at Knox mopping up the last of his stew with a crust of bread. Through the window the moon spied on them between the roofs of two houses. "I warrant you are weary yourself, sir, though you show your men unflagging energy."

He nodded. "Weary of the separation from my family. I miss my wee bairns."

He had children? She could not hide her surprise. She had never imagined him with a home and family. He was so consumed by his cause. So driven.

He seemed to catch her look. "Aye, Nathaniel's three. And baby Eleazer not yet one." He set his empty bowl on the floor. "And you? Have you young ones?"

"A son. Nicolas. He's four." Her throat felt tight. "The heart of my heart."

"I hear your longing. You miss the lad. Does he bide in London with your people?"

She nodded. She had no wish to confess that the Queen's trust in her was so thin she was holding Nicolas as a hostage. To change the subject she asked where his wife was.

"St. Andrews. And snug abed tonight, I hope. I pray God I'll see her soon, and my bairns." He looked at her. "Marjory is about your age. English, too, like you. Daughter of the captain of Norham Castle. Ach, I've gifted her with a hard life. Whisked off to Scotland. Exile in Geneva. Back to Scotland and this camp life, marching from town to town." There was unmistakable affection in his voice as he added, "She is dear to me, like my own flesh."

It moved Isabel. She thought of Carlos. *Like my own flesh.*

Yet could she truly believe Knox's tenderness for the woman in his life? Cecil had told her about the notorious book the man had written castigating female rulers. "You astonish me, sir, for the world says you detest women."

"I?" he said, surprised. "Never." Then he understood. "Ach, the blasted book."

"A blast, indeed." His book was titled *The First Blast of the Trumpet Against the Monstrous Regiment of Women.* In it he had called female rulers unnatural, unfit to govern, and ungodly.

"I had Mary Tudor in my sights when I wrote that, she who wrenched England down into the muck of idolatry and evil, and burned so many hundreds of our brethren at the stake. I was also looking over my shoulder at the coming of young Mary Stuart, Queen of Scots, another worshipper of idols. Never forget that the French want England, and that she, their queen, is their tool. *Those* women were my quarry." He shook his head in disgusted regret. "Ill timing that the book was printed just as Mary Tudor died and Elizabeth became queen."

"And so felt herself the object of your ire." Bad timing, indeed. Cecil had said that Elizabeth had refused to speak to Knox when he'd returned from exile in Geneva, or even to let him pass through her realm on his way back to Scotland. He'd had to sail.

"Do not believe everything the world says, mistress. I have many female friends. I correspond regularly with several in London and Geneva, wise and brave women who support our cause. They have my greatest respect. As do you."

A compliment, though given with his usual dour intensity. "Thank you," she managed.

He sat back, folding his arms and studying her. "If I believed what the world said of *you*, I would think you a mere idle lady of leisure. Pampered, waited on, and good for nothing but to fatten the purses of the trinket merchants. But I know better. I wonder, mistress, do you?"

She was astonished. "Pardon?" The liberties he took!

"I say that you do not know yourself. I have learned something about you since first we met. Your role in the Wyatt rebellion. I hear you undertook great dangers to assist Sir Thomas Wyatt in his noble intent to bring down Queen Mary. A go-between, were you not, for Wyatt with his scattered accomplices?"

She said nothing, unnerved, though she knew her silence was consent.

He nodded. "*That* is how you are meant to be. In action. God wishes it. It is your destiny."

She felt it like ice water dashed on her face. Abruptly awake. She tried to quiet the pounding of her heart. The voices that had been murmuring inside her—now she knew who they were. Wyatt's men, cut down when she had opened Ludgate and Queen Mary's men had set on them. "*We would have lived, but for you.*" And the voice of Tom, murdered because she had made him ride out with her. "*I would have lived, but for you.*"

Knox went to the door and closed it, then sat down again beside her. "I have had a letter from Sir William Cecil. The Queen's council are unanimous in urging her to help us, thanks be to God. And to Cecil, who has been our champion. But the Queen will not commit. She is fearful of Spain. I need you to go to her. Clearly she trusts you. You must tell her what you have seen with your own eyes, felt with your heart—our desperate need. It is no longer a question of aid. That is not enough, neither her money nor even some hundreds more men. We need an army. An English army. An army of thousands. Without that, we perish."

Isabel looked at him, her heart racing. To go back to London meant freeing Nicolas. She imagined swinging him up into her arms in a hug, taking him hand in hand to the customs wharf, boarding a ship bound for Spain, and sailing home to Peru. It's what Carlos wanted.

But she thought of Knox's men tonight standing in the church, their dirt-streaked faces resolute. What are they fighting for? she had asked herself, and then had realized the truth. For brothers, fathers, cousins, sons. For the women who waited at home. For kin.

She felt her troubled heartbeat settle as she made her choice. Nicolas was living in a palace. Lonely he might be, and sad, but he would be living in comfort and ease. True, the Queen could exact

her displeasure on him if she thought Isabel grossly disloyal. Former kings, enraged by unfaithful nobles, had sometimes thrown
the transgressor's young sons into the Tower with the father, there
to languish for years. But Elizabeth, though formidable, would
never be that cruel. More to the point, Isabel would never give her
cause to think her disloyal. Nicolas was safe.

She had watched Tom bleed to death in her arms. It had
brought home to her the menace of the French as nothing before
had, and now she knew she would do her all to prevent them
swooping down to conquer England. Her family would not survive
an occupation. She had seen Wyatt's men die. Seen Tom die. She
would see that her kin lived.

"You are right," she told Knox. "Her Majesty must hear this
news, and your plea. But I shall not deliver it."

He flashed her a look, startled, angry. "But you are—"

"Send a man she can relate to. Send Sir William Maitland. He
will state your case with accuracy and eloquence. As for me, I can
do you better service."

He blinked in surprise. "What?"

"You need information about the French at Leith. Their pre-
paredness. Their expectation of reinforcements. I will go there.
Into the garrison. I will get the facts you need."

He looked at her as if she were mad. "How?"

"My husband is with them. Sent as a military liaison for Spain. I
will visit him."

It so took him aback, his mouth dropped open. "You are married
to an ally of the Queen Regent?"

"My husband is completely neutral, sir. He is merely an observer. He takes no sides."

A new distrust seemed to dawn in his eyes. "Unlike you?"

She bristled at the implication. And forced herself to say the
words she had used so often since returning to England. "Trust
me."

Alone in her lodging Isabel undressed, shivering in the chill
night air, and at the thought of the task she had taken on so boldly.

Recklessly, it felt like now. But Knox had jumped at her offer, and she would see it through. She would.

At the moment, though, her thoughts were snagged on what she was looking at in her satchel. Balled up between her wool shawl and her last clean shift were the laundered rags she had brought from London for her monthly flow. When she had left London at Christmas her time was already almost two weeks late, yet she had not needed the rags in the days that followed. It was because of the tension, she had thought then, and the rigors of the journey. But now January was giving way to February, with no blood yet. Two months.

She sank down on the edge of the bed. How could she have been so blind? Her queasy stomach so many mornings. Her ravenous appetite, yet aversion to fatty food. She laid her hand on her belly and felt excitement flutter. It made her smile, for in a few months that flutter would be an impish kick. Flesh and blood. Hers. Carlos's.

She looked out the window at the moon, and its cold, sad light stole her smile away. In war, uncertainty was all that was certain. What country would her baby be born into? Scotland? England? Peru? And what kind of world? A sliver of fear slid into her heart. Her offer to Knox was going to take her into danger. She made a silent prayer. *Let me not endanger my child. My new wee bairn.*

❧ 17 ❧

Through the Enemy's Gates

Isabel tightened her grip on her horse's reins. She knew she should have expected what she was seeing, yet it took her aback. Edinburgh was swarming with French soldiers.

They swaggered down the snow-packed High Street. They strolled out of taverns. They regarded her with blatant interest as she trotted past them. Their wolfish looks gave her a shiver, for she was riding all alone. Two of Knox's men had ridden with her from Stirling, but the French patrolled the countryside and the closer she and her escort had got to Edinburgh, the more she had worried they would be stopped and questioned. She had a legitimate reason for coming—to visit her husband—but Knox's men had none. So, at the outskirts of the city she had sent them back to Stirling. She would not have the deaths of two more good men on her conscience.

Snow had been falling for the last few hours, shrouding the road and trees and the hovels of the poor in a ghostly silence. Dampness had soaked through Isabel's cloak at the shoulders and seeped through her leather gloves, leaving her wet and cold to the bone, and trying to tamp down her alarm as she trotted past a crowd of soldiers lounging beside Edinburgh's tollhouse. One of them eying her said something to his comrades and they laughed. She pretended not to notice, but her skin prickled. There were several guards posted at the doors, and she realized that the toll-house jail must be crammed with Knox's men captured in the horrible attack three days ago. Poor souls. They would almost certainly be hanged.

A church bell pealed. All the churches, of course, would have reverted to Catholic services. She caught glimpses of the townspeople going about their trade in shops and cookhouses, while on the street they clattered past her in carts and wagons. Knox had warned that Edinburgh was Catholic to its backbone, and the people that Isabel saw had a brisk attitude of business as usual, as though they felt well rid of the rebels. How quickly the French had made themselves at home! And how arrogant they were in their prowess. It galled her. Frightened her, too, for if she ran into trouble none of these citizens would rush to her rescue.

She was only minutes past the tollhouse when a stench reached her, so putrid it turned her stomach. She looked up at the church tower ahead and her breath snagged in her throat. Corpses were slung over the tower parapets. Half a dozen, hung by their heels like meat to rot. A lesson to any rebel-friendly townsfolk. That big fellow, she was sure he was the one who had given her some bread from his saddlebag that day of the retreat. Upside down, gaping in death, he was barely recognizable. She quickly looked away. Didn't trust herself to hide her horror.

But what she saw at the other end of the street only compounded her fears. Edinburgh Castle brooded on its high stone crag, and from its turrets the flags that lifted in the cold breeze bore the colors of the Queen Regent. Until now Lord Erskine, who commanded the castle, had observed a strict neutrality, fending off both sides in the conflict and declaring he would continue to do so until a Parliament could convene and give him his orders. But if the Queen Regent had taken up residence there, it had to mean that Erskine had gone over to the French. The impregnable castle had its cannons trained on the High Street to mow down any attackers. It gave Isabel a pang of dread. Knox and his men faced such terrible odds. Without help from England they were doomed.

"Pas si vite!" Not so fast!

Isabel gasped. A soldier had grabbed her horse's bridle and

brought her lurching to a halt. There were two of them, both red-cheeked from drink and barely steady on their feet. She understood their French, slurred though it was. The one who had stopped her stroked her horse's nose while leering at Isabel. "Very pretty," he crooned.

"Nice woman, too."

The first one laughed. "And a better ride."

"Unhand my horse, sir!"

He glared at her. Isabel cursed herself. *Speak French, like a lady.* "*Laissez-passer!*" she commanded.

She wrenched the reins, yanking the bridle free of the man's hand, then kicked her horse. It burst into a trot. She heard the men calling lewd names at her back. A sweat of fear chilled her. Was she brainsick to have come here? She hadn't even reached Leith yet, two miles away, and already this felt like a lethal mistake.

Find Carlos, she thought. He was her goal, her haven. Once she was with him she would be safe. It pained her that she would have to keep from him her real reason for coming. She longed to confide in him how crucial it was for England that Knox's rebels win back their country, and how desperately Knox needed the information she could supply. But she was sworn to secrecy and must honor that oath. Still, she was sure Carlos would understand what she was doing if he knew. Right now, all she wanted was to be with him, safe, and no longer alone.

But how to find him? Leaving Stirling, she had assumed he would be at the Leith garrison, but now she wondered if he might have been given rooms here in Edinburgh. Having taken back the capital, the French didn't need to stay bottled up in their seaside fortress, and it was obvious that hundreds were now billeted throughout the city. *Don't think of them as the enemy,* she told herself, trying to steady her nerves. *They've got to believe I'm on their side.* Should she stop one and ask if he knew where to find her husband? But rank-and-file soldiers would likely not know Carlos. He was above them, a kind of ambassador for Spain. Perhaps go into a tavern or cookhouse and inquire there? But if she wandered the streets on foot she could be taken for a whore. She had to stay mounted; the horse was a sign of her station. She tapped her heels against its flanks, eager to keep moving at a brisk trot. She had to get into the Leith fortress in any case to get the details Knox needed.

She rode out through the city gates and started across the open fields toward Leith. She was not alone on the road. A few farmers rattled by in carts, and some men and women trudged along on foot, but Isabel felt very alone. Memories flooded her of the last time she was here. Riding on one horse behind Tom. Hearing faint sounds of battle in the distance. "Seen enough, my lady?" he had coaxed. But she had insisted on going farther. If only she had been sensible, he would still be alive.

She was approaching the bridge. There, the deserter had stabbed Tom. There, she had killed the wretch. Too late, though, Tom already dying when she had gotten him back onto the horse. She steeled herself to see his body lying on the side of the road. But she reached the spot, then passed it. Where was he? She looked around on either side, almost frantic now. Had corpse robbers hauled his body away? But why? Did they sell cadavers? She refused to follow that vile thought. No, he must still lie here somewhere, hidden under the fresh, deep snow that blanketed everything. She tried to take comfort in the peacefulness of his resting place, but it was cold comfort. Her horse's hooves thudded hollowly over the wooden planks of the bridge, echoing the hollowness in her heart.

The high walls of Leith rose before her. Ghosts of snow floated off the ramparts and drifted in spasms, hostages to the wind. The central gates stood wide open, evidence of how invincible the French felt, and a straggle of country people plodded in and out, farmers' carts delivering firewood and coal, women carrying in baskets of root vegetables and cheese, peddlers pushing in carts of knives and crockery, and leaving with bones and rags. Isabel joined them, riding her horse at a walk in through the enemy's gates. Atop the walls the corpses of more of Knox's men had been strung up to rot as memorials of the conquest. Isabel almost gagged.

She was in, the gates behind her. The French had erected Leith's walls according to the most modern military science, she assumed, but the place they enclosed was a poor Scottish town. The narrow streets were paths of muck where skinny dogs prowled and dirty children, big-eyed with hunger, sat idle in doorways. Inside a rickety house on a corner, a baby screamed. Soldiers tramped past Isabel in twos and threes, a few of them eyeing her. She saw two rolling a cannon carriage toward a blacksmith's forge. One sat on a bench outside a tavern, oiling a musket.

She stopped at a stable where the hostler was leading a stallion to a water trough, and was about to ask him where the garrison was when she looked across the stable roof and saw her answer. A half dozen flags emblazoned with the blue fleur-de-lis fluttered from buildings that seemed near enough to walk to. Though faded by sun and wind, the flags were still a proud symbol of French power. She took a deep breath. The garrison was her destination. She could hardly wait to take refuge with Carlos.

"Stable your mare, mistress?" the hostler asked.

"I'm not sure." She told him she had come to visit her husband, a guest of the French commander.

"Ah, then you're but 'round the corner from him, and this is the place for your mare." She asked if he knew Carlos, and he brightened. "I do. A fine judge of horseflesh. He's out on the training course, yonder." He pointed up the narrow street. Between the houses Isabel could make out an open field where she glimpsed some horsemen cantering past. "For his sake," the hostler added, "I'll groom her myself."

Isabel started out for the training course on foot, and immediately felt more vulnerable down from her mount as soldiers passing her turned to look, and those lounging in doorways watched her go. She felt her exhaustion acutely, too, for her legs and back, cold and sore from the ride, ached with every step over the street's frozen wheel ruts, iron hard.

She smelled smoke, and turned to look down a narrow lane. Three men stood around a campfire. Beside them was a cart heaped with what looked like rags. She slowed to look only because the fire was so odd in that cramped space. The stone wall of a churchyard rose on one side, the brick wall of a house on the other, a wooden shed closing the alley. She saw that their cart was crammed with a jumble of breeches, boots, jerkins, caps, blankets. Booty, she realized in disgust, plundered from Knox's dead on the fields. They were burning the trash from the haul. The rest they would likely sell. Were they soldiers or villagers? Soldiers, it seemed, for they wore the uniform buff jerkin of the French infantryman. Except for the one nearest the fire. He was talking to the others, making sweeping gestures as though telling a grand tale, and the firelight lit up the jerkin he was wearing. Isabel froze. It was of sheepskin, its collar of red satin, and every move of his arms set the tattered gold tassels on the sleeves to dancing. Tom's!

Fury flooded her. Swamped her mind with raw rage. She was running. Tearing down the alley toward the villain, screaming, "Take it off!"

They turned to her in surprise. She reached the one in the sheepskin and grabbed hold of it at his chest. "You stole it from Tom! Take it off!"

"Christ on a stick," he said in dismay, his French a guttural patois. His arms shot up between them, easily breaking her hold. Isabel staggered back.

His mate grabbed her arm and spun her around. "Who's this little she-devil?"

The third one chuckled. "André, did you duck out of the whorehouse again without paying?"

Fury coursed through her. "What have you done with his body?" She lunged for the sheepskin again and clawed at its collar to unfasten it. "Tell me!"

"She's a lunatic," the man said, fending off her hands. "Get her off me."

The other one yanked her back again. He was a big lout and she was no match against his strength. But she shrugged off his hand and stood her ground, catching her breath, fired with rage.

"It's a lady, you idiots," the third one said, the runt among them. His words whistled through a gap where a front tooth was gone. "Look at her gew-gawed clothes."

"That's right," she spat, "I've come to see the commander." She pointed to the cart. "And when he hears of your thieving he'll have you all whipped!"

The three of them shared a look. Then a laugh. "I just sold him a plaid blanket nicely speckled with gore," said the one in Tom's jerkin. "Trophy for his wife, he said."

They were all grinning. Isabel swallowed. Rationality returned, and with it the cold realization that she had made a terrible mistake.

The men's grins hardened. Isabel's every muscle tensed for flight. But they surrounded her. The fire crackled behind her. She felt its heat. Two of the men moved in closer to her, the big one and the one in Tom's jerkin. She backed up, and stumbled in stepping around the fire. They moved forward, parting for the fire. They backed her up against the churchyard wall. Its rough stone surface snagged her cloak like a clutch of burrs.

The one in Tom's jerkin grabbed the edge of her cloak, his knuckles poking her breast. His clothes stank of pork fat, his breath of ale. She pressed up against the wall, the stone icy against her back. He fingered the fine wool. "This'd fetch more than half the bloody truckle."

"Here," she said, fumbling to untie her cloak. "Take it."

"I will." He wrenched it off her shoulders. He stepped aside with his booty, but before Isabel could move, the big one took his place. He jammed his knee between her legs. "Got something for me, too?" She stiffened in fear. Rape was in his eyes.

"Hold on, you blockheads," the runt said. "She's no doxy. What if the commander really is expecting her? One word from her and we'll be grubbing with the rats in the Hole."

The other two shared a worried look. Isabel rejoiced. It was *they* who had made a mistake, and they would pay for it!

"What do we do?" the big one asked, stepping back.

The runt said quietly, "She hasn't been there yet. Better she never does."

Terror gripped her so fiercely she could hardly breathe. Their way out was to murder her.

"I *was* there," she managed to blurt. "I'm on my way back. The commander knows that. He'll send men to look for me."

The runt moved in on her and studied her face, frowning. Then he looked at the big one. "She's lying. Snuff her out."

"And leave her here?"

"Cart her to the road. Highwaymen got her."

Spiked by terror, Isabel gave the runt's bony chest a furious push. He stumbled backward and she darted between the other two. She ran. Faster than she had ever run. She heard boots pounding after her. She was halfway up the alley when the two lunged in front and cut her off. They took a wide stance, hulking, their arms spread wide, ready for any move from her.

An oak tree rose above the wall and Isabel saw a scatter of wind-blown branches at the men's feet. Among them, a stick with a sharp end and as thick as her wrist. She lunged for it. The one in Tom's jerkin flinched as she straightened with the makeshift weapon tight in her hand. She held them at bay with it, and this pause gave her a jolt of power. The stick was sharp enough to gouge an eye, and they knew it.

The big one pulled a long knife from his side. He thwacked the stick with such brutal force, it shocked her hand to numbness and the stick flew from her grip.

She ran back the way she had fled. But ahead there was only the closed-off end of the alley, nowhere else to go. The runt watched her pass him. Pleased that her terror had made her lose her mind, he looked as satisfied as a cat torturing a mouse.

She made it all the way to the cart. She turned, panting, chilled with sweat. The fire beside her crackled. The three men watched her, their smiles returning. Three cats, with murder in their eyes. Isabel's heart thumped so painfully she thought it would crack her ribs.

She turned to the cart and scooped up a bulging armful of things helter-skelter—breeches, boots, shirts. She stepped to the fire and flung her armload into the flames.

"No!" cried the runt. The other two looked horrified. The three of them came running to rescue their booty.

Isabel scooped up another armload. Hurled it into the fire. The men converged on the fire and set to kicking boots out of the flames and pawing out garments.

She bolted past them. Ran toward the street. She heard one pounding after her, but his moments of delay at the fire kept him too far behind. She reached the street and ran past a housewife chatting with a priest who watched her in surprise. Everything in her wanted to dash into the first side street or alley and keep running. Or else find some corner to hide in and curl up in a ball so the men would pass her. But her best chance lay in staying on the street where people were. She headed for the field with the training course and forced herself to slow down, walk normally, calm her heaving chest. And not look back.

The moment she reached the field, she saw Carlos at the far side and could not hold herself back. She rushed toward him.

He was galloping, sword drawn, toward a straw effigy that sat on a sawhorse, while five men on horseback watched from the sidelines. Carlos was about to slash the straw man's neck when he spotted Isabel. His slash went wide of the mark. He hauled on the reins, stunned at seeing her. He turned his horse and cantered off the course toward her.

"Isabel!" He swung down from the saddle as he reached her.

She threw her arms around his neck, feeling her heart would burst with relief.

"Madre de Dios." He pulled her away to look at her, gripping her shoulders. "What are you doing here?"

Her rehearsed words spilled out without thought. "I came . . . to see you."

"What?"

"Came north with Frances . . . to her brother's, and then . . . here."

He stared at her, still struggling with it, and she knew what he was seeing—her disheveled hair, her face pale from fear and exhaustion.

"Carlos, I . . . missed you so."

It was no lie. And she saw the sincerity of it strike a chord in him, changing his stark astonishment to something softer—sheer wonder.

The love on his face was so welcome, his rough face itself so dear to her. And the bond of trust that held them both—it was all too much. She could no more hold back from telling him everything in her heart than she could hold back the ocean's tide. She would tell it all—about Nicolas, and Knox, and why she was here. It would be such a relief to share her burden! But without warning, her elation at finding him ebbed and her sorrow over Tom flooded in, swamping her. "Oh, Carlos, it was awful . . . so awful." She found herself sobbing.

"What was? What's happened?" His hands on her shoulders tightened in a protective clench. "You're all wet. Where's your cloak? Where's your horse?" He glanced behind her in dismay. "You came *alone?*"

"With Tom," she wailed.

"Who?"

"Tom Yates. My father's servant. He's dead!" She could not dam her tears, nor stop her body shuddering. "My fault . . . my fault! Carlos, I held him as he died!"

She threw her arms around his neck again and clung to him, her cheek against his chest, and when he wrapped his arms around her she felt a rush of joy. She pressed against him so tightly, the top buckle on his leather jerkin dug into her cheekbone. He was her rock, her refuge in this storm of war, and she clung to him as if for life itself. She breathed in the familiar smell of him, a mix of his body's earthy warmth, of leather, and of horse, and the comfort it brought drained her sorrow and her fear. The relief was so sudden it left her weak in the knees. She had to hang on to Carlos just to stay standing.

"Isabel, where did this happen? What did—" He stopped abruptly, and Isabel lifted her head to see why. The men on horseback who had been with him on the course had trotted over. Officers, clearly, by their superior mounts, their polished swords and tooled leather boots.

"Everything all right, Valverde?" one asked.

"My wife," Carlos said. The men bowed to her from their saddles with grave respect. "She's had a rough time getting here," he added, and she heard how he was forcing steadiness into his voice, still shaken by her being here and bewildered about how and why—details to get when they were alone. He did it well, the forced steadiness. So well, it made Isabel realize, with a pang of caution, something that she had not considered. Carlos would not let her tormentors escape. No, I can't allow that, she thought, her mind lurching ahead. The corpse robbers would tell how she had attacked the man in Tom's jerkin. Carlos must not go after them.

"Gentlemen, pardon my woman's tears," she said, trying to find some of Carlos's steadiness as she wiped her eyes. "They are for my servant. I lost him on the journey." She invented it on the spot—not just for the officers' sake, but for Carlos. A tale of setting out with Tom from the home of Frances's brother, crossing the border, and, as they approached Edinburgh, being set upon by a highwayman. The villain had been wrenching off her cloak, she said, when Tom had pulled his dagger to defend her, and had been killed. The villain had snatched the cloak and fled with Tom's horse.

The Frenchmen were full of indignation. One expressed his condolences, another suggested they ride immediately to retrieve her servant's body. Isabel said nothing, knowing that the deep snow would make such a search fruitless. Another offered his assistance in organizing a hunt for the murderer, an offer more passionate than rational, for it was obvious to all that the highwayman would never be found. Another insisted that Carlos and Isabel take his billet, more comfortable than Carlos's room, for the duration of her visit. She listened with dismay, for she saw that their concern was all because of Carlos. They considered him their comrade, their friend. They did not see him as a neutral Spanish observer. They saw him as one of them.

It chilled her. She felt she had come to her senses just in time. She now could not confide the truth to her husband. She *must* not. Though in spirit he was one with her, on the ground he was one with the enemy.

❧ 18 ❧

The Enemy Queen

That evening the officers' hall was festooned with flags for the
banquet, some emblazoned with the elegant blue fleur-de-lis,
some with the austere coat of arms of the Queen Regent. Servants
scurried with jugs of wine while musicians sawed and piped from
the gallery, though little of their music could be heard above the
banter and laughter of the officers. They were milling about, enjoying the fine burgundy and freewheeling talk before the
Queen Regent's arrival, when formal decorum would be necessary. There was little enough at the moment. A captain was bal-
ancing a spoon on his nose to the raucous amusement of his
friends, and a lieutenant was groping a girl in a doorway, a pretty
girl with rouged lips, as though he was getting all he could before
she was banished to the backstairs and the Queen Regent and
her ladies welcomed in.

"To the valiant Señora Valverde!" Captain Lescarbot made the
toast with panache, his glass held high. The dozen men around Isabel enthusiastically raised their glasses. "Señora Valverde!" they
chorused, and drank to her.

Isabel forced a smile of thanks, overwhelmed at being the focus
of such attention. The story of her ordeal on the road to Edinburgh
had spread through the garrison, embellished every time it was re-

told, until when it reached her ears again she heard that ten barbarian Scots had attacked her and Tom, that she had killed two with her dagger, and that before galloping off they had cut out Tom's tongue and hanged him from a tree. When she and Carlos had arrived in the hall, the men greeted her with an admiring "Huzzah!" as though she were some Amazonian heroine. She caught Carlos's eye and he winked at her, enjoying himself now that he'd had time to get used to her turning up out of the blue.

But that had taken a great effort on her part. He had brought her to his billet above the hall, a small room that he shared with an officer, and the moment they were alone she knew a barrage of questions would be coming. Her best course was to try to control it herself, so she told him again how she had come north with Frances. "She's staying with her brother at Yeavering, you see. From there Edinburgh is so close, I decided to come and see you."

"Yeavering?" He seemed utterly baffled. "But why didn't you go home like I told you?"

"I thought you understood. I promised Adam I would look after Frances."

"That was two months ago. She's had the baby. She has servants to help her."

"She's still not well, Carlos, not strong. I simply couldn't leave her."

He let out a puff of breath, struggling to take it in. "I wanted you to go. You and Nicolas. Away from all this."

"I know. But Frances needed me."

"Is he with her? In Yeavering?"

Nicolas. "No. It's a bitter journey north for a child. I left him in London." She hoped he would assume she had left him in the care of her mother. She did not dare say more. "Carlos, please understand. I made a promise."

He frowned. "I hope your brother appreciates it."

"He's not the only reason I stayed."

"What else?"

"You know the answer, we've been through it. My parents won't leave England, and I won't abandon them."

He shook his head, exasperated.

"Don't be angry," she said. "You would do no differently. You wouldn't desert me and Nicolas."

"Not the same."

"It is. We can never forsake the people we love."

She could see him making an effort to accept it. She moved closer to him. "Forgive me?"

He smiled then, though the smile was still tinged with exasperation. "For your loyalty to your family? Well, it's what brought you here, so it's not hard to forgive."

She felt the warmth in his voice, and it made her long to tell him that she was with child. But not now, when he already had so much to take in. Later, when they had time alone. It would make him happy, and she savored the promise of that.

He took her in his arms and kissed her—a hungry kiss that sent a spark racing through her. He held her so tightly she felt his hardness. She ached to give herself to his kiss, to him, but her lies somehow held her back. The words she had said were all true, but there was so much she was hiding—about Nicolas, the Queen, and Knox.

He broke off the kiss, looking as though doing so was a struggle. "After the feast," he said in a low voice. *"Mi amor."*

"Feast?"

"Tonight. A banquet for the Queen Regent. Unless you're too tired?"

She was, but she wanted very much to see Marie de Guise, the woman in whose name this army fought. "No, of course I'll come."

"Good." He grinned. "I want to show you off to these Frenchmen."

"But I have no gown." She had not thought of such things when she had packed her satchel. "Certainly nothing suitable to meet royalty."

"I'll send Pedro to forage something."

Pedro, another face from home. She longed to see him. "How is he?"

Carlos shrugged. "Hates winter. He curses the snow."

She had to smile. Her docile Indian lad was developing a mind of his own.

"He'll be glad to see you, Isabel. He was about to take Quadra my report the other day but a skirmish with the Scots kept him here and I sent it with a porter."

She shuddered inside. That "skirmish" had killed so many Scots.

"More wine, señora?" Captain Lescarbot asked now amid the noise in the banquet hall. He snatched a jug from a passing servant and tipped it to fill Isabel's goblet.

"No, no," she said with a laugh, covering the goblet with her hand. "My head is light enough already, monsieur." She was trying to act merry to match their high spirits, but it was hard. Her lies to Carlos made her feel tainted, as though she had swallowed wormwood. She hated deceiving him—it wasn't *her*. Tonight she was even *dressed* like someone else, for Pedro had indeed found her a gown, one offered by a French lady in the Queen Regent's entourage, another mark of how highly everyone here thought of Carlos. Isabel hated being obliged to the French for the clothes on her back, but she had no choice. In truth, she had to admit that the gown was lovely, of sapphire blue velvet, and she was pleasantly aware of how becoming was the fit. The men's looks told her so, Carlos's most of all. "After all," she went on to the captain offering the wine, "I must keep what wits I have if I'm to speak sensibly to Her Grace. I am not the brave veteran of the bottle that you and your friends are."

"Ah, but you *are* a veteran, madam. We've been skirmishing with the barbarians throughout Fife, and now you've done us the favor of chasing off a few. Huzzah, I say."

They all laughed and toasted her again. She pasted on a smile, but felt a shiver down her backbone. They were not frightened of Knox's men. Not even nervous. They felt confident. Arrogant. To them, the army under Knox and Glencairn and Arran and Lord James was merely an unpleasant bit of business, all in a day's work. And she had seen the horrific results of their day's work—the maimed men sprawled through the hall of Stirling Castle, moaning for water, for their wives, for God, for death. She was trying, for Carlos's sake, not to hate these Frenchmen, but she wished with all her heart that Knox and his men had the power to fall on them and send them limping back across the Narrow Seas. But Knox was weak and the French were strong, and both sides knew it.

"Have the barbarians proven difficult to put down?" she asked Lescarbot.

"Easy as swatting flies, until a few weeks ago. They had no artillery. But now they've been supplied with arms brought by a rogue English admiral, Winter by name, and a gang of his captains, damn their heretic hearts. But never fear, madam, we've rounded up a good number. We'll soon get them all."

She remembered riding in through the fortress gates where corpses had been hung high on the walls to rot. Her thoughts flew to Adam, sailing with Admiral Winter. He could become a captive. They could hang him. It gave her a sharp pain at her heart.

"You're mad to keep such a lovely wife alone in London, Valverde," said a mustachioed captain. "Englishmen are rank sinners."

Carlos let out a good-natured laugh. "My wife can take care of herself, Dupuis, I assure you."

"Ha," said Lescarbot, "Dupuis wishes he could say the same about his wife back in Marseilles."

They all laughed. Dupuis and his wife seemed a familiar topic of merriment, and even Dupuis cracked a smile. He said with stoic forbearance, "She took such good care of herself, she left not a sou behind when she rowed off with the sail maker."

"You'll have her back yet, man," Carlos said, and Isabel caught a gleam of thanks in Dupuis's eyes for his support.

"Care to wager on that?" a lieutenant asked.

More laughter, and within a moment the lieutenant was collecting bets. Carlos, smiling, shook his head at the foolery. "No, not me," he said when the lieutenant asked him to wager.

"Oh, why not fleece us some more, Valverde?" Lescarbot said with mock indignation, and they all joined in jesting about some gambling adventure in which Carlos, apparently, had been the big winner. Isabel saw that Carlos had the admiration of these men, even their affection. His camaraderie with them was hard to stomach.

She heard a commotion at the far end of the hall. A trumpet

sounded, announcing the arrival of the Queen Regent's party. There followed a brisk flurry of officers setting down goblets, tugging doublets into shape, lining up as though forming ranks, all eyes on the doorway as the Queen Regent walked in followed by a half dozen of her French ladies-in-waiting. She was escorted by a short, bullnecked officer—the commander, Isabel assumed, a Monsieur D'Oysel. She had a clear view of the Queen Regent, a petite, trim woman who looked about the same age as Isabel's mother, forty-five or so. She wore a moss green brocade gown with gold satin sleeves that were studded with pearls. Her dark hair was neatly coiffed, and a necklace of emeralds sparkled at her throat.

Isabel felt riveted. Here was the very face of the enemy. Marie de Guise, mother of the nominal monarch, sixteen-year-old Mary, Queen of Scots, who had married the teenage French King François. Marie de Guise governed Scotland in her daughter's name, while in France the young King was ruled by the powerful men of the Guise family, this woman's brothers, who were bent on enforcing their niece's claim to the throne of England. Sir William Cecil had made it clear to Isabel that the French meant to use Scotland as a stepping stone to launch themselves into England, and Marie de Guise had brought in the troops to do it.

A proud woman, Isabel thought, studying her. And yet, despite her elegant bearing she looked tense, her face pinched and pale. Was she ill? The Queen Regent stopped to greet a visiting French dignitary and the priest with him, and Isabel turned her attention to the short, bullnecked gentleman escorting her. He looked impatient, as though he wanted to be anywhere but at a banquet.

"Is that Monsieur D'Oysel?" she whispered to Carlos.

He nodded, frowning as he, too, watched the commander.

"Is he always so stern?" she asked.

"No. It looks like something's happened."

Isabel stiffened. Was that why the Queen Regent was arriving late? Had she and D'Oysel been shut up together planning another assault on Knox's men? Would they be marching out in force come morning to attack the Scots at Stirling?

The Queen Regent moved on past the dignitary, and Carlos whispered in Isabel's ear, "Come. Time to meet her."

She felt a flutter in her breast as she walked with him down the length of the hall. Officers stepped back to let them pass. When they came before the Queen Regent, she greeted Carlos with an affectionate nod. He bowed and introduced his wife. Isabel sank into a deep curtsy.

A smile flitted over the Queen's face, softening her drawn features. *"Très jolie,"* she said. Very pretty. She beckoned Isabel to rise, and switched to speaking Spanish, clearly as a mark of distinction to Carlos. "I can see, señora, that you have made your husband happy by your visit. You are very welcome here with us."

Isabel thought it only polite to answer in French, the lady's mother tongue. "You honor me, Your Grace."

Marie de Guise smiled at this touch of finesse. One of her ladies-in-waiting behind her whispered something in her ear. Her eyebrows lifted in mild surprise. She said to Isabel, continuing in French, "You were attacked during your journey? How dreadful. These brigands infest our realm. I hope you have recovered from your ordeal?"

"Completely, Your Grace, thanks to the kindness of your officers."

"You and Señor Valverde have come a long way from the New World, and we do appreciate his counsel. Tell me, in what part of Spain does your family live?" Before Isabel could answer, the lady-in-waiting whispered again in her mistress's ear. Listening, her face hardened almost imperceptibly. Fear gripped Isabel. Was the Queen Regent being told about her connection to the rebels?

"Forgive me." A touch of frost in the Queen Regent's voice. "You are English."

Isabel relaxed a little. "Yes. My father is Lord Thornleigh," she said with some pride.

Her tone did not please the Queen Regent.

Carlos intervened. "My wife has lived in several countries, madam, and from our home in Peru she came to visit her family in London. Like me, she is a loyal subject of His Majesty King Philip. And, like me, is honored to be your guest." He said it cordially, as though to clear up a mild misunderstanding. Isabel was sure that she alone had heard the fiercely protective note in his voice. She longed to kiss him.

This took the edge off the Queen Regent's mood. "London," she mused to Isabel, sounding as though her interest was waning. "You have traveled a very long way. Are the roads even passable?" She glanced at the tables set with silver plates and crystal goblets on white tablecloths, looking bored as Isabel explained how she had broken her journey with relations. "They live not far from Alnwick." That word caught the Queen Regent's attention.

"Oh? You have family in Northumberland?"

"In Yeavering, yes. My sister-in-law and her brother."

"And who is that gentleman?"

"Sir Christopher Grenville."

Silence from the Queen Regent, but a sudden look of keen interest. Isabel had no idea why, only that the change was striking.

A nearby official cleared his throat, looking anxious. He caught the Queen Regent's eye and made a servile gesture of welcoming her to be seated. A steward, perhaps—the food must be getting cold. The Queen Regent said to her commander, D'Oysel, "Well, monsieur, I suppose we should eat." But her eyes returned to Isabel, and this time there was warmth in them.

"Señora Valverde, tomorrow I hope you will do me the favor of a visit. It would be my pleasure if you would accompany me to mass."

Carlos closed the bedchamber door. "What a secret weapon you are!" he said with a laugh. He grabbed her by the waist and lifted her off her feet and whirled her around. "How did you do that? Three other wives have been here and she barely gave them a word."

Isabel held on to his shoulders to steady herself, still stunned by the Queen Regent's invitation. "I have no idea. It has to be because of *you*. A mark of her esteem."

He laughed again, squeezing her. "No, no, you can't shirk the credit. She likes your spirit."

"An Englishwoman who talks back to her?"

"My wife, who braved the Scots to get here."

"Your wife, that's what I mean—it's all for *you*. Everyone here thinks the world of you, especially her."

He ignored this and lowered her so her feet touched the floor. "Isabel, do you realize what this means for us? For my getting the council seat in Trujillo? Quadra will hear about the Queen Regent showing you such favor. He'll tell the King. That will do more for my application than all my scrawled letters."

Trujillo. The King of Spain. Her head was spinning. Those things, they meant little in this crisis. She was here for Knox. For Nicolas. For England. *But I can't tell Carlos any of that.* It felt so hard to deceive him. Felt impossible.

He took her face gently between his hands. "The King will give me the seat, and it'll be thanks to you." He kissed her. A brief kiss, but then he smiled with a gleam in his eyes, as though holding back to savor what lay ahead. They were finally alone for the night. The officer who had gallantly given them his quarters was the nephew of a marquis, and the room, though not large, was comfortably appointed with damask curtains, an ornate desk, and an inviting feather bed, plump with embroidered pillows. Isabel ached to sink into the haven of Carlos's embrace and into bed with him. To blank out all her troubles and lose herself in his love. But losing herself could lose her everything. She had to stay alert, rational.

"I hate that you're here," she blurted, unable to stop herself. Then added, to cover herself, "You can leave soon, can't you? You've done what the ambassador wants. You've been here for two months. You're not a soldier anymore, and he can't expect you to stay forever. And the situation is so dangerous."

He shook his head. "He likes my reports, wants more. And I must have his recommendation to the King. I need that seat to pay our debts. I have to stay."

"How long?"

He shrugged. "But *you* must go." He pulled her close. "Isabel, it's so good to see you. I'm glad you came. But this is no place for you. You must go back."

What? No! To get the information for Knox could take several days. She *had* to stay. She struggled to invent a reason. "The Queen Regent—"

"See her tomorrow, of course. Then start back the next morning. Take Pedro."

"But you said other wives were here, too, so—"

"They've gone. Listen, the old hands who watch the sky say a storm is coming, maybe a few days. Leave on Wednesday morning and you'll be in Yeavering before it hits. Once it's passed, head back to London for Nicolas."

Nicolas. He was why she was here . . . and Carlos had no idea. Yes, she would go back to London the moment she had delivered the information to Knox, but she could not leave Leith until she had something.

He gave her a quick kiss, then went to the window to close the curtains. The room was on the second floor of a tower, and windows in a twin tower a stone's throw away glowed with torchlight. As he tugged the curtains together Isabel came up behind him and pressed her cheek between his shoulder blades. "But I want to stay. I want to be with you."

She felt him pull in a breath, felt it fill his back.

"Please," she said, pressing her body against his. "Don't send me away."

He turned, his face tight with frustration, and took her gently by the shoulders. "It's not what I want. Believe me. But if things get rough, I want you and Nicolas away from it all." He held up his hands to forestall her objection. "Not to Peru, just to Spain. Stay with Beatriz's family in Seville. You won't be so far from your parents there, so you won't be abandoning them. They'll be just a short sail away."

"If things get rough? You mean, the French might win here, then invade England? Is that what you think?"

"Win here, yes, I'd bet on that. They have far superior forces. Invade England, hard to say. That's politics."

"How superior?" She had pounced on his word too quickly. She tried to sound vague as she added, "Of course, military matters—"

"Are best left to military men," he said with an affectionate smile. "So, tell me you'll go to Seville. Please. Do that much for me."

This was agony. She didn't know how to promise something she could not deliver.

"Isabel, I don't want to fight you about this. I have to know that you and Nico are safe. Just to Seville, all right? Truce?"

Why not? she thought, hating herself. She had already gone so far beyond the bounds of what he thought she was doing, what was one more deception? She nodded. "Truce."

He smiled. "Good." He brushed a kiss on her lips, then her ear, then her neck. The sweet, familiar tingle rippled through her. A small voice inside warned her to stay on guard lest she betray herself with a dropped word, but she could not resist caressing the side of his head. His close-cropped hair standing up like boar bristles always surprised her by its softness. He took her hand and kissed her palm. He untied the lacing at the cuff and peeled back the silk and kissed the inside of her wrist. She felt her pulse thrumming against his lips, and thrumming all through her. She lifted his head, impatient for him, and kissed his mouth. He pulled her tightly to him, his kiss hungry, and she slipped her hands up to his shoulder blades and pressed herself against him with a moan. She wanted this. No more talking, no more dissembling. She wanted him—that at least was the pure truth.

They broke off the kiss only to catch their breath, they were both so eager, and he grinned, then kissed the half-moon of her breast that swelled above her bodice. Then something stopped him. He said, his smile still warm, "I forgot to ask, what with all that's happened. Why did Queen Elizabeth want to see you?"

She froze. "What?"

"At the palace."

"When?"

"The night I left London. You said she'd summoned you. Why?"

She squirmed inside, struggling to stay calm. "Oh, just to meet me. For my mother's sake."

He ran his fingers into her hair, smiling at the feel of it even as a frown of doubt creased his brow. "Nothing more? Nothing about Quadra?"

"No. Just . . . for my mother. They're friends."

"I know. But why would she ask—"

She flipped open the top buckle of his doublet to stop him. "It was just a few pleasantries with her, then an hour with her ladies." She flipped open the other two buckles, then slipped her hands inside and slid her palms over his shirt at his chest and looked up into his eyes. "Do you really want to hear boring court gossip? Who's in and who's out? Who's marrying, who's quarrelling?"

"Isabel?" he said, still smiling, his hands on her hips to hold her close. "What are you not telling me?"

"Nothing. There's . . . nothing to tell." This was killing her. She could not let him go on with such questions. She pushed the doublet off his shoulders and was relieved to see that he was happy to let it fall to the floor.

He smoothed her hair. "Just be careful with the Queen. Her interest in the rebels is not in the interest of Spain. So if—"

"You're all knots, my love," she said brightly, smoothing her palms over his shoulders. "You worry too much about Quadra and Spain. Here, sit down. You need to relax." She took him by the hand and led him to the chair at the desk and sat him down, then moved behind him and massaged his shoulders. "All knots," she murmured as she kneaded his muscles, glad to hear a grunt of pleasure from him. She moved in close so that her breasts brushed the back of his head as she massaged. *Stop your questions,* she silently begged him. "There, isn't that better?"

"No complaints." He took her hand and led her around so she stood in front of him. "Remember, if Queen Elizabeth asks you—"

"Shhh. Not now." Resting the backs of her thighs against the desk, she leaned forward and massaged the muscle cords between his neck and shoulders. His eyes drifted over her breasts.

"Too much shirt here," she murmured. She untied his shirt strings and shoved the shirt open, exposing his chest almost to his navel. At the sight of his hard body she felt a yielding in every part of her. It was all she could do to think anymore. She slid her hands over his skin, starting with his shoulders. The heels of her palms radiated in gentle circles over the caps of his shoulders, then on to his breastbone and down his chest. He let out a low groan of pleasure.

She said, "This borrowed gown should come off, don't you think? Pedro can return it." She untied the lacing of the bodice and wriggled it down off her shoulders. She wore only a chemise beneath, and she shifted her weight against the desk, making her breasts move freely under the thin cotton fabric. Carlos watched, all attention now as she untied the chemise strings and slipped it off her shoulders and down off her arms. Now she was half-naked, like him, and the cool air on her bare breasts made her nipples tingle with desire. Carlos was breathing hard, and she saw his erection straining against his breeches. She leaned forward and laid her hands on his forearms on top of the chair's arms, pinning him in place. She kissed him. He thrust his tongue into her mouth and a quiver shot down to her belly.

She broke off the kiss to catch her breath. Then kissed him again, harder. Her hand moved down to his erection. It felt so hard against her palm. She rubbed.

He groaned, and caught her wrist and stopped her. But only to prolong the pleasure. He stood up, looming over her, making her breath catch at the power of his body, the force of his need. She leaned back against the desk and took his hand, and with her other hand lifted her skirt and put his hand between her thighs. She gave a small gasp as his fingers slid into the hot cleft, slick with her desire. The feel of his big fingers weakened every muscle in her, and she had to support herself on her bent arms. His fingers stroked her . . . and stroked her . . . until her arms would not hold her any longer and she lay back on the desk with a moan. He bent over her, and she gasped again as his tongue took the place of his fingers. She arched to spread herself, and his tongue licked and flicked and probed, and she cried out as she climaxed.

He gathered her up in his arms, her body still throbbing, and carried her to the bed and laid her down. She whispered, "Please," and he unfastened his codpiece, his hungry eyes on her. He pushed up her skirts and spread her legs, and when he lowered himself on top of her she threw her arms around his waist and cried out again as he thrust into her.

After, they lay on their backs, catching their breath. Isabel felt the sting of tears hot against the back of her eyes. She loved him so much. And was deceiving him like the most vile of liars.

He sensed the change in her and raised himself on his elbow to look at her. "What's wrong?"

"Nothing. I love you. You know that, don't you?"

He laughed. "If that wasn't love, I'll take whatever it was." He smoothed her hair back from her forehead. "Isabel, this won't go on forever. We'll get home soon. We'll be together, back in Trujillo. Life will be good."

She nodded, forcing a smile, misery roiling inside her. She had to turn away. He lay down again and scooped her gently against him, her back against his chest, and let out a contented sigh, settling down for the night.

She waited until he was sleeping, and then she wept.

Morning sunshine flooded the desk as Carlos's pen scratched the last words of his report to Quadra. Isabel had left the curtains wide open when she'd gone out, leaving him to his task. As usual, the writing had taken more time than he cared to spend, but finally it was done, and he tossed down the quill and flexed his cramped fingers. He smiled to himself, remembering the night's lovemaking. What a woman. Five years together, and it still amazed him that she was his. He would hate to see her leave, wished he could keep her by his side for just a few more days. But it could not be. If the rumor was true, things here were going to get rough. The sooner she got out, the sooner she could collect Nicolas and sail to Seville. He would take comfort in that.

He folded the letter and got up. The one small consolation in sending Isabel to London was that she could personally deliver his report to Quadra. Rumors had leaked from D'Oysel's quarters that morning and spread through the garrison like a line of burning gunpowder. Carlos had put in his report everything he had been able to find out, which wasn't much. D'Oysel had given him only a brief explanation before setting out for a closed-door meeting with his officers. So Carlos had told Quadra the bare facts that D'Oysel had told him: that Queen Elizabeth's council was unanimous in urging her to publicly declare a pact with the rebels, and Sir William Cecil was beating the drum loudest of all; and that if the Queen agreed, Cecil stood ready to put the Duke of Norfolk in charge of mustering an army of nine thousand foot soldiers and seven hundred horse under Lord Grey of Wilton. Quadra would surely know this already; in fact, if the Queen had agreed, it would by now be common knowledge in London. But Carlos wanted to be thorough, and had added his personal assessment that although the French had been poised to rout the Scots, England's entry into the fray with an army would change everything, so he would no longer hazard a prediction about the outcome. *God only knows who'll win this fight now*, he thought.

Bells clanged. He glanced out the window. Across the barracks rooftops he could see the bell tower on the garrison church. The bells were ringing not for mass, but for a muster. Had D'Oysel received another report? Better go and see. Where had Isabel gone, anyway? She had said she'd be back soon to await the Queen Regent's note summoning her to visit, but it had been two hours since she had left their bed.

He grabbed his sword, buckling it on as he crossed the room. When he opened the door he was surprised to find a woman, her fist raised, about to knock. D'Oysel's blond. Fenella.

"Going out, are ye?" she asked.

"Yes." She had visited him a few days ago saying she was collecting old shirts for rags, and had lingered to make a point of letting him know how unsatisfactory she found D'Oysel as a lover—"my wee frog," she'd called him. Carlos had sent her to Pedro for the rags. He said now, "If you're looking for my Indian boy, you'll find him in the stable."

"Nay, it's you I want. Are you looking for your wife?"

He knew she kept a keen eye on events around here, but her scrutiny of his affairs was a little unsettling. "As a matter of fact, yes."

She had not moved, stood blocking the doorway, and now she leaned one hip and shoulder against the doorjamb and twirled a thick lock of yellow hair around her finger. She gave him a lazy, sad smile. "Until she came, I was beginning to think you fancied me."

"Look, I have to go. If there's something—"

"She's not what she seems, you know."

"What? Who?"

"I was in town last night. Met some chums at the Spotted Dog. Dunstan was there."

"Who's Dunstan?"

"You've seen him about. Scruffy fellow with a beet nose. He does some watching work for my wee frog."

D'Oysel's spy, Carlos realized. The commander used a few in the town. Turncoat Scots.

"Anyway," Fenella went on, "he's an old chum of mine and we had a good chinwag. I mentioned your wife visiting you, gave him quite a pretty picture in words. Imagine my surprise when Dunstan says he's seen her before." She leaned closer to Carlos and lowered her voice, enjoying her knowledge. "I'll tell ye this, Master Spaniard. Your pretty little wife's been lying to ye."

❧ 19 ❧

The Second Hostage

Isabel's head swam with numbers, details of gun calibers, lists. For hours she had strolled the garrison under the pretense of taking morning exercise, making mental note of everything she saw: munitions, artillery, battlement layout, stores of victuals, the physical state of the troops. She had started early, when the place was quiet, but now church bells had begun signaling a muster and soldiers were hurrying past her on their way to form up. It gave her a shudder. Were they planning to march out and attack? Should she get out at once, ride to Stirling and warn Knox? But warn him of what? This might be no more than an inspection. She was being too panicky, she told herself. Calm down. Wait and see. At least with everyone's attention on the muster she was all but invisible.

But it was impossible to be calm when she felt almost sick with her private misery. Shame swept her at how despicably she had acted with Carlos. Her lies. Her evasions. Her promise to flee England with Nicolas when she had no intention of fleeing—England might be torn to pieces! Only, right now *she* was the one being torn apart, between Knox's cause and Carlos. But the only way was to keep going. Lies were all she could give Carlos.

She forced herself back to her task. Get the information. *The sooner I get it, the sooner I can go.* She had gathered a good deal already. She had peered through a barred window and counted the stockpiled lasts of gunpowder, and the stores of muskets and arquebusses. She had walked into the infirmary, pretending to look for Pedro, and seen dozens and dozens of soldiers lying ill on cots and pallets, weakened by a virulent flux. When a kindly surgeon ushered her out, saying she should not risk contagion, she thanked him, having seen enough to know that almost a full company of men was unfit to fight. She had walked the base of the fortress walls, and when she saw a lieutenant coming down from a watch-tower, a friendly fellow she had chatted with at the banquet, she struck up a conversation with him, asking what could be seen of the sea and the countryside from the tower. He had given her a description of the view, no more than he would give any curious tourist, but Isabel had gathered enough about angles of attack to be useful. When he had moved on, she'd scanned the fighting platforms on the towers and noted the number and caliber of the big guns, from falconets and culverins to demi-cannons and cannons.

It felt eerily familiar, noting munitions to report to a rebel leader. Five years ago she had carried the same information to Sir Thomas Wyatt. He had tried to prevent Queen Mary from making England a vassal state of Spain through a marriage to Prince Philip, but Wyatt's uprising had ended in tragic failure—in some small part, Isabel knew, because of her. When Wyatt's soldiers reached the walls of London, her father's life had suddenly hung in the balance, and she had made the tortured decision to help close Ludgate against the rebels. Queen Mary had crushed them, married Philip, and England then suffered through her harsh reign. Now the threat to England came from France, and this time Isabel was determined to do everything she could to halt that threat.

She was passing a small window at ground level when a sound reached her that made her stop. A low, guttural moan. The window, without glass, was not much bigger than her foot, and its iron bars were rusted. The foul stench that snaked through it, and the moans, more bestial than human, turned her stomach. A dungeon, she was sure. Captive men of Knox's army, in chains. She longed to crouch down and whisper some encouragement to the poor victims, but soldiers were tramping by all around her and she did not dare draw their suspicion.

A door opened beside her, forcing her to move back. A soldier stepped out, followed by D'Oysel, the commander, bullnecked but as short as Isabel. A wave of the prison stench rolled out with him. He was wiping his hands on a handkerchief. Isabel gave a little laugh. "Monsieur, you startled me." Her heart thudded. Had he seen her peering down at the dungeon in pity?

He made a slight bow, looking rather surprised himself. "Señora Valverde. Are you walking alone?"

"What safer place?" she said lightly. "The fact is, my husband has letters to write and I have learned not to disturb him."

He smiled. She saw that the handkerchief he was using to wipe his hands was smeared with blood. A rebel prisoner's blood. The threat of sickness rose up in her throat. She forced it down. "Monsieur, might I have a word with you?"

"Of course." He gave the soldier the bloodied handkerchief and a curt nod, at which the soldier saluted and walked away. "Forgive me, madam," D'Oysel said, "but I can give you only a moment. Our muster, as you see."

"That is my very question, monsieur." Feigning the alarm of a nervous civilian, she blurted, "What is it for? Do you expect an attack?"

"Not at all. Have no fear. A mere inspection."

"Oh, thank heaven for that. They terrify me, the rebels, I do admit. Such barbarians. Though I am sure that if they did attack, you are well equipped to repulse them. I only hope the disease that has felled so many of your soldiers has not left you undermanned. Have you sent to France for more troops?"

She could see the walls of his defenses rise. His businesslike smile said, *I cannot discuss that.* "Excuse me, madam," he said with a courteous bow, "I must see to the muster."

Isabel cursed herself for pushing too hard, too fast. "Excuse my foolishness, monsieur. It is only for my husband's sake. I long to see him home soon."

"Ah, now there I cannot share your sentiment, madam," he said pleasantly. "Your husband has been such a boon to us, I will be loath to see him go. I almost cannot do without him."

She didn't understand. "You mean, for his counsel? As a neutral observer?"

He laughed. "Neutral? Hardly. He was an enormous help when we marched out against the enemy. He cut a bloody swath of death through their ranks. Nobody leads a cavalry charge like Valverde."

She was so stunned, so furious, she barely noticed the soldiers she walked past. They were thick on the ground now, hurrying by her in packs. Her only thought was to find Carlos, demand an explanation. A cavalry charge! Her every footstep forged her dismay into white-hot anger. How *could* he? She banged a passing soldier's elbow and didn't even pause to acknowledge his apology as she hurried on. She had left Carlos writing to Quadra and hoped he was still there. The room was in a squat tower connected to an identical tower by an arched walkway, and as she approached it she saw him coming down the stairs. Halfway down he saw her and stopped.

She could not hold back her anger. "You fought for the *French?*"

He bolted down the last steps so fast, Isabel didn't have time to say another word before he grabbed her by the arm and hustled her into the arched stone passage beneath the walkway. Blocking the sun, the arch felt like a cave, but she could still see the hard look on his face, and dread crept over her.

"Why did you come to Scotland?"

"Carlos, you're hurting me. Let me go."

He tightened his hold. He almost shook her. "Why did you come?"

His cold fury frightened her. She winced at the pain of his grip. "I told you. To see you. I wanted—"

"No. You came to Edinburgh five days ago and met with the rebel leaders. Why?"

Her heart banged in her chest. *He knows.*

Seeing the pain in her face, he looked horrified that he was hurting her. He let her go. The sudden freedom made her stagger a step to get her balance.

"Please, Isabel, tell me I'm wrong. Tell me what I've heard is all wrong. That it was some other woman who met them."

Heard? How? She tried to think. It was hard to breathe. *Who betrayed me?* Sweat made her skin clammy. Only one thing was clear—she could not go on pretending. Her only hope was to trust him with the truth. She lifted her chin and mustered what steadiness she could. "If you heard that I brought Master Knox good cheer from the Queen of England, you heard aright. I was glad to do it. I would do it again."

He let out a sharp breath like he'd been punched in the stomach. "The *Queen?*"

There was nowhere to go but forward. She told him about Cecil's appeal for her help. About her mother taking her to see Elizabeth. About the Queen's wish to send money to the rebels in secret, and Isabel's offer to deliver it.

He stared at her, appalled. "You volunteered? *Madre de Dios.* What have you got yourself into?"

"A fight that must be fought. Carlos, we have to help Knox and his reformers. They have to win. Only they can keep the French from invading England."

"Knox and his—" He was scowling at her as though at a stranger. "You've been with them?"

"Yes. In Edinburgh, then in Stirling. That's where they're regrouping to—"

"You've been living among those men? In their camp?"

It sounded horrible, as though he thought her a harlot. She shivered at the revulsion in his eyes. "Carlos, you must listen to me—" But her words were drowned out by the tramping of soldiers along the walkway overhead, a din that echoed through the stone arch.

Carlos plowed a hand through his hair, shaking his head in shock. "I cannot . . . cannot believe you've done this. Lied to me—"

"You've got to understand, I *had* to—"

"Betrayed me. With the enemy!"

This was all wrong! *He* was wrong, talking like she was some traitorous slut. She had done nothing to be ashamed of. *He* had.

"It's *you* who's gone over to the enemy," she cried. "I just heard what a friend to the French you've become. You *fought* for them, for God's sake. Killed Knox's men for them! How *could* you?"

"How could *I?*"

"It's disgusting. Like you want the French to win."

"Of course I do."

She gaped at him. "How can you say that?"

"Because the King of Spain wants it. And our lives are in his keeping."

"Our lives are *not* in his keeping. Only our livelihood."

"It's the same thing!"

"It's not! You want that council seat, but we don't *need* it. We don't even need the *encomienda*. We have enough money. You could leave this wretched place today and—"

"Don't talk nonsense. Of course we need it. Our life is in Peru. And my son will grow up to be a gentleman, damn it, not a god-forsaken soldier. I'm helping here because the King of Spain wants a French win, not a Protestant Scotland, and *we are Spanish.*"

"*You* are Spanish. I am English."

He glowered at her. His next words were menacingly restrained. "You are my wife. We are the subjects of Spain. And you will do what I—"

He stopped as more soldiers jogged toward them on their way to the muster. Carlos pushed Isabel up against the arched wall to give the men room to jog past. Standing face-to-face with him, their bodies pressed close, she felt sickeningly disoriented. He was so brutal, so deaf to her words, when just hours ago he had made passionate love to her. She clung to that, the bond of their love. She *had* to make him understand. "Carlos, this is about more than us. Something bigger. England."

"Bah. A country is not flesh and blood."

"It is to me. You've never had a country. You've fought in so many. And always to destroy, never to build. You've never called a country home."

"Peru is home."

"No, Peru is your reward. Your pay. But no matter how much money you get, the Spaniards there will never accept you as one of them. They're obsessed with pedigree. You will always be beneath them. Can't you see that I'm fighting for the country that has *always* been mine? A country that *would* accept you?"

"Fighting? You don't know the meaning of the word. You're playing. Meddling. And it could ruin us."

He was *still* deaf to her pleas. She wanted to scream. How had this happened? How had he even found out? That thought shot a new fear through her, and the moment the soldiers had gone on she asked, "Who told you about me? Who knows?"

"A Scot. A friend of D'Oysel's spy. She came to warn me."

A woman? "My God, Carlos, she'll tell them about me." He might be furious at her, but he could not possibly want her arrested.

He shook his head. "I paid her to keep her mouth shut. Gave her enough to keep the spy quiet, too." He was looking at her as though seeing her clearly for the first time . . . and hating what he saw. It made her feel cold to her bones. "You haven't told me why you came *here*," he said. "Was it to spy for the rebels? For the Queen? Tell me." He almost snarled, "And don't dare lie to me again."

She could not find words. He wouldn't believe a denial, and she would not grovel to explain. *I did what I had to do*, she thought, but in her misery she knew that silence was her confession.

His eyes glittered with revulsion. "I see. You're on a mission. So last night was . . . more lies."

No! she wanted to cry, *I love you!* but his face was so hard. Her thoughts were a storm of confusion. "This is pointless," she said, struggling to think what to do next. She had to get away from here, that much was clear. The woman who had blabbed to Carlos could not be trusted not to tell the French commander. This place now held only danger for Isabel. She glanced at the massing soldiers. "Carlos, if the commander finds out about me, it will be bad for us both. I must get out. Right now."

"Sir, excuse me."

The voice startled them. A young soldier stood waiting. "Pardon, sir, but the commander asks if you will stand with the officers for the inspection."

Isabel could see Carlos pulling himself together. "Yes... in a moment. Wait over there," he said with a nod to the gravel path beyond the arch.

"Carlos," she whispered when the soldier was out of hearing, "come with me?"

"Don't you understand anything? This is my post. I have given my word."

Don't do this, she wanted to cry. She longed to reach out, touch his face, his arm—just a touch to tell him they were still connected, still man and wife, still *one.* But his face was a closed door. "Then," she said, a sharp pain at her heart, "we have no more to say. Go to your muster." She could not move him. And she could not tarry any longer. Tears scalded her eyes. *"Vaya con Dios,"* she whispered. She turned to go.

She gasped as he snatched a fistful of her dress at the back. He yanked her to him. "Going to report to the rebels?" His voice was a growl, kept low so the waiting soldier would not hear, but still tight with fury.

Humiliation at his manhandling brought her anger surging back. "You *told* me to go," she snapped. "Back to London."

"But that's not where you're going, is it?"

"I'll go where I want!"

His hand flew up so fast she could not have avoided the slap. He clenched his hand into a fist that hovered at her cheek. Her breath had stopped in shock. Carlos swallowed hard, then lowered his arm. Isabel sucked in air. They stared at each other, both knowing how near he had come to striking her. *Dear God,* she thought, *what's happened to us?*

Tears glinted in his eyes. It sent a sorrowful wave of love coursing through her. *His heart is breaking, just like mine.*

"Soldier, come here," he said, his voice raw. The man was back in a moment. "Escort this lady to Monsieur de la Salle's chamber, up there. Make sure she doesn't leave the room."

Isabel froze. "Carlos, no—"

"Quiet."

The young soldier looked puzzled. "You mean, keep her under guard, sir?"

"Are you deaf? Yes!"

"Your *wife?*"

Carlos slapped him. The soldier gasped, but said not a word. Isabel felt shaky, knowing that Carlos's rage was meant for her. He looked pale himself. Never before, she was sure, had he struck an inferior.

"Take her upstairs, I tell you, and hold her there. You hear me?"

"Yes, sir." The soldier grabbed Isabel's arm. "Come, madam."

"No! Wait—" He was pulling her up the stairs. She struggled to resist, but he was strong and dragged her up two steps.

"They'll know about me!" she cried in desperation to Carlos. "If you hold me here, they'll know! That will hurt *you.*"

"A marriage spat, I'll say." He turned to go.

This could not be happening! She was fighting the soldier, and Carlos was walking away!

"Carlos, wait! You *must* let me go! For Nicolas!"

He kept going, and said over his shoulder, his voice flat, "He's safe with your mother."

"He's not with her!"

He stopped. Then turned, frowning. "What?"

"He's not with my mother. And if I don't get back to London, I don't know what will happen to him."

He stared at her. "What are you talking about? If this is some new lie—"

"It's the truth." The soldier tugged her, and she dug her heels against the bottom of the next step. "Tell this man to let me go! I must talk to you. Alone."

"Let her go." Carlos was coming up the steps, taking them two at a time. When he reached Isabel he yanked her by the arm, taking her up to the room where they had spent the night. Over his shoulder he said to the soldier, "Go. Tell the commander I'm coming."

He shoved her into the room and slammed the door behind them. "Where is he? Where's Nicolas?"

She rubbed her arm, sore from his fingers. "At Whitehall Palace. With the Queen's ladies. Don't worry, they're talking good care of him. For now."

He gave a bitter bark of a laugh in sheer disbelief. "What fantasy is this? He's playing in a royal palace?"

"It's no fantasy. I brought him along when my mother took me to see the Queen." She remembered how Nico had seen horsemen of the royal guard riding into the courtyard and called out, *Papa!* She had to close her eyes for a moment. This was so hard.

"Why in God's name is he still there?"

"I offered to take the Queen's gold to the rebels, and—"

"You told me that. What's it got to do with Nicolas?"

"The Queen wasn't sure she could . . . trust me. Because of *you*. I'm the wife of a Spaniard, a Catholic. So, to be sure I would carry out the mission, she . . ." Suddenly, all the shame she had kept dammed up swept through her like a poison. She turned away, feeling faint. She could not look at Carlos.

"*Madre de Dios.* She kept him." He gripped Isabel's chin and wrenched her face back to him. "Look at me! She kept him, didn't she? He's a hostage."

She nodded.

He let go of her. "*You* did this. You've risked his life to—" He took a step back, as though from something vile. Never, ever had he looked at her that way. *Man and wife? Still one?* No, he had severed that bond. *Or did I?* a voice inside her wailed. They were as separate as strangers on a midnight street. She could not bear it. "Carlos, please—"

He grabbed her satchel from the floor. Threw it on the bed and wrenched it open. "Pack. You leave today. Now. You'll take Pedro. You will ride to London and get my son from the palace. You will take—"

A knock on the door. Carlos barked, "What!"

The young soldier poked his head in. "Excuse me, sir. The Queen Regent's chamberlain is below and asks—"

A portly man pushed the door open and stepped past the soldier. "I am Her Grace's chamberlain, Señor Valverde. Her Grace requests the pleasure of Señora Valverde's company."

Dread flooded Isabel. *They know! They all know! They're going to arrest me!* She looked at Carlos, and his clenched jaw told her he was horrified by the same thought.

The chamberlain added with grave dignity, "Would you kindly escort your wife, señor?"

Dear God, would they arrest Carlos too? Make him suffer for her sins? They shared a look, he tight-lipped with alarm, she feeling trapped. It was impossible to ignore the Queen Regent's summons. They followed the chamberlain down the stairs. Two soldiers waited to accompany them. Isabel almost recoiled. Guards to deliver her to prison? Carlos, too? Side by side she walked with him across the courtyard, the chamberlain leading the way, the guards behind them, the din of the mustering soldiers all around them. She wanted so much to feel Carlos take her hand to give her strength, but he marched on, eyes forward, his face as still and taut as if he were riding into battle. They reached the house appropriated for the Queen Regent and her entourage, and guards stood aside to let them enter. As she climbed the staircase to the Queen Regent's suite, fear so blanked Isabel's mind she saw nothing but the few feet ahead of her.

"Kindly wait here, Señor Valverde," the chamberlain said when they reached the antechamber to the Queen Regent's private rooms. "Señora, will you follow me?"

He opened the door. She followed, her legs feeling as spongy as if she were walking to her execution. The Queen Regent sat at a dressing table, flanked by two of her ladies who fussed at dressing her hair. She flicked her hand to dismiss them. Isabel dared to glance at the door. The chamberlain stood there, the door still open. Beyond it, Carlos stood rock still, his eyes on her. His struggle to appear calm was clear to her alone. He was too far away to hear. Or to help.

The Queen Regent turned to her. Her face had the pallid cast of chronic ill health, her eyes rheumy. "Thank you for this visit, señora."

Isabel curtsied, her legs as weak as willow saplings.

"Though I am sorry that it must be a short one," the Queen Regent went on. "I return to the castle today. I am not well, you see, and they can care for me better at the castle. So, sadly, I will not see you again—that is, assuming you intend your stay here to be brief. Or do you expect to remain long?"

She was almost too confused to speak. "Not long, Your Grace," she managed.

"Oh? When do you plan to depart?"

"In fact—" Her mouth was so dry she had to swallow to go on. "Today."

"Today! Gracious." She smiled. "Well, in that case I was wise to see you now. Tell me, will you journey to London?"

"To London . . . yes."

"And do you intend to break your journey with your relations near Berwick, as before? With Sir Christopher Grenville?"

Isabel's mind was spinning. They were not going to arrest her? It made her almost light-headed with relief. She glanced at Carlos. He had moved, but only to pace, for servants had come into the antechamber. He did not know that she was, apparently, out of danger.

"Señora?" the Queen Regent coaxed.

"Yes, pardon me, Your Grace. I will stop there, yes. At Yeavering." Her thoughts could not be further from this chitchat about her journey.

"In that case, might I ask a favor?"

She did not follow. "Your Grace?"

The Queen Regent nodded to her chamberlain. He went to a cupboard and returned with a package, a box-shaped object wrapped in silver satin and tied with a pretty bow of red lace.

"A christening gift. For the baby daughter of my friend, Anne, Lady Percy, the Countess of Northumberland. I am told that your relation, Sir Christopher, lives not far from their estate, and I hope you will entreat him to do me the honor of delivering my gift."

Isabel hesitated. It seemed an odd request. The woman had scores of servants to ride south with messages, so why not this gift? It took only a heartbeat to realize this request was about more than a baby's gift. What, exactly, she had no idea. But she was sure that friends of Marie de Guise—English friends in high places—could not be friends of England.

Again the Queen Regent prompted, "Señora? Can you do this favor?"

Isabel found her tongue. "Of course, Your Grace. You honor me with your trust."

The Queen Regent's smile had a touch of iron in it as she glanced at Carlos beyond the open door. "Ah well, you see, we so appreciate the company of your husband."

Her eyes locked on Isabel's, and Isabel felt a shudder to her very core. Elizabeth had Nicolas. Marie de Guise had Carlos. And both expected her loyalty to their cause.

She was with him again, going down the stairs of the Queen Regent's suite. She hardly knew how her legs were holding her up.

"That's all?" Carlos whispered tightly. "Just a gift?"

She was carrying it. It wasn't heavy, whatever it was. "Yes. Just this."

He shook his head as if to shake off his bewilderment, and with it all matters that were not essential. They left the building and walked in tense silence until Carlos was sure they were out of hearing of the Queen Regent's guards. He turned to Isabel. "Then do it. But don't stay long in Yeavering."

She hoped he would offer some word of kindness. Not forgiveness—she didn't expect that—but just a word to let her know that the rift between them might one day be bridged.

He didn't. "When you reach London, you will get my son from the palace. You will take him to your father's house and stay there, and when I come back I will take him home with me to Peru." He glanced at the soldiers across the courtyard lined up in their ranks. That was where he had to be. He gave Isabel a last, hard look. "And then, as you said, madam, you can go where you want."

PART THREE

Yeavering Hall

❧ 20 ❧

Out of the Storm

In the north of England people cherished the old ways. The hushed hills and dales of Northumberland, Durham, Cumberland, and York were remote from the clash and clamor of London, where volatile new ideas from the Continent, especially the German cities afire with Protestant zeal, arrived with every trading ship, heating a ferment of reform. That ferment did not reach the North, where the age-old rites and customs of the Roman Catholic religion were engrained in the country people's dawn-to-dusk working lives. Their local lords, too—the powerful families of Percy and Neville, whose ancestors had come from France five centuries ago with William the Conqueror—shared this bond with the old Church. Henry VIII's shocking break with Rome to create a new national church so he could wangle a divorce had wreaked a devastating change throughout the realm, and nowhere more than in the North, where his decree to break up the monasteries had thrown hundreds of thousands of acres of church-held lands onto the open market to be grabbed by the jumped-up new gentry.

Now, the young Queen Elizabeth's reformed Protestant religion had become the law of the land, and her Visitors, the authorized committee, had visited every nook of England to purge all churches of so-called idolatry. The people of Northumberland, Durham, Cumberland, and York had grudgingly obeyed, watching in mute shock as the Visitors' workmen had ransacked magnificent Durham Cathedral of its gorgeous rood screens and stained glass, its sacred paintings and alabaster saints, its engraved brasses and the bright, embroidered raiment of their priests. They obeyed, but felt bereft at losing these beauties and customs that had brought comfort to their days of grunting toil and brought meaning to their lives: the Jesus Masses that had been sung every Friday throughout the year, the great silver basins and crucifixes that had gleamed before the high altar, the candles that had burned continuously day and night, the tinkle of the sacring bell at all rites, from christenings to funerals. In every parish they remembered creeping to the cross on Good Friday, remembered the joys of saints' days and feast days, the quiet mysteries of holy wells and relics, and the robust pealing of the monasteries' bells ringing out across the dales to touch people's hearts in the upland hills and let them know that the monks, who were their sons and brothers, were praying for their souls. Northerners missed these things, and longed for their return.

Frances Thornleigh, coming north at Christmas, had seen inside the stripped shell of Durham Cathedral and felt revulsion at its desecration. She would never get used to heresy being the law of the land. Her strongest reason for coming to Northumberland to stay with her brother, Sir Christopher Grenville, had been to ensure that her baby, Katherine, would be properly baptized by a priest, for if the child should die without that sacrament her little soul would be condemned to drift for eternity in Limbo and never see the face of God. Catholic priests, however, had been made outlaws by the new regime. Most had capitulated to the new rules; many had gone into exile. But Frances knew that Christopher had given a few priests secret sanctuary on his manor estates. He had arranged the baptism soon after Frances arrived, a quick ceremony held privately in his library away from the eyes of the servants. Baby Katherine's soul was safe.

Afterward, Christopher told Frances that he had been displeased by her marriage and asked her not to mention her husband's name in his company. The war between the families—how she hated it! But he had made his request with urbane restraint, so she told herself to be grateful to him, and she was, for the baptism and for much more. It was her first visit to Yeavering Hall, his home, and she had found the place truly grand. Christopher had married well. The house was immense: three stone stories rising into the cold, blue Northumberland sky, with acres of pleasure grounds and gardens—though they huddled now under crusted snow—and views that swept up to the twin-peaked hill of Yeavering Bell and down to the frigid River Glen. Despite the home's magnificence, its chambers, tastefully decorated by Christopher's late wife—he was a widower—felt cozy and intimate. Especially the solar. This bright family room on the third floor where Frances sat now with Katherine was her favorite place, for she liked to know what was going on in the household, and while the solar's north windows overlooked the snow-swept Cheviot Hills, its south windows kept tabs on the domestic activities in the courtyard.

Still, she did not know *all* that was going on—that was her thought as she tugged her needle and thread through a silk cap she was sewing for Katherine and rocked the cradle with her foot. Lately she had begun to wonder how far her brother's passion to preserve the old religious ways had taken him. She had heard murmurings about secret musters among his scores of men-at-arms, and had seen neighboring gentlemen arrive for meetings with him behind closed doors. When she had asked him about it, Christopher said the musters were in preparation for a strike against a Scottish clan of cattle-thieving border raiders, while the meetings were gatherings for Christian fellowship. Frances believed none of that. The raiders did not merit such force, and the grim faces of the gentlemen traipsing in and out of Christopher's library were not suffused with Christian contentment. And then there was the surprise visit last week from the Earl of Northumberland, Thomas Percy. Christopher was well respected in the shire, so dealings with the earl were nothing extraordinary, but for his lordship to arrive practically alone, with no retinue and only five men-at-arms, and not even stay to the supper that Frances had ordered in a flurry of instructions to the kitchen, was odd, to say the least. It made her quite anxious. In spirit she was with her brother in his deep love of the old Church, but the laws of Queen Elizabeth demanded a compliance that Frances knew was wise to obey.

Katherine sneezed. Then sneezed again, so violently it stopped her breath. Frances dropped her sewing in alarm and scooped the baby out of the cradle. Katherine sucked in a breath, and Frances hugged the little body in relief. "There, there, sweet pea," she cooed.

A kitten, one of five newborns barely a week old, mewed from their basket beside the hearth. Frances looked at the gray balls of downy fur nuzzling their mother's side for milk, and she felt a tug of indecision. She had promised Christopher that she would dispose of the kittens, for his nose got stuffy and his throat scratchy whenever a cat was nearby. But the kittens fascinated baby Katherine, so Frances had kept the basket with the mother cat and her brood in a nook beside the hearth. She would have to find a home for them soon, though. Perhaps the wife of the household marshal would take them. In her sizable house she would need mousers.

Sleet lashed the north windows. Frances looked out at the barren hills. A storm had raged down from Scotland for three days, and wind moaned in the casements as though making an anguished escape from the border's bleak wastes. It was five in the afternoon, the winter daylight beginning to fade toward frigid night, and Frances felt grateful for the warmth and comfort of Christopher's home. The glow from the hearth's blazing oak logs rippled over her baby's face, the tiny eyelids trembling on the brink of slumber, and in her daughter's features Frances, as always, saw Adam. How she missed him. This unholy war in Scotland still kept him away, doing she knew not what. That barbarous country was so near, a curlew on the wing could cross the border by nightfall, yet her husband seemed a world away. And in worsening danger, too, she feared, for the war had intensified. News had come that Queen Elizabeth had made an open pact with the Scottish rebels and mustered an army ten thousand strong to join them in fighting the French. They were marching north at that moment under the command of Lord Grey. They would soon tramp through this very shire.

It made Frances shudder. Which side was she on? The rebels were heretics. In their brutal sweep through Scotland they had desecrated churches from Perth to St. Andrews to Glasgow, killing priests and looting monasteries. The French had beaten them back to Stirling, but now that an English army was on its way to join them the rebels might take the country, force out the French, and press every Scot into heresy. That would be grotesque—an entire country, right on England's border, spitting at God.

But beyond the hills outside her window lay the North Sea, and on it Adam aboard his ship. She *had* to hope for an English victory, for his sake. A victory for the heretic Queen—that thought turned her stomach, but she knew she must swallow her aversion to Elizabeth. Men's fortunes were made by the Queen's friendship. Or rather, her lust for handsome young adventurers. Men like Adam. Frances knew all about the shameless interest Elizabeth had shown in Adam, and she despised the woman for it. But that was in the past, behind them now. He was married, and a father, and Frances was not such a fool as to risk his chance of advancement by visibly holding a grudge.

There was no choice, really. She knew in her heart that she had made her choice the day she first saw Adam and fell desperately in love. She would be loyal to him, even if it took her to the gates of hell. Her life was one with his, so his cause was hers. And his cause was the Queen's.

She hugged her baby closer and told herself not to pine. She would write to him, and she wanted no melancholy to creep into the letter. She settled Katherine in the cradle and sat down at the desk and arranged paper and pen and ink. She began,

My Dear Husband,

Then hesitated. What to say? God only knew when, or even if, the letter would reach him. She could only send it to the Admiralty in London and hope. What if—God forbid—he had been killed?

No, she would not allow that demon thought to terrify her. He will survive, she told herself, and he will come back. For Katherine, if not for me. *And when he does, I will somehow make him love me.* She dipped her quill in the ink and began again on a fresh sheet.

Dearest Adam,

She told him how comfortable she was at Yeavering, and how busy, for her brother had encouraged her to oversee the household almost as though she were mistress of the manor. Christopher had been without a wife for over a year and Frances was proud to call herself a very capable manager. She told Adam what a joy Katherine was, and how she was thriving and growing. Told him that she prayed daily that God would keep him unhurt and send him home soon. Told him how dear he was to her, blushing as she wrote it, adding that he must allow her to say such things because today was Saint Valentine's Day, when the church, in its infinite wisdom, encouraged the sending of affectionate letters to a beloved.

She heard a shout outside. She moved to the south windows and peered down. The film of sleet on the glass made the shapes in the courtyard look wavy and indistinct. Four or five servants surrounded two figures, a young man and a woman, who stood bundled in cloaks beside a horse. The couple had apparently just come in, for the gates were still wide open, causing sleet-stiff wind to gust across the courtyard and the servants to hunch their shoulders against it. Despite the distorted glass, Frances could see the lowered heads of the couple and their shaggy horse, too, as though all three were bowed with fatigue, as well they must be, she thought, traveling in this foul weather. Were they tramps? Parkins, the master butler, was waving an arm toward the outside world as if interrogating them on where they had sprung from. But why was no one moving? The servants seemed dumbstruck.

She would have to deal with this herself. The tramps must be given shelter for the night, at least, in the stables or one of the outbuildings. The bakehouse would be warm. She was about to go down and give these orders when she saw the woman beside the horse look up at the windows. Frances gasped. Though the face was a blur, she knew so well that tilt of the head.

She ran down the stairs, not even stopping to grab a cloak as she hurried past two chambermaids on their knees scrubbing the foyer floor. She dashed out the front door, calling, "Isabel!"

Her words were lost in the wind, a frigid blast that stung her face. The young man beside the horse, hugging himself against the cold, saw her coming and said something to Isabel and she turned.

Frances was shocked by the look of her. White-faced with cold, her lips almost blue, she was shivering horribly. Her cloak was plastered to her body, and ice was clumped on strands of hair that had escaped her sodden hood. She blinked at Frances as though trying to focus, and when she tried to speak her words were slurred. "Fra—? Is it—you?"

"Oh, Isabel, my dear! Where have you—? Come inside, out of this wind!"

"I—we—"

"Don't talk, dear. Come inside this moment."

Isabel slumped against the horse's side, looking too weak to take another step.

"*Señora,*" the young man pleaded, "*debemos parar aquí. Está enferma.*"

Foreign words. Frances didn't understand any of it. "Isabel, we must get you inside." She turned to the butler's fellows. "You men, take her arm. Help her in!"

But Isabel did not budge. "Give . . ." Her teeth chattered, slurring her words more. "Give . . . Pedro . . . drink, and . . ." Her lips kept moving, but making no sound, like she was a lost soul in Bedlam. Her eyelids trembled. Her eyes rolled up in their sockets. She collapsed.

"Isabel!" Frances cried.

Two serving men caught her. "Carry her inside!" Frances ordered them. One lifted Isabel in his arms. "Gently!" She grabbed the foreign young man's arm. "Dear God, what has happened to bring her through this storm?"

He gaped at her, shivering. Did he not understand English?

"Parkins," she said, "fetch Signor Carelli." The Italian had been there for days, visiting Christopher on business, and must know some Spanish. "And send someone for Doctor Harcourt." She hurried after the servant who was carrying Isabel, and called over her shoulder to Parkins, "And get word to my brother at the Palmers'!"

Frances and Christopher stood on either side of the bed, silently looking down at Isabel's still form. Frances felt shaken by Isabel's condition, especially after hearing that the doctor was not available, had gone to Bamburgh. She was relieved to have her brother near. He had been at the neighbor's two miles away, discussing with Henry Palmer their defenses against the Scottish border raiders, when the footman had brought the news about Isabel. He had left immediately, but the treacherously slick roads in the dusk had slowed him, and he'd got home just fifteen minutes ago. His fair hair was still damp with melted ice.

He regarded Isabel with somber interest, for it was the first time he had seen her. Frances had told him how she had regained consciousness soon after fainting in the courtyard, but then had lapsed into listless, blank-eyed shivering through all the ministrations of the women servants. They had peeled off her sodden clothes, dried her, dressed her in a clean nightdress, and settled her gently in the bed. Frances had been dismayed to find that Isabel's skin was hot to the touch, and perspiration slicked her forehead. She was suffering not just from the cold, but from fever! Her fingers and toes, though, were icy, and frighteningly white.

First things first, Frances had told herself, taking charge, for she had heard of frostbite killing the body's extremities. In severe cases, fingers could turn black and drop off. When she saw one of the servants rubbing Isabel's fingers to warm them, she ordered her to stop, and when a girl brought in two pig's bladders of scalding water to lay at Isabel's feet, Frances pushed her away. Heat and friction were the enemy, she told the wondering servants. Frostbitten flesh had to be slowly and gradually brought back to normal.

She made the women follow her precise instructions. They folded Isabel's arms over her chest and tucked her hands into her armpits, and they swaddled her feet in soft, thick wool cloths. Then they covered her with a quilted blanket, tucking it up to her chin, while others laid a fire in the grate. But through this flurry of activity Isabel had been near delirium with fever, and had soon slipped into unconsciousness. Frances had sat on the side of the bed, watching over her.

Now night had fallen, shrouding the hills and river around Yeavering Hall, and still Isabel had not opened her eyes. She looked so pale, her lips drained of blood, her body jerking in fevered shudders. Frances was beyond fearing that she might lose a finger or toe—she now feared for Isabel's very life.

"One horse, you say?" Christopher asked. "They rode it together?"

He kept his voice low, as though to keep from waking Isabel. If only we could, Frances thought.

"The boy's horse was stolen at the last inn they stopped at," she said. She had gotten this information from Isabel's servant, for that's who he was, the Indian lad she had brought from Peru. He had told of their ordeal as he gulped warmed wine in the kitchen, his Spanish translated by the Italian houseguest. "That was last night," Frances went on. "They set out this morning on the boy's horse—though why Isabel would push on in this storm, I know not."

"Did you ask him?"

"He just kept saying over and over that she wanted to get to London."

Christopher frowned in sympathy. "Not in this weather. And not in her weakened state."

Frances found a shred of hope in his response, for he had not said *She'll die.* "According to the boy, the Cawthorpe bridge had collapsed, and as they forded the stream the horse went lame, so they walked the last four miles. Imagine. Walked!"

"Madness."

Frances's fears surged back. She could not bear to lose her

sister-in-law. Isabel had stood up for her against Adam's parents. And during the awful childbirth she had saved Frances's life and her baby's life, of that she had no doubt. She owed Isabel so much.

"So," Christopher said gravely, studying the pale face, "another Thornleigh."

Frances heard the new edge in his voice. The old feud. She knew it was up to her to protect Isabel. "She is one of us, Christopher. I assure you."

He looked at her, an eyebrow raised in skepticism. "With those parents?"

"She is not like them. Truly, she is a loyal Catholic. In London she joined me at mass in the Spanish ambassador's chapel. And her husband is with the French in Scotland as a military adviser, helping them."

"He's a Spaniard, you said?"

"Yes, and the Spanish are the most pious people on earth. Isabel has come from visiting him in Edinburgh at the Leith garrison. Believe me, she is a faithful daughter of the Church."

Christopher considered this gravely. He gave his sister a slight smile. "Then I bow to your superior judgment." She felt the hidden barb—weeks ago he had made his opinion clear that she had shown *no* judgment in marrying Adam. And yet, as he looked down at Isabel lying so still, pale as an alabaster saint, he murmured with obvious sincerity, "She's actually quite lovely, isn't she?"

A twitch tugged Isabel's brow, some fevered nightmare clawing at her in the depths of her unconsciousness. Sweat glistened on her face. Desperate to help, Frances dipped the linen cloth she'd been using into the basin of water and laid it on Isabel's brow to cool her. Her skin was alarmingly hot.

"Yes, do what you can for her," Christopher said with an earnestness that touched Frances. "We must not lose her."

Morning came. Frances sat slumped in the chair by the bed, bone-weary from her sleepless vigil, and from her fears. All night, Isabel had not moved.

Frances got up, rubbing her stiff neck, and pulled open the

heavy damask curtains. The wind had died, and a pale sun struggled past the edge of the heavy, massed clouds that were slowly departing, leaving the field like a mighty enemy whose power is spent. The storm was over. Frances glanced back at the still figure in the bed. Isabel's storm was still upon her.

Children's laughter startled her. Then the scuffle of small feet scampering by outside the chamber. She hurried to the door and opened it to see a trio of children running past—her niece and nephew and their playmate, the chamberlain's daughter.

"Hush, there!" she whispered. "Keep your voices down!"

The elder girl slowed. "Beg pardon, Aunt Frances, it's the mummers! They've just come! Master Horner says we may watch them get ready. It's to be Saint George and Beelzebub!" They all giggled and ran on.

Foolishness, Frances thought, closing the door. The arrival of the traveling actors' troupe had already set the servants to chattering. Nan, who had brought Frances her breakfast of bread and a slice of cold beef a half hour ago, had whispered excitedly about it even as Isabel lay in the depths of fever. It shook Frances that the life of the household could go on so blithely when Isabel lay near death.

The listless day dragged on. Downstairs in the great hall the actors were setting up a makeshift stage for their nonsense, and laughter and snatches of drumming and piping snaked up to the bedchamber, setting Frances's teeth on edge.

Dusk settled over Yeavering Hall. Hour after hour, she watched Isabel's face for any sign that her spirit was returning, but her skin had become horribly pallid, the fever sweat giving a waxen sheen, and Frances despaired.

Night fell. Isabel lay as still as death.

❧ 21 ❧

The Secret Gift

"Nico!" Isabel cried. Her eyes sprang open. The sunlight hurt. She squinted to fend off the glare. Each blink felt like sand grating under her eyelids. Her throat felt shredded by a razor. Her head throbbed. Her stomach roiled. She struggled to take in the unfamiliar chamber. Wainscoted walls of gleaming oak. A ceiling painted in rosy hues. The perfumed bed she lay in. She felt a lurch of panic. *Where am I?*

"God be thanked," a man said.

She jerked her head on the pillow to find him. It made the room spin. He sat in a chair by her bed. He was leaning toward her, a hopeful smile on his face.

"Good morning," he said.

"Who—" It was pain to speak, her throat was so parched. Her mouth felt caked with dirt. She tried again. "Where—"

"Here, have a little water." He reached for the goblet on the table beside her. "Can you raise your head?"

She did, and it sent hammers pounding in her skull. The cool water was heaven on her dry lips and parched throat. She gulped it down.

"Not too fast," the man said with a gentle laugh.

Isabel sank back on the pillow, exhausted from her effort, her stomach still rocky.

"You see?" he said. "It's wise to go slow."

"Yes. Thank you." Who *was* he? His steady blue eyes on her
made her uneasy. To cover herself she tried to tug the blanket up
to her shoulders, but her arm was so weak that her hand trembled.
She looked away, disoriented at feeling helpless, confused.

"Do pardon me," he said gently. "It must be awful to wake up
to a strange face in a strange house. But it was my turn to watch
you. Frances was needed in the dairy house. A milkmaid cut herself, and Frances is clever with salves."

Frances! It came to her in a rush. The freezing walk in wind-
driven sleet. Fingers and toes numb, legs aching, brain fogged
with fever. Stumbling through the gates of Yeavering Hall to
strange faces calling questions. Pedro shivering—

"Pedro! Where—"

"Your Indian boy is fine, don't worry. He was up and about the
next day, none the worse for wear. He's busy in the stable, doctor-
ing your lame horse. Even slept with the animal."

"Next day? I've been here . . . for two days?"

"Three, as of this morning." He nodded to the bright sunshine
streaming through the windows. "Pardon me again, I am doing a
poor job of introducing myself. I am—"

"I know." His resemblance to Frances was unmistakable. This
had to be Sir Christopher Grenville, head of the house of Grenville
in fact if not in law, since his dead brother's sons were underage.
Horrible images rushed in of how that other Grenville had tortured
her mother and chained up her father . . . how her mother had
killed the brute.

He frowned in concern at the change in her. "What is it? Pain?"

She knew not how to answer.

"Ah," he said, nodding sadly. "You feel . . . how shall I put it . . .
unease at being my guest?"

Unease? Paltry word! Not only because of him; he seemed all
kindness. But civil words failed her as the terrible memory of
Leith suddenly rushed back. Carlos's brutal words. His unforgiving glare as she had ridden out of the garrison with Pedro. She
turned her face away from Grenville, overcome with anguish.
Thoughts of the last days in Scotland tumbled through her mind.

She had ridden straight to Stirling Castle, her heart breaking, and had given Knox all the information she had noted about the French guns and fortifications and troop strength. She had said nothing about the Queen Regent's gift. No need to. On the way, burning with suspicion, she had opened the box and found that her suspicions were wrong about a dark connection between the Queen Regent and northern Englishmen: the gift was a silver rattle, a christening gift for Lady Percy's baby, exactly as the Queen Regent had said. Nothing incriminating—that had been her overwrought imagination. She left Stirling wanting only to get to London, get Nicolas, and end this nightmare. She had set out just as the storm clouds gathered over her head. By the time she and Pedro had crossed the border, the storm was so bad she had made for the shelter of Yeavering.

Nicolas. "I must go . . ." She pushed off the blanket and threw her legs over the edge of the bed. The sudden move rucked her nightdress up above her knees, but there was no time for modesty. There was only her driving need to get to her son. She pushed herself out of bed.

"What?" Grenville cried. He rose and grabbed her arm to steady her, for the moment her feet touched the floor her legs had begun to give way.

"Let me go. I must get my son!"

"Madam, you are not well. Please, let me—"

"No . . ." But she was dizzy. And short of breath. The room wavered. She collapsed in his arms.

He lifted her and laid her back in the bed, his hands sliding under her bare legs to settle her. Looking embarrassed at his impropriety, he pulled the blanket up to cover her to her shoulders, and tried to lighten the moment with a jest. "Awaking to my rough face has frightened you, I dare say. But do not let it force you to flee."

Not rough at all, was her wandering thought. For weeks she had been among soldiers, unwashed men with bristled chins and scabs and scars. Grenville was as smooth-faced as a courtier. He even smelled like one, a faint scent of lemon thyme rising from the fresh linen shirt beneath his doublet of russet satin.

Isabel's head was pounding, her nerves were frayed, her stomach threatened to heave, and she felt like a fool. "Pardon me, sir. You are right, I will rest first. And please accept my thanks, for I believe your care these past days has saved my life."

"Oh, I did nothing but assist Frances, I assure you. She did it all. Nursed you, and wept like a mother when we thought we were losing you." Looking down at her, his jesting smile now gone, he said somberly, "We have you back, thanks be to God. It is a sign, I dare to think, that He would like us to be friends. For my sister's sake, and for mine, will you join me in putting past griefs behind us? My brother, I am ashamed to say, was a vicious man. I beg you not to judge all our family by his example."

She felt his sincerity, and it moved her. Forgive and forget? Why not? Why should the two of them continue a feud they had taken no part in?

She thought of Carlos, and misery swamped her again, all but crushing her spirit. Could he ever forgive and forget? Could *she?* It was impossible to forget his merciless words. *"I will take Nicolas home with me to Peru. And you may go where you want."* Tears stung the back of her throat. She beat them back, anger spiking her misery, for she refused to regret what she had done. It was necessary— for England's safety, her parents' safety. How could Carlos not see that?

"Forgive me," Grenville said, "I should not have brought up such a painful subject."

"No, no, it is not you. You are most kind, sir. Believe me, I am most grateful for your friendship."

"Good. And please, do let me know if there is anything at all I can do for you."

She thought of the package in her saddlebag. "Might I further entreat your kindness to deliver a gift?" She wanted to get this task over with. Every thought of Leith was painful. She wanted it behind her. "It is for the Countess of Northumberland, for her baby. I believe the earl's home is not far from you."

He was clearly taken aback. "You are acquainted with Lady Percy?"

"Not I, sir. I am only the messenger. I have come from Leith, where the Queen Regent did me the honor of entrusting this small task to me. The gift is hers. I understand the two ladies are long-time friends."

The change in him was astonishing. His look of gentle amiability vanished and in its place was intense curiosity. His face, his body, his every muscle fell into a new alignment. It put Isabel in mind of a hunting dog excited at sniffing the prey and pointing with nose and tail. She felt as though Grenville had lifted a mask and she was seeing the real man.

"Where is it?" he said.

"In my saddlebag. Or it was. Pedro will know and—"

"I'll get it myself." His eyes glittered with suppressed excitement. "Madam, you are more welcome than I can say, for you have brought more joy than you can know."

Something cold slid down her backbone. All this for a rattle? She said carefully, "A christening is, indeed, a joyful thing."

He grinned as though delighted at her being his accomplice. In what, she had no idea, but felt that it could only be bad.

The players settled in at Yeavering Hall. The whole household assembled in the great hall for the nightly performances that brightened their spirits in these dead days of winter. The mummery, as the people called the age-old plays, took the form of a different tale every evening, though each was a variation of a virtuous hero vanquishing evil. Christopher Grenville presided for the first night's performance, then rode the next day to Kirknewton for the assizes where he was a justice of the peace, leaving Frances to represent him in the great hall.

Isabel still felt too weak to attend the play. Frances sat by her bed during the day and read to her and chatted, though Isabel sensed that something was troubling her. Did she, too, wonder about her brother? Frances never said, and Isabel could think of no way to bring it up, so they kept their talk to household matters, mutually complicit in not mentioning their misgivings about Grenville. Frances did, however, tell her some wonderful news. Queen Elizabeth had mustered an army of ten thousand foot soldiers and seven hundred horsemen and they were marching into

Scotland at that very moment. That had cheered Isabel greatly. *May it save Knox and his men.*

But she suffered during these days. Her body was healing, but not the wound in her heart. Nights were the hardest. In the daylight she had Frances for company, but in the darkness, all alone, she was tormented by nightmares. Carlos throwing her out of Leith, his sword raised against her. Carlos carrying Nicolas away to a ship. Nico crying and squirming, reaching out to get back to her. She would wake up weeping, wildly confused, and feeling so bereft, so empty, she felt half-dead.

On the morning after Grenville went to the assizes she made herself get out of bed and get dressed, shaky though she was. She longed to set out for London right now and reclaim Nicolas, but knew that she was too weak yet to sit a horse. A day or two more, then she would go. She climbed the stairs to the third floor, and in the solar she found Frances sewing while rocking Katherine's cradle with her foot.

"You're up!" Frances exclaimed in delight.

"A little shaky, but on my feet at last." She took Frances by the hand. "Thank you so much for all your tender care."

Frances squeezed her hand in return. "Without you, my dear, I would not be here to care for anyone."

"Ah, look at my pretty niece." Isabel took a ball of scarlet yarn from Frances's sewing basket and dangled it above the cradle. The baby gazed at it in fascination and tried to touch it with her tiny fist. Isabel smiled and thought ahead to her own baby's birth. It would be August, high summer, fields of green, flower-scented breezes. But where would she be? Where would Carlos *allow* her to be? Would he really take Nicolas to Peru without her? Would her new baby grow up fatherless? Such thoughts were torture. The future was a fog, what lay ahead unknowable. All she could do was get to London, get Nicolas, and pray that Carlos would come to his senses. She forced her mind back to the here and now. "She is a beautiful babe, Frances."

Frances smiled with pride, and patted the chair next to her. "Sit you down and take your rest. You are not yet strong."

They spent the day sewing baby clothes for Katherine, reading, chatting, enjoying the antics of the gray kittens, soft as dandelion fluff, who tumbled on the floor with the yarn until they got quite tangled in it. Isabel gazed out at the snowy hills that bordered Scotland and remembered what Knox had said to her, that the idle life of a lady was not for her: *"You are meant to be in action. God wishes it. It is your destiny."* Extraordinary, his tone, like some prophet. Well, she had done all she could. The rebels' fate—and England's—now lay in the hands of others. She did not dare discuss the war with Frances, for she wondered about her sister-in-law's divided loyalties. She knew how much Frances loved Adam, and was sure that she feared for his safety, but Frances was also a devout Catholic, and Grenville's sister. If Grenville was involved in some way with the Queen Regent, did Frances know that? Was she encouraging it?

But *was* Grenville involved? And if so, how? Isabel had nothing to go on except his extreme reaction, his evident excitement, when she had told him of the Queen Regent's gift for Lady Percy. Which was nothing, really.

That night, she could not sleep. She longed to be on her way to London. With Nicolas safe in her arms, and both of them back in her parents' house, she would find the strength to take stock, decide what to do next. Here she felt so alone. Frances was a good friend, and Grenville, despite Isabel's vague suspicions, was kindness itself. She was grateful for everything they had done, but they were not her family. They could not fill the hollowness in her heart. She had to get home.

Staring at the moon through her window, she heard the creak of wagon wheels. Many wagon wheels. She got up and went to see. Her room overlooked the rear of the stables and the armory. The wagons stopped, five of them ranged in a line. A man came out of the armory with a torch, and Isabel watched as at least a dozen men unloaded crates. Who would be making deliveries at this late hour? The crates were sealed, but a drayman who went to unload the second wagon slid the top off the first crate, perhaps to verify its contents, and Isabel could plainly see moonlight glinting off the steel barrels of arquebusses and muskets. So, a delivery of weapons.

Every large landowner kept an armory stocked for his tenants to defend the manor in a crisis, but the number of guns being unloaded seemed astonishing. If each crate held this many, there must be hundreds. Another drayman flipped back the canvas cover of his wagon and she saw that it was filled with bundled spears and staves, enough to equip a substantial company of fighters. Another wagon was piled with bows and sheaves of arrows, thousands of arrows. The man with the torch looked up at her window, and Isabel quickly stepped back, out of view. But from the shadows she watched as the men uncovered the final wagon. Her breath caught at what it held. Three bronze light cannons: a falconet and two demi-culverins.

This was no defensive preparation for tenants. This was the groundwork for war.

She tried to impose order on her racing thoughts. Perhaps Grenville was organizing forces to join Queen Elizabeth's army marching to Scotland. That would be perfectly legitimate, a patriotic duty of which he could be proud. But why, then, make no mention of it? Why this secretive, middle-of-the-night activity? No, he was stockpiling weapons for some other purpose. The Queen's troops would be passing through Northumberland about now. Was he planning to attack them? It seemed too astonishing. Yet she felt sure there was some dangerous connection between Grenville, the Queen Regent, and the powerful Percy family.

Her thoughts flew back to London and St. Paul's that day Adam had rescued her from the assault. In telling her about the crisis in Scotland he had said that Elizabeth had dismissed Thomas Percy, Earl of Northumberland, as Warden of the East and Middle Marches, which was basically the whole Scottish frontier. "He's a known Catholic," Adam had said, "and she can't trust him if it comes to choosing sides." Had the earl chosen sides now, with the backing of the Queen Regent? Was Christopher Grenville his right-hand man? Were these men planning—the deadly word hovered in her mind: *treason?*

Slow down, she told herself. Her fertile imagination might be linking things that had no link. The Percy family were Grenville's near neighbors, and through him the Queen Regent was sending her friend a gift—all innocent enough. If there was a darker link to be found, she had to know more.

She whirled on a robe and went barefoot down the passageway. Though unfamiliar with the house, she did not have far to go. Frances's bedchamber was next to hers. She tiptoed in and shook her sister-in-law by the shoulder to wake her.

"What is it?" Frances cried in alarm. She looked to the cradle at the far side of the bed. "Is it Katherine?"

"No, the baby's fine," Isabel assured her. "Frances, something's going on outside. Something I don't understand." She explained about the weapons.

Frances looked astonished. "Really?" she said, sitting up. "Are you sure?"

"Yes, I saw. What do you think your brother means by it?"

Frances was about to speak, then seemed to catch herself. A mask of wariness hardened her features. "I believe there is a simple explanation. Christopher and the other local gentry are banding together to fight the Scottish reivers."

Isabel was skeptical. "All those arms to go after mere cattle raiders?"

"The brutes are a constant threat. Burning and looting and murdering throughout the borderlands. Christopher is organizing a counterattack. I have heard him say he intends to deal with the menace once and for all."

"With cannons?"

Frances shrugged.

"Come, you know this is not logical," Isabel said. "The government has deputies posted at garrisons along the border. It is their job to deal with the Scottish outlaws." Though she did not say it, they both knew that the government would consider any Englishman who took such matters into his own hands to be equally an outlaw. So what could such a hoard of weapons be for except a purpose *beyond* the Queen's laws? A queen that many northerners considered illegitimate, and a heretic. A queen that France wanted to supplant with their own queen. "Frances," she said, "what do you *really* think is happening?"

Frances looked away. Her tone was frosty. "I do not think we should discuss this."

Isabel felt a shiver of caution. Frances knew what her brother was up to and meant to keep it secret. It grieved her to be in conflict with Frances; she was Adam's wife. But Grenville was her brother, and the Grenville family had always been devoutly Catholic. The tender ties of the heart could not match the iron bonds of blood and faith.

She said a dispirited good night. The next day she kept to her bed. Frances did not visit her. Isabel was not at all sure she had interpreted Grenville's actions aright, but she was burning to know—and intended to find out. She waited all day in an agony of impatience. That evening, while the household sat at supper in the great hall, she left her room and went in search of answers. She did not know the house at all, and the rooms she looked into held nothing beyond the trappings of domestic life. A clerk's messy office. A pantry where dried herbs hung. A children's nursery. Clothes cupboards. A games room.

Then she opened a door on the ground floor and paused. Grenville's library. No one was there. She glanced back down the way to the hall where the diners' laughter and chatter and clacking of knives on trenchers carried on. She went in and closed the door, instantly muffling the household sounds. She looked around at the two walls of books. Many had spines of beautifully tooled leather of green and burgundy, their titles stamped in gold. She thought of her mother, always a bookworm, getting happily lost in perusing these shelves. Or perhaps not; though books were neutral, Mother might consider these tainted by their Grenville home. The elegance of the room did not stop at the books. A gorgeous tapestry adorned a third wall. The fourth had three windows that looked out on the courtyard, and their colorful stained glass was worked with the heraldry of the house of Grenville. Candles burned in a hanging brass candelabra, burnishing the room with a soft glow, and herbs gave off their sweet scent from the fresh floor rushes. There was a solidly built oak desk where papers were spread. A globe stood on a waist-high pedestal. A table held maps.

Isabel went to the desk. She had no idea what she was looking for. Anything that would give her a clue to Grenville's connection to the Queen Regent, Marie de Guise—whatever that might look like. She gingerly lifted papers and scanned them. A letter from a lawyer about Grenville's son's school. A bill from a wine merchant. A deed to a manor house in York. A list of accused men appearing at the Kirknewton assizes. Not a single thing connected with Scotland. She opened a drawer. Quills, a pot of ink, a pen knife, a letter opener that was a slender blade of ivory, a few loose farthings that clinked as she closed the drawer again. She opened a lower drawer. There it was—the silver rattle. The satin wrapping and lace bow were gone. This gift was staying with Grenville, at least for the time being.

She lifted the rattle out. It was superbly crafted with filigree, the work of a master silversmith. She held it by the handle and shook the bulb, and heard the predictable *whooshing* sound of tiny pebbles. She held it up to the light under the candelabra and examined it for an inscription. There was none. That seemed odd. A gift from one aristocratic lady to another should carry some floridly etched words, perhaps a biblical quote, a date—a name, at the very least. This was no gift, at least not for an innocent christening. It had some other purpose. Isabel tried to loosen the bulb by unscrewing it. It would not budge. She turned it over and looked at the base of the handle. Embedded in the end hole was a semi-precious stone of green malachite. She got out the letter opener and tried to pry the stone loose. The slender ivory tip did not seem strong enough to dislodge it, and she was looking around for something else to use, when the malachite stone dropped out. It fell to the floor with a faint clatter. Isabel dug her baby finger into the handle, the only finger small enough. She felt something—paper—and eased it out. It was a scroll no longer than her forefinger. Her heart beat faster as she unfurled it. Words. Lines of words. But in some language that made no sense. It was gibberish.

Pins and needles crawled over her skin as she realized—the message was in cipher. Only the person it was meant for could decipher it. Grenville. The scenario she had feared now loomed fully formed in her mind. Grenville was planning armed insurrection with the backing of the Queen Regent, and the mighty Earl of

Northumberland was the power behind it. The timing was ideal, she realized. With the Queen's commanders marching her troops north to Scotland, and her treasury too depleted to hire more, her defenses at home were weak. Isabel's thoughts lurched ahead. When were these traitors preparing to strike?

A *clunk* startled her. It came from the passage outside the door. Quickly, she rolled up the paper, her fingers trembling. Footsteps sounded, coming this way. She slid the paper back up into the hollow handle. She was jamming the rattle back into the drawer when she realized—the malachite! She dropped to her knees and groped in the floor rushes, searching for the green stone. She found it! The door opened. She stood.

Grenville walked in. He stopped, startled to see her.

"Sir, we didn't expect your return tonight." She held the rattle behind her back, trying to jam the stone into the hole.

"How wonderful to see you restored to health," he said, coming to her with a smile. "The bloom is back in your cheeks. And, if I may say, it puts the rose's bloom to shame."

They were standing face-to-face, and he tilted his head slightly to look behind her back. His smile vanished. "Have you found what you were looking for?"

❧ 22 ❧

Captives

The alarm bell clanged in the courtyard, a warning loud and frantic. Listening from the stable, Carlos felt a stab of dread. *Isabel. The French have caught her.*

He tried to tell himself that no, the alarm couldn't be about her. *It's been three weeks. She'll be near London by now, beyond their reach.* He went back to brushing his horse. It was late and he was alone in the stall with Noche, working under the lantern hooked on a post. Usually, brushing the horse calmed him, but not tonight. Three alarms in the last four days. No attack, though—just jittery Frenchmen jumping at the sound of the bell. With an English army on its way, every man in the garrison was as tense as a taut bowstring. Carlos, too. He could live with the prospect of battle. It was his lying wife that was killing him.

He took another pull on the bottle of brandy that was keeping him company. He'd been turning to the stuff a lot, though it did nothing to drown the wild nightmares. Isabel captured, writhing in chains on a French ship, bloodied from rape by the crew. Nicolas tumbling from a tower of the Queen's prison, plunging into the Thames. Sometimes in the nightmare all three of them were in their house in Trujillo as it went up in flames, the King of Spain screaming orders to make ashes of Carlos and his family.

He wiped the brandy off his mouth with the back of his hand. The alarm in the courtyard kept on. *Gong! Gong! Gong!* What had set off the French this time? Yesterday, it was to close the gates against their own after an infantryman sank a knife into the gut of an officer and the search was on for the murderer. They'd found him and he would hang. Two days before, it was to open the gates for a scouting party returning the corpse of the garrison priest who'd visited a village inn outside Edinburgh in rebel territory; the landlady had pushed him into a washtub and held him under until he drowned. The third alarm had been a false one after some green recruit saw shadows in the moonlight and imagined English soldiers scaling the ramparts. Carlos thought the men in the barracks must be getting dangerously accustomed to the bell, like the villagers in the old tale of the boy who cried wolf. Would these troops be alert enough if the enemy mounted a surprise attack?

Do I care anymore? he wondered. A furious confusion had plagued him since Isabel had gone. Who was the enemy now, for him? The Scots with their new English muscle? Warfare was simple: fight or be killed. But now it was the French he had to fear, because if they found out about Isabel it would threaten her, threaten Nicolas, threaten the whole life Carlos had built for them. That felt worse than simple death. What she had done—he could not comprehend it with anything less than frustrated rage. He took another pull of brandy. A barrel of it wouldn't be enough to make him forget his wife's betrayal.

He tossed the brush aside and grabbed a hoof pick. He stroked the stallion's rear leg from hock to cannon bone to signal his intention, then lifted the hoof and wedged it between his knees. *Gong! Gong! Gong!* from the courtyard. If it was something serious after all, he'd better go see. Yet he heard no commotion, just indistinct shouts. Another false alarm? Or could it be a courier with *good* news for the commander? He knew D'Oysel was hoping for reinforcements from the French king. But that was before they'd heard of the events that had recently stunned France.

"Huguenots," D'Oysel had groaned to him the evening the report had arrived. "God-cursed Protestants." They had been playing cards, although the commander's concentration was barely on the game. Carlos knew that pockets of Protestants had been gaining strength all over France. Now, it seemed, a cabal of them had struck. "They tried to abduct the King," D'Oysel had said, clearly shaken. "He was at Amboise, at the chateau, and the Huguenot forces stormed the place. Tried to arrest the King's uncles, too, the Duc de Guise and the Cardinal of Lorraine. The King's men cut down the heretics, of course. Hung the leaders' corpses on the chateau walls. But, God in heaven, what a monstrous conspiracy was uncovered. They say it's thousands strong." Carlos knew why it meant so much to D'Oysel, and religion had little to do with it. It was because the extent of the conspiracy had forced the King and the Duc de Guise to concentrate their forces at home. That meant sacrificing their troops in Scotland. In war, Carlos thought grimly, timing is everything.

And so is knowing your enemy. His bitterness roared back as he cleaned Noche's hoof. He had thought he knew Isabel. He'd been wrong. It made him sick to think how wrong. She had lied to him. Lie upon lie. She had agreed to a pact with Queen Elizabeth. Left their son as a surety, a hostage. Brought the Queen's aid to the rebels, and then lived among their soldiers—that thought turned his stomach. And then she had spied for them, right here under his very nose. Had she been scouting the garrison before they'd made love, or after? Or both? A fist of sickness threatened deep in his throat. He would rather she had gone insane and shot him in the head than betrayed him.

He let go the horse's leg and upended the brandy bottle in his mouth, almost choking as the liquor poured down his throat. *Choking on her lies.* He swallowed, and spat, and took an unsteady step back. He had to flatten his shoulders against the wall for balance and focus on the lantern above him, its yellow light blurry. Too much liquor. He hadn't realized he'd had so much. It was cheap stuff, a foul rotgut. Watching the lantern flame dance, he saw Isabel smiling as she lied to him, and he felt a lash of sorrow. Did their marriage mean nothing to her? Did intrigue and danger mean more than her life with him and Nicolas? After everything he had done to build a secure life for them? *I am done with her,* his rage had told him that day when she had ridden away.

He let the bottle slip from his fingers. Alongside his anger and sorrow was a squeeze of shame about Fenella. Brandy—that's how it had started with her. A bottle of D'Oysel's finest. It was the day after he had sent Isabel away. Just after dawn. He'd had no sleep, and Fenella had found him here, brushing Noche, channeling his fury into the task. *Or else I'll hurt someone,* he had felt with a wild despair.

"Thought I might find you here," she had said, strolling into the stall.

He threw her a glance, then went back to brushing. He was in no mood for talk.

She leaned back against the horse's neck, throwing one arm along the ridge of its back. "Hard times with the wife, I hear."

He glared at her. Did everyone in the place know he'd thrown Isabel out? Then a far worse worry hit him—had Fenella kept her word? He had paid her to keep quiet about Isabel's link to the rebels, and she had given her promise, but there was still a risk. After all, she shared D'Oysel's bed.

"Och, you're well rid of her," she said lightly. She held up a bottle, offering it. "Brandy? It's the best," she added with a wink. "From the private stores of my wee frog."

Why not? "Thanks."

As he drank, she toyed with the buckle on the sleeve of his leather jerkin. "Now that she's gone, gives me a chance, I hope." She eased herself between him and the horse.

There had never been any mistaking her broad invitations, and her interest in him gave Carlos some confidence now that she would do what he wanted and keep quiet about Isabel. Her breath smelled ripe with brandy. She was so close he could feel her body's heat. The thought lingered: *She'll do what I want.*

Did he want her? They were alone. No one to see. And his wife had just shown him how little he meant to her. He took another swallow of brandy and let his gaze range over Fenella's tangle of yellow hair, carelessly bound up with a red ribbon as though she had just come from bed. A few long, loose strands hung down, touching her full breasts.

He read the gleam of excitement in her eyes. "Here, let me help you with this," she said, taking the brush from him. She turned in the tight space between him and the stallion, and brushed the horse's back. With every stroke her backside rubbed Carlos, her ass grinding against his groin.

"I warrant your beast likes the feel of this," she said, brushing. " 'Course I can't do it hard like you do, strong fella that you are." She glanced over her shoulder and winked. "Hard is best."

She turned to face him, her breasts brushing his arm. She stroked a fingertip down his throat and into the V of his shirt. He let it happen, his body already there. "So, you do like me a little," she said with a sly smile. Pressing her hips firmly against him, she chuckled. "Och, a lot!"

Why not? he thought, desire and bitterness surging. He tossed the bottle onto a pile of horse blankets and pulled her close. "You're an easy woman to like. You don't lie."

She smiled, tossing away the brush. "I can lie. Or stand. Or bend over. Whatever way you want it, lover." She leaned in to kiss him.

But he didn't want to kiss her. He only wanted to fuck her. He pulled her over to the manger, a hip-high trough for fodder where his saddle was slung over the edge. He bent her facedown over the saddle and shoved her skirts up over her buttocks and loosened his codpiece. She braced herself, gripping the saddle's pommel and cantle. He grabbed her by the hips and rammed into her, driven by a fierce need to exorcise his fury and his sorrow.

When he was done, his fury, at least, was spent.

He stepped back, getting his breath, retying his codpiece. He had a bad feeling that he'd been too rough, might have hurt her. "Sorry," he said.

"What for?" She had straightened up and was tugging her clothes back into place.

Carlos heard a scraping at the far wall that abutted the next stall. In the gloom he could make out a pair of dark eyes low down between the slats. The damn stable boy, watching. Carlos grabbed the horse brush and hurled it at the wall. "Get out, you little bastard!"

They listened as the boy scampered out of the stall and out the stable door. Fenella snorted a laugh. "Never mind him. Watching is the closest he'll ever get his wee prick to me."

Carlos sat down on the stacked horse blankets. He felt strangely lost. His fury was spent, but he had not expected how mercilessly his sorrow would surge back, stronger than before. He didn't want this woman. He wanted Isabel. But she had stepped beyond the borders of his trust, had moved herself beyond the reach of his love. He was without her, alone.

Fenella picked up the brandy bottle from the blankets and sat down beside him, patting her hair into place. "Good," she said. She sounded cheerful, as though they had finalized a mutually agreeable business deal.

He looked at her, surprised by her breezy mood, but relieved, too. She didn't expect anything more than the base coupling they'd just done. She was a woman who did what she wanted. He admired that.

She took a long pull from the bottle, then handed it to him. "Drink?"

He took a swallow.

"The fellows around here say your job won't keep you in Scotland much longer," she said, brushing a bit of straw off his sleeve. "Good thing, eh? To get out of this stinking country?"

He had to agree. "When I do go, I won't be sorry." He handed her back the bottle. She drank. They listened to the morning sounds around them. Hooves clopped at the far end of the stable as someone led a horse out for exercise. Outside, a wagon rumbled by.

"Know of a place called Marseilles?" she asked.

Odd question. "French seaport," he said.

"Close to Spain?"

"Not far. Why?"

She grinned. "We get along fine, you and me. When you leave

here, how would you like to take me to Spain? No strings, I promise. If you patch things up with your wife later, I'll clear out. Just take me with you when you go, that's all I ask."

He looked at her. He hadn't expected this. "I'll be going home to Peru."

"And where in Spain is that? Anywhere near Marseilles?"

"It's not in Spain. It's across the Ocean Sea. In the New World."

She gaped at him, her face blank with shock. "Across the . . . ?" Her body slumped, heavy with disappointment. "Bloody hell."

It was suddenly clear to him. "That's why you've been after me? To tag along to Spain?"

She heaved a weary sigh. "To France. That's where I have to be. No chance of that with my wee frog. He's stuck here."

Carlos had to chuckle. "So you tried me instead." So much for feeling bad at using her. Instead, he'd been her fool. His chuckle gave way to a full-blown belly laugh.

She glared at him, still smarting at her mistake. "What's so funny?"

"Me. I thought you couldn't resist me."

She made a face, a good-natured sneer. "You're a fine cock of a man, lover, but I promise you, you're nothing new."

"Quite the compliment."

They looked at each other. He had almost made her smile.

"Why France?" he asked.

"What?"

"Why do you want to go to France?"

She took the bottle from him and drank, then handed it back to him. "My brother's in Marseilles. He's dying." She wiped brandy off her mouth. "I want to go take care of him. I'm all he's got."

Carlos stared at her. He had never thought of her as anything more than D'Oysel's woman, a good-looking woman, a flirt. Not someone with a life and problems like everyone else. "I'm sorry I can't help you," he said. It struck him that they were both captives. He wanted out, but had to stay to win Quadra's backing. She wanted out, but was too poor to go on her own.

"I hate this bloody country," she said, staring at the cold lantern on the post. "What the hell are these frogs fighting for, anyway? What's this godforsaken, sodden land to them?"

A stepping stone to England, Carlos thought. "But you didn't want to join the rebels?" he asked.

"Christ, no. They'll lose. A sorry lot of fools, dying for nothing. I'll stick with the winners."

"You're not worried about the English?"

"Why should I be? If they win, I warrant an Englishman likes a soft body in his bed as much as a Frenchman does. But I will say this for the Scottish fools—at least they're fighting for something they care about. This is their home. What do the bloody French care about?"

Her words sank into him. *What do I care about?* It used to be Isabel and Nicolas. He would have died for them. He still would for Nicolas. And Isabel? *She cares.* Fighting for her parents, she said. For England. It shook him, remembering the passion in her voice. England was the home of her heart, not Peru.

He knocked back another drink, wanting to forget. "I'll say this for D'Oysel, he has damn good brandy." He offered her the bottle.

She stiffened as though she remembered something terrible. "Oh, Christ. If he finds out about us . . ." She jumped up, tightening her shawl around her as if she felt a chill. "I was sure I'd be getting out of here with you. But now . . ."

Carlos saw fear in her eyes. "Don't worry, he won't find out."

"It's not just me he'll take it out on. He's a mad one, he is. You watch your back."

Rodriguez's words came back to him, the tale of a man who'd spent the night with Fenella. *"D'Oysel cut off the jackass's ear."* Carlos stood up. "Fenella, I promise you—"

"Don't you come near me again. You hear? Don't even talk to me."

In a moment, she was gone.

The courtyard alarm clanged again. *Gong! Gong! Gong!* Carlos shook off the memory and that morning with Fenella . . . and his tortured thoughts of Isabel. Better go see what the commotion was about.

The night was clear and cold, the moonlight so bright the wall torches flaring outside weren't even necessary. Carlos welcomed the bracing air. It helped clear his head as he set out along the alley that ran from the stables to the main courtyard. When he reached the archway at the end, he stopped to take stock of the activity in the courtyard.

It looked like a play. Thirty or forty soldiers made the audience, standing in a semicircle well back from the "players"—about a dozen soldiers looking proud as their captain exhibited three captives in chains. D'Oysel was hurrying down the staircase from his quarters, followed by several of his men, some still buckling on their swords, the scabbards clinking. And now, making an entrance on the balcony of the royal apartments, came the Queen Regent, flanked by three of her ladies, some looking like they had dressed in haste. Among the watching soldiers a few young recruits hissed at the captives and yelled jibes. The older veterans looked on in grim silence. Carlos knew why, for he shared their experience. They could recall campaigns where they had almost fallen into an enemy's hands, and knew that a fate like these prisoners' might still one day await them.

Carlos moved in among the men, trying to get a closer look at the captives. Usually, the rebels brought in were the kind too slow or stupid or unlucky to flee the raiding parties that D'Oysel sent into the countryside. But the Queen Regent wouldn't be called out in the middle of the night for rabble like that, nor would D'Oysel. These prisoners had to be important.

"English," a pock-faced soldier beside Carlos said.

That surprised him. "Outriders?" he asked. The coming English army could not have advanced much farther than the Tweed River at the Scottish border.

The soldier shook his head with the smile of one who knows. "Sailor boys. From the English Queen's navy."

They had been roughly treated, Carlos saw. All were filthy, and all were bowed by the chains that connected the manacles on their wrists to those on their ankles. One wore a thick, tattered bandage around his thigh, and blood crusted his mouth and nose. Another had his arm in a dirty sling, the bloody, mangled hand hanging like meat. He was swaying on his feet, almost too weak to stand. The third, whose back was all Carlos could see, wore a leather jerkin slashed from the shoulder to the opposite hip, the slash black with grime and blood.

The pock-faced soldier talked on about the capture. Captain LaFollette had caught the English ship offloading weapons to the rebels at Grangemouth some fifteen miles west along the estuary. But Carlos was barely listening. His eyes had not left the third prisoner, who had turned around to look up at the Queen Regent. The soldier said, "That one's their bloody captain." Carlos's heart thumped as he saw the short black beard and recognized the face.

Isabel's brother. Adam Thornleigh.

Adam's pain-filled gaze, taking in the courtyard, fell on Carlos. Their eyes met in a shared moment of shock.

Isabel held the silver rattle behind her back, frozen at Grenville's words. *"Have you found what you were looking for?"*

Impossible to pretend she had *not* been looking. She forced her hands not to tremble as she brought the rattle around in front of her. Her mind was afire, trying to think. What was *he* thinking? Was he shocked to find her looking through his private papers? Or did he believe she had known all along about the scroll? Her best hope lay there.

"I was worried that *you* might not have found it," she said as steadily as she could. She slid the scroll out of the handle to show him.

Grenville looked at it blankly. Was this the first time he was seeing it? Isabel's heart crammed up in her throat. Had she just condemned herself? But it was too late to go back. "I wasn't sure," she pushed on, "since you said nothing about it."

He took the paper from her. Then looked into her eyes. "Forgive me for that. Business took me to Kirknewton. I should have told you before I left how very welcome this news was."

She thought her legs might give way in relief—but relief shot with horror that she had been right. Grenville was plotting treason, and the Queen Regent was backing him!

He held the scroll up to the candelabra and touched it to one of the candles' flames. The paper smoked, then caught fire. He lowered it between him and Isabel and they watched it burn. She could hardly hold back from asking, *What did she write to you? Instructions?* The paper shriveled to ash. Grenville dropped the last scrap of it onto the floor rushes and ground the ashes under his boot.

She needed to know more. And to get it she had to *dare* more. "Shall I take a message back to the Queen Regent at Leith?"

He blinked in wonder. "*Could* you?"

It was the last thing in the world she would do. *Just tell me what you're plotting.* "Easily. My husband is one of her favorites."

He considered it. Then shook his head. "No, Lord Grey's troops will reach them soon. In the garrison, you would be in danger."

Dread roiled inside her. That Carlos would be in the fighting. That Grenville considered her a trusted fellow traitor. That there was nothing she could do to stop any of it!

He smiled. "Don't worry, it really is not necessary. We are ready."

She almost gasped. Who was *we?* Ready to do what?

"You seem amazed. I understand. You marvel that you and I, a Thornleigh and a Grenville, should find ourselves united." He nodded as though in wonder. "In truth, it is passing strange."

She swallowed. "God chose us, sir. It is His will."

His face lit up. "And we obey!" He smiled, the admiration in his eyes unmistakable. "Isabel," he said quietly. She was as startled by his use of her Christian name as if he had touched her body. "Frances was right. You are one of us."

Frances, a co-conspirator! It rocked her.

"Are you sure you are quite recovered?" he asked in concern.

"Yes. I am very well. I am only eager to know how you will proceed . . . Christopher."

She saw a flicker of excitement at her use of his name. But he smiled and said nothing. He was careful, as well he had to be, she thought. To get him to speak would take more than merely asking.

"Come," he said, opening a drawer. He took a candle out and lit it from the candelabra. "I know what will give you cheer. Follow me."

He opened a door and beckoned her into a darkness. It seemed to be a tunnel. Isabel forced a smile, saying, "My, you are full of surprises." She stepped into the dark space, and her skin crawled as Grenville closed the door behind them. His candle was the only light. The tunnel was a crude passage with rough planks shoring up the earthen walls and narrow ones laid down as a floor. The air was cold and smelled as dank as a grave. They walked. Roots were exposed between the wall planks, and in the flickering candlelight they seemed to grope at Isabel. They reached a door, which Grenville opened, ushering her in. She entered a stone room like a large prison cell, the ceiling low, the walls clammy, the light dim, the air musty. She was surprised by the noise, a rushing sound of water, almost a roar, and a constant *Slap! Slap! Slap!*

Grenville seemed amused at her bewilderment. "The river," he said, raising his voice above the din. "This is our mill."

She turned and saw an iron shaft creaking as it went round and round—an axle powered by an outside paddlewheel. A dam on the river forced the water against the wheel, churning it so it struck the water with that *Slap! Slap! Slap!* Two huge millstones were idle at the moment, not engaged. Along thick beams in the ceiling, empty burlap sacks hung from iron hooks. In the gloom they looked like starved, dead children.

"This way," Grenville said. She followed him down stone steps into the belly of the mill. The noise below was even louder, and as they crossed the dusty floorboards Isabel felt a gust of cold, wet air and glimpsed the dripping paddlewheel plunging. Grenville opened a door no higher than his shoulders. He bent and went in, beckoning her to follow. She bowed her head and stepped through the door into a brick passageway barely high enough to stand up in. They made their way along it for several paces, Isabel following in mute wonder. This tunnel, she thought, must lead right into the riverbank. When they reached the end and straightened up, her breath caught in her throat.

Before her was a room as big as a rich man's bedchamber, and it was filled with treasure. A cross of gold as tall as Grenville lay at an angle, propped against shelves. On the shelves were hundreds of objects sacred to the rites of the Catholic church. Jeweled crucifixes. Chalices of gold. Pyxes and pattens of sheened silver. Rood screens of intricate carved beauty lined a wall, stacked back to back, over a dozen of them, each one almost the length of the room, each one a priceless work. In the far corner stood a congregation of saints, perhaps thirty, some of the whitest alabaster, some painted in gorgeous colors of scarlet, gold, sea green, and blue. A doleful Virgin Mary had pride of place at the front. Life-sized, carved of wood and painted in gold and sapphire blue, she spread her arms in a gesture of tenderness, welcoming all who were wracked by life to take comfort in her embrace. Coins lay scattered at her feet.

Isabel was in awe. Possession of any of these articles was illegal. At Queen Elizabeth's ascension to the throne she had sent her agents—the Visitors—into every corner of the realm to strip all churches of "popish" objects. People caught hiding them had been fined. The unrepentant had spent time in prison. Some would never come out. And here was such a hoard!

She said to Grenville, "You rescued . . . all this?"

He nodded, looking pleased. "Before the Visitors arrived. Throughout Northumberland, from cathedrals and churches and chapels and chantries."

The sheer feat of organization was amazing. Hundreds of people must have been involved.

"Yes," he said, as if reading her thoughts, "the faithful risked their lives. We are waiting for the day when England throws off her heretic pall and returns to the one true faith."

"And surely," she probed, "that day is coming."

"God willing. For every one of the faithful who acted then, a thousand are ready to follow now."

His confidence deepened her dread. Thousands. He could not lead so many alone. Other gentlemen must be involved, all coming together under the banner of the earl. Thousands . . . armed . . . prepared to rise up in rebellion.

"Come," he said. "I think we are in time."

"For what?" she managed.

He laid his finger over his mouth with a conspiratorial smile. They went back up the stone steps to the millstone room. Isabel heard a faint shuffling above her head. People moving about on the floor above? Grenville took her by the hand—she tried not to squirm at his touch—and led her up a narrow set of wooden stairs. She smelled the dust of grain in sacks even before they reached the room above. It was as cramped as an attic, but alongside the grain sacks it held people. Four men—clerks, perhaps, or scriveners by the look of their tidy clothes—and three women, one old and stooped, another a plump, well-dressed matron, another young but careworn, perhaps a laborer's wife. They stood in two rows, like supplicants. It was the fifth man, standing before them, who held Isabel's attention. He was dressed from head to foot in the sumptuous raiment of a Catholic priest, including a snow white alb and an embroidered silk stole. He looked straight at her, and Isabel felt a shiver at his long white face and crow black hair and eyes as dark as wet stones.

"Father York," Grenville whispered in Isabel's ear. "He suffered in the Queen's prison." He led her forward to the front of the little congregation, revealing a woman kneeling on a cushion, looking up. Frances! Isabel's mind tripped as their eyes met. Frances must have slipped out of the supper hall and come down the tunnel before Isabel had gone to the library.

She wished she were a hundred miles away, far from these traitorous Grenvilles! But Frances, looking almost as startled, moved aside to make room for her. Grenville knelt, and Isabel, following his lead, sank to her knees between brother and sister.

The others knelt, too, and Father York led the mass. Isabel went through it by rote. The prayers. The elevation of the Host. The consumption of the body and blood of Christ. The priest's invocation, beseeching God to smite the heretic female who had usurped the throne of England, and to keep safe the rightful monarch, Mary, the young Queen of France. Isabel closed her eyes, trying desperately to keep a calm face as she pieced together what she knew and what she suspected. The weapons stockpiled here, and likely in the armories of Grenville's fellow Catholic gen-

try, too. The fighting men among their tenants and retainers, training for the day they would strike. The earl's gold paying for it all.
The Queen Regent, Marie de Guise, promising the leaders rich
lands and titles once they had wrested the English throne and in-
stalled her daughter on it. A Catholic regime—a French regime—
triumphant in Scotland and England.

Where would they strike first? And when? After helping Wyatt
five years ago, and John Knox now, Isabel knew how rebel leaders
strategized. As soon as their men and munitions were ready they
set a date to attack, because every day that they waited put them
and their cause in peril. Grenville and his fellows would be waiting
only for a signal. Who would give it? The earl?

Sorrow flooded her, for she realized what she had to do. She
could not go home for Nicolas. Not yet. She had to stay with
Grenville. Had to uncover the essential facts of his plot, and then
warn Queen Elizabeth. She lowered her head, afraid she might
weep.

The service was over. The people bowed to Grenville and then
silently filed down the stairs. Isabel was glad to see Frances leave
with them, for she was so dismayed by her sister-in-law's dis-
loyalty, so appalled for Adam's sake, she would not know what to
say to her. Father York gave Grenville a questioning look, and a
glance at Isabel. Grenville returned a brief, reassuring nod. The
priest said nothing, and went down the stairs. Isabel was alone
with Grenville. The way he was looking at her made her so uncomfortable she almost wanted Frances back. She did not yet
know how to get the information from him. She needed time to
think.

"Thank you for this," she said. "It was cheer indeed." She
started for the stairs.

He stepped in to stop her. Her heart thumped. Why was he
frowning?

"You did not join the prayer," he said.

"Pardon?"

"For Queen Mary. Why did you keep silent?"

"Did I?" Sweat prickled her back. It sprang from fear, but
something else too. Anger. People were always setting tests for

her! "I'm afraid my mind was elsewhere. On something more important."

"What could be more important than a prayer for our Queen?"

She wished she could spit at him. "Something closer to home, I should say." She lowered her voice like a co-conspirator. "Christopher, I want to do more. To help."

He looked at her, unblinking. *That's right*, she thought, her pulse quickening. *This time I shall set the test. And I shall snare you in it.*

"Please, let me help you. To redeem—" She broke off, lowering her head. "To redeem my soul. For the sins of my family."

She heard him take a breath of surprise. "You really feel that?"

"I do," she said, lifting her face to him. "You asked me not to judge you by your brother's actions. I now ask the same of you. My path is not the path of my parents. I will not lie to you—I love and honor my mother and father. But they have been lured to a false religion. That, I cannot abide. Let me help you fight for God's cause here in England."

He was studying her as if hoping to see what he wanted. "Help me . . . how?"

"My mother is Queen Elizabeth's friend. She introduced me to her. Through my mother I have pathways to knowledge about the Queen, knowledge useful to you. The doings of the court. The movements of her commanders in the field. Even Her Majesty's private comings and goings. Please, I ask only to continue to be a part of your great undertaking. Believe me, I can help you."

He had not taken his eyes off her, and in them she saw a piercing interest warring with caution. In the next moment, she felt certain, he would leap one way or the other—and decide her fate.

In the solar, Frances could not get warm. The night was so cold the servants had built up the fire with the stoutest oak logs the hearth could hold. The flames leapt and crackled as Frances sewed the lace cap in her lap and rocked Katherine's cradle with her foot. Christopher sat beside her staring at the fire, his arms crossed, his legs stretched out in front of him. He coughed, then rubbed his nose.

The chill that Frances felt came from more than the drafts from the casements. She felt shaken from seeing Isabel at the mill. She was glad they shared a devotion to their religion—that bond would not change—but why was she spending time with Christopher? Frances knew he was plotting something, and she feared he had enmeshed Isabel in his conspiracy. She had been unable to discover any details of what he was up to, but her suspicions about his secretive meetings, and the earl's visit, had been confirmed when Isabel told her she had seen Christopher stockpiling arms. Frances had lied to her—it's to fight the raiders, she had said—because she feared Isabel was on the side of the French. How could she not be, when her husband was with them in Leith? Isabel had to support Carlos's cause, just as Frances did Adam's. For a wife who loved her husband, there was no choice.

Christopher coughed again. He pulled a handkerchief from his breeches and blew his nose. "Must be touched with a cold."

Frances said nothing, knowing she was at fault for the discomfort of his congestion. The cat and kittens. She had not yet taken them to the marshal's wife. Her mind turned back to his plot, and she decided that tonight she would demand to know. She was his sister, she would say, his closest family—he could trust her. She was nervous, but her mind was made up. She started by asking if he expected the earl to visit again, when Christopher held up a hand to quiet her.

"Shhh. What's that?" he said, cocking an ear.

A mewing sounded across the room. Frances stiffened. She had moved the basket of kittens there, shoving it behind a screen, hoping he would not notice. He so rarely spent time with her in the solar. Before she could explain, he was on his feet, moving across the room. Straight to the basket. He shoved the screen aside. Then shot a look at Frances. "I told you to drown them."

"There's no need for that, Christopher. Margery Cowell says she'll take them. Good for keeping down the mice, she says. I promise you, I'll take them to her tomorrow."

Christopher picked up the basket. The cat and kittens tumbled among themselves at the violence of the motion. "Not tomorrow, Frances. Now." He carried the basket toward the hearth.

She shot to her feet, horror flooding her. Surely he was not going to . . .

"No!" she cried, and lunged to stay his arm.

But he was quicker and yanked the basket clear. Missing him, Frances staggered off balance. Then froze in shock as he tossed the creatures into the fire.

❧ 23 ❧

Letters

Carlos sat waiting to see D'Oysel. To steady his nerves he worked with his knife, using the tip to dig grit from under his thumbnail. The clerk at the desk across the room had told him that the English prisoners had been taken to the lockup beneath the armory and put in the Hole, the dungeon with the tightest security. Carlos had asked for this meeting with the commander, but he was well aware that he had no authority to intervene. Prisoners were a matter completely under D'Oysel's control. All Carlos had was the goodwill he'd built with the man. D'Oysel owed him for leading Renault's company of horse in the January strike against the rebels. He could only hope it was enough to buy him what he had come for. Adam's life.

The door to the commander's private rooms opened and the Queen Regent came out. Carlos got up, but she swept on out without noticing him. She looked tired but triumphant, which gave him the awful certainty that his task would be that much harder. In Sir Adam Thornleigh, she had a prize prisoner.

"Ah, Valverde," D'Oysel said when the clerk ushered Carlos in. D'Oysel stood at his desk pouring a goblet of wine. He had shaved too quickly, leaving one jowl streaked with stubble above his bull neck. His eyes were bloodshot from lack of sleep. "Wine?"

Carlos held up his hand. "Thanks, but no." He had already had too much brandy. He needed a clear head.

"We face a sea of troubles, Valverde. The English army already across the Tweed. A quarter of my men sick with the flux. No reinforcements coming from France. Still, we take comfort where we can." He raised his goblet in a cheerless toast. "To LaFollette." He took a swallow. "He says the English captain led him on a chase across the beach to let his crew escape. They disappeared into the woods, but we got him and a couple of his gunners. Got his ship, too." He allowed himself a satisfied smile. "She's worth a vineyard in the Loire, eh?"

"Congratulations." By the laws of war, the captured ship was D'Oysel's to keep and sell. "The English captain," he said. "Will you ransom him? He'll fetch a fat purse."

"Thornleigh?" D'Oysel shrugged. "I don't know yet."

"He's no use to you rotting in the Hole. Better to be rid of him and make a profit."

"Maybe I'll send him to enjoy the brief life of a galley slave. Fair punishment for the aid he's brought the enemy."

"Wasted opportunity, though."

"Maybe I'll keep him here in chains."

To suffer and die—that's what he'd left unsaid. "He's a friend of the English Queen, did you know? One of her favorites. Is it wise to antagonize her?"

"He's a *pirate*," D'Oysel said sourly. "And since the army that his Queen has thrown at us will arrive any day, it's a little late to kiss her ass."

"Let him go, D'Oysel. Send him back for ransom. You'll get your price, I promise you."

D'Oysel regarded him with a skeptical frown. "Is that why you're here? Why do *you* care about the fellow?"

The only argument left was the truth. "He's a relation. My wife's brother."

D'Oysel's eyes widened in surprise. "Great heavens. Of course. I *knew* I'd heard the name Thornleigh somewhere." He eyed Carlos as if realizing this offered an interesting new opportunity. "Your wife's English family—makes things rather difficult for you, doesn't it?"

"Let him go. Please. I'd consider it a personal favor."

"Yes, I see," D'Oysel said, intrigued. He sat down on the corner of the desk, goblet in hand, his eyes on Carlos, gauging the situation. He went on, lowering his voice as though to be considerate about this private matter, "To tell you the truth, that is something I wanted to talk to you about. Your wife. I hear she's been a problem."

A warning rippled through Carlos. Had D'Oysel heard about Isabel's tie with the rebels? No, he thought—if he'd gotten wind of that he would have called me in earlier, furious. "Problem?" he said cautiously.

"Ah, Valverde, what fools these women make of us, eh?" His tone was sympathetic, man to man. He turned to the bedchamber door and called, "Fenella!" Carlos stiffened, his eyes on the door, as D'Oysel went on, "Take it from me, there is only one way to deal with an unruly female."

The door opened with a creak and Fenella shuffled into the doorway. Carlos sucked in a breath. She had been beaten so badly that one eye was a swollen slit and her lower lip was crusted with a scab. She wore only a sleeveless shift, showing bruises that mottled her shoulder and arm. Her hair hung down, disheveled. Seeing Carlos, she was suddenly alert. And frightened.

"Come here, my dove," D'Oysel said with mock tenderness. She shuffled to his side. He put his arm around her waist and asked her, while keeping his eyes on Carlos, "You were telling me about Valverde's wife, remember? What was it?"

So this *was* about Isabel and the rebels, Carlos was sure of it now. He wished he could grind D'Oysel's neck under his boot. Who could blame Fenella? To save herself she had told the bastard everything she knew. Isabel would be safe in London by now, thank God, but Carlos knew this would blast his reputation to hell. Far worse, how could he possibly hope to get Adam spared?

"Well?" D'Oysel urged Fenella.

"They had a row," she answered steadily. "Him and her. A

great, bloody row. Couldn't hear what it was about, but everybody in shouting distance heard the ruckus."

Carlos shot her a look. That was all? Nothing about Isabel helping the rebels?

She added with emphasis, "Even the bloody boys in the bloody *stables* must have heard."

He suddenly knew what she was telling him. The stable boy who had seen them. He imagined the trail—the boy telling a groom, the groom telling a lieutenant, the news reaching the commander's quarters. Fenella was warning him that D'Oysel knew.

"Marital squabbles in public—not wise, Valverde," D'Oysel said as if giving friendly advice. "Best we deal with our women in private." He jerked his chin at Fenella. "This one was whoring with another man." His cold glare at Carlos made it plain that he meant him. Still, he kept his tone affable, a man of the world. "Now she's learned the consequences. You see? All quietly settled in private."

Carlos wanted to ram his knuckles into the man's face. There wasn't a thing he could say.

"Go," D'Oysel told Fenella.

Carlos gave her a look of earnest thanks. If she had not told about Isabel under the brute's fists, she never would.

When she was gone D'Oysel refilled his goblet, then took it around the desk to the chair. He sat, leaning back, regarding Carlos. "About your wife's brother. Such a worry for you." He took a slow swallow of wine, savoring it. "I have my own worries. Perhaps we can help each other."

Carlos didn't know what the man was getting at, but he jumped at the chance. "How?"

"Are you sending a dispatch to Ambassador de Quadra any time soon?"

"Today," he said. Where was this going?

"Good. I need troops, Valverde. If France cannot spare them, perhaps Spain can. Everyone knows your king hates the rebels for their heresies, and with good cause. If they wrest control of Scotland with the help of the English Queen, this whole poxy island will be a breeding ground for heretics, and then they'll set out to infect *our* God-fearing lands. France and Spain should make common cause, stop them here and now. Bishop de Quadra listens to you, and he has King Philip's ear. What I want is for you to write to him, make the danger clear so he'll urge the King to send us troops, and fast."

It was a major request. Carlos was here as an emissary, a neutral observer. Meddling in affairs of state could have dangerous repercussions. Lesser interferences had led to wars. But he saw how much D'Oysel wanted his partisan report. "If I do, you'll let Thornleigh go?"

"I would send him home safe this very moment, for your sake, if it were up to me. Unfortunately, though, the Queen Regent has taken an interest. So it might take a little time. But I assure you, we'll work something out."

Can I trust him? Carlos thought. He had seen the hatred in the man's eyes when he'd made it clear he knew about him and Fenella. No, to punish me, he'll never free Adam. "I'll have the letter on its way by sunrise," he said.

"Excellent. Thank you."

"Let me talk to Thornleigh?"

D'Oysel smiled, magnanimous. "Of course."

Grenville's library felt as cold as death to Isabel. Seven men stood between her and the fire that burned in the hearth, and not a touch of its heat reached the dread, like ice, at her core. This was the hardest thing she had ever done—listening to their talk of treason, showing them a quiet delight in their strategy, pretending her admiration for Grenville's brilliant organizing. He had brought her into the meeting an hour ago, and with his encouragement she had made her case to the group. It had excited them, and she had answered their barrage of questions, and now she felt nearly faint with the effort, dizzy with dissembling. Surely at any moment they would see through her lies and turn on her.

"Where in Norfolk?" one of them asked her. Was it Donaldson? Or Ives? She found it hard to remember each man's name. Except Father York. His participation in the cabal had shocked her. A man of God, plotting sedition. He sat on a stool across the room, listening intently, never speaking, his long white face as still as a death mask. But each of them glanced at him from time to time as if to a touchstone to strengthen their commitment.

"Now that, sir, I do not know," she replied. "Before I left for Scotland my mother told me only that Her Majesty intends a visit to Norfolk later this month."

"Norwich, most likely," said another man. "To reward her heretic clergy at the cathedral. They have been diligent in suppressing the faithful."

"Aye," said another with a flash of anger. "My wife's cousin lies in the cathedral jail, seven months now, for attending a mass."

"And they fined my brother's business agent just for—"

"We all have friends who have suffered," Grenville interrupted, "but that is not the point. Let us stick to what *is*—getting close enough to the Queen to do what must be done. Mistress Valverde has given us this extraordinary opportunity. We must seize it."

That quieted them. Grenville was clearly their leader, Isabel had observed. It was not a matter of rank. All these men, gentry who hailed from counties throughout the north, had landholdings as rich as his, yet all seemed to understand and accept that he would give the eventual signal for their uprising. He never raised his voice, but they seemed almost to fear him. Isabel's own fear was hard to control—a constant worry that she would not be able to keep up her lies without slipping. She had had enough time with these men to digest their plot, but it brought her so near to nausea it was hard to think straight. Under the banner of the earl, having gathered all their forces, they planned to assault Durham, unite there with more forces raised throughout the north, then march south en masse and seize London. And assassinate Queen Elizabeth.

She forced a calm face. "The place and time are easily discovered, gentlemen. I shall simply ask my mother where the Queen intends to go, and when."

"Are you sure she will tell you?" a man near the fire asked. "They keep the Queen's plans private for as long as possible."

"Not from my mother." She looked to Grenville to support her.

"Sir Christopher knows what a dear friend my mother is to Her Majesty." He gave her a smile of solidarity that made her feel grateful, which shook her—she was in so deep, she hardly knew her own heart anymore. "So, here is what I propose," she went on. "I shall write to my mother that I am returning to London and wish to be allowed, on my way, to come to Her Majesty in Norfolk to present her with a gift. That will please my mother greatly, and she will arrange it. She will tell me the Queen's destination, gentlemen, I warrant."

They all regarded her soberly. Isabel was sure they saw her mask slip, saw her falseness.

One man said to her, as though struck by a thought, "Since you are allowed this special access—"

"Just what I was thinking," said another with growing excitement. "We planned to enlist one of the faithful at court—a gentleman server, or an ambassador's clerk. But now . . ." He fixed his eyes on Isabel. "Mistress Valverde, could *you* do the deed?"

They all watched her, waiting. Rational thought fled her mind. Assassinate Elizabeth? She was so horrified, she could find no voice, no breath.

Grenville saved her. "No, no, gentlemen, it is too much. This good lady is doing all she can. The rest must be our work."

Mercifully, they released her. They thanked her for her courage. Father York even blessed her.

In her bedchamber she sat down at the desk to write. It was a struggle to force her hand to stop trembling.

> *Dear Mother,*
> *My servant brings you this letter, for he knows your house and you. I would that I could impart to your face the dire information contained herein, for there must be no blunder or fault in the telling, lest you misbelieve the dreadful threat. Only the need to remain at Yeavering Hall to gather further details of the conspiracy prevents me from standing before you. Therefore, let my telling herewith be perfect.*

She looked in frustration at what she had written. Get to the point, she thought. She continued:

> *You will gape at my words—threat, conspiracy. My pen rushes ahead of my thoughts. Thoughts that every day fly to London, to my son. I long to see him.*

She stilled her hand. Closed her eyes. Why was she babbling about her son? She tried to subdue the frightened beating of her heart and calm her jangled mind. She dipped the pen in ink again and scratched out the last lines. Then wrote:

> *The threat I speak of is to Her Majesty the Queen and to her realm. Divers gentlemen here in Northumberland, adherents of the Catholic faith, are secretly prepared to rise up with a host of followers almost three thousand strong, mightily armed, and strike against Her Majesty's authority. Their intent is to rally in force and capture Her Majesty's city of Durham, there to gain further strength in numbers, treasure, and arms, and then strike with full force at Her Majesty's capital city of London. With the realm thus in disorder, unstable and confused, they mean to murder Her Majesty, and then to welcome her successor, her royal cousin, the Queen of France and Scotland, to ascend the throne of England. The conspirators have assurance from friends at the court of the Queen Regent of Scotland and from the King of France that the King encourages their plot.*
>
> *You will be dumbstruck at what you read. But I assure you every word is true.*
>
> *I write in haste, for this letter must go to you today. I still lack much detail on the plotters' intended date to strike, their precise stratagems, and the locations of their mustering, for I have not been privy to all their deliberations. I will try for all of this. Meanwhile, I judged it needful to apprise you instantly of the threat so that you may alert Her Majesty, and she may move against these traitors posthaste.*

The men I know to be plotting are as follows: Sir Christopher Grenville, who is their leader. Henry Palmer. Sir Ralph Donaldson. Sir Cyrus Pinkerton. Charles Ives. William Conroy. Father Thomas York. I believe there are more, but I know only of these. I am told they will rise up in the name of the Earl of Northumberland, though I have not seen his face. I entreat you, show this letter to Her Majesty.

God keep you well, and my good father, and my dear son. If you are allowed, kiss my boy for me. I know not when I shall lay eyes on him again.

Written by my hand this eighteenth day of February,
Your loving daughter,
Isabel Valverde

She sealed the letter, then left her room to look for Pedro. She would trust none but him to take it. Going down the stairs she stumbled, so shaky was her balance, and she had to sit for a moment on the step, hugging herself to quell her trembling muscles and brace her mind for what lay ahead—more meetings with Grenville and his fellow traitors. Every hour in his home was agony. But she would stay and watch . . . and long for the day when she could leave.

The lockup beneath the armory was so cold, ice crystals frosted the stone walls. Carlos quickly surveyed the layout as he came down the stairs. Four cells ran along each side of the dim corridor. All were empty. The rebels they had held had recently been hanged. The Hole was a narrow cell facing him at the far end, hard to see in the dim light. The stairs he had come down seemed to be the only way out. He looked through the gloom toward the Hole. If he hadn't known the English captives were there, the sharp stink of piss would have told him. The cell had no window, and the space was so narrow that if a man were on horseback his knees would touch the side walls, while the horse's nose and tail would touch the ends. Behind the barred door Carlos could just make out the shadowy forms of two men. One sat on the floor, knees up, forehead on his knees. One lay curled on the floor as if asleep. Three men had been brought in, so where was the third? Had Adam been taken somewhere else?

A lone turnkey lounged on a stool halfway down the corridor. Carlos hoped he was French, not a hired Scot. Everything depended on that. Seeing Carlos approach, the turnkey got to his feet in deference to this visitor in gentleman's clothing with a fine sword at his hip. Carlos noted the iron keys on an iron ring hooked to the man's belt.

"Are those the English?" he asked in French. He pointed at the two men in the cell, shadowy in the dim light. The one with his head on his knees heard him and his head shot up. It was Adam. Relieved, Carlos added, "I'm here to speak to their captain."

"Yes, sir," the turnkey said. "May I see the order?"

Carlos handed him D'Oysel's note, and then asked, switching to English, "Were you posted down here when the prisoners were brought in?"

The turnkey's puzzled frown was all the answer Carlos needed. The man knew no English. He switched back to French. "I speak English. More effective for questioning them."

The man's frown cleared. He understood—the prisoners would better appreciate threats in their own tongue. "Yes, sir. This way, sir."

Carlos followed him to the Hole. Adam blinked up at him, and Carlos gave him a fierce look that said, *Keep quiet.*

The turnkey unlocked the door. Carlos said, "Better wait down the corridor. They may not talk if you're near."

When they were alone, Adam struggled to his feet. He stared at Carlos with a look of disgust and sorrow. "I was hoping I'd imagined it . . . seeing you out in the courtyard." The sorrow gave way to sheer contempt. "So, have your French masters sent you to me?"

Carlos bristled, but he had no time to explain. He glanced at the man lying curled on the floor, his eyes closed. His mutilated hand had turned black. Gangrene. His face was as white as a corpse. "There were three of you," he said.

"Dawkins died in the night." Adam took a steadying breath. "My crew—what happened to the rest of my crew?" He looked as if he barely trusted Carlos to tell the truth.

"They got away."

Adam bowed his head in relief. "And my ship?"

"Confiscated."

Adam nodded, accepting it. He was shivering, hugging himself, his side pressed against the wall as if he needed its support to hold himself erect. He looked up, his disgust returning. "And you . . . gone over to the enemy. Show me the gold they gave you, Carlos. I'll shove it down your throat."

"Save your strength." He was trying to judge how bad Adam's condition was. He looked almost as pale and weak as the sick man on the floor. When they'd been brought in Carlos had seen the crusted blood on the back of Adam's jerkin slashed through from shoulder to hip. "How bad is your wound?" he asked. "Can you walk?"

Adam snorted. "For a stroll in the garden?"

"Could you make it down to the shore on your own?"

Adam gaped at him. "What?"

"Could you manage sailing a boat?"

"What are you talking about?"

Carlos glanced down the corridor. The turnkey sat on his stool a half dozen paces away, watching them, his face blank. Could he hear? Did he understand English after all? *If so, Adam and I are both dead men.* He lowered his voice even more. "I'm here to get you out. Answer me, could you sail a fishing boat?"

Adam looked at him with a dawning dread, as though Carlos were the hangman come for him. "I'm not going anywhere with you."

That threw him. He had expected hostility, but not downright refusal. It was suicide. "Damn it, you've got to trust me. If you don't—"

"Oh, I'm sure they think you're the perfect man to make me trust. So you can deliver me to the rack, is that it? Turn the screws to make me talk? Break me on the wheel? Well, haul me out if you're going to, but I'm not walking. I'd rather trust Satan himself." The effort had drained him. His head lolled back against the wall.

Carlos didn't know what to do. Everything in his experience told him to abort. The odds of getting Adam out to safety were terrible, even if Adam was ready and willing to try. *Without* his cooperation, the attempt was madness; Carlos would be courting his *own* suicide. He'd done his best, but he couldn't do the impossible. If he had any sense he'd accept that reality, call the turnkey, and get the hell out of here. But what did sense have to do with it? He was awash with feeling. It was Adam's face that did it. Dirty and bruised though it was, in it Carlos saw Isabel. That same proud tilt of the chin. The same knowing, clever eyes. It hit him hard. He knew where that pride in her came from. He had accused her of betraying him, but now, looking at her defiant brother, he knew that what she had done sprang from something deep inside her—a need to help. Her parents. Her country. Her defiance had confounded him when they'd stood face-to-face, because she had set herself against *his* need, a need to safeguard their future. She had lied to him, and as he had writhed at that wound she'd inflicted, he had thought he would never forgive her. But now, seeing her in Adam, knowing that her bravery was no less than her brother's, he knew that he already had. Forgiven her. Wanted her. Would take steel in his belly for her.

"I'm going to get you out," he told Adam. "Tomorrow, if I can. You have to believe that."

"Believe you? Why should I? Why would you risk the wrath of your French paymasters?"

Carlos gritted his teeth. He would see this through. "For your sister."

The scorn left Adam's eyes. Carlos saw a glimmer of trust. Then, suddenly, Adam slid down the wall, too weak to stand any longer. He sat, looking dazed. "Good try . . . but I'll stay."

Carlos wanted to kick him. "You *have* to get out." He squatted beside him. "They're going to hang you."

Adam shook his head. "They won't. I'm worth a ransom. They know that."

"Christ, is that what you think?"

"They're like you. They won't pass up the gold."

"You're wrong. You don't know this commander." *He'll hang you to spite me.* "Listen, forget how angry you are at me. This is about your neck. Believe me, this man will break it."

Adam frowned, the words sinking in. *Finally,* Carlos thought.

"So you've got to be ready to move when you get my signal. Before that, I'll send you word of the plan." *Once I have one.*

Adam thought about it for a long moment. Then, warily, "What's the signal?"

Carlos let out a breath of relief. He'd convinced him. "You'll know it when you see it." He stood up. At the door he called to the turnkey to come and let him out.

Adam struggled to his feet again. He said very quietly, "All right. We'll be ready."

Carlos spun around. *We?* He glanced at the sick man on the floor. "No. Just you. You can't risk being slowed by a man who's almost dead."

"That's not possible. I won't leave Braddock behind."

The turnkey was at the door. "Everything all right, sir?"

"Yes . . . fine." Carlos turned back to Adam and said in a fierce whisper, "Only *you*. Understand?"

Adam's anxious eyes flicked to the turnkey unlocking the door, then back to Carlos. He looked down at his crewman on the floor. The door was open. When he looked back at Carlos he shook his head, grimly resolute. *No.*

Isabel crossed the courtyard, looking for Pedro. In the kitchen they had told her he had gone out to the dairy house. She passed an oxcart creaking past with a load of the miller's grain. A half dozen of Grenville's mounted men-at-arms were trotting in through the main gate. She pulled her shawl tightly around her. It had looked like such a clear, bright day from her window she had not bothered with a cloak, but the moment she had stepped outside, the air's cold sting reminded her that winter still held Yeavering by the throat. She had just reached the alley that led to the outbuildings when a man called after her, "Mistress Valverde. Stop a moment, please."

She turned. Grenville's grizzled steward, Peter Hardy, strode to catch up to her, his breath steaming in the cold. He said with polite concern, "Cook said you were looking for your foreign lad to make a delivery. I assure you, there is no need to go to the trouble. We have porters to do that for you."

"Thank you, Master Hardy, but I prefer to send Pedro. He knows the house it is bound for. Really, it is no trouble at all."

"But then you would be without your servant. Please, allow me to take the parcel to our porter. Do you have it with you?" When she hesitated he added, embarrassed at having to make his meaning clear, "I am sorry, madam, but it is my master's request that nothing leave Yeavering Hall without I see it. I hope you understand."

"What nonsense. It is only a letter."

"Good. I will see that it is safely delivered." He held out his hand, waiting.

She pulled it from her shawl and handed it over. He slid his forefinger under the wax seal, breaking it. She moved to stop him, saying, "How dare you—" when a horseman trotted alongside them. Grenville.

"Isabel," he said. "What are you doing out in the cold? Is there a problem, Hardy?"

"This, sir." He held up the letter.

Grenville ignored it, looking annoyed at the man. "No, no, not this lady. Do forgive the intrusion, Isabel. Hardy can be over-careful of my safety." He scowled at his steward. "Let the letter pass, man."

"Are you sure, sir?" he insisted, handing it up.

Grenville took the letter, impatient to end the matter. He scanned the writing. Then slowly folded the letter. "That is all, Hardy."

The man bowed and walked away.

Grenville looked at Isabel. "You are taking this to your servant, I gather." He added with feeling, "God speed him." He handed the letter back to her. "When you're done," he said with a smile, "get you into the house and get warm." He turned his horse and trotted for the stables.

Isabel walked on down the alley, tucking the letter back into her shawl. It read:

> *Dear Mother,*
> *I trust this letter finds you in health and contentment. I hope to swell that contentment, for I have bought a gift for Her Majesty the Queen which I believe will delight her. I know her love of music, and my gift is a viol crafted from an ancient wood of this shire and delicately wrought. I am so eager to deliver it unto her, I entreat you to write me posthaste when Her Majesty will make her journey into Norfolk . . .*

She walked on, her heartbeat calming as the other letter brushed her thigh—the letter hidden in her petticoat pocket.

❧ 24 ❧

New Friends, New Foes

The Earl of Northumberland's role in the plot. Names of the plotters in Yorkshire. The date Grenville had set for the strike. Who, when, how? There was still so much Isabel did not know. Wrestling with these thoughts, she skirted the great hall, her mind in turmoil. How was she to find out what she needed? How much time did she have? Rain drummed the house in a downpour, for the temperature had shot up overnight, and her head ached from it. A wave of laughter followed her from the hall, the servants preparing for a performance by the actors, who were still in residence. She tried to block out the ruckus. She needed to think. She passed the library, its door closed. Grenville was in Kirknewton—on business, he had said. Meeting with the earl, Isabel was sure. If only she could be at that meeting!

She heard footsteps and looked back to see Frances leaving the library. She hurried on toward the staircase, hoping Frances had not seen her. The last person she wanted to talk to was her sister-in-law, a traitor like Grenville, perhaps not an active member of his conspiracy but a willing confederate, just as bad. She started up the stairs, eager for the refuge of her bedchamber. *Think.* There had to be a way to get Grenville to take her to the earl. As the most powerful lord in the north, and the one with the connection to the Queen Regent and therefore France, he was surely the lynchpin of the grand plot. She *must* get that proof for Queen Elizabeth. But what reason could she give Grenville? Perhaps if she said—

"Isabel, stop," Frances called.

She kept on up the steps, head down, pretending she had not heard. A lie. Her head felt crammed with lies . . . so hard to keep track of them all, her smiling-faced dealings with these people when she wanted to scream at them . . . she almost felt she was losing her mind.

"Stop, I say!" Frances caught up to her and snatched her wrist.

Isabel lurched to keep her balance. *Let me go, all you Grenvilles!* It was hard to keep a civil face as she pulled her hand free. "Frances, you startled me."

"I want you out of this house."

Isabel blinked at her. "Pardon?"

"You heard me. I want you gone." Another wave of laughter from the hall. Frances nervously glanced over her shoulder. There was no one around. Still, she lowered her voice. "I know that Christopher is trying to corrupt you. He may have already succeeded . . . I don't know." She looked pale, distraught, her hands clasped together as if to steady herself. "But all these men coming here—and the stockpiled arms—it is not about the border raiders, of that I am sure."

Isabel could not find words. Frances knew nothing about the plot?

"I sniff treason," Frances whispered, "though it pains my soul to say it. Whatever Christopher is planning, I cannot stop him. But you . . . *you* I will stop. I demand that you leave."

"Are you saying"—*Wait. Go carefully*—"that in a crisis, you would not stand with your brother?"

"Like you, standing against yours?" The vehemence of the outburst left Frances unsteady. She clutched the newel post for support. "I never thought I would see the day that you would plot against Adam."

"Let me understand—"

"He is fighting for England! If you strike at England you strike at him!"

"Shhh, keep your voice down." She could hardly believe what

she was hearing. But fervor shone in her sister-in-law's face. Adam was the sun of her world. Isabel was suddenly ashamed that she had ever doubted her. "Frances, I . . . I have misjudged you." A fresh energy coursed through her. To find an ally in Frances, after all! She grabbed her hand. "We cannot talk here. Come." She pulled her up the stairs.

Frances balked. "No. You cannot hoodwink me with your smiles and soft voice. Christopher has made you his confidante, and I will not—"

"My friendship with your brother is a sham. I am with you, Frances. For England."

"Ha. I do not believe you. You were in Leith with the French. You *said* so. Your husband is on their side."

"He is—but I am not!" It had burst from her, the wound from Carlos still raw.

They stared at each other. Footsteps sounded, coming from the hall. "But . . . I have seen you with Christopher," Frances stammered. "At the mill. And with his fellow—"

"Not here. Come." She tugged her. "Please!"

Up the stairs they went. The moment they were in Isabel's bedchamber, she shut the door and pulled Frances to the window across the room, far from servants' ears. She sat her down on the window seat and sat beside her and gripped her hand. "Your brother is plotting a massive uprising. Under the earl's banner. He and those men you've seen—they plan to strike at Durham, then London, kill the Queen, and take the realm."

Frances's hand flew to her mouth. She shrank back from Isabel, a look of horror on her face. "How can you know this unless"—she got to her feet—"unless you are with them. You *must* be!" She took an unsteady step back, looking for the door.

Isabel jumped up. She could not let her go! "I have *pretended* to be with them. You must believe me." The details tumbled out of her, the whole tale. Cecil urging her to help. Her meeting with Elizabeth. Her mission to take the Queen's gold to the rebel leaders. Her meeting with Knox in the rebel camp. Tom's death, and the terrible retreat to Stirling. "It was awful . . . awful," she said, almost breathless as she finished. Reliving it made her shudder, yet it was a relief to share her burden with a friend. She had been alone with it so long.

Frances looked stunned. And not convinced.

"I know you are amazed," Isabel said, "but you *must* believe me. Look, I'll prove it!" She dashed to the wardrobe and pulled out her brocade satchel, dug under the false bottom and into the hidden pocket, and pulled out a paper. "Here, look. It is the receipt Knox gave me for the Queen's gold. Signed by his hand. Look!"

Frances took the receipt, her hand trembling. She looked up at Isabel, and all the doubt drained from her face. She murmured in awe, and revulsion, "The heretics."

"Reformers, they call themselves. Frances, they are England's only bulwark against a French invasion."

"I know. Strange bedfellows," she said unhappily. "But Adam is fighting for them, and I know it is for England." The sadness in her eyes deepened to pure compassion. "Oh, Isabel—what risks you have taken."

Isabel felt shaky still. She had told everything, except about Nicolas. She could almost hear again his cry to her when she had left him, and it wrenched her heart. "For Nico . . ." she said. She now told Frances how the Queen had kept him as a surety, and as the words tumbled out she could not stop the tears.

Frances reached out to her in pity. "Your son! Oh, my dear, how terrible!" She guided Isabel back to the window seat and they sank down on it together and Isabel fell into her arms, sobbing. Frances held her. "And Carlos?" she asked. "Does he know?"

Isabel cringed. She could hardly bear to speak of Carlos. "He does . . . and hates me for it." She heard Frances suck in a breath of shock. Isabel straightened and looked at her. "I do not know . . . where I stand. He will not have me back. But, Frances, I am with child."

Frances embraced her in a rush of pity. But Isabel forced her sobs to a halt. She did not dare sink into weeping for Carlos. If she let it, that pain would destroy her. She sat up and wiped her wet cheeks with her hands. "Enough . . . enough," she said, mastering herself. "It is your brother we need to speak of."

Frances looked still overwhelmed by Isabel's anguish. But then she nodded, shifting her thoughts to the crisis. "Yes. You're right. How can we stop him?"

"I have written to my mother telling her everything I know. Pedro is on his way with the letter. Mother will warn the Queen."

"Ah, that is good! But it will take so long. Is there not something we should do here? I know the sheriff. Dawkins. Should I ride to Kirknewton and tell him?"

"No! He is one of them! I have heard them speak of him."

Frances looked appalled. They were silent for a moment, lost in the immensity of the plot.

"Isabel, I fear you may be in danger. If Christopher discovers that you—" She stopped as though the prospect was too awful. "He can be cruel when crossed. You should leave."

"I wish I could! But I must have more information. I need proof—there is just my word against the word of all these powerful men. The moment I have it I will fly from here, I promise you." She gripped Frances's hand. "But you should go. When they strike, you should be far away, lest, as his kin, you be tainted in the eyes of the law."

"No, I will not leave you."

"Frances, think of your baby. Take Katherine home." It was hard to say, for when Frances was gone she would be alone again. But there was nothing her sister-in-law could do, and Isabel did not want to put her in danger. Despite her fears she forced a smile. "I swore to Adam that I would look after his wife and child. Do not make a liar of me, Frances. Go home."

The Leith garrison had clanged with activity day and night, nonstop preparations to withstand the assault of the approaching English army. Lord Grey of Wilton, commanding nine thousand foot soldiers and seven hundred horse, had crossed the River Tweed three days ago and was now just twenty miles from Leith. The King of France had sent no reinforcements, concentrating all his forces instead on stamping out the Protestant menace at home—the Huguenots—whose plotters had come so close to abducting him and wreaking havoc throughout France. From dawn to curfew the gates of Leith stood open, heavily guarded by archers on the ramparts, as wagon after wagon rumbled in with barrels of brine-cured beef, crates of live rabbits and hens, bushels of cabbages, kegs of ale, and sacks of grain. The garrison forges belched smoke and ash as blacksmiths sweated, hammering at cannon carriages. Teams of soldiers grunted over picks and shovels, fortifying the citadel's breastworks. The inhabitants of Leith knew they were in for a siege.

Carlos followed Fenella as she left a cookhouse. She made her way along the smoky alley between the armory and the bell tower. He caught up with her and grabbed her elbow and pulled her into a dark, narrow cul-de-sac straddled by a building above.

She snatched her arm free, crying, "Good Christ, what the—" She saw who it was. "You!" Then, in a fierce whisper, "Get away from me! You want him to *kill* me?"

Even in the dim light Carlos saw her fear. "I want to thank you. For keeping quiet about my wife."

"Forget it." She poked her head into the alley and looked both ways, as furtive as a cornered animal. "I told you to stay away from me. I can't be seen with you." The way was clear, and she was about to step out.

"Wait. I have to talk to you, that's all."

"Talk's enough to get my teeth knocked out."

"Fenella, listen. I can get you away from here. Out of the country."

She looked at him, stunned. "What?"

"That's what you want, isn't it? To get to your brother in Marseilles?"

Her eyes lit up. "You're leaving? You'd take me?"

"No, but I can get you out, and across to France."

That threw her. "How? What can—"

He held up his hands to stop her. "But I need you to do something first."

She studied him, eyes narrowed in suspicion. "And what would that be?"

"The storeroom in the cellar beside the armory. Does D'Oysel have keys to it?"

"He's got bloody keys for every bloody door in this bloody place."

"Could you get one? A key to the storeroom?"

"What for? You plan to help yourself to some turnips and bacon?"

"I'm going to help a fellow next door."

"In the armory?"

"Beneath it. There's a prisoner who'd like some air."

Her mouth fell open in surprise. "You want to spring one of the English? Why?"

"Doesn't matter why. All you need to know is that he can sail a boat. It will be waiting for you, a fishing boat, in the cove below the ramparts. Get me the key to the storeroom and I'll see that he takes you to France."

Four infantrymen tramped down the alley in front of them. Fenella ducked back farther into the gloom and snatched Carlos's sleeve to pull him after her. The stone vaulting above them was so low he had to bend his head. The soldiers tramped past.

"I . . . I can't," she said, her voice wavering, her bravado gone. He saw that she was shaking. "If he caught me stealing keys . . ."

"He won't. You've got quick wits. And he has to sleep sometime."

"Not him. He's the very devil. Watches every move I make."

He took hold of her shoulders. "Fenella, you can do this. Get clear of the bastard. Go to your brother. Live."

She looked at him, hope warring with her fear. The fear won. She shook her head in misery. "I can't. He'd break my neck."

"And if you stay? You know the English are coming. Have you ever seen a siege? I have. Starvation is a slow and painful death. People start eating horses. Then rats. Then, late at night, they start digging up fresh corpses. Get out now—it's your best chance, believe me. Stay, and you'll be a corpse, too."

Horror flooded her eyes. Her head lolled back against the wall in defeat. She groaned, "You're a cruel bastard, you are."

He saw that he had her. "The key. That's all."

She looked at him. "When?"

"Tomorrow night."

"How will we get out past the watch?"

"I'll see to that." He looked out into the alley, ready to go. It was clear. "Get the key to me by sundown tomorrow." He looked back at her. "All right?"

She hugged herself as though trying to come to terms with the overwhelming risks. "So, you and me and the Englishman, out on the briny deep."

"Not me. I'm staying."

She frowned. "And starve to death? Why not bolt with us?"

Duty, he was about to say, but that wasn't true. He had come to this God-cursed place for one reason only—to win the prize in Peru that he needed. Quadra could get it for him, and he'd be damned if he was going to give that up. Anyway, he'd soon be done here. He had written to Quadra his intention to be out before the English arrived. He would have fulfilled his mandate. The man could expect no more. "I'll leave, but not yet," he said.

"Suit yourself." A noise—a window banging open. "Oh, God." Fenella shrank back beside Carlos, terrified of being seen with him.

"I'll go first," he said. "Remember. Sundown."

He was walking back to his billet alone when a lieutenant caught up to him. "Sir, Commander D'Oysel would like to see you."

Carlos felt a jolt of fear. Had the turnkey overheard his talk with Adam and told D'Oysel? If so, he could join his brother-in-law in swinging from a gibbet. "Now? I'm on my way to send an important dispatch."

"He asked to see you immediately, sir."

No way out. He crossed the noisy courtyard crowded with soldiers drilling, and climbed the steps to D'Oysel's quarters. When he walked through the door, his fear dug in. The commander was on his feet in conference with a half dozen captains, and with them was the Queen Regent.

"Ah, Valverde," D'Oysel said smoothly.

The Queen turned to Carlos, a fevered look in her eyes. He knew she had some kind of chronic sickness, but at the moment she looked more keyed up than ill. All the officers' eyes were on him, and they, too, looked strangely excited. Something had happened. He bowed to the Queen. "Madam."

"Señor Valverde, we have received joyous news."

Joyous? He looked to D'Oysel for an explanation. D'Oysel met his gaze but said nothing. He was leaving this up to the Queen.

"God has answered our prayers," she said. "Your mighty king has been moved by our plight. A wise and pious monarch, he sees the terrible threat to Holy Mother Church here in my daughter's homeland realm. As a remedy, he is massing ten thousand troops to come to our aid in our fight against Satan."

Amazing. Exactly what D'Oysel wanted. "Do I understand you, madam? *Spanish* troops?"

"The very best. Veterans of King Philip's holy wars. They are sailing to us even as we speak." She smiled that fevered smile. "You look amazed, señor. As are we all. Amazed, and utterly grateful to your noble king. I wanted you to know immediately, for you have so honorably and faithfully represented His Majesty here with us."

He bowed again to be polite, thinking how extraordinary the news was. Spain throwing its weight into this war would change everything. The Queen of England, young, untested, and drowning in debt, could never match the might of Spain. He thought of Isabel, and her fear of England being conquered. She had thought France was the enemy, but England had far more to fear from Spain. If Spanish troops claimed victory in this island, they would never leave it, they'd be here to stay. Spain with its boot on England's throat—it rocked him. Isabel was more right than she knew.

"Lady Frances, is this the one you want for tomorrow?"

Frances looked up from folding the baby's smocks on the bed. Her maid, Nan, held up a garnet brocade gown. "Yes. And my new cloak—" This was hard, acting as though all were normal, as though

Christopher were not plotting treason in this very house. "The one with the sable trim." She set the folded smocks onto the pile to be added to the trunks that Nan was packing. She felt terrible about leaving Isabel in these dreadful circumstances, but Isabel's letter would soon reach the Queen, and then government officers would step in, take over. Meanwhile, Isabel was right—Frances had to think of Katherine. And of Adam. There must be no taint of suspicion on him because of his wife. Now that the decision was made, she wanted only to see morning, when she could be on her way to London. Home. Katherine would be safe there. "Have you packed your own things, Nan?"

"Soon as I'm done here, my lady."

The baby made a fussing sound from her cradle by the hearth, and Frances went to check on her. Katherine's tiny hands flailed in excitement at seeing her mother's face. It made Frances smile. "Are you eager to get home, sweet pea?" she cooed. She picked up the teething coral nestled in the blanket and offered it to the baby. It gave her a sad pang. The coral was Isabel's gift. Dear Isabel— how courageous she was. But what risks she was taking!

A knock on the door startled her. Her nerves were so on edge. And it was late. "Yes?" she called.

Her brother walked in. Frances fumbled the coral. "Christopher."

"I may not see you in the morning," he said. "I'm off at first light to Wooler. Thought it best to say good-bye now."

"Ah. That is thoughtful."

He looked at the trunks. "All ready, then?"

"Almost."

He looked at Nan. "Leave us, please."

Nan bobbed a curtsy and bustled out. Frances wished she could have held her back. She did not want to be alone with her brother.

He went to the cradle and gazed down at the baby, but with a blank look, his thoughts elsewhere. Fixed on treason, Frances thought. If she were a man she would strike him to the ground.

"That Indian boy of Isabel's, have you noticed anything odd about him?"

"Pedro? Well, he's foreign, so I suppose everything about him is odd." She went back to folding the baby's clothes on the bed. Anything to keep busy.

Christopher picked up the teething coral from the cradle and turned it absently in his hands. "He said something to Father York after mass."

"Pedro attended the mass?" Frances herself had organized the service at the mill for some of the servants, the most pious, but she had not known that Isabel's Indian lad had gone.

Christopher nodded, toying with the coral. "It was something he said in confession that's got me wondering."

Frances was shocked. "Father York broke confession?"

He gave her a look of scorn. "Don't be naïve, Frances. These are perilous times. Father York knows that better than anyone, and he came to me with this information. He said Isabel's Indian talked of his time in Scotland, and he confessed to lusting after a wench in Stirling."

Frances almost laughed. A mighty sin, indeed! "Poor little fellow," she said.

"Did you hear me? In *Stirling*. That's where the heretic rebels are. Or were—they're on the march eastward now to meet up with the English army." He crossed his arms, still holding the coral, and gave her a probing look. "Did Isabel tell you where she had been in Scotland?"

Frances's mouth had gone dry as canvas. "Leith," she managed. "To see her husband. You know that."

"Yes, but did she mention anywhere else?"

Could she throw him off the scent? She forced a tone of indignation. "Really, Christopher, you surprise me. Isabel is faithful to her husband and his cause. How dare you imply that she might be wanton."

"I am implying no such thing. Heaven forbid. I only wonder what her servant has been up to behind her back." Irritated, he tossed the coral back into the cradle as though tossing aside the topic. "Well, don't let's squabble. I came to wish you Godspeed." He came to her and made a small dart to kiss her cheek. She froze, allowing the kiss, and said, "Thank you."

"Write to me when you reach London." He started for the door.

Frances went back to folding the little smocks, waiting to hear the door close after him so she could breathe again.

He stopped. "Why would you say his cause?"

"Pardon?"

"You said, her husband and his *cause*." He turned. "Who said anything about causes?"

She gaped at him.

His eyes flashed with interest. "You know something."

"I?"

"Is it something about Isabel?"

She said as steadily as she could, "Isabel? I know that her heart is pure and—"

"Enough of that. You know something. Tell me."

Frances clasped her hands at her waist. Now that it was up to her, she was surprised that she felt no more fear of him. Nothing on earth could make her betray Isabel.

He gave a grunt of sudden understanding. "So that's it." His voice rang with wounded disgust. "She is a Thornleigh after all."

"That is nonsense, Christopher. You know her to be a good Catholic. If you are worried that she might speak to her family about Father York, I assure you she will not. Her first allegiance is to God."

"This is not about York. And you are lying."

"How dare you!"

"Tell me what you know of her."

"I don't know what you are talking about, and I want you to leave."

"No?" He went to the cradle and lifted the baby out. "You will tell me what you know about the woman. Do it now, before I stop this child's breath."

She did not understand. He held her daughter so gently in the crook of his arm, like a loving uncle. Yet his cupped hand, as big as the baby's face, hovered an inch above her mouth.

"Frances?"

She watched, terror crawling over her.

"*Now*, Frances." His hand came down, clamping over the baby's mouth and nose. Katherine did not move. Not a whimper. But her eyes sprang wide open.

"No!" Frances lunged to wrench his hand away. He stepped back, out of her reach. She lurched for him again. Again, he stepped back.

Katherine's face was turning blue.

"*Stop!*" Frances screamed.

❧ 25 ❧

The Postern Gate

Carlos struck the flint. The spark jumped to the thin cord he held, then burst into a flame the size of his thumb. It cast a flickering light over this corner of the dark, stone cellar beneath the garrison's great hall. The vaulted space, as long as a jousting yard, was stocked with victuals laid in for the expected siege. The quartermaster's orderly rows of sacks, barrels, casks, and crates smelled of musty hemp sacking and brine-soaked barrels of salt pork. Fenella had done her part, delivering the storeroom key to Carlos at his billet. Now the rest was up to him.

He shifted the burning cord to his other hand and glanced at Jorge Rodriguez, his comrade-in-arms from Continental campaigns a decade ago. He'd been happily surprised to find the Portuguese artilleryman here in Leith when he'd arrived at Christmas, but there was nothing happy about tonight's mission, and any surprises now could get them killed. Rodriguez knew it, too, and had been reluctant at first when Carlos had taken him aside in the alehouse yesterday and asked for his help. But he'd admitted that after a year and a half in the Leith garrison he was itching to get home to Lisbon and his wife and six children. "If I stay longer," he'd said, "when I get back, there may be a seventh." The purse of gold crowns that Carlos had dropped into his palm had clinched the deal. Rodriguez would get home with more money than the French would pay him in a year.

Now, in the cellar, they had shoved heavy sacks of grain into a heap, hefting them up as high as their shoulders, then had cleared a space around the sacks so the mound stood like a castle keep surrounded by a dry moat. Sweat glistened on Rodriguez's forehead from their burst of labor. Or maybe from the thought of their chances of getting away with this, Carlos thought grimly. The odds were not good. The plan depended on so many things going right, and when did that ever happen? He wasn't even sure Adam would cooperate.

He pushed his worries to the back of his mind. "Ready?" he said.

Rodriguez gave him a nod, looking dour but determined. "Ready."

Carlos stepped close to the flour sacks and dropped the burning cord. The sacking instantly caught fire. He turned to Rodriguez. "Let's go."

They took the back stairs and reached the ground floor of the great hall, keeping to the screened passage that led to the kitchens. The way was dimly lit by the spill of light from torches in the hall where soldiers were taking their ease before curfew. A wolfhound padded past Carlos. He and Rodriguez turned into the hall and walked through the crowd of men. Some sat in small groups, cleaning weapons. Others stood in knots, trading tales. Carlos nodded a greeting to a couple of men he had played dice with last night and stopped to talk to them. The casual face he showed them was a mask; he was very nervous. He had hoped to do this after midnight, when most of the garrison would be asleep, but the fisherman whose reeking little boat he had bought had said that after ten o'clock the tide would turn, challenging any vessel that set out into the estuary. Carlos had to get Adam Thornleigh out and on the water before ten.

They walked on, and Rodriguez nudged Carlos's elbow and jerked his chin toward a staircase leading down to the cellar. Carlos saw wisps of smoke rising from the stairs. No one else appeared to notice.

They stepped outside into the broad inner ward. Curfew was near, but some of the garrison's workers were still hard at it under torchlight. The quadrangle echoed with the clang of hammers, the jangle of harnesses, and gruff, tired voices.

"We'll give it a little time," Carlos said.

Rodriguez cast an anxious look at the armory that stood adjacent to the hall, butted up against its west wall. In preparation for siege, the armory was storing extra gunpowder. "If you're wrong about this, Valverde," he said in a low voice, "we'll all get blown to kingdom come."

Carlos wasn't worried about the fire spreading. The cellar was stone, and they had created the dry moat as a firebreak, and if this worked, the fire would be located soon enough and put out. A mixed blessing, that. What worried him more was the brightness of the rising moon. He looked up at it sailing out from behind scudding clouds. Though on the wane, it gave enough light that he could make out the faces of sentries patrolling the high walkway along the fortress's outer wall. He tried to convince himself that the moonlight was a good thing—there would be no need for a torch to light the fugitives' way down to the cove. But in fact it made him more nervous. If the French went after Adam, in this light he would be easy prey.

He took a deep breath to clear his head of such thoughts. He could not control the moon.

"That's time enough," he told Rodriguez. He motioned him to follow, and led the way next door to the armory. They opened the heavy doors and stepped inside. It was quieter there, the day's inventory done. Moonlight shone through the windows and glinted off racks of pikes and staves, muskets and pistols, breastplates and helmets. The massed longbows and stacked sheaves of arrows gave off a smell like fresh lumber, and there was a sharp tang of gunpowder in the air. What Carlos hoped to smell was smoke. The storeroom under the great hall ran under the armory, too. He had set the fire directly beneath it. He sniffed, and was glad when he caught an acrid whiff.

The watchman, round-faced and no more than twenty, got up from his bench where he was munching an apple. "Help you, sir?" he asked, jamming the apple in his pocket.

"Can't you smell that, soldier?"

"Sir?"

"We could smell it outside, for God's sake. Smoke. There's a fire. And it's somewhere near."

The watchman's mouth fell open in horror. They were standing inside a powder keg.

"Raise the alarm," Carlos ordered.

"Aye, sir!" The fellow grabbed a big brass hand bell from the bench and clanged it.

"Fire!" Rodriguez shouted out the open door.

Soon over a dozen men were pounding into the armory, and drifting smoke was visible from a loose floorboard beside the musket racks. The armory became a chaos of shouts and tramping boots, of questions and confusion, with more men arriving and jogging through in search of the smoke's source, while others outside shouted, "Fire!" In the din, Carlos and Rodriguez slipped downstairs to the basement lockup.

The stone staircase wound down to the corridor that held the cells. Carlos stopped halfway down and gestured to Rodriguez to halt. Fenella stood at the foot of the stairs, her back pressed against the wall so that the turnkey along the corridor could not see her. She had been watching for Carlos and she looked ready, but very frightened. She cast Carlos a questioning look, her eyes flicking to the armory above them where the thuds and shouts, though muffled, carried the sound of panic. Carlos nodded to her. She seemed to steel herself, then nodded back. She left the wall and ran down the corridor, shouting, "Fire!"

The turnkey stationed on his stool outside the Hole jumped up in alarm. He had heard the commotion above, not knowing what it was about. "Where is it?" he cried. *"Where?"*

She gasped and pointed to the Hole. "Look!"

He twisted around in fear. "Flames?"

Carlos and Rodriguez took the cue. They sprinted down the corridor, and Carlos grabbed the turnkey from behind and pinned his arms behind his back. The man cried out, unable to see who had attacked him. Rodriguez whipped a cloth around his mouth, gagging him, and Carlos dropped a burlap sack over his head. The turnkey struggled, but Carlos held him firmly while Rodriguez tied his wrists with a leather strip. Carlos snapped the iron ring of keys off the man's belt. He turned to Fenella. She looked terrified by the violent scuffle and had pulled out a stiletto. She crouched, on her guard against the trussed-up turnkey and against Rodriguez, too. The fear in her eyes was so frantic, and her grip on the knife so tight, Carlos was afraid she might lash out with it. "It's all right," he said to calm her. "You did fine. Put that away."

"Who's he?" she demanded.

"Rodriguez. He's with me."

She let out a wobbly breath, getting control of herself. She slid the knife into a sheath at her belt. *Everyone's too nervous,* Carlos thought. He looked through the gloom toward the Hole. Adam was on his feet, clenching the cell bars, watching them. Carlos tightened his grip on the squirming turnkey, and Rodriguez said, "What do we do with him?"

Fenella pointed to the empty cells. "Bring him here. Come!"

Following her, Carlos and Rodriguez dragged the hooded turnkey to an alcove between the cells. She opened a door to what looked to Carlos like a dark cupboard until the stink told him it was the turnkey's privy. They pushed him inside and Carlos closed the door. So far, so good, he thought with relief. The turnkey had not seen his face.

"Sweet Jesus, listen to that," Fenella said in fear, lifting her eyes to the ceiling. Soldiers pounded over the floor above them. "Sounds like half the garrison."

"The more the better," Carlos said quietly. "Did you bring the cloak?"

She picked up a bundled cloak of gray homespun wool, the kind an infantryman might have. It would cover the gash in the back of Adam's jerkin where he'd been wounded. Carlos took it and strode down the corridor to the Hole. Adam still gripped the bars, watching him come. He looked pale and gaunt, his eyes red-rimmed. He was eyeing Rodriguez and Fenella with a wild look of

confusion and suspicion. "What's happening?" he said. His condition made Carlos very nervous. The wound, and this foul place,
had sapped a lot of his strength. Was he too weak to make a run for
it? Could he even walk?

"We're getting you out," he said, unlocking the door. He thrust
the cloak at him. "Put this on."

Adam ignored it. He backed up, as wary as a cornered dog.

"I told you," Carlos said, "there will be no ransom. If you stay
here they will hang you."

"Why should I trust you? You're with the French."

"Not tonight. Believe me, I'm the only friend you've got."

Adam looked to be in an agony of doubt.

"Adam, there's a fishing boat waiting for you. All yours. You'll
be down to the shore before they know you're gone. Fenella
knows the way. Rodriguez will be your mate. They're sailing with
you."

Adam licked his cracked lips, trying to decide. Then flashed a
skeptical look at Rodriguez. "You know a sheet from a halyard?"

"No. But I can take orders."

Adam grunted, unimpressed. He took one last, hard look at Carlos and seemed to realize that this was his only hope. "All right."
He moved to his crewman, who lay curled up on the floor. Carlos
saw that the man's mutilated hand had gone black all the way to
the elbow. Gangrene. And his face was as white as a maggot. He
was so near death he hadn't moved despite the scuffle around him.
He was unconscious. "We'll have to carry him," Adam said.

Christ. "Too dangerous. I told you—just you."

"And I told *you*, I don't go without Braddock."

"That man?" Rodriguez said in disbelief. "He'll be dead by
morning."

"Shut up." Adam's bloodshot eyes looked fevered. "And get the
hell out of here, all of you."

"Adam—"

"Get away from me, Carlos. All of you, get away!"

Carlos shoved the cloak back into Fenella's hands and said to
Rodriguez, "Help me take him."

They came for him. He swung a fist at Carlos, but Carlos

ducked. Adam jabbed Rodriguez in the jaw. Rodriguez staggered from the blow, but quickly found his footing. Adam crept backward, hulking like a wrestler, waiting to take them on. But a man weak from a wound is no match against two who are fresh. They rushed him, each taking one of his arms. Grappling him between them, they yanked him toward the cell door. In a frantic burst of energy Adam swung both legs up and braced his feet against the bars with a thud that shook Carlos and Rodriguez and almost made them lose their balance. "Not without Braddock!" he cried. His bloodshot eyes were desperate as they fixed on Carlos. "If you *are* a friend you know I can't leave him!"

Carlos glared at him. Damn it, there was no time for this! Adam had a surprising reserve of strength, and if he kept resisting they'd never get him to the boat. Carlos yanked him backward so Adam's legs fell from the bars and dropped back down to the ground. "If we bring this man you'll come quietly?"

Adam was out of breath from his effort. "Yes."

Carlos went to the sick man and bent and lifted him in his arms. He felt like a sack of bones and stank of death. Carlos slung him over his shoulder and stood. "Now, come," he ordered Adam.

"What?" Rodriguez looked appalled. "How do you explain *him* if they stop us?"

"Say we're taking him to the infirmary. Say it's plague, then they'll keep clear."

"Are you brainsick, Valverde? Our chances are bad enough already. Leave him. I won't be hanged because of a dead man."

"Good Christ, leave the man!" Fenella said in horror. "If we don't go now, they'll find us and hang us *all!* And before they do, D'Oysel will have us screaming for mercy with his torture toys." She was hugging herself, shaking with fear. "Leave that man and let's *go!*"

Adam staggered a step, suddenly too weak to stand, and stumbled against Fenella. She grabbed him with both arms and steadied him. He got his balance and made an effort to stand tall.

"If you do this," Rodriguez told Carlos, "I'm out. You can have a dead man or me. Not both."

Carlos had never felt so torn. Rodriguez *had* to go with Adam.

Adam was too weak to sail to France on his own. "You hear that?" Carlos told him. "You are going to need Rodriguez. You won't make it alone." He went down on one knee and laid the crewman back on the floor. "This man stays." He got to his feet. "And you are coming." He jerked his chin in a signal to Rodriguez and again they came at Adam.

Adam whipped a knife from his sleeve. Carlos and Rodriguez froze. Where had he got that blade?

Fenella cried in surprise, "My knife!" The stiletto, Carlos realized. Adam's stumble against Fenella had been a feint.

Adam flashed the blade, flicking it toward Carlos, then Rodriguez. His grip was firm, and in his fevered look was the desperation of a wounded animal, unpredictable, dangerous. Carlos knew they could not reach him without someone getting cut, maybe killed.

"Stand back!" Adam warned. "I won't leave this man. Not while he draws breath!"

There was shouting, loud, right next door. Shouts of victory.

"Mãe do Deus," Rodriguez whispered in fear. "They've found the fire."

Fenella's hand flew to her mouth to block a scream. She cowered as if the soldiers could see her through the stone wall.

Carlos's back was clammy with cold sweat. *They'll soon find us.* He took a stiff breath and made a decision. It made him sick, but he forced down the bile in his throat before he could change his mind. He went down on one knee beside the dying crewman and made the sign of the cross over the man's face. He took hold of his head in both hands and gave it a sideways wrench. The neck snapped. The body gave a feeble jerk. Then lay still. Carlos, his hands shaking, looked up at Adam. *There. No more breath.*

Adam let out a grunt of shock as though he'd been punched in the stomach. He stared at Carlos, too stunned to speak. The others did, too.

Carlos felt a dizzying rush of shame and rage. Rage at Adam. *You've made me a murderer.* He sprang up and went for the stiletto Adam still held. He chopped Adam's wrist, and the blade flew from his hand and clattered on the floor. Fenella snatched it up.

Carlos drew his own dagger and pressed its tip at Adam's throat. "If it weren't for your sister I would leave you to rot," he growled. "Come quietly, and help these two who've risked their lives for you, or I swear I will finish you. I'll tell the French I stopped you escaping and I'll be a hero. So, resist and get your throat cut, or sail to France and live to see your daughter. It's up to you."

Adam blinked as if he had just recovered his wits. He walked out stiffly but peaceably, Carlos and Rodriguez tightly flanking him in case he resisted again. Fenella led the way. She took them up the stairs toward the armory, but halfway up she opened an arched door and they followed her into a dank, windowless room that held instruments of torture. The rack, branding irons, whips, the press. The place stank of excrement. Adam balked in fear, as though seeing his worst suspicion about Carlos come true.

"I said you're going to France, and I meant it," Carlos said. "Follow her."

Fenella led them through the torture chamber and up a narrow staircase that brought them to another door. She opened it a crack, and as she looked out the three men waited in uneasy silence. Carlos tried to steady his nerves. The next step would be the hardest. This door would lead them outside. The place swarmed with soldiers now organizing to carry water to put out the fire.

Satisfied that the way was clear, Fenella motioned them to follow her, and they stepped out onto the grassy space of the outer bailey. No soldiers in sight. They were at the back of the armory, and the back of the fortress. A long stone's throw away rose the outer wall. It was darker here. The shaggy grass between the high outer wall and the armory looked black, silvered with the faintest sheen of moonlight. An ox bellowed. There was a smell of sheep dung. Animal sheds hulked against the outer wall.

"What now?" Fenella asked in a tight whisper. Carlos was listening to the clamor of voices in the inner ward at the far side of the armory where the fire-fighting continued. That's where the well was. But the voices were getting louder. Fenella, too, heard them coming. "The cistern," she said in horror.

Carlos shot her a look. What cistern?

"By the sheep sheds. Rainwater."

Christ! Soldiers would come around the corner soon to fill their buckets. *It'll be a miracle if we get through this.*

He motioned for them all to stay tight against the armory wall, and pointed to the walkway atop the outer wall to show why. Two sentries stood there, black silhouettes as the moon hid behind the clouds. He pointed diagonally down from the sentries, across to the postern gate in the outer wall. "That's where you're going," he said. The low, narrow door was always open for fishermen delivering the day's catch, and for servants going to do chores in the town. It would stay open until the English arrived. "Wait here," he said. "Watch me. When you see my signal, go. Fenella knows the way."

He strode across the wet grass to the outer wall and climbed the stairs set flush against it two stories high. He could hear the growl of the ocean on the other side, waves kicking up in the estuary, and when he reached the top he felt the salt-tanged wind hit his face. The two sentries on the wall walk heard him and turned. Carlos knew one of them. Bouchard. He'd played dice with him last week in the alehouse. Fraternizing with the lower ranks was something the French officers, all the sons of aristocrats, never did. Carlos was glad now that he had.

"Bouchard," he said, "did you see the fire from here?"

"Monsieur Valverde. Yes. Well, we saw the smoke. Christ, was it the armory?"

"I don't know. So much confusion." All three of them looked down at the inner ward. Carlos could see the front of the armory where men swarmed with torches and buckets, and dogs ran around barking, excited by the crisis. He could also see its east wall and the corner that led to the back, but he couldn't see Adam and Fenella and Rodriguez pressed up against the back wall, waiting. "Thought I'd join you fellows up here until it's out," he said to the sentries. "If the armory blows, those poor bastards will land in Edinburgh in pieces."

They smiled at his dark jest. "What started it, do you think?" the other sentry asked.

Carlos shook his head. "Don't know." He caught sight of D'Oysel leading a gang of soldiers with buckets out the armory's front door. He was in shirtsleeves, striding ahead, waving as if giving orders—

and leading the soldiers to the east end of the building. Carlos's heart thumped in his chest. Soon D'Oysel's gang would turn the corner and then reach the back wall.

It has to be now.

To distract the sentries he pointed across the inner ward to the blacksmith's shed. "Look! Is that more flames? In the smithy?"

Bouchard and the other man took a few anxious steps closer to get a better look. It was enough for Carlos. He took a quick step back until he could see the three fugitives, mere black shadows against the dark wall. D'Oysel's gang was almost at the corner. Carlos waved to the fugitives, a clear signal. The three shadows dashed across the grass toward the postern gate. Carlos flinched as the moonlight hit them like a beacon.

They were halfway across the grassy space when Fenella stopped and turned. Carlos saw her face, her look of alarm. She was hearing D'Oysel and his soldiers coming. *Madre de Dios, Fenella, don't stop!* She turned back to Adam and Rodriguez and jerked a signal to them to carry on. The two men ran for the postern gate. Fenella turned back again just as D'Oysel and his men swarmed around the corner. She hurried to D'Oysel and reached him, making frantic gestures, leading him back toward the building.

Carlos held his breath. What was she doing? Distracting him? Or informing on Adam and Rodriguez? The two fugitives slipped out through the gate and closed it. They disappeared into the night.

"Can't see anything at the smithy," Bouchard said, rejoining Carlos.

"No?" Carlos said. It was hard to find his voice. Fenella had saved Adam and Rodriguez. He was sure of that. But she had sacrificed her own chance to flee. He swallowed. What would she do now?

"Seems the commander's got it under control," Bouchard said.

Carlos watched as over two dozen of D'Oysel's men rushed to the cistern to fill their buckets. D'Oysel sent a couple of men into the building through the same door Carlos and the fugitives had used to get out, no doubt to check that no stray sparks posed a danger to the lockup. Which meant they'd soon find that Adam was gone. Meanwhile, D'Oysel took Fenella by the elbow and led her back toward the inner ward.

Carlos forced himself to exchange more quips with the sentries, who were glad, they said, to resume their standard, boring watch, the more boring the better. He bade them good night. Questions battered his mind as he went down the wall stairs. What had Fenella told D'Oysel? She was smart, so maybe she had said she'd gone behind the armory to check the cistern. How long until the soldiers who'd gone down to the lockup brought D'Oysel word of Adam's escape? Then he'd send out search parties. Did Adam and Rodriguez have time to reach the cove? Could they even find it without Fenella's help?

It made him more nervous than he'd ever felt. How could he pretend to act normally when the whole escape might be blasted to hell? If D'Oysel caught Adam, he would torture him to tell who had helped him escape. Torture Rodriguez, too. And whether they divulged anything or not, D'Oysel would hang Adam. Carlos couldn't live with that. And Fenella—what would D'Oysel do to her? What would *she* divulge?

He had to find out what was happening.

Pedro was afraid he had failed Señora Isabel. Yesterday, his first day on the road, he had made good speed, had ridden almost non-stop even though the spring mud caked his horse's legs and spattered Pedro's, too. He had stopped last night for just a few hours of sleep in a farmer's byre before setting out again in darkness before dawn. But this afternoon he had come to a river where the bridge had fallen in from all the rain, and that had stopped him. A team of men were working to rebuild the bridge, but it would take time, and the señora had said he was to get to London with her letter as fast as his horse would carry him. He did not know how far he would have to go to find another bridge, or even which way to try. He had asked the men, but it was hard to understand their impossible language of English. So he had waited. Dismounted, and sat on a tree stump, and watched them work, and waited.

They had finished the job by dusk. Now he was on the road

again and it was dark. Had he failed the señora? He remembered her face, how earnest she had looked, and how sad since she and her lord, Señor Valverde, had fought. Pedro thought she was pretty, and she always smiled at him even though she was sad, and thinking about her now made him want to do what she wanted. But he hadn't stopped for *that* long. She would understand.

Under the bright moonlight the land stretched out in long, lonely, brown hills that looked tired of life. So different from the peaks behind Trujillo with bright snow on their heads and glossy jungle at their feet. He liked that place better. A happier place to live. But then he thought of the milkmaid, Liza, at Yeavering Hall, and the way the tip of her tongue showed pink between her teeth when she laughed. Maybe the place you lived in did not matter so much. Thinking of her, he wanted to deliver the letter in London and get back as fast as he could to Yeavering Hall.

He was leaving a poor village where big trees grew around a graveyard, when he heard the sound of horses behind him. He turned in the saddle. Five men, riding toward him. He was astonished to see the man leading them. The lord of Yeavering Hall.

"Halt!" the lord called. "You, boy! Stop."

Pedro's stomach seemed to drop. The señora had said, *"Let no one stop you. No one."* But how could he disobey the great lord of the manor? He had already slowed to look at them. It seemed only right and proper to stop.

But the señora's words filled his head again. *"Let no one stop you."* He kicked his horse's flanks and bolted down the road, away from the great lord's horsemen.

They came galloping after him, the lord shouting at him, angry. "I said stop, you wretched heathen!"

That made Pedro angry. He was a God-fearing Christian, no heathen. A good rider, too, and much lighter a-horse than those big beef-eating men, so he galloped on.

But some devil drove them, and he heard the hooves getting closer, heard their horses breathing like bellows. They caught up to him at the edge of a fallow field. Surrounded him. His horse shied in fear. Pedro hung on. They were all around him. What was happening?

"Get it," the lord told his men.

One reached across and grabbed for Pedro. He lurched back and the man's grab missed. But a hand from behind snatched his collar and yanked him with a savage jerk. Pedro's foot twisted in his stirrup as he tumbled.

❧ 26 ❧

The Cove

Carlos crossed the courtyard, heading for D'Oysel's quarters. All around him soldiers were milling, everyone in high spirits after putting out the fire. He went through the mess hall and climbed the stairs, trying hard not to hurry, not look anxious. He was ready for D'Oysel to suspect him of some involvement in the escape; that had been inevitable—Adam was his brother-in-law, and Carlos had asked D'Oysel to spare his life. But his status as Quadra's emissary was too solid for D'Oysel to make such a damning accusation without proof. All Carlos had to do was stick to his story: he'd been talking to soldiers in the hall when the fire had broken out and the escape had happened. If asked, they would innocently confirm that he had been there. So D'Oysel had no proof—unless Fenella talked.

In the antechamber he found D'Oysel's clerk, Fontaine, in a hushed discussion with a couple of captains. Carlos nodded to them. "Lescarbot, any news of how the fire started?"

"No, but that's not the worst of it, Valverde. The English captain who was in the Hole—he's escaped."

Carlos feigned surprise. "How?"

Lescarbot shrugged. "Don't know. The commander has ordered search parties. They'll be combing the town. He can't hide for long."

The town. Thank God. Not the cove. If Adam and Rodriguez had found the boat, they would soon be under way and safe.

The commander's door opened and a man shuffled out. Carlos stiffened—it was the turnkey from the Hole. Two guards flanked him and his hands were tied behind him. He looked cowed, terrified. D'Oysel had clearly given him a rough time, and he was almost certainly headed for a cell. As he moved through the room with the guards he looked straight at Carlos. Carlos held his breath, half expecting him to point and say, *"That's the one."* But nothing registered in the man's eyes beyond his own misery, and the guards led him away. Carlos relaxed a little. In the Hole he had been careful to not let the turnkey see his face when he and Rodriguez had gagged and hooded him.

He was daring now to hope that this might work out. If D'Oysel had no proof against him, and Adam had gotten safely away on the water, maybe the whole thing would blow over. With the English army almost at their throats, D'Oysel had far bigger problems to deal with than one escapee.

There was muffled shouting behind D'Oysel's door. Fontaine and the captains shot uneasy looks in that direction. Carlos asked, "Who's in there with him?"

"His woman."

His heart thudded. Fenella, the turnkey *had* seen. She had expected to be safely away with Adam by now. He wiped a bead of sweat off his upper lip. "What a night," he said to the clerk. He nodded to the wine decanter on the desk. "Mind if I help myself?"

"Of course, señor, allow me to—"

"No, don't bother, I'll get it." The desk was near D'Oysel's door and he wanted to hear. His hand was a little unsteady as he poured wine into a goblet. More shouts sounded behind the door. D'Oysel's voice, in a rage. Carlos could make out only a few words, but that was enough: "You were *there* . . . Who put you up to it? . . . Who?"

Carlos knocked back the wine. A devil's voice inside him said, *Stay out of it. Deny everything. D'Oysel has no proof, just the word of a whore who'll say anything to protect herself. Go back to your billet. It'll blow over.*

Then he heard reality—Fenella's voice. Her words were harder to hear, indistinct, her voice too soft. Was she confessing? But then D'Oysel yelled again, "Tell me, you lying bitch!" and Carlos knew that she had not told him a thing. It amazed him. He closed his eyes in shame. *She saved Adam and Rodriguez, and now she's saving my skin, too.*

D'Oysel's shouts got louder, shriller. The clerk and the captains set to talking even more loudly, as though to block out the unpleasantness happening beyond the door, not get involved. D'Oysel yelled something furious, but he had moved farther from the door and Carlos couldn't make it out. Then Fenella's voice . . . crying?

A crash. Fenella screamed. There was a sickening thud.

He's going to kill her.

Carlos threw open the door. Fenella was on the floor, moaning, struggling to get up. Blood covered the side of her face. D'Oysel stood over her with a broken wine bottle, its jagged edge gleaming with blood. He was breathing hard, and his eyes were bright with fury. He shot a look at Carlos. "Thought she was a pretty piece, Valverde? See how you like her face now."

Carlos closed the door. "Let her go, D'Oysel. She's not the enemy."

Fenella had made it up onto her hands and knees and was crawling away from D'Oysel, trying to reach the desk to hide beneath it. He kicked her in the ribs. She toppled, whimpering, and curled into a ball.

"Enemies *within*, Valverde." He bent and grabbed a fistful of Fenella's hair. "Like this lying cunt." He dragged her by the hair. She screamed in pain.

Carlos lunged for him and hauled him away from her. "I said let her go!" He threw D'Oysel against the desk.

D'Oysel staggered, but got his balance and turned on Carlos, his voice a snarl. "She was part of the escape! I'll get it from her yet. And if you're involved, Valverde, I swear I'll have a piece of your hide before your fine friends intervene!"

He twisted back to Fenella. She lay on her back, moaning. He still held the broken bottle, and he stood over her, the jagged glass poised to gouge her face.

THE QUEEN'S GAMBLE   333

Carlos grabbed two fistfuls of D'Oysel's collar. "Stop. Or I'll stop you forever."

"You wouldn't dare—you son of a whore." He shouted to the antechamber, "Fontaine!"

Carlos grappled him tighter. "Shut up."

"Fontaine! I need—"

Carlos snatched him by the hair and smashed his face down on the desk. Bone cracked. D'Oysel slumped to the floor, blood gushing from his nose. Coughing blood, he groped for Carlos's boot. Carlos kicked him in the head. D'Oysel sprawled on his back. He jerked in a convulsion. His eyelids fluttered, then closed. He went still.

Fenella struggled to her hands and knees, staring at D'Oysel's inert body, his bloodied face. Her own blood smeared her mutilated cheek and matted her hair. She sank back on her heels and looked at Carlos, stunned. "Sweet Jesus," she whispered.

He felt so shaky he was afraid he might fall. *Another murder.* No, wait—he could see D'Oysel's chest move. *He's still breathing.* Relief flooded him. His body was clammy with sweat. He took deep breaths, fighting to get calm. *Think!* He looked at Fenella. He had to get her out of there before D'Oysel came to. Her only hope was the boat. But had Adam already sailed? "Can you walk?" he asked.

She was so disoriented she looked like she didn't understand. Her cheek was bleeding badly.

He gripped her arm to help her up. "We have to get you to the boat. Now."

She blinked as if waking up. "Yes . . . I can walk." With his help she struggled to her feet.

Carlos grabbed D'Oysel's wrists and dragged him behind the desk so no one could see him from the door. He looked around. A folded shirt lay on a sideboard. He grabbed it and handed it to Fenella. "Press hard. To stop the blood." She did as he said. He went to the door. "We do this fast. You're my captive. Say nothing. All right?"

She straightened up and took a ragged breath and nodded.

He opened the door. The clerk and the two captains turned.

Carlos said, "The commander fell. He'll need some help." They looked in surprise toward D'Oysel's room. Carlos shoved Fenella out, holding her roughly by the arm. "I'm taking her to the lockup." He marched Fenella past the men. They were already on their way in to see to D'Oysel.

Across the inner ward they went, Carlos holding Fenella's elbow to support her—and himself, too. She was so rocky on her feet she stumbled several times, but he got her around to the back of the armory and across the grass, and they slipped through the postern gate. They had made it out.

But Carlos was horribly aware of the bright moonlight on them as they went down the stone staircase. The wind was stronger here outside the fortress walls. The staircase turned twice with sharp angles. They reached the bottom, where the stony ground was the flat top of a crag above the ocean. A main path led to the left, toward the town.

Fenella stopped, in pain, and leaned against him. But her eyes shone with relief. "We did it."

Holding her to support her, he looked back up the steps for any soldiers coming after them. "Not yet."

"Don't worry, they'll be swarming the town, that's where he sent them." She lowered the blood-soaked shirt from her cheek. "I'm glad you did him. I wanted to. Couldn't get out my knife."

"You did enough." He only hoped Adam hadn't sailed yet. "Which way to the boat? You're the leader now."

She pointed to the right where a faint trail led through trees that hugged the ridge of the crag. They set out along it. Mercifully, the trees hid them from the moon. The trail wound down the crag through scrub brush, and finally to the rock-strewn cove. A stony beach fanned out in a crescent where waves washed in, mumbling over the stones. There on the water, three boat lengths from the beach, the fishing boat stood at anchor. Rodriguez stood at the water's edge, his eyes on the boat. Hearing Carlos and Fenella, he turned, astonished to see them.

"Good Christ, you made it!" He frowned at Fenella's blood-smeared cheek. "But not without a fight, eh?"

"We won," she said proudly.

Adam got up from a boulder he'd been sitting on. He looked surprised to see Carlos. "You came."

Carlos said, almost as surprised, "You waited."

"For her," Rodriguez said. Then he jerked a thumb at Adam. "*His* call."

Carlos felt too much to speak. Adam's code: He didn't leave crew behind.

Rodriguez said, "Enough talk. Let's be off!" He ran for the water and splashed out knee deep.

Fenella threw her arms around Carlos's neck and kissed him. She let out a happy laugh. "So, lover, it's you and me to France after all, eh? Come on." She ran into the water after Rodriguez, hiking up her skirts and calling to him, "Wait up, you lousy Portugee. We're coming!"

Carlos and Adam stood alone on the beach, face-to-face. The lapping waves nudged the soles of their boots.

"Your friend is right, we have to set sail," Adam said. "The tide will soon turn."

Carlos nodded, glad that Adam looked stronger now that he was free. He glanced at the battered little boat rocking in the waves. "Is it seaworthy?"

"I've been aboard, had a look. She'll make it."

"And this wind is good?"

"A fresh breeze, yes. It'll be fair on our quarter."

"Go, then. No time to waste."

Adam frowned, surprised. "You're not coming?"

Carlos shook his head.

"Are you sure? You've taken a big risk, Carlos. They'll be after you."

"I know. But the water's not for me. I'll ride."

"Where will you go?"

"Never mind about me. How about you?"

"I'll take them to Amsterdam. They can go on from there. I'll be coming back."

"What? Why?"

"To fight for England."

England again. "You sound like your sister."

"You sound like a man with nothing to fight for."

It took him aback.

"Captain, come on!" Rodriguez called from the boat.

"Coming!" Adam called back.

No more time. Carlos held out his hand. Adam clasped it. *"Vaya con Dios,"* Carlos said. Go with God.

"And you."

He watched Adam wade out to the bobbing boat and climb aboard. Watched Rodriguez haul up the anchor. Watched Adam raise the sail with Fenella's help, and then take the tiller and steer the little craft out toward the sea.

Now he was alone. Adam's question stuck with him. *Where will you go?* He looked out at the dark water. He had just destroyed his own future. Cut himself adrift from everything he had come to Scotland for. He had done Quadra's bidding with the French for one reason only—to win the Trujillo council seat. It would have brought enough cash to pay all his debts. Make him a member of Peruvian society. Secure his son's future. Instead, he had helped a prize French prisoner escape, and had all but killed their commander. There would be no seat now. No advancement, ever. The King would revoke his *encomienda*. The King's agents might even arrest him. He might make a convincing case that he had attacked D'Oysel in self-defense, since the bastard's temper was well known, but all dreams of a lordly life in Peru were blasted. If he managed to evade a jail cell and make it back to Trujillo, he'd be lucky to end up owning a mule.

Yet he didn't feel like cursing his fate. He felt strangely calm. No, better than calm. He felt buoyed up, felt good for the first time in months. Like he had cut the chains that had kept him striving for Quadra's reward, like some plow horse in harness. Adam had escaped a dungeon, but Carlos felt like the one who had been set free.

He looked out at the silver stars of moonlight snapping on the waves. Looked up at the vast sky of moon-silvered clouds. He listened to the waves shushing over the stones, and felt the wind tingle his skin. The air held a faint smell of wood smoke—the smell of hearth and home. The place seemed beautiful. He suddenly knew why. Isabel. Her spirit had brought him to this beach.

Adam's words came back to him. *"To fight for England."* And what Fenella had said days ago: *"At least the Scottish fools are fighting for something they care about. Their home."*

Isabel cares. She's fighting for something that matters. Why had he not seen how extraordinary that was? He had been so sure of what *he* wanted, so sure it was the *right* thing to want—wealth and status, a life of leisure delivered by docile Indian semi-slaves. Wanting success like that kept most men striving all their lives, slaves themselves in their hunger to get it.

Not him. Not now. Now he wanted what Isabel wanted. To fight for something that mattered. All his life as a soldier he'd been hired to destroy. Isabel was fighting to build. England. And England was in more jeopardy than she knew if Spanish troops were on the way. He wanted to be on her side in this. Wanted it almost as much as he wanted her. It sent a ripple of excitement though him. To be *for* something, standing with her.

Only, he was so far away from her. She was in London. He had sent her there in his fury, thrown her out—and burned the bridge between them. It made him shudder to remember her riding away in tears. He was a bastard as brutal as D'Oysel. Could Isabel ever forget that? Could she ever forgive him?

He could no longer see Adam's boat in the darkness. The wind was cold. He suddenly felt very alone on the beach.

Time to move. A search party could come this way at any moment. He turned and walked away from the water. He needed a horse.

❧ 27 ❧

The Players

The wind rattled the windows of Yeavering Hall as Isabel left her bedchamber to check on Frances. A ferocious wind it was this evening, a lion roaring in with March, making Isabel's headache worse, a pounding pain. For days she had scarcely slept. Nor could she eat much, though she feared the lack of nourishment might hurt the babe in her belly. She was so tense from her weeks of watching Grenville, so worn by worry, so alone with her fears, she felt as hollow as a husk that the wind might spin away.

One of her worries was Frances, who had not left for London as planned. She was ill with a fever—so the chamberlain had told Isabel yesterday morning, stopping her as she had knocked on Frances's bedchamber door. Frances had not answered. The door had been locked. Isabel had not seen her since. She felt terrible that sickness had struck Frances, and even worse that it was forcing her sister-in-law to stay in this dangerous house.

She reached the door now to find a man standing guard, a dull-eyed Grenville retainer armed with dagger and sword. A chill touched Isabel's scalp. Was the man on some kind of death watch? "How fares Lady Frances?" she asked.

"No better."

"I would like to see her. Please, it would do her good."

He shook his head. "No one goes in. Master says the fever would spread."

Isabel heard Frances's baby cry behind the locked door. That made no sense. If Frances was wracked with fever she would never keep the child nearby, for fear of infecting her. The cry was followed by a woman's muffled murmuring, tense and low. Surely it was Frances. The baby's cries stopped. What was happening? The stony face of Grenville's man told Isabel nothing—except that she would not get past him. She turned away and went downstairs, more anxious than ever. If the woman behind the door was Frances, she was not fevered. And if not fevered, why was she being kept in seclusion?

So many troubles—Isabel felt overwhelmed by them. She had failed to discover anything more about the planned uprising, yet had an awful sense that the time was near. Grenville, though always gracious to her, had been careful to keep the organizational details secret. She knew that he and his co-conspirators planned to ride in force to Durham to raise the revolt, but she did not know when. She knew there were perhaps a dozen more powerful men of Northumberland, Yorkshire, and Cumbria who were ready to join them in Durham with their forces, and then all would march on London, but she did not know who they were. She knew that the Queen Regent of Scotland was involved, preparing the way for her daughter to seize the English throne, but Isabel did not know how. All she had learned was that Grenville and his plotters had scheduled their next meeting for Sir Ralph Donaldson's home near Wooler eleven miles away. The location was more convenient for the other men, Grenville had quietly told her at breakfast, since the heavy spring rains had left the roads around Yeavering like muddy bogs. Isabel was not invited.

She was in misery. Had her attempts to help Queen Elizabeth been worth the heartrending choices she had made? Because of her, Nicolas remained a hostage. Because of her, Tom Yates was dead. Because of her, Carlos had turned against her, their marriage shattered. The loss of his love still reamed her heart as though he had dug his dagger into it. And here at Yeavering Hall she faced terrifying consequences if Grenville should come to suspect her double-dealing. She could not wait to leave this suffocating place! If she stayed one more day she felt she would break from the strain. And why *should* she stay? If Pedro was making good speed to London, the Queen would soon have her letter and know about the plot. Why should Isabel risk her life to get proof? The crisis was out of her hands. She could leave. She *would* leave, tomorrow. Making the decision brought a blessed relief.

She would see her son! A bubble of joy broke through her swamp of worries. She imagined pulling his sturdy little body into her arms and finally taking him home.

Home? Her stomach lurched as she remembered Carlos's contempt. Would he bar her from their home in Trujillo as he had threatened? Would he take Nicolas back with him and forbid her to see him? Was her parents' house to be her home now, like a childless widow with nowhere else to go? It brought a surge of anger. Carlos had not even *listened* to her reasons.

"You're just in time for the fun, Mistress Valverde," a young maid said gaily, coming up the stairs with a tray of food as Isabel reached the bottom step.

Isabel blinked at her, then realized—the actors. They had been Grenville's guests for as long as she had been here, and tonight they were to give their final performance before they traveled south. She nodded at the covered dishes the girl was taking up. "Is that for Lady Frances?"

"Yes. Too bad she'll miss the play."

Isabel asked if she had seen Frances, but the maid said no, her orders were to leave the food at the door. "A fierce fever, I warrant, poor lady." She hurried on up the stairs, leaving Isabel even more confused and worried about Frances.

She found the great hall humming with excitement. Maid-servants scurried with goblets of wine and pots of foaming ale. Footmen had dragged the communal dinner tables against the walls and now were shoving benches into position in front of the makeshift stage. The chamberlain's men, perched on ladders, were stringing curtains on either side of the stage to mask the ac-tors as they prepared, and behind the curtains the sounds of tuning lutes and viols lilted above the chatter of the household folk who were streaming in from the kitchens, stables, dairy house, bakehouse, and brewhouse, eager to take their seats.

It was the last place Isabel wanted to be. She had intended to stay in her bedchamber all evening, but Grenville's footman had delivered a note to her door late that afternoon, a friendly invitation to join him for the festivities. She had been at great pains to show him an amiable face, to keep him believing she was in harmony with his plot, and could not risk marring that impression now. She saw him standing near the stage, arms folded, watching the preparations. She took a breath and moved through the hall past the bustling servants, and joined him.

"Ah, Isabel," he said. "Eager for the entertainment?"

She felt the warmth of his smile on her and found it bizarrely comforting. Bizarre that he, unlike Carlos, harbored her no ill will.

She forced a smile in return. "Well, sir, your people surely are." The hall rang with the high spirits of the household folk at this welcome break from their dawn-to-dusk chores. Grenville had ensured a good supply of ale, and as fast as the tapster and his helpers filled mugs from a row of barrels, the throng of men-at-arms, maidservants, grooms, footmen, clerks, officers of the household and their wives quaffed it down. Their children darted about like fish in shallows, and dogs trotted from one handout of food scraps to the next. A maid curtsied to Grenville and held out goblets of wine to him and Isabel. Grenville took one. Isabel declined.

"How is Frances?" she asked. "They will not let me in to see her."

"No, I would not have you fall ill, too. But she is greatly improved today, rest assured."

She was relieved. It explained why Frances had the baby with her. Yet there was something in Grenville's eyes, a darkness, that made her uncomfortable. "Yet you still fear for her health?"

"No, it is not that. I have had news, Isabel. Momentous events in Scotland. My clerk galloped back from the market in Kirknewton, where he heard it. Queen Elizabeth's army has reached Leith and is preparing to lay siege."

Isabel felt it like a cold hand at her throat. Carlos was inside

Leith. Her anger at him vanished, and fear for him swelled in its place. He was an experienced fighter, but even veteran soldiers dreaded a siege with its threat of death from starvation or disease.

"But take heart," Grenville went on. "The Queen Regent's soldiers will staunchly defend the fortress. And there is wonderful news from Antwerp. Thirteen ships with eight thousand Spanish troops, veterans of King Philip's wars in the Low Countries, are set to embark for Scotland to support God's cause there. We must pray that they arrive soon."

Isabel nodded, pretending to agree, but this news stunned her. Spain and France combined, against England! It was horrible. She had never felt so torn. English defeat could bring down Elizabeth, her parents, Adam. Yet English victory could mean Carlos's death.

Grenville lowered his voice to an intimate, urgent murmur. "I see that you feel the deep significance of this moment, its bearing on our grand goal. This is not a night for stage foolery, not for you and me. I have asked Father York to meet me at the mill to say a private mass. You will join me, will you not? We will pray God to give strength to the righteous defenders of His creed."

He asked so fervently, Isabel did not see how she could refuse. And why *not* go? It was impossible to sit here pretending an interest in silly theatrics. In the desert of merriment around her, she felt the little chapel in the mill beckoning like an oasis. A place to unburden her heart to God. Grenville would pray for an English defeat. She would pray for the opposite—and for Carlos's life.

Grenville drank down his wine and handed the goblet to a passing maid. He offered his arm to Isabel. "Shall we?"

She hooked her elbow around his. *One last night*, she told herself. *With the morning sun I'll be riding to London.*

They crossed the length of the hall, making for the family quarters at the north end where Grenville's library was. From it, the tunnel led to the mill. Grenville opened the library door for her. She took a last glance over her shoulder—and what she saw made her halt.

A man had come in at the far end of the hall. A tall man, standing with his back to her. The moving throng blocked a clear view of him, but she glimpsed muddy riding boots, a dark blue cloak, a sword at his hip. He turned to scan the crowd, and when she saw his face her heart leapt. Carlos! She could hardly believe her eyes! It seemed impossible . . . yet there he was, looking around, stopping a passing clerk to speak to him. Questions swarmed her. Had he deserted? Why was he here? Had he come for *her?*

"What is it?" Grenville asked. His gaze followed hers. "You know that man?"

She turned to him, smiling in wonder and bewilderment. "My husband!"

His face clouded. "Good heavens."

She turned back, eager to spot Carlos again through the mass of people. Every muscle in her yearned to run to him. She could not stop herself from calling out, "Carlos!"

Grenville's hand clamped over her mouth, gagging her. She staggered at the shock of it. His other hand roughly gripped her upper arm. He yanked her into the library. Her eyes above his hand flicked in panic to Carlos. He was talking to the groom. He had not heard her. Grenville shut the door.

His bailiff was waiting. Morton, a bear of a man with a shaggy beard.

"Hold her here," Grenville said. "Let no one in."

Carlos saw that he had walked in on a household feast.

"Not as such, sir," the clerk explained when Carlos asked. "The players are set to enact the struggle of Saint George against Beelzebub." He pointed to the stage. "It's a favorite 'round here."

Carlos was about to ask where he might find the lord of the manor when he noticed a finely dressed man striding toward him. Chances were it was Grenville. As if to confirm it, the clerk made a quick, fawning bow to the man, then hustled away. "Sir Christopher Grenville?" Carlos asked as he reached him.

"I am, sir," Grenville replied with a friendly smile. "I'm afraid you have me at a disadvantage. I do not know your name."

Carlos introduced himself, then said, "I've come for my wife." He had been riding hard from the Scottish border, hoping he could cover the miles to London in a few fast days. Isabel would be there, at her father's house. But in Alnwick he had stopped at an inn for a meal and learned that she was with her relations at Yeavering Hall. The talkative landlady had beamed with delight at being in the know. "Every soul hereabouts has heard of the Spanish-English lady what staggered into the Hall, sir, half dead from the storm. Black and white she was with the frostbite, so I heard."

Carlos had knocked back his ale in pained silence. He hated to think of Isabel suffering so. Hated himself. He had cast her out into that storm.

"Ah, don't you fret, sir. My husband's cousin delivered a wagon of coal to the Hall and he saw the lady. You'll find her hale and hearty now."

Grenville said cheerfully, "Señor Valverde, it is a pleasure to meet a kinsman. For that is what you are, sir. Since you married a daughter of the house of Thornleigh, and my sister married Sir Adam, we are one family, under God."

Carlos mustered a smile. "True." He appreciated the man's goodwill but had no stomach for chat. He only wanted to see Isabel.

"Pardon me," Grenville went on, "but I am somewhat confused. I understood you were in Edinburgh, serving his Majesty King Philip at the fortress of Leith."

"My services were no longer needed."

"May I ask when you left?"

"Yesterday." He was looking around for Isabel.

"And can you tell me how things stand there? We heard that the Queen's army will shortly lay siege. Do her forces seem strong enough to vanquish the French?"

"Strong, by all reports, but not strong enough if Spanish troop ships arrive to take them on."

"So that report is true?" Grenville sounded almost eager. But the note of satisfaction changed to soberness as he added, "Then we must double our prayers that the Queen's commanders prevail."

Carlos got the sense that Grenville had mixed feelings about it. He didn't know why, and didn't really care. "My wife," he said. "I heard she was staying with you. Is she here?"

"She was."

Carlos looked up to the ceiling. "Gone up to bed?" *Madre de Dios,* what he would give to open the bedchamber door and see her. Tell her what a fool he had been. Ask her to forgive him.

"I am sorry to disappoint you," Grenville said, "but I'm afraid you have come a day too late. Your wife left yesterday for London."

It knocked Carlos back. If he hadn't heard of her being there and detoured to come for her, it wouldn't have felt like such a heavy disappointment. But having got his hopes up, this felt like he had lost her all over again.

"Will you stop and rest the night, as my guest? You would be most welcome." Grenville's eyes glinted amusement. "Or do I sense a husband's keen desire to ride on to London to be with his wife?"

Carlos almost smiled. Was he that obvious? But the smile died in him. There were still over three hundred miles to cover before he saw Isabel, and the distance seemed ominous, as though he might never close up the awful chasm between them. He had been fantasizing about her forgiving him, even getting the reward of a soft smile, but what if she could *not* forgive? What if she never smiled at him again?

"Your offer is kind, sir," he said. "But I have a fair moon. I'll ride on."

Grenville grinned. He gestured toward the doors. "Let me see you to your horse, and from there I shall wish you Godspeed."

She scanned every window and door, looking for a way to escape. Morton stood with his back against the door to the great hall, his arms crossed, his eyes on her. He had sat her down in a chair at the center of the library where there was no object she could touch. The desk with its ledgers, its books, its lantern—things she might somehow use to defend herself—was at least ten feet behind her.

The merry din from the hall seeped in around the door that Morton guarded. Impossible to get past him. There was one other door, at the far side of the room. It opened to the tunnel that led to the mill. Could she reach it before Morton stopped her? Was it locked? If not, she could bolt down the tunnel. Morton was strong, but he had the lumbering body of a wrestler gone to fat. Running fast, she might have a chance. But the door seemed so far away.

The windows? They were to her right, three tall windows in a row, their gold brocade curtains pushed to either side, revealing the main courtyard. Each one was big enough to climb through. But all were shut, snugged tight with an iron latch. And each held nine panes with lead partitions—she could not smash an opening big enough. There was another window, smaller, higher. It was open an inch, and a draft of the night wind touched her face, a special torture, for this window was too small—only a child the size of Nicolas could climb through it.

Two dairyhouse maids hurried past the three large windows, arriving for the play. In the moonlight they slipped past like ghosts. Giggling ghosts. Isabel heard them as they hastened for the door to the great hall. She heard that door grate open, then shut. Then silence. At the far side of the courtyard, by the main gates, a horse in the shadows whinnied.

She looked at Morton and swallowed. "Is he coming back?"

No reply. He watched her with calm indifference, arms crossed, as if merely keeping an eye on a wagonload of his master's belongings at the fair. She knew the answer in any case. Grenville would be back. He had found out about her. How, she did not know. The fearfulness she had suffered for days now hardened into bone-deep terror. Grenville was a careful planner of treason. He would have a plan for her.

The tunnel. That was her only hope. To have a chance, she had to make Morton come to her.

She stood up. Morton's arms dropped to his sides, ready for action. "Sit," he said. "Or I'll make you sit."

Ignoring him, she dragged the chair over to the tall windows.

"Christ," he growled, and started for her.

She jumped up on the chair and reached for the window latch. A mad move, they both knew, for he was within two steps of her and would easily lift her down and drag her back.

But he was near, that was all that mattered.

She grabbed the curtain and whipped it around his head. He

pawed at it to rip it off. She leapt off the chair and dashed for the tunnel door. She was almost there when she heard him pound after her. He snatched the back of her dress and wrenched her, spinning her with such force it sent her tumbling. She hit the floor on her back, and pain shot up her spine. He grabbed her arm with a brutal grip and hauled her to her feet, then dragged her over to the chair, grabbed it with his other hand, and dragged both back to the center of the room. He pushed her down into the chair. "Sit."

She thudded onto the seat, catching her breath. She braced her hands on the seat's sides and tried to force down the panic that threatened to close her throat.

She heard voices outside the windows. Men's voices. She and Morton both looked. Moonlight shone on two figures leaving by the main door. Isabel's heart jumped. Carlos! He was with Grenville. They were walking toward the gates. Chatting like friends. They reached the horse tethered in the shadows. Carlos swung up into the saddle. He was going to leave. No! She was about to scream, *Carlos, stop! Help me!* She could shout that much before Morton stopped her. And Carlos would come.

She strangled the cry in her throat. If she called out to Carlos, Grenville would act. There were a score of his armed retainers in the hall who would rush to the call of their lord. At his order they would stop Carlos. He would fight them. They would take him prisoner. Or kill him.

He reached down from the saddle to shake Grenville's hand. Isabel clamped her hand over her trembling mouth to keep the scream from bursting out. Every fiber in her craved to see Carlos leap from his horse at the sound of her voice and come running to her. But if he did, Grenville would have him cut down.

She shut her eyes and pressed her palm against her mouth so hard her teeth dug into her lip. *Keep still. Keep quiet. He must not hear you. Must not see you.*

But her eyes sprang open. Her need to see *him* pulled her up from the chair. The need to see him go, to make sure he got safely away.

Morton's meaty hand pushed her back down onto the seat. "Have it your way," he said. He pulled a length of leather cord from his pocket and wrenched her arms behind her back and tied her wrists. The leather bit into her skin. She twisted her head to see Carlos. He had reined his horse around and was starting for the gates at a trot. Grenville waved to him. Carlos rode out through the gates, his cloak rippling behind him, and was swallowed up by the night.

Isabel felt as if her heart had been dragged from her body. Carlos was gone. Whatever Grenville meant to do with her, she would have to face it alone.

He came back, buckling on his sword. He had thrown on a cloak and was booted and spurred, ready for a journey. "Thank you, Morton," he said, eyeing Isabel's bound hands. "Well done."

She said with forced bravado, "You have no right to treat me thus."

"Oh, but I do. Of that I am quite sure."

"You are mad. You cannot hold me here for long."

"I do not intend to." He took her by the elbow and pulled her to her feet. "We were on our way to the mill, remember? Shall we continue?"

She dug in her heels. "My husband came for me. He'll be back. With my kinsmen."

"I wouldn't count on it. Bit of a blockhead, isn't he?"

She spat at him.

He slapped her face so hard it wrenched her head sideways. Pain exploded up her neck. With her hands bound she had to fight to keep her balance. But she made herself stand tall. They stared at each other. He wiped her spittle off his upper lip. Isabel's stung cheek was on fire.

"Your treason will not prevail. The Queen will stop you. I wrote and told her everything."

He almost smiled. "You wrote, but she will not read it." He pulled a paper from his pocket. She saw the broken seal. Her letter! "Your Indian put up a surprising fight. Rather comical, really. My men made short work of him."

Pedro! "Dear God," she cried. "What have you done to him?"

"What was necessary."

"You *killed* him?" She swayed at the shock. Pedro . . . dead . . . following *her* orders. Tears scalded her eyes.

"You weep for one heathen," he said in contempt. "You, who would send hundreds of brave Englishmen to hang."

"A traitor's death for traitors—it's what you deserve!" Her voice was a croak, her heart breaking for Pedro. "I hope they hang you and cut you down alive and disembowel you. Monster!"

He was not listening. He opened a drawer in the desk, shoved the letter in and closed it, then picked up the lantern and carried it to the tunnel door. "Morton," he said, opening the door, "bring her."

❧ 28 ❧

Treasures of the Mill

From her bedchamber window Frances watched Carlos reach down from the saddle to shake Christopher's hand. Then he turned his horse and rode out through the gates. Christopher walked back toward the house. He glanced up at the window. Frances lurched back a step, out of sight. She was so horrified, she felt almost numb.

Carlos must have come for Isabel! Christopher, smiling, had sent him away. What had he told Carlos? *What has he done with Isabel?*

She paced from the window to the bed, back and forth. Had he locked Isabel away? *Like me—locked in, unable to warn her.* She hugged herself, cold with the knowledge of her sin against Isabel. *My fault . . . my fault.* Back and forth she paced. *Like a caged animal . . . that's what Christopher has made of me.* She buried her face in her hands in misery. No—no animal could suffer the lashes of guilt she suffered.

What has he done with her? Think like he does. He would not let Isabel loose to warn the Queen of his plot. No, he would keep her a prisoner. Maybe even . . . kill her?

Dear God, would he go so far? She looked at the cradle where Katherine lay, and shuddered, remembering the horror. He *would* have gone that far with her baby. Frances had stopped him . . . had told . . . had put Isabel's life in peril.

Katherine began crying. Frances scooped her up and held her close and swayed with her to soothe her. To soothe herself. She looked out the window as she swayed, trying to muster strength. By now, Carlos would be turning onto the road to London. Everything was up to her. She was not an animal. A sinner, yes, but still human, with free will. She could act. *Must* act. If Christopher had been ready to kill her baby for his ends, none of them were safe.

It gave her a jolt of determination. And cleared her mind. Hurrying now, she snatched her warmest shawl and bundled Katherine in it. She pulled the coverlet off the bed and yanked the linen sheets away. Taking scissors, she snipped each sheet, then tore them into wide strips. She tied together all the strips except one, forming a makeshift rope. Holding Katherine tightly against her breast, she wound the last strip around herself and the baby and tied it snug. All she could see of Katherine was the top of her little head. Frances dug a purse of coins out of the desk drawer and snugged it in with the baby.

The window, almost as tall as she was, opened easily. The March wind gusted in on her. She pulled a chair close, climbed up with the sheet rope, and climbed through.

She stood on the ledge, clutching Katherine to her, her own heart drumming wildly against the child. The wind rushed around them with a roar like the sea. Bright moonlight washed over them. Below, the roof of Christopher's library jutted out. Three servant girls were hurrying across the courtyard, making for the main door, eager to get to the play. Frances waited until they had gone inside. Her baby squirmed against her.

Just a short drop to the library roof, she told herself. But she was stiff with fear. Would her baby survive the fall? No, this was madness! Katherine let out a cry as if she knew, and Frances caressed the small head to comfort her. She could not bear to hear Katherine cry. But neither could she keep standing here—the crying could alert Christopher's men. With a rush of resolve, she hugged her baby tightly. *Do it now!*

She jumped.

Her feet hit the roof with a spasm of pain. She lost her balance and fell, tumbling to the edge, one foot tangled in the rope of sheets. She stopped herself just in time to brace herself from going over. The violence of it silenced Katherine. Frances's heart stopped. *I've killed her!*

Katherine gasped a breath and let out a wail. Frances almost wept in relief. She realized now, too, that the sound of the wind riding through trees and across the rooftops was so loud it masked her baby's crying. No one below would hear.

She untangled the rope of sheets. A gust caught it, but she snatched it back. She got to her feet, her ankle so painful when she put her weight on it that tears sprang to her eyes. She bit back the pain and hobbled across the roof, carrying the makeshift rope to the library's chimney. A loop around the chimney, a knot, and it was done. She took the rope to the edge of the roof and tossed the end over, but saw in dismay that it reached only halfway down. Was that enough? It had to be—she had no choice. She tested it. It felt strong. She stood on the roof edge and said a prayer. For Katherine . . . for Isabel . . . for her sinful self. With trembling arms she gripped the sheet rope and eased herself over the edge.

So hard to hold on! The linen jerked through her hands, burning her palms. But she held tightly enough to slow her descent. The rope ran out. She let go. She hit the ground on her hurt ankle and almost cried out at the pain, then staggered to get her balance. Hobbling, she made her way around to the front door. She did not dare go in and be seen—the chamberlain had orders to keep her locked up. She stopped a young groom hustling in for the play.

"I need your help," she told him, catching her breath.

He gaped at her disheveled state and the baby bound to her breast. "What's amiss, my lady?"

"Do you know my maid, Nan Rouse?"

"Aye."

"Fetch her. Tell her to come to the stable. Mark you, tell no one else. No one!"

The play had not yet begun when Frances rode out through the gates. She was alone. Nan had the purse and orders to hide the baby until morning, then take her to the inn at Kirknewton, stay there, and hire a wet nurse. Whatever happened now, Katherine would be safe.

*   *   *

Grenville opened the tunnel door at the mill end. The roar of the river rushed at Isabel like a blast of wind. Morton pushed her in, her wrists bound at her back, and she stumbled to keep her balance. Grenville hooked the lantern over an iron ring on a wood beam. Under its light Isabel shrank back so he would not see her straining to loosen the leather tie at her wrists. Coming down the tunnel, she had worked at it so frantically the leather had cut her wrist.

Grenville went to the staircase that led downstairs and called down, "Father York." Morton stood by Isabel waiting for orders. Outside, the big waterwheel hit the river with a constant *Slap! Slap! Slap!* that sent a tremor from the floorboards up into the bones of Isabel's legs. The iron shaft powered by the wheel creaked as it went round and round. The air was dank, and she saw why. Where the shaft met the waterwheel there was a gap between the wall and floor, a space as wide as a table, and through it she could see down to the river. Swollen by the rains, the water churned in a white froth around the wheel. Fear crawled over her skin.

The priest came trudging up the stairs. He was dressed to travel as Grenville was, in riding boots and heavy cloak, with a black scarf wound below his long, white face. He carried a full burlap sack slung over his shoulder, heavy enough to make his final steps up the stairs an effort. He set it down and Isabel saw that it bulged with sharp angles. He looked at her with eyes as hard as wet coals. "Surely you are not bringing the woman," he said.

"Of course not. Forget her," Grenville said. He indicated the sack. "Where is the rest?"

The priest pointed across the room. In front of a wall of sacks plump with grain and reaching almost to the ceiling were three sacks that bulged with angular objects. "Those three are sorted," he said. "Two more to come up." Resting against them was a cross of gold as long as the priest's leg, and studded with gems. Isabel remembered it from the room downstairs that held the secret hoard of sacred objects. Greenville and his people had saved them from dozens of churches all over Northumberland before the Queen's agents could confiscate them. The priest's sacks, she realized, were crammed with some of that treasure.

"And horses?" Grenville asked.

"Ready at the door, for us and the load."

"Good." He looked at Isabel. "Now, just one last task."

He jerked his chin at Morton, a command. Morton gripped Isabel's elbow and yanked her to the riverside wall so that she was only a step away from the gap. Sickness shot up her throat. He was going to push her into the churning water! She balked, but he held her firmly. There was no way she could fight him, and the turning iron shaft at her hip boxed her in. If he pushed her, her only chance in that water was to get her hands free. In panic she was straining with all her might against the leather cord, grating the skin raw, and she felt a warm trickle of blood—but the cord was loosening! She just needed time! She called to Grenville, "Wait!" Her voice was a thin reed against the roar of the water and the slap of the wheel.

"Yes, do wait, Morton," Grenville said calmly. "Some insurance is needed." He pulled an empty burlap sack off a hook on the wooden beam and took it over to a rubble of broken millstones.

Isabel felt the cord loosen a fraction. Just a little more time! "Where are you taking that treasure?"

"Why, to Newcastle," he said with mock surprise. "Did you not learn that in your spying? The sacred objects will gladden the hearts of our fighting men." He was loading the sack with fist-sized jagged stones. "Some final organizing to do there. Seven hundred men are waiting for the call, and once we have them we go on to Durham. But, of course, that you know. Twelve hundred more stand ready to join us there. With God's grace, we will raise our banners at Durham Cathedral on St. Joseph's Day and march on London."

He took a rope from a shelf and with it tied the throat of the sack, leaving a length of rope that he looped and knotted. He carried the sack over to Isabel. Her heart was banging so hard she felt it would crack her ribs as he hung the sack around her neck. It was so heavy she had to fight against it pulling her down. "In London," he said, "thousands will rejoice to see us depose this bastard queen."

"Please . . ." She was shaking. Her voice was a quaver. "I beg you. I am with child. Spare its innocent life."

He looked disgusted. "Another Thornleigh whelp? There are too many of your blood already." His voice was thick with anger. "A family of murderers. My father, dead. My brother, dead. Your blood is black with sin." He brought his face so close to hers she felt his hot breath. "I should have let you die in the storm."

He yanked her closer to the gap. She stumbled, unbalanced by the weight, and almost lost her footing at the edge. A gust that rose from the churning water jerked her skirt, blowing icy mist on her bare leg. She tried to bolt forward but Grenville blocked her. The iron shaft barred the way to her left, Morton barred the way to her right. She and Grenville stared at each other, she panting, straining against the sack's weight like a yoked animal. It swung between them, a dying pendulum.

He stepped back, leaving Morton with her. Morton again gripped her elbow. Grenville went to the sacks of church treasure beside the grain and picked up the big gold cross and held it in both hands outstretched before him. Its gemstones gleamed in the lantern light, and he gazed at it as if drawing inspiration. "Is it not beautiful? I shall hold it high before me, just like this, as we march into Durham Cathedral. I shall return this cross to the altar, its sacred home."

He looked at Morton and nodded. A signal.

"Wait!" Isabel cried. "Give me a moment to pray, I beg you!" She was shivering so hard she could hardly force out her voice. But the leather was almost loose! A few moments more and she might wrench her hands free. "Give me that much, in Christian charity."

He shrugged. "Why not."

She dropped to her knees and shut her eyes, half expecting Morton's boot to push her plunging into the water. She was not praying, only struggling in terror to loosen the leather.

"Enough," Grenville said. Isabel's eyes sprang open. He had set down the cross and bent now to pick up one of the treasure sacks, ready to go. "Morton, do your office."

"Father!" Isabel cried to the priest. "Your blessing, at least, before I die!"

Father York regarded her with a look as cold as stone. "All who support the bastard Elizabeth are heretics. There is no grace for a heretic." Done with her, he said to Grenville, "Help me bring up the last loads."

The two of them went down the stairs.

Morton yanked Isabel to her feet. She froze, dizzy with terror. He gripped both her shoulders.

There was a crash at the ceiling, a pounding of boots on the floor above. Isabel flinched, but she could see nothing, Morton's body a massive block before her. She was pushing against his hands with every ounce of strength in her. She heard the boots come pounding down the stairs. Morton was wrenched backward. Isabel fell forward at the sudden freedom. Strong hands grabbed her to steady her. She looked up though her dizzied vision, and gaped in shock. Carlos!

Morton got his balance and grappled Carlos by the throat. They staggered back together, wrestling.

Isabel was too stunned to breathe. Frances was running toward her, crying, "Isabel!" Frances pulled her away from the gap. Isabel's legs gave way in shock. Frances struggled to hold her up.

Morton had wrestled Carlos close to the gap and now wrenched him around to its edge. Carlos's heel slipped over. He lurched away and got his balance, backing up to the turning iron shaft. Morton plowed a fist at him, but Carlos vaulted over the shaft. Morton staggered, lost his footing. He plunged through the gap and down into the water.

Grenville was running at Carlos's back, his sword held high.

"Carlos!" Isabel screamed.

He spun around, drawing his sword. The two blades clanged.

Frances was struggling to pull the stone-weighted sack off Isabel's neck. The moment Isabel was free of it she cried, "Cut my hands loose!" Frances tugged at the leather, but Isabel's wrists were slick with blood, making Frances fumble. Grenville and Carlos swung their swords, scuffling, Grenville grunting with the effort. The blades clanged and scraped.

The priest came charging up the stairs, a long dagger in his hand, and rushed at Carlos. Carlos saw him and jerked clear of the attack even as he kept fending off Grenville. Isabel watched in agony. Carlos's sword against one man could chop off an arm, but against two men ferociously attacking in close quarters he could not get the room. As soon as he backed Grenville against the stairs, the priest came at him from behind. Carlos twisted from one to the other, fending off one, attacking the other.

"Hurry, Frances!" Isabel cried. Carlos was keeping both men at bay, but they fought fiercely. He could not keep them back forever. The moment he tired, one would reach him.

"There!" Frances cried, and Isabel felt the leather cord snap. She was free! Carlos had turned to fight Grenville, and she saw the priest about to plunge his dagger into Carlos's shoulder. She snatched an empty sack from a hook and ran at the priest and flung it over his head. He clawed at it, his dagger flailing. The tip swiped Isabel's neck. A prick of pain. Carlos looked in horror at her blood, and in that moment Grenville swung at him. Carlos parried, but Grenville's blade slashed his forearm. Blood gushed through Carlos's sleeve. He flinched but then attacked, fending Grenville off.

Frances cried, "Stop!"

The priest flung away the sack that had blinded him. He turned on Isabel and plowed his fist into her stomach. Frances again cried, "Stop!" Isabel crumpled, hugging herself at the pain. York raised his dagger over her, poised to stab. Carlos twisted to go to her. Grenville slashed at him. Carlos ducked but lost his footing and staggered.

"Stop!" Frances screamed at the priest. She grabbed the lantern off the hook and hurled it at him. It glanced off his shoulder, then went hurtling and hit the stacked sacks of grain. The flame leapt onto the burlap. Flames shot across the mound of sacks, engulfing the sacks of treasure.

Grenville looked in horror at the fire. He ran to the treasure where the gold cross lay. Frances was in his way and he struck her face with the back of his hand, knocking her down. He stood over her and kicked her. "Fool!" Twisting around to rescue the gold cross, he bent to grab it from the flames, but cried out, his hands scalded.

Carlos was helping Isabel up. He looked horrified at her bloodied neck, but she said, "A scratch—look out!" The priest stabbed Carlos's sword hand. The sword fell from his grip.

The priest kicked it away and he and Grenville both came at Carlos and wrestled him to the floor. Flames leapt from the stacked grain to the wooden posts, torching the empty sacks that hung there, flaring up to the ceiling beams. Isabel ran to help Frances, who groaned on the floor, so dazed from her brother's blows that Isabel could not get her to her feet. She watched in horror as the three men wrestled, Carlos beating the other two back, the two ganging up to bring him down again, Carlos hurling them off, only for them to come at him again. All the while the fire spread, roaring over the grain, rippling along the floor, crackling across the beams.

"Get out, Isabel!" Carlos yelled.

Grenville coughed at the smoke. "The treasures!" he cried. He bolted down the stairs.

Isabel's eyes burned. The heat . . . the smoke. She could not rouse Frances, who moaned, too stunned to move.

The priest staggered back from Carlos, appalled at being left to fight him alone. He ran for the stairs that led up and outside. Flames shot across the floor in front of him and he lurched to a stop. He turned and ran back toward the tunnel that led to the house. A flaming beam thudded down in his path, blocking the door. He froze in panic.

Isabel was dragging Frances by the wrists, but she could barely see in the billowing smoke. It had engulfed the priest. Carlos was suddenly at her side, pulling her away from Frances. "Go!" he told her. "Get out!" He lifted Frances in his arms.

"Yes, this way! Follow me!" Isabel said, and ran for the staircase that led up and out. But near the steps she balked at the knee-high flames eating the floor in front of her. She heard a crash, and turned. The staircase leading down to the treasure room had collapsed in a thunder of flames and sparks. Grenville would be trapped down there.

"Go!" she heard Carlos yell again. She saw him lumbering through the smoke with Frances in his arms. Isabel bolted through the flames and up the stairs, frantically batting sparks from her skirt.

She staggered out the door, coughing, and onto the riverside path. The cold night air was bliss to breathe. But where was Carlos? She was so shaky it was hard to stand, and the heat was fierce on her face. She saw Carlos barrel out the door, and tears of relief stung her eyes. He reached the path and dropped to his knees and set Frances down on the grass. She looked half-dead. Isabel fell to her knees beside Carlos. "Is she—?"

"She'll be all right," he said, catching his breath. "Are you?"

She looked up at him. She could not stop trembling. "Yes. And you? Your arm—"

"I'll be fine. Isabel, I . . ." His voice choked.

"Oh, my love!" She threw her arms around his neck. He held her so tightly against him she could hardly breathe.

The building was a roaring billow of orange flame and black smoke, the heat blistering. Three horses nearby whinnied in fear at the fire. Tethered to a railing, they strained and stamped to get loose.

Frances sat up, coughing.

"Can you stand?" Carlos asked her. "We can't stay here."

She nodded. They both helped her to her feet. She looked back at the mill. "Christopher—"

"We ride," Carlos said, making for the horses. "Before his men stop us." He untied the horses.

As they rode away Isabel looked over her shoulder at the mill blazing in the darkness. She saw with a shock—was it her fevered imagination?—a man stagger out the door. It looked like Father York. He was limping, dragging something. The flames lit it up . . . the golden cross.

*   *   *

The inn was old, of oak and mossy stone, snugged into a quiet, wooded valley. The wind had spent itself, and all was still. A soft rain whispered on the roof. An owl hooted from the woods.

The chair by the fire's embers held Isabel and Carlos, both naked, he sitting, she straddling him. He was inside her, and she did not move as they caught their breath. The lovemaking had been slow, gentle, exquisite, for their bodies were both so bruised, but they had wanted each other too much to stop. Now, with her hands on his shoulders, his hands on her hips, they looked into each other's eyes, savoring the time together after the hard ride to this valley.

They had picked up Frances's baby with her maid and then set out for London, for Isabel had told Carlos about the plot and they were on their way to warn the Queen, with no time to lose. She had told him, too, about Pedro, and saw that it hit him as hard as it had her. She felt that Grenville perishing, trapped in that inferno, was simple justice. As they had covered the miles on horseback, past fields, across bridges, up hills, down valleys, she had felt nightmare images of the mill galloping after her. The churning water that would have drowned her . . . the searing heat of the blaze . . . the white-faced priest limping out of the flames and into the night.

But here at the inn, when Carlos had closed the door and they were alone, she had put it all behind her. They had found each other. They were man and wife again—they were one. Nothing else mattered.

She let her heartbeat settle and heard his breathing calm, both still looking into each other's eyes. His gleamed with happiness, but she also saw a shadow of remorse. "Isabel," he said, his voice so low she could still hear the whispering rain. "Can you ever forgive my—"

"Shhh," she said, laying her fingertips on his mouth. She felt so full of contentment, she wanted to give him more. "Carlos, I am with child."

She watched emotions chase each other across his face. She knew him so well she could name them. A thrill of joy. Shame at how he had treated her. Anxiety because of her previous miscarriage.

"I promise you," she said, her own voice as soft as the rain, "we will not lose this child."

A smile wobbled on his lips. He lowered his forehead onto her shoulder and she felt him struggle to hold back a sob. She wrapped her arms around him, and murmured, *"Mi amor."*

PART FOUR

The Threatened
Queen

❧ 29 ❧

Return to Whitehall

L ondon's church spires rose into the morning mist like beacons
to the three arrivals, and beyond the city walls a church bell
was pealing as though to greet them. Isabel let out a sigh of relief.
They had made it. The days of hard traveling had left every muscle in her body sore, but she and Carlos and Frances had reached
the capital in time to warn the Queen about the Northerners' plot.
She had no doubt that Grenville's co-conspirators planned to go
ahead without him, but they would not succeed. As soon as the
Queen knew of it, the traitors would be rounded up. Despite Isabel's aches, a fresh energy coursed through her at being so near
the end of her journey. She smiled at Carlos riding beside her.
"We'll soon see Nico," she said.

He nodded, doing his best to return the smile, but Isabel saw
the worry gnawing at him. He had told her there could be serious
consequences for what he had done in Leith. She and Frances had
listened in amazement as he had told them how Adam had been a
captive of the French and how Carlos had secretly freed him, but
in doing so had done violence to the French commander. It was a
grave offense, yet all Isabel felt was overwhelming gratitude to
Carlos. To think of Adam suffering in that Leith jail and facing the
gallows! Carlos had risked his life to save her brother. How she
loved him for that.

"Yes, you shall see your son," said Frances, "and, God willing, I shall soon see Adam, home from France. And he shall meet his daughter."

Poor Frances, Isabel thought. She looked exhausted. In making such haste to get to London, they had left the maid Nan with baby Katherine two days' ride behind them. Frances was determined to accompany Isabel to the palace, keen to assure Queen Elizabeth in person that she had nothing to do with her brother's treason, for any such taint could hurt Adam. What a whirlwind we've been through, Isabel thought, looking at her sister-in-law. When Frances had confessed that she had betrayed her to Grenville, Isabel's fury had been sharp, but also brief, for Frances had looked so utterly desolate in telling her. Besides, Isabel knew she would have done the same if anyone had threatened to smother Nicolas. She and Frances were friends again.

They were nearing Bishopsgate, the traffic thicker on the road now. Draymen driving wagons, farmers walking cattle in for slaughter, merchants on horseback, bustling foot traffic of housewives, water carriers, apprentices, laundresses—they tramped and trotted and rattled their carts in and out of the city. Geese bound for market squawked from crates. Cattle bellowed under the farmer's whip. A listless breeze carried smells of fish and sawdust. Isabel and Carlos and Frances passed through the gates and on down Bishopsgate Street. As they approached her parents' house she saw a maid shaking a Turkish rug from a third-story window, and she thought how wonderful it was going to be to bring Nicolas back to the house, wash off the dirt of the road, and finally rest. But not yet. Not until they had warned the Queen.

They carried on westward through the teeming square mile of activity that was London. Past the Mercers' Hall, past the church of St. Mary-le-Bow, down Paternoster Row and past St. Paul's they went, and then out Ludgate, past the Belle Sauvage Inn and across the Fleet Ditch with its stink of entrails slopped from the slaughterhouses and tanneries. They were approaching Charing Cross on the Strand, where the luxurious town-house gardens of rich nobles spread down to the river, when Carlos slowed his horse. "I'll say good-bye here," he said. Isabel and Frances stopped with him, Isabel casting an anxious look at the grand edifice of Durham House, the Spanish embassy. She and Carlos had agreed to this on the journey. "I should see Bishop Quadra right away," he had told her. "My best chance is to tell him myself, before D'Oysel's report reaches him."

Isabel understood how serious the situation was. The ambassador could punish Carlos for assaulting D'Oysel, could even recommend that the King revoke their *encomienda*. "It may not be as bad as you think," she had said, trying to be optimistic. "It sounds like no one knows you were behind Adam's escape, at least."

"No one but D'Oysel," he had said grimly, "whom I almost killed."

Now, at Charing Cross, he reached for her hand and squeezed it. "I'll do my best. Go, do your duty with the Queen, and then bring Nicolas home. I'll see you back at your father's house."

She pressed his hand to her cheek. No matter what lay ahead, she felt no despair about their future, only happiness. They had found each other. They would soon be reunited with their son. She felt aglow from the life growing inside her, and her faith in Carlos was stronger than ever, with or without the *encomienda*. Nothing could shake that happiness. Carlos brought her hand to his lips and kissed it, then turned his horse, heading for Durham House.

Isabel looked at Frances.

"I'm not going anywhere," Frances said.

Isabel smiled, glad to have her company.

A mile farther they rode into the rambling precincts of Whitehall Palace. Isabel remembered how struck she had been at its sprawling diversity when she'd been summoned by the Queen before Christmas. The palace was a village unto itself with its houses and shops, stables and barracks, tiltyard and tennis courts, towers and turrets. Leaving their horses at the stables, they made their way through the north courtyard bustling with merchants, vendors, lawyers, and clerks. Ballad-mongers and pamphlet printers called to customers, waving their tracts. A dirty little girl sang out her song of mincemeat pies for sale.

Yet, for all the normal bustle, Isabel sensed a new tension in the air. Through an archway under the clock tower she glimpsed soldiers of the Palace Guard massing in ranks, and heard an officer barking orders. The clerks scurrying everywhere looked tired and anxious. She shared a look with Frances, who clearly felt the tense mood as well. "Something has happened," Frances said.

Inside, making their way to the royal apartments, they found the staircases and corridors and galleries crowded, as usual, with courtiers and servants, but there were no merry faces. And no music. The Queen was known for her love of music—Isabel's mother had said that lutes and virginals and viols could be heard all day long and into the night—but not today. Only tense, hushed voices and bursts of anxious arguments.

They reached the antechamber of the Queen's suite. A woman was coming out of the inner chamber with a bundle of papers. Isabel remembered her—Katherine Ashley, the Queen's former governess and longtime friend. She looked as fretful as everyone else, almost haggard.

"Mistress Valverde?" she said in surprise. "Bless my soul, it *is* you. Your mother was speaking of you just yesterday. But I thought you were in—"

"Is my mother here? Good Mistress Ashley, please let her know that I am come. It is urgent."

"I'm sorry, but she left last night to see the Earl of Shrewsbury on Her Majesty's behalf. Every peer and gentleman who can muster a company of soldiers is needed. Her Majesty's council has vowed to raise five thousand troops by Sunday."

"Why? What has happened?"

"Have you not heard? The courier brought the news from Scotland this morning."

Isabel's heart tripped. "Scotland?"

"Weeping, he was." Mistress Ashley looked on the verge of weeping herself. "Oh, the shame of it, for England! The Queen's forces under Lord Grey have been cut down."

"Cut down?"

"At the French fortress of Leith."

"But they were to lay siege. How—?"

"No. No siege. Instead, Her Majesty ordered Lord Grey to mount an all-out attack. He did so . . . to disastrous results. Our brave soldiers scaled Leith's walls only to find their ladders too short. The French hurled our stranded men from the ramparts in glee, with the help of even their *women*. Thousands of our soldiers were broken on those walls to bleed and die."

Isabel was so appalled she could not speak.

"There's worse," the distraught lady went on. "A fleet of Spanish ships has embarked for Scotland with thousands of troops. They will help the French attack the remains of our poor army."

Frances exclaimed, "God save us!"

Mistress Ashley's eyes flicked to her, a stranger. Isabel quickly introduced the two. Her mind was in turmoil. What a horrendous defeat! And a Spanish army on the way! The Queen was weakened and foundering, just as the northern traitors were poised to strike at her in her own realm. *Thank God I can prevent at least that*, she thought. "I must see Her Majesty," she said. "I had hoped my mother would bring me to her. Mistress Ashley, you must do this office for me."

"Her Majesty? Impossible. She is closed up in earnest conference with her council."

"Then you must take her a message. Tell her I *must* speak to her."

"Madam, you do forget yourself. These grave matters of state—"

"There is only one matter of state, and that is the safety of the realm. Her Majesty faces a new peril"—she held up her hand to forestall an interruption—"No, not just in Scotland. A peril from *within*."

Mistress Ashley tensed. No person near the Queen could dismiss a charge of treason. "You have . . . information?"

"I do."

"Whom do you suspect?"

Isabel trusted the lady, but there were many other people between this room and the Queen, and she feared the damage that loose tongues could do. "Forgive me, but this report is for Her Majesty's ears alone."

The lady hesitated. Frances said, "I beg you, madam, urge Her Majesty to give audience to my sister-in-law with the news she brings." She added, with a quaver in her voice that showed how much this cost her, "To the eternal shame of my brother and his house."

Mistress Ashley looked so shocked at this confession, it was clear she was convinced. "All right," she said to Isabel. "I shall deliver your request. But it may take some time. I cannot barge in on Her Majesty. Please, wait here."

She left the room. Isabel squeezed Frances's hand in solidarity and whispered, "Thank you."

She noticed they were not alone. Two young maids of honor sat together on a window seat, one embroidering a cap, the other stringing a length of catgut on a lute. They were far enough away that they could not have overheard the talk about treason, but their nervous glances at Isabel and Frances showed that they had picked up on the tension of the exchange. Isabel recognized one of the girls, a pretty blond. She had played with Nicolas that day Isabel had brought him here, had tossed a ball back and forth with him, laughing. There was no laughter now. The news from Scotland had rocked everyone.

"Mistress Arnold, is it not?" Isabel said, going to her.

"It is, madam."

"We met at Christmas. You were kind to my son, Nicolas."

The girl smiled. "Sweet boy."

Isabel felt a clutch at her heart. "Do you see him often? Is he all right?"

"Have you not seen him since then?"

"No. I have been away." She could not hold back from asking, "Who takes care of him? Where does he stay?"

"Oh, he's in the rooms above the orangery. Old Mistress Dugan has the keeping of him."

"The orangery?"

"Beside the tennis courts." The girl nodded to the window. "Just around the corner." She put down her embroidery. "I'll take you, if you like. I need to see the Lord Chamberlain's maid, and your boy's room is on the way." She got to her feet. "Come."

Isabel hesitated. What if the Queen sent a quick reply?

Frances said, "I shall stay, Isabel. I'll send for you instantly if word comes. Go, see your son."

She needed no persuading. Off she went with Mistress Arnold, downstairs, outside, past the vacant tennis courts, and into the bright, glassed gallery of the orangery. Upstairs, along a darker corridor, they reached a closed door. "There you go," Mistress Arnold said, and added with a smile, "sweet boy," as she went back down the stairs.

Isabel knocked on the door. There was no answer. She opened it to a bright room bathed in spring sunshine from a tall window. A desk was littered with books, quills, and inkpots. Toys lay scattered on the floor. A plump matron sat in a chair by the window, reading aloud in French. She looked up at Isabel in surprise. "Oh!"

"Pardon me," Isabel said, coming in. "I knocked but—"

"I am somewhat hard of hearing, madam." The woman raised herself from the chair with some effort because of her bulk, while saying, "May I ask who—"

"I am Lord Thornleigh's daughter. Is my son—"

"Mama!"

Isabel whirled around. Nicolas sat on the floor, a red tin top spinning between his outstretched legs. He gazed up at her as if she were an apparition.

"Nicolas!"

He scrambled to his feet and hurled himself at her, throwing his arms around her waist. "Mama!" He buried his face in her skirts.

She hugged him to her. "Nico! Oh, my dear boy!"

"Madam," said the lady, smiling, "you have found us in the midst of the adventures of Monsieur le Lapin. Your son is anxious to know if our furry hero shall escape through the lettuce garden." She made an arthritic curtsy. "I am Agnes Dugan. The boy's tutor is ill today."

"Mistress Dugan, I am very glad to meet you." Tears of relief pricked her eyes at finding this kindly matron instead of the bully taskmaster with a stick that her imagination had conjured. She pried Nicolas away from her leg to ask, "How are you, my love?"

"Look!" he cried, and pulled her over to the scatter of toys on the floor. He grabbed a wooden horse the size of his hand, painted a shiny black and frozen in proud mid-prance. "It's Noche. Papa's horse!"

"So it is," she said with a laugh. She kneeled down and took his face in her hands. He looked utterly happy and healthy. How could I ever have thought the Queen would do otherwise? she realized. Her Majesty was no tyrant. Keeping Nicolas had been mere prudence, a judicious ruler being careful about the threats she faced. Now those threats had multiplied, and Isabel pitied the Queen. From Nicolas's sunny face she took hope that Her Majesty would overcome the crisis in Scotland, and prevail. "Now tell me, what have you been doing while I've been gone? Who is this tutor the lady speaks of?"

"He brings me peppermints."

"Master Chandler," the lady explained. "He sees to the boy's arithmetic and grammar, madam. And Master Nicolas and I have just begun our French lessons."

"And do you see your lady grandmother, Nico?"

"She hears my sums." He rolled his eyes. "Over and over."

"Lady Thornleigh visits every morning, madam, without fail."

Isabel was delighted to hear it. And yet she felt a pang. Nicolas was so well settled and content, it was almost as though he had not missed her, had hardly noticed she'd been gone. *Foolish thought,* she chided herself. *And selfish.* She banished it.

But he had seen the changed look on her face. She was still kneeling, and he threw his arm around her neck and smiled into her eyes as if to reassure her. "Can we go home now?"

Her heart swelled. She pulled him to her, holding him tight. "Soon."

He tugged free. "But I want to go home *now*. I want Pedro. Where's Papa?"

"You'll see Papa soon. I promise."

"And Pedro?"

She could not bring herself to tell him. He loved Pedro so. "Nico, there has been—"

"Madam."

The male voice behind her made her look up in surprise. Sir

William Cecil stood in the open doorway. "Madam," he repeated sternly, "you are not allowed here."

"Sir William!" She had not seen him since he had sent her to Scotland with the Queen's gold. She got to her feet. "Oh, I am heartily glad to see you, sir." Nicolas looked shy and pressed against her leg. She gave his shoulder a squeeze. "Greet the gentleman properly," she told him. "He is our good friend."

Nicolas bowed. Cecil ignored him. Isabel did not wonder at the man's careworn face. As the Queen's most trusted councilor, he was carrying the weight of the national crisis on his shoulders. Isabel was thankful that she could help him cut down at least one looming catastrophe. "Sir William, I have so much to tell."

"Indeed." He looked at the matron, who had curtsied when he had appeared. "Leave us," he told her. She padded out. Cecil came closer to Isabel. "You have been mightily busy in the North."

"I have, sir. Master Knox and the Lords of the Congregation rejoiced to receive Her Majesty's aid, and I pray that, despite the recent setback, they may eventually prevail alongside her army. But I am come to warn her that she faces another danger, one as great or greater than the French. Will you take me to her? I must speak with her right away."

He gave a snort of incredulity. "To what possible end?"

"I know she is busy with dire matters of state, but hear me, sir, and be the judge." She poured out the broad outline of the traitors' plot. How they intended to take Durham with the musters they had, almost two thousand strong, and there to gather more disaffected Northerners in the thousands and with them march on London. How they planned to kill the Queen and bring over her cousin Mary Stuart, Queen of France and of the Scots, and proclaim her Queen of England. "This foul plot, sir, they intend to spark mere days from now. There is not a moment to lose. I beg you to take me to Her Majesty."

"Names?" he said quietly.

She stared at him in frustration. "Sir William, we must not stand idly talking. Every moment of delay brings the traitors closer to their goal. Let me see the Queen. To her I will gladly unburden my heart of names and places, dates and stratagems. You, by her side, shall hear it all. Only, please, take me to her!"

His face hardened. "So that you may fulfill your mission?"

"Yes!"

He looked as if he wanted to strike her. "Guards!" he called.

Five men in glinting breastplates and helmets marched in.

Isabel instinctively clutched Nicolas closer to her. What was happening?

"Captain, arrest this woman," Cecil said.

She gaped at him. *Arrest?* Her thoughts flew wildly. Was it about Grenville? His death in the fire? Was Cecil arresting her for . . . murder?

He held up his hand to momentarily halt the guards. "Come away from the child," he told Isabel.

"No!" She lurched back a step, clasping Nicolas against her. "Sir, I was involved in a terrible thing, it is true. But, believe me, I could do nothing to prevent—"

"So, you confess your crime?"

"I beg you, let me explain everything to the Queen!"

"To increase her misery? The French cheer her downfall. Spain rattles its swords at her. And now *you*—" He stopped as if too sickened to go on. He turned to the captain as if about to order him to take Isabel away.

"Please!" she cried. "You must let me speak to Her Majesty!"

His voice was low with menace. "I know what you would speak."

Her heart crammed up in her throat. She forced her voice out. "What happened at Yeavering demands examination, I accept that. But before I am put away you must first hear what I have come to—"

His slap came so fast it knocked her head sideways. In shock, she fought to catch her breath. Pride forced her not to touch her burning cheek, and to lift her gaze to Cecil, face-to-face.

His eyes glittered with the emotion of betrayal. "I trusted you. Brought you into Her Majesty's presence. Trusted you with a mission. Well, I have learned my lesson." He straightened his shoulders, getting control of himself. "As has Her Majesty, a hard lesson indeed—how to deal with the jackal when he strikes. Months ago, when the peril was fresh, she hesitated. She will not hesitate again. She will strike down these French marauders before they can rage across our borders. Just as I will strike down any traitor who would harm her. Like you."

Isabel froze. "I?"

His lip curled in contempt. "A traitor, and a fool. I know you have come to kill her."

"Kill—? God in heaven, no! How could you think—"

"A clerk in Sir Christopher Grenville's house is my spy. He arrived this morning with his report. He heard you stand in Grenville's library and tell eight of your confederates how you would wheedle information from Lady Thornleigh, and with it contrive to get one of their agents close enough to Her Majesty to take her life. Perhaps *you* are that agent. Perhaps not. No matter, you are finished, along with your fellow conspirators. Grenville has slipped beyond us to a greater judgment—God's. He has perished in a fire. But the others will soon be in our custody, and in chains."

She stared at him, stupefied. "But . . . I never meant Her Majesty harm, I swear it!"

"So," he snapped, "you told those men no such thing?"

Her words on that day of plotting swarmed in her head like hornets. "I did, but only to bait them. To draw them out, and so warn—"

"Spare us your lies, *Señora Valverde.*" He practically spat the Spanish name. "We will have the truth, if not from you, then from the others. One testimony is sufficient to convict for treason."

Treason. The penalty was torture . . . disembowelment. Her stomach twisted and she felt her legs would buckle. "I swear before God, sir, I only *pretended* to join those men. It was the only way I could uncover their plot!"

"So say all traitors."

This cannot be happening. "Send for my mother! She will vouch for me!"

"I dare say, poor lady." He shook his head in disgust. "How

right Her Majesty was to mistrust you. Enough wrangling. I am done with you." He jerked his chin at the captain of the guard, the command to take Isabel away.

A guard yanked Nicolas from her. "Mama!" he wailed. She groped for him, but two other guards gripped her arms. She stiffened, resisting them. "Sir, my son is an innocent! Let my mother take him home, I beg you!"

Ignoring her, Cecil told the captain, "Post a guard at the door. I would have the boy closely kept." He cast a withering look at Isabel. "Sins of the father. Or mother."

The guards dragged her across the room and out the door. She strained to look back at her son. "Nico, I'll be back!"

The door slammed shut. She heard him cry in panic, "Mama!" as they dragged her down the stairs.

Durham House, the Spanish embassy beside the Thames, rose up around the bend from the palace. Frances fumbled a coin into the hand of the boatman for ferrying her to the wharf, then hurried up the stairs from the landing. She found crowds of men swarming the embassy's public rooms, English merchants and Spanish traders alike, all clamoring for information from the ambassador's clerks about Spain's intentions in the war in Scotland. Frances pushed through them, their din hammering her terror for Isabel into a painful rivet in her breast.

A clerk stopped her as she approached the ambassador's private rooms and requested that she state her business. Breathless from her hurry, she struggled to compose her jangled thoughts. "Señor Valverde . . . he has come to see Ambassador Quadra . . . I must see him . . . must tell him . . . *please*, let me through." Her desperate babbling made no impression on the clerk. He was all politeness, but explained that he could admit only those who had scheduled business with the ambassador or his secretary.

Clear thinking, Frances told herself, that's what is needed. Panic will only breed more panic. She said that Señor Valverde needed her information for *his* scheduled business, and she was about to invent a reason when she realized that she recognized this clerk. She had seen him in Ambassador Quadra's private chapel.

That Quadra held regular masses for his staff was a perquisite of his rank in this Protestant land, and some of the English faithful slipped in to attend if they dared. Frances had dared. That's where she had seen the clerk—praying. She lowered her voice and mentioned this to him, spoke of their bond of loyalty to the one true faith. His stern face softened. "Just bringing a message? In and out?"

"In and out, I promise." She was right—the bond was enough. He let her through.

The corridor was even more crowded, and the men here were shouting even more loudly. As Frances made her way through she glimpsed two men in a fistfight. Then, at the far end, she saw Carlos. He sat alone on a bench, elbows on his knees, hands clasped. He kept his eyes down with a scowl on his face as though trying to ignore the chaos around him. He was waiting to get in to see Ambassador Quadra.

She halted, held back by a flood of emotions. How much she owed him for saving Adam's life . . . and how he loved Isabel! She remembered the day she had met them both, Adam's sister and this fierce-looking Spaniard, newly returned to England. The family had been so merry together that night, Carlos laughing along with them. Dear God, how was she to break to him this piteous news?

He noticed her with a look of surprise and got to his feet. They both pushed through the crowd to reach each other. By the time they met, his surprise had darkened to worry. "What is it? What's happened?"

"Oh, now is the time to pray," Frances said in misery. "Pray God for His mercy, sir. The Queen has arrested Isabel for treason. They have taken her to the Tower."

❧ 30 ❧

The Plan

A cold spring rain lashed London. Thunder boomed like cannon and lightning flashed from steely clouds mustered above the Tower. Carlos hunched his shoulders against the downpour as he stood watch at the street railing above a stairway that ran down to Billingsgate Wharf. From a Dutch ship at anchor, boats were loading passengers and ferrying them to the wharf. He scanned the people climbing out of the first boat, ten or so, as they scurried along the landing toward the shelter of the sheds and shops. Through the slanting rain he caught sight of the one he was looking for as the man stepped out of the boat—tall, gray-haired, with an eye patch. Carlos set off down the stairway, calling, "Thornleigh!"

Isabel's father heard him and looked up. They hurried toward each other and met in the middle of the stairs. Carlos was shocked at Thornleigh's haggard face. In the week since he had sent word to him in Antwerp about Isabel, her father had aged a decade. *I must look like that, too,* he thought. For a moment neither spoke, too weighted down with feeling. Then questions rushed out of Thornleigh.

"Have you been allowed to see her? Is she bearing up? Has Honor talked to the Queen?"

Carlos shook his head, didn't answer. He wasn't here to commiserate. There wasn't time. "Come." He led Thornleigh to a chandler's shop. Under its gabled roof they could stand out of the rain.

"The trial," Thornleigh said, agony in his eyes. "Were you there? Who testified against her?"

It made Carlos sick to remember, but he saw how much it meant to Thornleigh, so he told him. How the spy Cecil had put in Grenville's house swore that Isabel had plotted with the co-conspirators to kill the Queen. How a footman at the Spanish embassy swore he had seen her before Christmas at a mass in Ambassador Quadra's chapel, and had seen her in hushed private talk with Quadra. A would-be assassin and a confederate of Spain—that's how they had painted her. And convicted her. She had been sentenced to hang along with eleven men.

Listening, Thornleigh was ashen. He looked across the waterfront's low rooftops to the Tower, its gray stone walls and turrets hulking in the rain. Carlos followed his gaze. Isabel was locked up behind those walls. The Tower was almost close enough that he could let fly an arrow and strike it. A hundred arrows, a thousand, guns, cannon—he wished he could blast the place to rubble to get Isabel out. But that was fantasy. Her only possible hope lay with his plan. He would not let himself think how uncertain a hope it was. It *could* work—if every piece fell into place.

Thornleigh could barely get out the next question. "When are . . . the executions?"

"Eight days."

"Of course," he said bleakly, "Palm Sunday tomorrow. They don't dare do it in Holy Week. It would inflame Catholic sympathizers."

Carlos pulled his eyes off the Tower. Talk like this would not help Isabel. "So we have just seven days to prepare."

Thornleigh blinked at him. "For what?"

Carlos hesitated. Could he really trust the man? Thornleigh loved his daughter, but he was also known for his loyalty to the Queen. If he informed, they would arrest Carlos, and then he could do nothing for Isabel. But the strategy required his father-in-law. He *had* to trust him. "What would you give if we could save her?"

Thornleigh's eyes narrowed. "What? How?"

"Answer me."

"To save my daughter's life? Everything!"

"You swear it? You would give up everything? Your lands? Your title? Give up England?"

"Good God, man, are you saying you have a plan? What is it? Tell me!"

"Swear first."

"I swear!"

"The ships you own. Where does the nearest one lie?"

"Colchester Harbor. What does—?"

"Can you pilot it yourself?"

"Of course."

"How long would it take you to bring it here?"

A clerk at the Admiralty told them Adam was across the river in Bermondsey. They walked over London Bridge to the south shore, then past the riverside bear-baiting grounds, and found Adam in a boat-building shed. He stood beside a new ship's naked ribs, talking to a couple of workmen. He looked bleary-eyed, as though he was bent on constant work, no sleep, to keep his mind off Isabel's fate. He had returned from Amsterdam only to hear that she had been tried as a traitor and convicted.

When he saw them coming, he left the workmen and embraced his father in silent misery. They had not seen each other in the three months since the crisis in Scotland had sent them on different missions for the Queen. Carlos watched him, thinking: Where does Adam's deepest loyalty lie? His devotion to the Queen is stronger even than Thornleigh's. To make sure, he was about to ask a few probing questions, when Thornleigh suddenly said to his son, "Carlos has a plan."

They both looked at him, cautious but eager. Carlos decided to barrel ahead. In the din of rain drumming the roof, he laid out the details. When he'd finished, he could see a spark of hope in Adam's eyes. But he also saw the struggle going on inside him. What meant more to him, his sister or his queen?

"I need you, Adam," Carlos said. "If I don't make it through this, you might. You can get her to your father's ship, and then to his house in Antwerp. But we all know what it would mean for you." Rupture from the Queen's navy. Disgrace. Exile. "So, tell me now if you can't do it."

Adam looked at him for a long, hard moment. He turned to his father, and Carlos saw the look of anguished solidarity between them. Adam took a deep breath and said to Carlos, "There's work to do in Antwerp for the Queen's cause. What do you need?"

Carlos let out a breath of relief. Adam was with them. "Fighters," he answered. "You know where to find them. And you'll be leading them."

"The taverns by the bear garden are our best bet. The Black Whale. The Horn. How many?"

"Eight is best, but only if we're completely sure of them. Six or seven, at least."

"When do we do it?"

Carlos looked at Thornleigh, who gave him a grim nod of encouragement. Carlos said to Adam, "That depends on your mother."

That evening the Thornleighs' house on Bishopsgate Street was as silent as though its people were already in mourning. Carlos had asked the two Thornleigh women to come downstairs and meet him in the parlor. He stood before the fire's embers in the hearth and watched them come in. Frances was first. She looked drained, from worry or weeping or both. Isabel's mother came in a moment later, pale and stiff, as though her iron will alone was keeping her from collapsing. Carlos saw Isabel in her, that same strength of will, and it wrenched his heart.

"Close the door," he told her. Then, to them both, "Sit down."

They sat in chairs close together, their eyes on him in tense expectation.

He pulled a stool close to them and straddled it. He lowered his voice so he could not be heard beyond the door. "I've talked to your husbands. We're going to try to rescue Isabel."

Frances gasped. Isabel's mother did not move a muscle, but her eyes were alight with a stark hope as she asked, "How?"

He held up his hand in warning. "It will take every one of us. Me, your husbands, and both of you. Even then, I must tell you, our chances of success are not the best."

The women shared a glance of dread. Then Isabel's mother said, her voice strong, "Tell us what to do."

He blessed her for that. He explained the plan, detailing the parts that Thornleigh and Adam would play. Then he told Frances hers. "Can you manage it?" he asked.

She lifted her chin and said without hesitation, "Yes."

"How many servants would you need?"

"Just one. A reliable manservant."

"Take Arthur," Isabel's mother told her. "He knows our Antwerp house."

Frances nodded. They both looked back at Carlos, waiting for the rest of his instructions. He explained to Isabel's mother the task that she must undertake.

"Lady Thornleigh," he said, seeing Isabel in her face, "everything depends on you."

Yeavering Hall, the building, looked the same, but nothing else seemed the same. That's what Pedro felt as he limped across the courtyard, still weak from his ordeal. He saw days-old heaps of stinking slops outside the kitchen. An open stable door, banging in the wind. A line hung with laundry that had fallen into the shrubbery. Somewhere a baby was wailing. Everywhere, neglect.

Pedro was headed for the dairy house, but he stuck to the shadows and kept a lookout for the great lord, Grenville. If Grenville should see him, this time he might finish him. But Pedro was determined. He had thought about it all the way here. His duty was to Señora Valverde but he had failed her, had let the great lord take her letter. He had tried to fight Grenville's three men, but it was impossible against their fists, and he had crumpled and curled up in the mud. They had kicked him, taken his horse, and left him on the side of the road, so beaten and bloody he had felt near death. A farmer leading his donkey to market had found him and taken him back to his cottage, and the man's wife had tended Pedro's cuts and bruises with some sticky, foul-smelling herbs. That had helped, and after a few days, as soon as he felt well enough to get up, he thanked the people and set out back to Yeavering Hall to confess his failure to the señora. It had taken over a week, for he was on foot and not yet strong, and he'd had to find cow byres to sleep in. Every mile made the pain in his knee throb worse.

"Pedro!" It was Liza, the milkmaid, coming out of the dairy house. Seeing her bright face, he felt light with relief. He poured out his troubles to her, trying to find the English words, though it came out mostly in Spanish.

"Your mistress?" Liza asked, catching that much. "She's gone, Pedro. Oh dear, you don't know everything that's happened." She was almost breathless as she told him, and he struggled to follow the English. "A fire at the mill . . . Sir Christopher perished . . . a treasure hoard, the gold melted . . . fished Will Morton's body from the river . . . the Queen's agents rode in with soldiers . . . treason plot . . . arrests at the neighboring manor . . . all the folk here in an uproar—"

Pedro stopped her. "Señora Valverde. Where did she go?"

Liza shrugged. "To London?"

Pedro thought of the letter. His duty. If the great lord was dead, was the letter lost? He asked Liza where her master kept his papers. She was not sure. "His bedchamber?" she suggested.

They went into the house, passing servants who looked idle. The place smelled musty, not clean. Pedro was not worried anymore about being caught. The great lord was dead and he was glad. No one stopped them as they went up the stairs and into the great bedchamber. Pedro searched through chests and drawers as Liza ran her hand in awe over the sumptuous bed hangings. Pedro could not find the letter anywhere. "Where else?" he asked. Liza frowned, thinking, then said, "He has a room of books and such. Downstairs. The library, they call it."

In the library Pedro looked through the papers on top of the desk. No letter. He pulled out every drawer and rummaged through the papers. In the lowest drawer he found it. He knew the señora's seal. It had been broken. The lines of scrawl on the paper meant nothing to him. He could not read.

"Give it here," Liza said. "I know me letters." She puzzled over the words and Pedro thought that she, too, could not tell what they meant. But then she looked up at him at if someone had slapped her. "Your mistress wrote of treason . . . hatched in this very house."

Pedro knew his duty. First, Liza took him to the kitchen where he ate some cold beef and bread and then wrapped some hunks of both in sacking to take with him. He said good-bye to her, and went out to the stable, and saddled a horse. No one stopped him as he rode out through the gates. He had sworn to deliver Señora Valverde's letter, and this time he would do it.

ॐ 31 ॐ

The Tower

Holy Week ended with a foggy Easter Sunday. Monday morning dawned bright and clear. Carlos took heart at the sunshine, an omen, he hoped, as he crossed the north courtyard of Whitehall Palace. Everything was in place. Everyone was ready. This *had* to work. Today was the last the convicted traitors would see of the sun. Tomorrow morning they would hang.

The courtyard bustled with clerks, merchants, lawyers, servants, vendors. Carlos ignored them, but his pulse thumped as he passed a company of soldiers of the Palace Guard marching in under an archway. He forced a calm face, didn't even rest his fighting hand on his sheathed sword. He made eye contact with no one and headed straight for the orangery, following the graveled path past the tennis courts. At the orangery he climbed the stairs and could not help hurrying now, taking two steps at a time.

The hallway was deserted except for a lone guard at the closed door. About age forty, Carlos guessed, with a beer gut. He was yawning. When he noticed Carlos striding toward him, he stifled the yawn.

Carlos didn't slow down. He grabbed a fistful of the man's hair and slammed the back of his head against the door. The man twitched, dazed. Carlos wrenched him around and rammed his face against the door. Blood gushed from his nose. Carlos let go. The man dropped to the floor and lay still.

Carlos stepped over the body and tried the door handle. It wasn't locked. He pushed the door open, drawing his sword. Nicolas sat at a child's desk, pencil in hand, eyes on the door in wonder at the commotion. When he saw Carlos his face lit up. "Papa!" He jumped off his chair and ran to him. Carlos took in the room, saw that Nicolas was alone. He sheathed his sword and scooped up his son in one arm, leaving his fighting hand free. "Hang on, Nico," he said. Carrying him out, he took off down the stairs.

He forced himself to walk calmly past the tennis courts, passing two courtiers in a heated argument, a knot of gossiping ladies, a limping clerk. Nicolas hugged his neck. "Papa, are we going home?"

"Soon." He held him tight as he crossed the courtyard. A toothless old servant carrying a basket of turnips smiled at Nicolas and waggled her fingers at him.

Carlos went down the wharf stairway to the palace landing. It was busy with courtiers and clerks, some milling, some stepping in or out of the wherries and tilt boats at the water stairs. A gentleman called out to a wherryman, "Oars, ho!" Carlos made for the far end of the landing where a tilt boat waited. Frances ducked out from under its awning.

Carlos set Nicolas down. "Go with your aunt Frances." He straightened to glance behind him. No one coming. Yet.

Nicolas looked stricken and threw his arms around Carlos's leg. "Where are you going? Aren't we going home?"

"Not yet. I have some business first." He couldn't hide the ache in his voice. God only knew if he would ever see his son again.

Frances held out her arms to Nicolas, beckoning him into the boat. "Come, Nicolas, we're going on a big Dutch ship to visit your grandfather's house in Antwerp. Your baby cousin Katherine is already aboard." She lowered her voice. "Don't worry, Carlos." She indicated her manservant in the shadows under the canopy. "We'll take good care of him. Now go. And may God keep you and Adam safe."

Nicolas did not move. Tears brimmed in his eyes, and his lower lip trembled. He asked Carlos, "Where's Mama?"

"You'll see her soon. Go on, now, into the boat with your aunt."

But the boy would not let go of his leg.

Carlos went down on one knee so he could speak to him face-to-face. "You've been brave, Nico, being shut up all these months. That was hard, and you've been good. I'm proud of you."

A shy smile broke through the boy's tearful look.

"I need you to keep being brave now. It's important." He kissed his son's forehead. "Go with your aunt."

Isabel's pen scratched another line of words. Her hand prickled, almost numb from writing. Her neck was cramped from bending over the paper. Her Tower cell had no desk, no chair, only the cot on which she sat. The few shilling coins she'd had with her when they brought her here had been enough to buy paper, pen, and ink from the jailer, but nothing more.

It was a struggle to keep the paper flat on the straw mattress. She had been writing since the feeble light of dawn had reached her through the small, high window. There was full morning sunshine now—she could tell from the sharp shadows it cast on the thin section she could see of the western wall—but, in here, still barely enough light to write by. The letters she had finished lay at her side. To her parents. To Adam and Frances. She was taking great care over this one to the Queen. The care needed with a tyrant. The next letter, to Carlos, would be the last . . . and the hardest. She dipped her quill in the inkpot on the mattress and bent her head to continue.

Lastly, she wrote, *I humbly entreat Your Majesty to take pity on my innocent child, my son Nicolas, and release him into the care of his father.*

Wait. Would the tyrant allow that? Carlos, a Spaniard. Think! What would she allow?

Or, she wrote quickly, *suffer him to go home with my lady mother, who is your devoted and loyal servant. She loves my son dearly and will bring him up in the ways of learning and charity.*

Tears scalded her eyes. To never see Nico again . . .

She swiped the tears away. *Don't.* She looked up at the barred window, trying to gauge the hour by the sun's shadows. How many hours did she have left? It was so quiet today. Yesterday, Easter

Sunday, London's bells had clanged all morning and into the evening. It had shaken her to her core—the joyous pealing for life resurrected, while she was trying to ready herself for death. But this morning's silence seemed worse. As though the city held its breath, awaiting tomorrow's hangings.

She laid her hand on her stomach. The evening they had locked her in after the trial had been the first time she had felt her baby quicken. She had been sitting on the edge of the cot as the daylight faded, trying to hold in the scream that threatened in her throat, her hands clasped so tightly in her lap the knuckles were white, and that was when she had felt it—the faintest gentle wave in her belly. The joy that had leapt in her had lasted only a moment as horror beat it down: This child would never be born. She had curled up in the cold and wept until she retched.

Now, hand on her stomach, she realized that she had felt no further quickening since then. Seven days. Why? Was the baby suffering because she could not keep down the cold porridge they gave her? Because of the fear that made her nauseous? A new horror crept over her. Had she lost the child already? Was it a black husk, shriveled by the evil spirit of the tyrant Elizabeth? She shook her head with a fierce will to stay rational. Such savage thoughts would drive her mad!

Finish the letter. Write. She jabbed her quill in the inkpot with such force she knocked it over. Ink poured onto the straw. *No! I have to write to Carlos!* She snatched the pot. Stuck in the pen. Empty! It filled her with fury. *She robs me of everything! My son! My last words! My life!* She hurled the inkpot across the cell. It crashed against the wall and fell, clattering on the stone floor.

She scrambled on hands and knees to salvage it. Even a few drops would yield a few words! What else was there to do but sit and quake in this torturing silence? She sank back on her heels, desperately cradling the inkwell in her palm, when she heard voices outside the door. A man . . . and a woman.

Mother's voice?

She shut her eyes tight. A cruel hallucination—more torture.

The door opened with a clanking of keys. Isabel squinted up at the bright sunlight that shone on two figures at the doorway. She blinked in disbelief. "Mother?"

"Isabel!" Her mother rushed to her. "Darling," she murmured as she helped her to her feet. Isabel wanted to fall into her mother's arms, sobbing, but a man in a breastplate stood in the doorway, watching, and she held back. Held on to the last thread of determination to stay strong.

Her mother said loudly, officiously, "Isabel, this is Sir William St. Loe, captain of the Tower Guard. He is here—and I am here—to escort you to Whitehall. You are to have an audience with Her Majesty the Queen."

She did not understand. Questions flailed in her head. No words came. Only a hoarse "What?"

"Sir William, may I have a moment with my daughter? She is amazed, as you can see, and your presence is somewhat fearful." She guided Isabel to the cot and gently sat her down. "Please, sir, allow me a few moments to calm her. If she cannot speak sensibly, Her Majesty's time will be wasted."

"As will my time, Lady Thornleigh, if you tarry long. Be quick." He moved away from the door. Isabel heard the footfalls of his boots become faint.

Alone with her mother, she felt her thread of willpower snap. "All for nothing!" she cried. She could not dam the flood of anguish. "I stayed with Grenville, all for nothing! Cecil had his spy there all the time. I did the work of a fool! A stupid, useless fool!"

"Shhh! Isabel, shhh!"

St. Loe was back in the doorway. "What's amiss?"

"Nothing, sir, nothing at all. Just let me calm her. Leave us, please."

He scowled, but he moved away again.

Despair and rage made Isabel sob, "All for nothing . . . nothing . . ."

"No, Bel. It was not." Her mother went down on her knees and took hold of her hand. "We try. We do our best to do what's right. Right outcomes do not always follow. But the trying is everything. My darling, the trying is life itself."

Isabel blinked at her. She held tight to her mother's hand, hungrily grateful for this absolution.

Her mother pulled out a handkerchief and busily wiped at the ink on Isabel's palm. "Bel, there is so little time to tell you everything." Her voice was so low it was almost a whisper. "Take heart, my darling. You are to be freed."

Isabel flinched.

"No, do not move. Make no sound, lest St. Loe hear. But hear *me*, and take heart. Carlos has arranged it all. At his suggestion I begged the Queen to grant you this audience, and she relented for the sake of our friendship. It is a chance to defend yourself, to explain the truth, and entreat her to pardon you. If she does . . . well, nothing would be more wonderful. But if she does not—which, my darling, is the more likely—I tell you, do not despair, for we are prepared. All of us. We are going to free you." She glanced over her shoulder. No sign of St. Loe.

Isabel was trembling, her hope so exquisite it felt like pain. She managed to ask, "We?"

Her mother turned back, lowering her voice even more. "First, let me assure you that Nicolas is safe. Carlos got him out of the palace this morning."

Isabel gasped. "Out? How?"

"He simply took him, and no one stopped him. He delivered him to Frances, who was ready with a boat, and she will now have Nicolas aboard a Dutch ship bound for Bruges. They will go to our house in Antwerp. Bel, your boy is safe."

She could not hold back the tears. Carlos. Was there anything he would not venture for her and their son? Hope flooded her. "What now? Where is Carlos?"

"Outside, masquerading as my manservant. He will come with us in the Tower barge as St. Loe and his yeoman guards escort you to Whitehall. At the palace wharf Adam stands ready with seven fighting men they hired. They are waiting at the tavern on the landing. If, after hearing you, Elizabeth will not relent and orders St. Loe to bring you back here, Carlos and Adam and their men will attack on the wharf, overcome your guards, take the barge, and carry you away. Your father has his ship *Gannet* ready at Billingsgate Wharf. He will sail you to Amsterdam."

"With Carlos and Adam!"

"With Carlos and Adam."

"And you?"

"I shall quietly leave the palace and make my own way across to the Low Countries. We shall all meet—the whole family—in Antwerp."

Isabel felt such a flood of joy she threw her arms around her mother's neck, trembling with excitement. They stood up together.

"Now, are you ready? Can you show a penitent's face to St. Loe?"

Isabel nodded. "Yes. Ready."

They left the cell, St. Loe leading them. When they stepped outside the sunlight was so strong Isabel had to shield her eyes, but its warmth on her face was like balm. Eight guards fell in, surrounding her. Her mother followed. Down the stairs they went, along a narrow, cobbled way through the Tower precincts to the western water gate. At the water stairs the open barge bobbed in the choppy waves. Its ten rowers sat waiting at their shipped oars. Water sloshed and ebbed over the landing's stone edge.

She saw Carlos standing beside the barge. Dressed like her mother's footman in a plain brown tunic with the Thornleigh emblem of a russet thornbush, he kept his eyes lowered in proper servility. Isabel was glad, for if he were to look at her she was afraid her joy would show. As she reached the barge she slipped on the wet stone landing. Carlos lurched to grab her, but a guard reached her first and caught her, then scowled at Carlos for overstepping his station.

They settled into the barge, Isabel seated in the middle, the guards standing fore and aft of the rowers, St. Loe taking a seat in the bow. Her mother sat in the stern, Carlos standing behind her. Once settled, Isabel did not dare turn to glance at them. It was hard enough to keep a calm face.

The barge nosed out into the water traffic, and Isabel gazed at the life of the river, feeling fresh delight at its vitality—the wherries and tilt boats carrying apprentices to work, merchants to their shops, a family to the south shore bear gardens, visitors to the quays from their arriving ships. She heard a child's laugh. Heard the slap of a dirty sail on a fishing smack as it beat against the spring wind. Off the customs wharf the barge passed through the fleet of big merchant ships that rode at anchor, their flags snapping with the colors of Portugal, Sweden, Venice, Poland. Their rigging squeaked and sang like a choir of crickets. Off Billingsgate Wharf she caught sight of her father's ship *Gannet*. Was that him, standing at the stern rail, watching the barge go by? She gripped the edge of the seat to ground her excitement, to beat back a smile.

They neared London Bridge, the incoming tide frothing the water around its twenty stone arches. Isabel looked up at the tall houses and shops that crammed the bridge. She could hear the traffic on it—the tramping people, riders, oxcarts, the bleating of a flock of sheep being driven across. They passed under the bridge, and she turned her face to the warm southerly breeze that had sailed across distant fields with spring scents of wet earth and grass. She felt a faint flutter in her belly. Her baby, stirring! It brought a jolt of happiness so strong she ached to turn and look at Carlos. *Not yet . . . not yet.* But oh, to think that in high summer, late August, this child would come into the world!

She looked ahead. Soon they would be past the city. Around the bend in the river lay Whitehall Palace. She could not see it yet. The wait felt hard, so hard. She bent her thoughts to her audience with the Queen. She would defend herself resolutely, but she expected nothing—the tyrant had granted the meeting only out of affection for her mother; there would be no pardon. She worked her thoughts on playing her role well in what would follow. The guards would take her back to the barge to return her to the Tower. That's when Carlos and Adam and their band of fighters would attack. She would be prepared to run with them.

The sun slipped behind a cloud. The water darkened. Isabel felt a shadow creep into her. Something was not right. Something about the stark joy she had felt since leaving the Tower. It had enveloped her like a bright light that she could not see beyond. Now, in shadow, she sensed that something was not right.

The sun flashed out, leaving the cloud behind, and her hope shot up again, riding high with the warm breeze. *Don't think. Let Carlos's plan unfold. Live!*

The turrets of Whitehall gleamed. Atop them the Queen's flags rippled, signaling she was in residence. The palace wharf was as crowded as ever with throngs of men come to do business at court, but as the Tower barge came alongside the landing and the guards got out, people moved away, eyeing Isabel, a prisoner about to come among them.

She stepped out onto the landing. Her guard formed around her. St. Loe led the party toward the stairway that led up to the palace, with Isabel's mother and Carlos at the rear. People eddied to let them pass. Isabel noticed soldiers of the Palace Guard on regular duty, perhaps a dozen, posted at the foot of the staircase and along the landing. Another half dozen soldiers idly watched from the top of the stairs. She looked across at the sheds and taverns that barnacled the wharf, where servingmen lounged in the sun with their ale. Adam was in one of those taverns with his hired fighters. How many had her mother said? Seven?

Her footstep faltered. Seven—with Carlos and Adam that made nine. Against the eight guards of St. Loe plus all these palace soldiers? Terrible odds. Carlos and Adam would try, but could they . . . She suddenly stopped walking. Her mother's words from the Tower echoed. *"Trying is everything."*

"Move on," a guard said, nudging her. Isabel walked on, but her blood had gone cold. She suddenly knew what was not right. Her mother was wrong. Trying is *not* everything. Trying can fail.

Up the staircase she went with the guards, her every footstep as stiff as her fear. Soldiers were posted everywhere. At doorways, under arches, on terraces. *Carlos and Adam cannot possibly prevail. The plan is impossible. To attempt it is suicide.* She imagined them attacking her guards, wounding many, killing some, and the palace soldiers rushing in to fight them. In the skirmish Carlos and Adam would be cut down. If still alive, they would be tried for murdering the Queen's men, interfering with the Queen's justice. Her father, too, and her mother. They would all be condemned. They would hang. And she would hang.

It was so clear. *If they attack, they will die.* The next thought was even more starkly clear. *If they don't attack, I alone will die.*

A voice inside her wailed, *Just try! It might work! Try!*

She stifled the voice. Killed it. To go on hoping for rescue was to condemn her family to death. She could not *let* them try.

It was agony. To not turn to Carlos, not reach out for him. To force herself to keep walking in the sunshine when she knew she was already dead.

"Where'd you spring from, goblin?"

Pedro did not understand the question. He was so tired from seven days of riding almost nonstop he could barely stay upright in the saddle, but he had made it to the walls of London. And now, to be held up at this roadblock outside Bishopsgate made him angry. Five armed men in breastplates manned it. Why were they stopping everyone from going into the city? "Goblin?" he asked. "What is that?"

The men laughed and one said, "You are, you runty little redskin."

"Get a move on!" a woman on a donkey called out from the cluster of people waiting to get through.

The man in the breastplate ignored her. He asked Pedro, "What's your business in the city?"

"Business? No business. Letter to give."

"Hand it over."

Pedro would not. He shivered when he remembered the beating the last time men had demanded this letter, but he was sworn to deliver it to the señora's mother and this time he would do it even if they beat him black and blue. Instead of taking the letter from his pocket, he countered with a question. "Why stop people?"

"Looking for papist troublemakers. Sheriff don't want nothing to mar the hangings tomorrow morn." He eyed Pedro's dust-white breeches and jerkin and his lathered horse. "You a papist looking for trouble?"

"Papist?" He had heard that word before and knew it could lead to fighting. "No, just servant."

"Aw, let him through," an old man groused from the throng. "At this rate none of us will get to see the hangings." He added cheerfully to the young farmer beside him, "They say there's a woman among 'em. I never did see a woman swing. That'll be something."

The man in the breastplate glared at Pedro. "The letter. Give it over."

"Sergeant, forget it," a breastplated man on horseback said, trotting up to him. "The runt would quake at his own shadow. Let's move this lot through."

"Aye, sir."

Pedro rode in, glad to be past such men. He was tired and hungry and sore, but so happy to be near the Thornleighs' house he kicked his horse for one final sprint down Bishopsgate Street.

But at the house his hope was dashed. Lady Thornleigh was not at home, the steward said. She had gone to Whitehall Palace. Pedro sat down on a bench in the courtyard, every muscle aching, and puzzled over what to do next. Take the letter to Lady Thornleigh? Or wait for her to come home? The smell of onions cooking in the kitchen made him want to stay and wait. Get some food. Some ale. Rest. Besides, if he went, how was he to find the lady at the great queen's court?

He pushed himself to his feet. He had to try.

Following St. Loe, the eight Tower guards marched along the corridor of Whitehall Palace, forcing Isabel, boxed in at the center, to keep up, though she felt her legs might buckle. Her mother was at the rear with Carlos, but Isabel did not dare glance back at them. They reached a double door with palace guards posted on either side. St. Loe gave an order and the guards opened the doors. The Tower party marched through.

They entered a long gallery, bright with tall windows. The guards tramped to a halt, and Isabel almost staggered at the sudden stop. There was a wave of laughter from the far end where a few dozen men and women sat with their backs to her and the guards. She looked past the people to a stage. A play was in progress. Actors dashing about. A beet-nosed buffoon, tumbling. At the center of the audience, on a hip-high dais garlanded with roses, in a gilt chair, sat Queen Elizabeth. St. Loe beckoned his men to stand at ease, and Isabel, struggling with her fears, tried to make sense of what was happening. St. Loe would not interrupt the performance that the Queen and her courtiers were enjoying. He was waiting for it to end.

The wait was torture. She felt disoriented by the merriment . . . the perfume in the air . . . the ladies' rustling silks . . . antic actors banging drums and tweedling pipes. Some of the actors looked familiar. A barrel-chested, strutting man in a lawyer's black cloak with cape. Another one, lean, with a crafty face. The players from Yeavering Hall, she realized. On the night of the fire they had been about to start south. There was a drumroll, and an actor's mock scream, and more laughter rocked the gallery. The Queen's shoulders, however, were still. She was not laughing. Elizabeth the tyrant, Isabel thought. How she hated the woman.

She was aware of Carlos and her mother moving slowly along the window wall, coming alongside her guards, getting closer to her. She fought to order her fractured thoughts. Carlos and Adam planned to attack when the guards took her back to the wharf. She had to tell Carlos to call it off. A shudder went through her bowels at the thought of going to her death tomorrow . . . the hangman's rope . . . snapping her neck. But unless she stopped Carlos and Adam, she would be sending them to *their* deaths, and likely her parents, too. She could not let everyone she loved die for her. She had to make them abandon the rescue attempt. *Dear God*, she thought in a daze of misery, *give me the strength to hold fast*. But how was she to tell Carlos? Eight guards surrounded her, and he was so far away.

The players cavorted to more laughter. Isabel stole a look at

Carlos. He kept his eyes lowered, playing his servile role—or maybe because he did not trust himself to look at her. The people's laughter burst out in a crescendo. Then a rush of applause. The players lined up at the front of the stage and bowed, sweating and smiling. The courtiers and ladies clapped and chattered. Then all heads turned to the Queen. There was silence.

" 'Twill serve," Elizabeth said, no smile in her voice. "Master of the Revels," she said to a nearby official, "next time, no drums." The players, chagrined, bowed deeply to her. She rose from her chair. All the courtiers and ladies rose, too. St. Loe went forward to the Queen's dais and bowed and said something to her. She turned to look at the Tower party. Her eyes met Isabel's. Her face hardened.

St. Loe motioned to his two men at the vanguard and they stepped to the side, leaving the way clear between Isabel and the Queen. Elizabeth came down the dais steps, ignoring the arm that St. Loe offered. She said something to another official. He hastened to pass the word along to the crowd, and the courtiers and ladies began quietly chattering, preparing to leave.

Isabel stiffened as the Queen approached her. Dark circles under Elizabeth's eyes made her look both fragile and pitiless.

"Your Majesty," her mother said, coming to them. "I thank you most humbly for granting my daughter this audience. It shows you as the merciful monarch you are."

Elizabeth barely nodded in acknowledgment. She regarded Isabel coldly. "Well?" she demanded. "Speak."

Words jammed in Isabel's throat. The chattering courtiers . . . Carlos moving nearer . . . an image of him dead on a gallows. Dazed, she could only mumble, "I am not . . . please, Your Majesty . . . I am loyal. I am innocent."

Elizabeth was unmoved. "So you claimed at your trial, I am told. Claimed it *ad nauseam*. No one believed you then. Why should I now?" Her dark eyes flashed with contempt. "Traitors, spawning pernicious discontent to eat at the good people of my realm and rob them of their native pride. And how vile of you to come at us now, like jackals, when we are so low, weakened by war. I will not suffer traitors."

It lit a fuse of anger in Isabel. To think that she had tried to *save* this woman from the traitors. Save a tyrant! Near the stage all the courtiers and their ladies remained standing, watching her and the Queen in fascination. The actors, too. No one was leaving.

Elizabeth's eyes narrowed on Isabel in suspicion. "You took on much in Northumberland, emboldening your fellow traitors to come at me. Did you devise that stratagem alone? I think not. Who put you to it? Answer me. Was it your husband? Your Spanish husband in the pocket of Spain? Where is he now, eh? Has he deserted you to stand alone?"

The accusation stunned Isabel. She did not dare let her gaze flick to Carlos, but he had moved so near she saw him from the corner of her eye, his hand on his dagger hilt, his knuckles white. Panic leapt in her. Elizabeth's suspicion, unchecked, could taint him, taint her whole family. She saw terrible danger for them all. She had to speak up, and now.

"Alone," she blurted. "Yes. I acted all alone."

Elizabeth frowned in surprise. "What?"

"I confess. All of it. Plotting. Sedition. Treason. I am a traitor to Your Majesty. I, alone of all my family."

Her mother gasped. "Isabel! What are you doing?"

"Quiet, Mother. I am guilty as charged."

Carlos had frozen. Courtiers had turned to look. Isabel forced herself to breathe.

"No!" her mother cried. "Your Majesty, I beg you . . . my daughter is not well. Her wits, in the Tower . . . do not listen—"

"I am listening only *because* of you," Elizabeth snapped. "Now, at last, we are getting the truth." Her eyes flashed at Isabel. "Out with it."

"The truth . . . yes. I confess to it all. I conspired with Sir Christopher Grenville to murder Your Majesty. No member of my family knew it, I swear it. They are all Your Majesty's loyal subjects."

She heard a tortured groan dragged from Carlos. She plowed on, "My poor mother—she loves me, that is her only sin. Loves me so much she begged for Your Majesty's clemency. So much, she will plead with you now beyond all reason. So much, she may even dream of rescuing me from Your Majesty's justice. Of course, that cannot be." She looked straight at Carlos. "I would not *allow* it. If it were attempted, I would refuse to flee." She tore her eyes from his ashen face and looked back at the tyrant. Her banging heart made it hard to breathe. "I accept Your Majesty's justice. And the sentence. The treason is on my head alone. Let your wrath fall on me, and be there confined."

Her mother fell on her knees with a cry, "Stop! Isabel, stop this! Elizabeth—"

"Lady Thornleigh, collect yourself," Elizabeth said, appalled. "Rise this instant."

"Isabel, take back these lies!" she wailed. "Elizabeth, you cannot believe—"

"You, man," Elizabeth ordered Carlos, "see to the lady. She is unwell."

He stood like stone, agonized, his eyes locked on Isabel.

Elizabeth glared at him. "I said see to your mistress, oaf!"

St. Loe gave Carlos a shove. "Your mistress, man."

Carlos turned on him in fury. St. Loe stiffened at such a defiant response from a footman. Carlos's hand was a fist around his sheathed dagger hilt.

Carlos, don't! Isabel looked around wildly for someone to break the impasse. Courtiers stood watching, and actors had come forward on the stage, everyone transfixed by the drama around the Queen. Among the actors was a face that made Isabel gape. A long, white face, eyes like wet coals. Father York! How could he be *here?* He wore a black cloak like the actor who had played the lawyer. Between it and his leg he held something alongside his knee. A tube of metal that gleamed in the sunlight. A pistol. His eyes were locked on Elizabeth.

Isabel's heart seemed to stop. *He has come to kill her.*

She looked in amazement at St. Loe. The guards. The courtiers. None of them noticed York. Everyone was watching Carlos in his aberrant standoff with St. Loe. Her mother was still distraught on her knees before Elizabeth. Elizabeth was reaching to raise her to her feet. Her back was to York, an unobstructed target.

The words burst from Isabel before she could think. "The priest!" she cried, pointing. "Carlos, look! He has a pistol!"

York jerked the pistol into the folds of his cloak. The guards instinctively moved in on Isabel. The actors looked about in alarm.

"There!" she cried. "Stop him! He'll shoot!"

Carlos bolted toward the stage, dodging the courtiers who were moving about in confusion, their voices rising in panic with cries of, "Pistol! . . . Assassin!"

York dashed along the stage behind the actors, raced down the steps, and disappeared into the throng of courtiers. St. Loe shouted orders and guards burst into action to surround Elizabeth. Isabel saw York pushing people aside, coming her way. Men shouted, and one grabbed for him, but York knocked him down. He was heading for the dais. In the melee it was the only vantage point for a clear shot.

"Carlos! The dais!" Isabel lurched forward, arms outstretched to shield the Queen. Guards seized her.

A woman screamed.

York was atop the dais. He raised the pistol. Aimed.

Carlos charged him, knocking him down. The priest tumbled off the dais. There were screams. People ran in panic. Carlos rolled across the dais to get to York. Guards rushed toward them.

The priest struggled to his feet. He raised the pistol, his arm jerking and bobbing in an attempt to get a clear shot at Elizabeth behind her screen of guards. The pistol pointed at Isabel. She saw the blackness down the barrel.

Carlos lunged for York. They fell to the ground, wrestling. The guards shielding Elizabeth were marching her away to safety. Other palace guards were rushing in. Two guards still gripped Isabel and she struggled to turn her head to see Carlos fighting the priest on the ground.

A gunshot.

People ran in panic, leaving space around the two men on the floor. York staggered to his feet. Carlos groped at the priest's leg. Palace guards reached York and seized him. Isabel strained to see past them. "Carlos!"

Carlos let go of York's leg and fell back. Blood soaked his side. He sprawled on the floor on his back. Isabel screamed, "No!" as his eyes closed.

❧ 32 ❧

Home

Three months had passed since the hangings. It felt to Frances like a year, so much had changed. The war in Scotland was over, and Adam was coming home.

She stood waiting on the landing at the Old Swan Stairs, looking out at the river traffic for his boat to appear. She was so eager, her skin felt flushed, an extra heat that she did not need on this sweltering June afternoon. She dabbed her moist upper lip with a handkerchief, thinking the last thing she wanted Adam to see was sweat dampening her face like a fishwife's. In the heat, wherrymen lounged in their boats, some napping, as they waited for trade. One pulled a net out of the water and fished from it a leather bottle of ale. Frances envied him the cold drink he upended in his mouth. She had been waiting in the sun for over an hour. The two footmen she had brought to carry Adam's luggage waited on a shady bench under the awning of a fishmonger's stall, but from there the view of the river was blocked by people buying the catches of shad, salmon, and eels, and others coming and going in boats. Frances wanted to stay at the wharf edge to catch the very first glimpse of her husband.

The church bells of All-Hallows-by-the-Tower rang out in the still air. She glanced across the waterfront rooftops at the Tower. She felt no pity for the twelve traitors who had died that April morning, not even for Father York, a man of God sickeningly corrupted by his hatred of the Protestant Queen. She thought of her brother Christopher. If he had not died in the fire, he would have been hanged alongside his wretched fellow conspirators, and neither could she muster a shred of grief for him. She was only thankful, deeply thankful, that Isabel had been spared. Frances had been about to sail on the Dutch ship with Nicolas and Katherine when Lady Thornleigh's messenger had come alongside in a boat with the extraordinary news. Isabel's action and Carlos's bravery in saving the Queen from Father York, followed by the arrival of Isabel's Indian servant with her letter, had proved her innocence beyond all doubt. The Queen had pardoned Isabel while bestowing her flustered thanks. What a change was there! And how welcome was the news that had reached Frances the next day, that Carlos had survived his wound.

The changes had been no less extraordinary in Scotland, where just ten days ago the tide had turned for England with an unexpected and resounding victory. The feared Spanish ships bringing an army to help the French had never arrived. Philip of Spain, in his ferocious ongoing war with the Turks in the Mediterranean, had suffered a disastrous defeat there just as his troops in Antwerp's port were about to embark for Scotland, and so, instead, he had sent them south to throw against the Turks. The French, bottled up in Leith, hungry and weakened by sickness after months under siege, and dispirited by Spain's abandonment, had surrendered to the English commander, Lord Grey.

Adam! There he was! Standing in the bow of the boat, his men rowing. Frances waved. He did not wave back. He must not have seen her. Or had he? She had a chilling memory of his cold aloofness when she had said good-bye to him on this very wharf at Christmas. She had hoped for just one tender look before he'd sailed off into danger, but his mind had been on his mission, not her.

"Come," she called to her footmen, beckoning them to follow. She pushed through the people hailing boats and reached the wharf edge as Adam's boat nudged the water stairs. He hopped out. She kept back a few paces as he spoke with his men. Then he turned and saw her. "Frances," he said with smile. He came to her. "How are you?"

"Very happy, now that you are here." Her heart swelled, for he looked so hale, his face burnished by sun and wind from the months at sea off Edinburgh where he and his fellow captains had been blockading the entrance to Leith. "And you?" she asked as his men began unloading his luggage.

"Me? Could not be better." He looked so pleased, she hoped it might be partly from seeing her, but she knew better. It was because of the victory. "The peace negotiations," he said, slinging a satchel over his shoulder. "Have you heard?"

"About your father? Yes, it was quite an honor." Lord Thornleigh was in Edinburgh as one of the delegation led by Sir William Cecil.

"It's done. Astounding terms, and France has agreed to every one. No French troops to be left in Scotland, not one outpost, not a single soldier. The Leith garrison to be torn down, walls and all. Plus—and this is the crowning glory of Elizabeth's victory—she has forced her cousin Mary, Queen of Scots to foreswear calling herself the rightful queen of England. It will be there in black and white, her renunciation forever of any such claim, signed by all parties. Ha! Elizabeth has not only ousted the French, she has put all of Europe in awe of her prowess."

Frances managed a smile, though it hurt to see him so animated whenever he spoke of the Queen. Elizabeth, he always called her. How could Frances compete with that young and beautiful creature? Life at court, they said, was lively these days with her banquets of triumph amid music and dancing and entertainments. The Queen especially loved to dance. Frances supposed that Adam would be asked to attend.

"What a wonderful outcome," she said. "You must tell me all about it." She gave instructions to the footmen to go on ahead with the luggage, then asked Adam, "Are you free to come back to the house now? I have had everything newly cleaned and fresh floor rushes laid, the best quality, in just this morning from Kent. And I've had cook prepare partridge the way you like it, with wine and blackcurrants. And Katherine—just wait until you see how she crawls about!" She knew she was rattling on foolishly, but Adam was looking at her in a new way, a look both gentle and intense that made her babble. "She grins when I coo to her. And when I offer her the spoon she can—"

"Frances," he said, stopping her. The tenderness in his voice sent a spark through her. "I want to thank you for all you did for Isabel. She wrote me, said she would be drowned at the bottom of Grenville's millrace if you had not fetched Carlos. And then, when she was in the Tower, I know how you stood ready, despite all the dangers, to take their son to safety." He lifted her chin, bringing her face closer to his. "What you did was not only good, it was brave."

He kissed her. A kiss of warmth. The very first. She could not move a muscle.

"Buy some eels, sir?" a boy asked, coming to them with his basket.

Adam looked at the boy, but Frances did not take her eyes off Adam. She could scarcely breathe for joy.

"No," he said, and then with a smile at Frances, "I have a better supper waiting." He slung his satchel higher on his shoulder. "Come. Let's go home."

"Bel, watch what you're doing. Oh, dear, you've nicked yourself."

"It's nothing," Isabel said, sucking the bead of blood from her fingertip. She and her mother were on their knees training a thorny rosebush onto the garden trellis, but when she had let her concentration slip to look at the door to the house, a thorn had jabbed.

"You will not make him come home any faster by constantly checking the door."

Isabel mustered a smile. "I suppose not." She wiped perspiration off her brow with her sleeve. It was so hot, and now, in her seventh month of pregnancy, she keenly felt the heat. "I'm just on edge after all the waiting." It had taken three months for the grinding wheels of Spanish bureaucracy to reach a decision about Carlos, and that morning he had been asked to the Spanish embassy to hear it. Our fate, she thought. If the King had forgiven Carlos his transgression with D'Oysel, they would be going back to Peru. A happy outcome, of course. Perhaps she would actually feel it once she knew for certain.

"Nicolas," her mother called across the garden path. "Come and help me, darling. You too, Pedro, since your mistress is no use to me today."

Isabel looked to the fountain where Nicolas and Pedro were playing. They had been sword-fighting with sticks, but now Pedro had found a pile of large, smooth stones that the gardener had left for starting a border and he was juggling three of them, to Nicolas's delight. Dear Pedro, she thought in wonder. That he had searched for her letter and found it, that he had raced to London with it, that he had reached her mother at Whitehall in that chaos of terror over York, and by delivering the letter had saved her life—it still left her in awe. How grateful she was to him!

And how good he had become at juggling, she thought with a smile as she watched him now. Tom Yates's legacy. Despite her deep well of sadness about Tom, it did her heart good to see how his skill at foolery had taken root in Pedro. It was branching out in all manner of little jests. Like yesterday morning. When Nicolas had come to breakfast, the servants had burst into laughter. While Nicolas had slept, Pedro had taken charcoal and drawn a mustache on him.

"They don't hear me," her mother said as Pedro kept juggling and Nicolas jumped to swipe a stone and missed. "Well," she said, abandoning her roses and getting up off her knees, "this labor of love is lost. Come, up with you, Bel, and let us take some rest in the shade."

She helped Isabel to her feet and they strolled arm in arm to a bench under an apple tree. "Don't fret, darling. Elizabeth's commendation of Carlos will have done a world of good, you'll see."

Isabel knew her mother meant to encourage her. In gratitude for Carlos stopping York, Elizabeth had written a note in her own hand to Philip of Spain, praising Carlos. As well she should, Isabel thought, shuddering at the memory of him being felled by York's pistol shot. His recovery had been long and slow from the bullet's ravages, including two broken ribs and a horrible loss of blood. For days they had not known if he would live or die. "I am sure you are right," she said now. The Queen's intervention on Carlos's behalf had been extraordinary. "And if so, the path is clear for us to return to Peru."

"From the Old World to the New," her mother murmured. They sat down under the leafy apple boughs that arched over their heads. The shaded grass felt cool where it touched Isabel's ankle. In bright sun at the garden wall, bees hummed among the tall irises and climbing columbine. The ginger cat prowled through a dense patch of lavender, releasing its perfume. Isabel felt her mother's probing gaze on her. "And yet, that does not seem to cheer you."

"It does . . . yes, of course it does. Trujillo is so beautiful. And I love our house. And it means so much to Carlos. But . . ."

"But it does not feel like home?"

How she sees through me, Isabel thought, unnerved. And then, *If only I could untangle my feelings.* She watched a chaffinch peck at seeds on the grass, then flutter up into the apple tree to a forked branch where its nest was tucked, a tidy cup pressed from moss, grass, and feathers. She remembered a day in spring when she was five or six, and Adam had pulled a ladder to a beech tree and showed her a chaffinch nest. Perched on the ladder, she had been entranced at him explaining how the nest was bound with spiders' webs and lined with feathers and wool, and decorated with lichen and flakes of bark.

Home, she thought. Peru. She said, "I didn't come to stay."

"No. You came for me." Her mother took hold of her hand. "I am so glad you did."

Isabel looked into her eyes. Whatever happened, she was part of this family forever. But something else was nagging at her. Something that her parents' young porter, Henry, had told her. He had taken a gift of honey from her mother to Adam and Frances, and had heard the story from a groom who had recently left Yeavering Hall to join Frances's household. At the time of the fire at the mill, the groom had been on an errand at the port of Bamburgh, and the day after the fire, he said, he'd seen a man boarding a ship bound for France, the man hunched over, looking furtive, as if to avoid being seen. The groom swore it was his master, Sir Christopher Grenville. "All burned his face was, red and raw, the hair half burned away." That had chilled Isabel. But was it true? The groom had sworn it, Henry said, but then had added that the groom was infamous among the servants for his tall tales. Was it nothing more than a made-up tale for a dark night by the kitchen fire? She had not repeated the tale to anyone.

"Papa!" Nicolas sang out.

Isabel jumped up. Carlos was coming out of the house. Because of his wound, he still walked favoring one leg to take the pressure off his side. She held her breath. What was the verdict? It was impossible to read his face. Nicolas ran to him and Carlos picked him up with a slight wince at the residual pain in his side. "Are you helping your mother and grandmother?"

"No, they just play with flowers. I'm learning to juggle. See?" He pointed to Pedro, who was still at it.

"Go on, then." He set him down, and Nicolas ran back to Pedro, calling, "Let *me* try!"

Isabel waited. Carlos looked at her. He shook his head. "Bad news."

"How bad?"

"Could not be much worse. The King revoked our *encomienda*."

Her hand flew to her mouth. This was a shock. The land grant with its Indian laborers was the basis of all wealth and status in Peru.

Her mother had stood as well, and she asked, "What does it mean, Carlos? For you?"

He let out a tight sigh. "Leaves us with nothing there but the house."

"Oh, dear. I am so sorry."

He managed a mirthless smile. "The price of bashing an ally commander's head."

"And freeing Adam," she countered, "for which all of us can never thank you enough." She squared her shoulders. "Well, this does change things." She called to the house, "James!" then turned back to Isabel and gave her elbow a squeeze. "I am going to see Elizabeth. It's time she did right by you." The footman appeared at the door. "We're going upriver," she called to him, and went inside.

Isabel and Carlos looked at each other. She could see his deep disappointment.

"I'll sell the house," he said. "Sell my share in the mine, too. It will pay most of our debts. But after that . . ." He shrugged. "No point in going back. Without land, there's nothing for us there."

"My father will give us something."

He nodded. She saw how much it rankled him. One stroke of the King's pen had knocked him down from grandee to poor relation dependent on his father-in-law. He laid his hand on her swollen belly. "Isabel, I'm sorry."

But she was not. She was happy. She was loath to show him *how* happy. Now that it was decided, now that they had been cut off from their life in Peru, she realized it was exactly what she had been hoping for. It felt as if she had been cut free. Free to stay where she wanted. In England. Home.

Her mother was as good as her word. That very evening, after supper, a messenger arrived from the Queen summoning Carlos and Isabel to Whitehall. Isabel was bubbling with hope as they dressed for the audience, and she could tell that Carlos was hopeful, too. Told by her friend Lady Thornleigh of their plight, the Queen seemed ready to reward them for saving her life. There was every reason to expect she would be generous.

It was dusk, yet still sweltering when their hired boat rowed them past the city and around the bend in the river toward the palace. Church bells were pealing from Lambeth on the southern shore, and as their boat approached the palace wharf, it was clear that something extraordinary was happening. The wherries and tilt boats and barges were so thick, it was hard for their man to row through the traffic, and the wharf itself was a whirl of courtiers, ladies, footmen, musicians. Men called for boats and women laughed and chattered as they milled about. Isabel saw a pet monkey chittering atop a lady's shoulder. Torches bobbed in the hands of a dozen servants in the Queen's livery who were hurrying down her private stairs. "What is it?" Isabel asked the boatman as they came alongside the jetty and he shipped his oars. "A banquet? A masque?"

"It's late for supping, my lady. From the sound of the Lambeth bells, I'd say Her Majesty is going out. They ring whenever she goes on the river."

"You're right," Carlos said. "Look."

Isabel saw what he was pointing to. Past the throng of people a gorgeously decked barge waited at the far edge of the wharf. Torchlight gleamed over its gilt prow, its garlands of silk roses, its windows paned with glass, its gold embroidered cushions, and its canopy of green silk that rippled in the faint river breeze. Carlos handed Isabel out of their boat and they made their way through the throng and up the stairs. Torches flared all along the gravel walk, and more servants with more torches and lanterns scurried toward the wharf. Isabel and Carlos had not even reached the palace doors when a small group of young ladies and gallants burst forth, laughing. The finery on men and women alike was a dazzle of colors—popinjay blue, scarlet, sea green, and gold—and in the center was Elizabeth in a blaze of gold and black, with silver slippers and silver spangles in her hair. Laughing too, she skipped like a schoolgirl.

"Aha!" she cried merrily, seeing Isabel and Carlos. "You are tardy, good people. Another moment and you would have found me gone. 'Tis too hot for staying behind doors, and the night is young." She stopped when she reached them. Isabel curtsied and Carlos bowed. Elizabeth's ladies and gentlemen waited behind her, maintaining their cheerful looks. Elizabeth beckoned Isabel to rise. "Now, where is your lady mother?" she asked, looking about her party. "What, no sign of good Lady Thornleigh? I saw her not a half hour ago. Well, no matter, she has done her office." She lifted her head with a regal smile and added, "Now, I shall do mine. You, sir," she said to Carlos. "I am very glad to hear of your ill fortune." Isabel thought she had misheard, but saw that she had not, for several of the courtiers looked startled, too. Elizabeth paused, enjoying the suspense she had spun. "Why? Because

Spain's loss is my gain," she said with satisfaction. "You shall remain in England."

Isabel relaxed and caught the smile of relief that Carlos shot her.

Elizabeth laughed. Then she said soberly, "In truth, good people, the loyalty you have shown me deserves not my jests but rather my heartfelt thanks. Which you have, indeed, in plenty." A sly smile played on her lips. "However, madam, your mother has let me know that my thanks will not buy you a house, nor furnish your table with meat. Therefore, I hereby name you, sir, lord of a great property in my realm, including its manors, fields, forests, and mines, and all pertaining rents and revenues, which include, I understand, a profitable glass-making enterprise."

Isabel and Carlos shared a happy glance. He said, "I thank Your Majesty most humbly."

"Nonsense, sir, I owe you my life, and that is a thing I rather cherish." She grinned at her friends, and they laughed. "And here is the best aspect of my gift. It has been rescued from the grip of the traitor, Sir Christopher Grenville. His lands were forfeit by his treason, and by a bill of attainder they have reverted to me. I give them now to you." She beamed at them.

Isabel was so taken aback she could not find the wit to speak. Carlos, though, answered quickly with another expression of his gratitude.

"Nay, thank your wife's mother, sir, for it was Lady Thornleigh who persuaded me of the justice of this arrangement." She gave Isabel a stern look. "Mark you, madam, let this gift be an end to the discord between your families, Thornleigh and Grenville. The slate is now wiped clean. England's war is done. Let yours be, too. I command it."

Isabel sank into a curtsy. "Yes, Your Majesty."

"Good." She turned her attention to Carlos and went on like a diligent businesswoman, "Go, sir, and take lordship of Yeavering Hall without delay. Affairs there are in limbo, I am told, and the people in disarray. Their court-leet awaits a lord to rule on manor business, and the county assizes await a justice of the peace. Good government is needed as much at home as in my wide realm. Go posthaste, get yourself sworn in, and see to restoring harmony."

"I will, Your Majesty. With thanks."

The Queen looked satisfied. "Now," she said, turning to her friends, her business done, "to the water, and a blessed cool breeze!" They flocked around her as she made her way down the wharf.

Isabel and Carlos, left behind, looked at each other in wonder. "Rescued," he said with a grin. "The property is vast. And rich."

"Yes. It's wonderful." She was trying to sort through her emotions. The reward was great indeed, and the delight it gave Carlos made her very happy. Yet she felt uneasy. Yeavering Hall seemed tainted by Christopher Grenville.

Carlos clearly had no such misgivings. "What a night," he said. "Let's get a boat and join the fun."

She smiled. "Let's."

The wharf was a madhouse of gaiety. People jumped into boats. People in boats called to friends ashore. The magnificent royal barge pulled out into the river, the rowers' work made easy by the placid water. Musicians on three separate barges followed with trumpets and pipes and drums, sending music dancing across the river. Isabel and Carlos found their wherryman in the cheerful chaos, and Carlos gave him a shilling to keep rowing them wherever the Queen's barge went. Downriver the motley flotilla coasted, past Durham House, past Baynard's Castle, past the Old Swan Stairs. They were in merry company, for Londoners in boats all along the river cheered the Queen as she went, and on the shore trumpets blared and flags flew and people ran from their houses and crowded the jetties and called out, "God save the Queen!"

Isabel settled against the cushions, and Carlos snugged his arm around her. The cool river breeze was delicious, and stars crowded the dark sky as though they, too, had come to hail the popular young queen. "Look," Isabel said, pointing at a constellation. "There's Cassiopeia." Her father had taught her about the stars on his ships, and she was proud to name them and know them.

"They're shining on Northumberland, too," he said, and she heard the satisfaction in his voice.

"I am glad to end the wretched feud," she said. "But, Carlos,

I've heard something troubling. About Grenville." She told him the story. "Do you think it could be true?"

He shrugged. "What difference, dead or alive? He can never come back. He'd hang." He hugged her closer to him and laughed. "You worry too much, Isabel."

His confidence was irresistible, and her misgivings evaporated like river mist at sunrise.

She settled against him with a sigh. Music and laughter eddied around them. All of London seemed to have thrown off the pall of war and had tripped out to make merry. Isabel looked above the waving banners and flags, up at the stars. It felt as though all her hard journeying in the last months had been leading her to alight here, in this boat, on this river, under these stars. The stars that smiled on England.

AUTHOR'S NOTES

Fact and fiction are intertwined in the novels of my "Thornleigh" series. The characters of the Thornleighs, Valverdes, and Grenvilles are purely my creations, but their lives weave through real historical events and around real historical personalities.

The first book in the series, *The Queen's Lady*, features young Honor Larke, a fictional lady-in-waiting to Catherine of Aragon, Henry VIII's first wife, and follows Honor's stormy love affair with Richard Thornleigh as she works to rescue heretics from the Church's fires. *The King's Daughter* introduces their daughter Isabel, who joins the Wyatt rebellion against Queen Mary, a true event, and hires mercenary Carlos Valverde to help her rescue her father from prison. *The Queen's Captive* brings Honor and Richard back from exile with their seafaring son Adam to help the young Princess Elizabeth, who has been imprisoned by her half sister, Queen Mary, another true event.

Fact and fiction also intermingle in the book you now hold, *The Queen's Gamble*. All the events of the war in Scotland happened as they occur in the novel, including the countrywide rampage of John Knox's army backed by a score of Protestant nobles, among them Lord James (the late King's illegitimate son) and the Earls of Glencairn, Argyll, and Ruthven; the Queen Regent's response of bringing in thousands of French troops; the alarm that this French military buildup caused Elizabeth and her council (which prompted the Spanish ambassador in London to write to his master, "It is incredible the fear these people are in of the French on the Scottish border"); and Elizabeth's clandestine financial support of Knox's rebels. Also true are Elizabeth's sending Admiral Winter's small fleet into the December gales to intercept French ships bringing more troops; Knox's capture of Edinburgh; the Queen Regent's successful counterattack that forced Knox's army to retreat to Stirling; Elizabeth's decision to send an English army into Scotland, to disastrous results at first when they attacked the French at Leith; then the English siege that resulted in the surrender of the French and total victory for the English.

The novel also refers to thousands of Spanish troops boarding ships in the Netherlands (a Spanish possession at the time), ordered by Philip of Spain to sail to Scotland to help France put down Knox's rebels. This, too, is a fact, and if the Spanish had arrived, the fate of Scotland, and of England, could have been very different. But also true is the concurrent, shocking defeat of Philip's army in the Mediterranean by the Turks, a devastating setback that made Philip halt his northern troops about to sail to Scotland and reroute them to fight the Turks. On such surprising hinges does history often swing.

Into these factual events I have set the actions of my fictional characters: Isabel and Carlos, Adam and Frances, Honor and Richard, and Christopher Grenville.

The plotted uprising organized by Grenville under the banner of the Catholic Earl of Northumberland is fiction, but it is based on truth, for in 1569, nine years after the novel ends, the Earls of Northumberland and Westmorland did raise the northern Catholics in a massive armed revolt. Leading five thousand men, they took Durham Cathedral and were preparing to march on London to depose Elizabeth. She sent a force under the Earl of Sussex to put down the uprising, which he did with great brutality, hanging over six hundred rebels. Elizabeth executed Northumberland.

What follows is a brief account of what happened, after the novel ends, to the real people who appear in the story.

Marie de Guise, unwell throughout the war with Knox's rebels, did not survive her troops' surrender in Scotland; she died at Leith in June, 1560. Her daughter, Mary Stuart, Queen of France at the time, refused to sign the Treaty of Edinburgh, one article of which was her relinquishing her claim to the English throne. Her refusal infuriated Elizabeth, and thus began their nineteen-year feud.

D'Oysel, commander of the French garrison at Leith, survived the English siege. My research tracked him down: A few months after the French surrender, acting as a French emissary at the English court, he asked Elizabeth to grant safe passage to Mary Stuart to travel through England on her return from France to Scotland. Elizabeth refused, a punishment to Mary for not signing the Treaty of Edinburgh, and D'Oysel took this message to Mary in France. D'Oysel has my apology for shamelessly besmirching his reputation; his sadistic streak in the novel is purely my invention.

John Knox secured the Scottish Reformation with the English-Scots victory over the French, and became his country's most influential religious leader. He died in 1572, having changed the course of Scotland.

After less than two years as Queen of France, Mary Stuart was widowed at age eighteen when her young husband, King Francis, died just months after the French surrender in Scotland. With little status in the new court of her brother-in-law King Charles, Mary left France for her birthplace, Scotland, arriving at Leith by sea in August 1561, and took up her birthright, the Scottish throne. A devout Catholic, Mary was always at odds with Knox, and hoped to reestablish the Catholic faith with help from France or Spain, but Scotland had become a Protestant state, and no foreign power was prepared to help her reverse this.

Sir William Cecil continued as Elizabeth's first minister for almost four more decades. A brilliant political strategist, Cecil was tireless in his efforts to maintain Elizabeth's security and extend her power. His urging her to intervene in Scotland against the French was the first implementation of what became his policy, eloquently stated by historian Conyers Read, of "keeping Elizabeth safe by making fires in her neighbors' houses." It was a policy that Cecil and Elizabeth pursued next in France, helping the Protestant Huguenots in their fight against the French government, and then in the Netherlands, helping the Dutch Protestants fight their Spanish overlords, all of which undermined those foreign powers, England's adversaries. Cecil's service to Elizabeth spanned almost the whole of her long and peaceful reign; theirs was one of the most successful political partnerships in history. His death in 1598 was the only occasion on which she was publicly seen to weep.

Elizabeth's victory over the French in Scotland, where *The Queen's Gamble* ends, was a turning point in her fledgling reign, and its significance cannot be overemphasized. Despite her initial vac-illation, the decision to defy the great powers of France and Spain, and to gamble on intervention, was hers alone. Her victory de-stroyed French domination in Scotland, and made English influ-ence there permanently predominant. Furthermore, it elevated Elizabeth's status at home and in the eyes of all Europe, whose leaders had to acknowledge her as a formidable ruler. She did this at the age of twenty-six, in just the second year of her reign. Never-theless, with the return of Mary Stuart to the Scottish throne the following year, Elizabeth's problems with Mary, her cousin and fel-low queen, had just begun. Their nascent feud drives the next "Thornleigh" novel.

A note about the actors' troupe in the book. All her life Eliza-beth loved plays, but at this point in history these were mostly pri-vate entertainments enjoyed by royalty and the wealthy. *The Queen's Gamble* takes place in 1559–1560, before the flowering of the great age of theater that we call "Elizabethan." Shakespeare was born in 1564, and it would be almost three more decades be-fore he and his fellow theater men built the famous public London playhouses: the Swan, the Rose, and the Globe.

Readers have sent me wonderfully astute comments and ques-tions about the characters, real and invented, in my "Thornleigh" novels and about the history of the period. This partnership with you, the reader, makes my work a joy. If you'd like to write to me, I'd love to hear from you. Contact me at bkyle@barbarakyle.com.

THE QUEEN'S GAMBLE

Barbara Kyle

ABOUT THIS GUIDE

The suggested questions are included to
enhance your group's reading of Barbara Kyle's
The Queen's Gamble.

DISCUSSION QUESTIONS

1. Given the threat of a French invasion from Scotland, did you think Isabel was right to offer to take Queen Elizabeth's gold to the Scottish rebels to help them fight the French? Or, instead, should she have stayed out of danger and gone home to Peru as Carlos wanted her to?

2. Elizabeth was skeptical of Isabel's loyalty since she was the wife of a Spanish Catholic. Did Elizabeth go too far in holding Isabel's son as a hostage to ensure that she would fulfill her mission?

3. When Frances was fearfully preparing to give birth, did you sympathize with her need, as a Catholic, to trust an "old-school" Catholic midwife?

4. Once Isabel delivered the Queen's gold to Knox and therefore could go back to London for Nicolas, she offered instead to go to the French fortress at Leith and spy for Knox. Did you think she was being brave or foolish in going into enemy territory?

5. When Isabel arrived at Leith, ostensibly to visit Carlos, she lied to him and kept secret her mission to get information for Knox. Did you feel she was right to lie to safeguard her mission?

6. Did you think Carlos had a right to be furious at Isabel when he learned of her involvement with the rebels? Was he justified in virtually throwing her out?

7. Adam refused to leave the Leith garrison jail unless Carlos let him bring his dying crewman, but Carlos knew the burden would endanger them all so he killed the crewman. Did you feel Carlos was justified in this act of murder?

8. When Isabel realized that Grenville was plotting to rise up against the Queen, she needed proof, so she stayed in his house to find out more about his plot. Did you think she was doing what was necessary, or was she taking too great a risk?

9. How did you feel about Carlos's brief infidelity with Fenella? Should he have confessed it to Isabel, or do you sympathize with him silently putting it behind him?
10. Condemned to hang, Isabel rejoiced at hearing of Carlos's plan to rescue her, but then realized that if he tried, he and her brother and father would likely be killed, so she made an agonized decision and refused to be rescued. How did you feel about Isabel's choice?
11. In Tudor England, Catholics and Protestants both felt justified in their religious zeal. How does this compare with the religious tensions in our own time?

GREAT BOOKS, GREAT SAVINGS!

When You Visit Our Website:
www.kensingtonbooks.com

You Can Save Money Off The Retail Price Of Any Book You Purchase!

- **All Your Favorite Kensington Authors**
- **New Releases & Timeless Classics**
- **Overnight Shipping Available**
- **eBooks Available For Many Titles**
- **All Major Credit Cards Accepted**

Visit Us Today To Start Saving!
www.kensingtonbooks.com

All Orders Are Subject To Availability.
Shipping and Handling Charges Apply.
Offers and Prices Subject To Change Without Notice.